Eebygum͏

Bolsover

UK

www.eebygumbooks.co.uk

Front cover from a sketch in Derby Local Studies and Family History Library, used by permission.

Design and layout: John Young

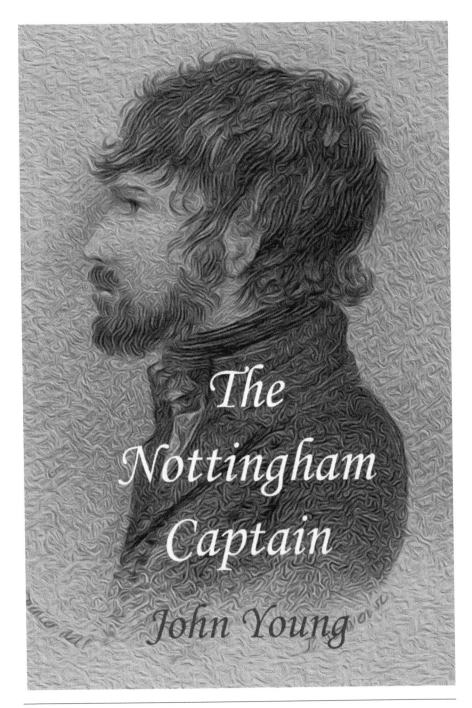

The
Nottingham
Captain

John Young

Foreword and Acknowledgements

I became aware of the Pentrich Revolution around 1980 and soon began researching the events and personalities involved. Over the years I have tried to tell the tale in several different ways: as an academic history, a school play, a TV script (co-authored with Director Norman Hull) and in song (together with Dr Keith Jones). Along the way pictures of the Pentrich rebels seemed to develop in my mind and this novel is the result. The plot stays close to historical fact, but must be read as a work of fiction.

My grateful appreciation must go to my friend Paddy McEvoy for close reading and constructive criticism of this work, not all in approval of the events portrayed and to Dan Healy, whose kind but astute observations helped me stay on track.

Eternal thanks are due to my son Paddy Young, my patient sounding board and partner in endless discussions and to my sister Margaret for her perceptive comments and close reading of the text.

Much gratitude to my daughter, Christy Young and her friend, Amy Downer, two rebel women, well-capable of bringing down any government! Christy scanned the different generations of text, while Amy, who was born in Sutton in Ashfield, was t' dialogue coach.

Finally, my sincerest thanks and appreciation to my dear friend and comrade the mighty Ray Hearne, who invested so many hours adding quality to this book. Without his inspired editing of every sentence this novel would have been immeasurably poorer.

As we approach the 200th anniversary of the Pentrich (and South Wingfield!) Revolution I hope this book will help readers understand and empathise with the people behind the events.

John Young,

Bolsover, May, 2016

Table of Contents

The Marchers' Route

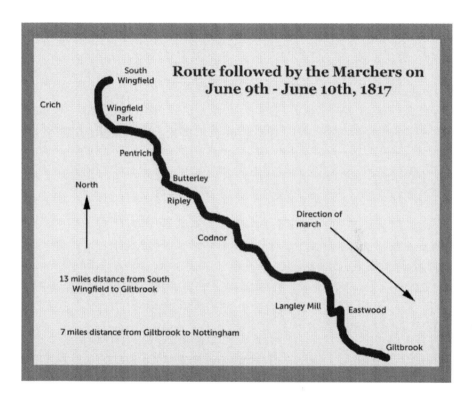

Chapter 1: Flight

Jeremiah Brandreth

Hawks were hovering over south east Derbyshire on the morning of June 10th, 1817. The heavy overnight rain had washed the sky clean and the sunshine made it a great day for hunting voles and field mice.

Hawks were not the only predators out that day. Along the Nottingham road, from Giltbrook, through Langley Mill, Codnor, Ripley, Pentrich and South Wingfield, terrified and fleeing men were being hunted, members of a shattered band of defeated insurrectionists beaten from their cover by friends and neighbours, to be chased down and taken by mounted Hussars and yeomanry.

For those who looked carefully there were yet other, more solitary, hunters searching for prey. A fox never walks aimlessly; this one was unhurried, as he picked his cautious path upwards to the lip of the old quarry. He sniffed his winding way through the damp ferns and bushes until he reached the skyline. Poised and attentive, he tasted the air for a moment or two, and then was gone.

As the fox departed Jeremiah Brandreth closed his eyes and felt the rain drip down upon him through the branches above. He shivered, more from the wet and his own exhaustion than any real coldness. His whole body ached. Branches and bushes had snagged his clothes, torn his skin and bruised his body, and now his numb fingers picked hopelessly at the thorns which throbbed in his palm.

The shivering overcame him once more and he thought again of standing up to pace around the glade. The effort involved was more than Jeremiah was prepared to endure. He shrank back even further into the meagre comfort of his sodden coat. Finding a little warmth there, he nudged the hat brim down over his face, and began to surrender to the onset of sleep. Moments before he dozed, something came to his mind and he felt inside the grubby shirt for the little blue scarf that was hidden there: it was a present from Ann and he found it gratefully.

Sleep brought back the old nightmare. Seven men were standing on a scaffold, awaiting execution. They had been brought there on a ridiculous, wheel-less wagon pulled by two horses, called a "hurdle". As they were taken up, nooses were placed around their necks. Some of them bore it well; others trembled. The last was a fine-looking man dressed in good boots and a dark brown greatcoat. He stood calmly as he was noosed and then adjusted the position of the knot so that it was under his left ear. This would cause his neck to break when he dropped and save him from slow strangulation. The crowd was restless, jeering and cajoling the soldiers who guarded the scaffold.

"Nelson spoke for him, Jeremiah", said the Corporal who stood next to him. The young Brandreth's wide eyes were fixed on the face of Colonel Despard, the seventh of the condemned. This man had shared Lord Nelson's tent and umpteen dangers when both these heroes were young men. Awed and silent, the hundreds in the crowd strained to hear his last words.

"Citizens, I hope and trust, notwithstanding my fate, and the fate of those who no doubt will soon follow me, that the principles of freedom, of humanity and of justice will finally triumph over falsehood, tyranny and delusion, and every principle inimical to the human race."

These words unleashed thunderous cheers and applause causing the nervous sheriff to wave his arms frantically and shout inaudible instructions to the guards who were beginning to look anxiously at each other. He screamed at Despard demanding he stop inflaming the crowd. Jeremiah gripped his musket tightly.

Nodding and smiling, the Colonel concluded: "I have little more to add, except to wish you all health, happiness and freedom, which I have endeavoured, as far as was in my power, to procure for you and mankind in general."

Transfixed, Jeremiah gazed at this brave man; he removed his cap and inspected the morning sky like a shepherd trying to determine the mood of the weather. It was a warm day and the crowd made its own heat, but Jeremiah was shivering as he and the rest of the onlookers stood in reverent silence. Then he joined in the collective gasps and screams as Despard dropped through the trap, to die with less suffering than some of the others. Later on, the Colonel's body was cut down and an incompetent surgeon tried to behead him with a knife. Impatient, the hangman pulled and twisted the corpse until he had the head ripped clear. Jeremiah had averted his tear-filled gaze before the bloodied head was waved by its hair toward the crowd and Despard was denounced as a traitor.

He jolted awake from that recurring nightmare, not sure in that first sensible instant of where he was. The blue scarf was tight around his fingers and he was hot inside the darkness of his stovepipe hat. His first thought was that he may have been discovered and he held his breath, listening intently. After a tense minute no voice had come to menace him, but a rustling in the bushes threatened danger. He sat up abruptly and looked around to find nothing more fearsome than a dozen alarmed rabbits scampering away, disturbed by his noise, and interrupted in their foraging after the rain. Those nearest hopped away, to continue feeding on the further side of the little clearing.

Jeremiah breathed out, relieved that there was, for the present, no danger. The sun and the innocent joy of the little animals relaxed him once again. After a moment more, he sank back into his muddy greatcoat to doze on into the warm morning. Wood pigeons cooed in the distance, reminding him of a mother shushing her baby. A memory of Ann came to him as he lay back in his own reverie.

He remembered them lying in the first sleep of their marriage from which the sounds of the morning birds had woken him. He had slipped softly from the bed to peep through the shutters into the new day. It was early and there were none yet stirring in Sutton in Ashfield, but the birds were celebrating his wedding. He was twenty five years old then, full of health, and the world was a place of singing and joy.

Ann had slept on and he had leaned towards her to feel her soft, even breath on his face. Her features were hidden by a web of golden hair and he was sorry that he could not see her. It was quite cold and he slid back into the bed and cupped his body around hers, amazed to find how warm she was. He had not stayed awake many minutes more, but had, in that brief time, discovered a memory that came now to comfort him when he was cold and alone and many miles away from where he ached to be.

Now in this lonely place, on the boundaries of his slumber, tears filled his eyes and he succumbed to helpless grief. He lay like a terrified child, small, clenched and silent, unable to sleep, but refusing to wake, powerless to stop the awful images which invaded his mind. There was moonlight through a hole in the curtain, and he followed its path to find it glowing on a cradle which shuddered slightly each time his baby son coughed in the cold. He remembered the patterns that the lines of damp formed on the walls, as he lay looking over Ann's thin shoulders, knowing that she too was sleepless and seeing hellish visions of her own.

Some days he had lain in bed, long after he would have risen to go about his employment, had there been any, noticing that each week another piece of their cheap furniture was gone. He recalled a time when he had imagined the edges of their bed were the shores of their world, knowing that each time he left it, he joined a legion of angry, frustrated men unable to find work in a land of hungry, listless, weeping children. Despite the constant sacrifices he and Ann made, there seemed always to be less food on the bare table and they had gone to rest, night after night, with no comfort in their stomachs, and only their despairing embraces for warmth.

There were better memories too threaded among the unhappy ones and as Jeremiah sat drowsily in his concealment, they came to offer solace. After the hopelessness of workless days and hungry nights came ideas promising a better world. He had walked among like-minded friends while the sun shone, united with talk of a better world waiting to be seized, caught up in their outrageous talk and revolutionary cause. Folk that had little shared all they possessed. They were Despard's heirs pledged to unbreakable fellowship; children had laughed as earnest-faced parents emerged, bright-eyed, from smoky, conspiratorial meetings.

His spirit had raised itself up from the floor of the cell of life, all too briefly soaring higher than it had ever dared before. Recollections of those bright times dispelled for a moment the ghosts that flitted through the grey, remorseless days and warmed his heart a little, while the wakening sun dried his clothes and energized his aching bones. Alive again, he rose carefully from his bivouac amongst the ferns and edged carefully up the slope of his quarry refuge.

William and Edward Turner

From their celestial view-point high above the road from Giltbrook, the hawks scanned the travails of the fleeing men who had invaded their hunting fields. Where the road between Derby and Nottingham prepared to enter the village of Langley Mill, two brothers lay in a ditch. They had run this far until their legs had betrayed them and then sought the cover of the long grass and bushes which now obscured their fugitive bodies from pursuit. Years ago, they had played hiding and hunting games, but William and Edward Turner were no longer boys, and their need for concealment was more urgent than the imagined dangers they had invented in their childhood.

They had secreted themselves here in the early morning and endured the rain teeming down, soaking the branches of the bushes that bent above them. Their tiredness was desperate, but both knew that to remain much longer in this spot would expose them to great danger.

"Let's be off," said William.

A tall, handsome man, now graying at the temples, William was the elder of the two by some years, had fought Napoleon in Egypt and generally made the decisions. Edward nodded his agreement and began to wriggle through the soaking vegetation to obtain a view of the road. He parted the long grass on the verge of the roughly-surfaced track and peered out, scanning from side to side. There was nothing to see, and except for the shrilling of hedge birds, the world was strangely quiet. Even the breeze seemed to be waiting for something to happen as Edward worked his way backwards to the little den where his brother waited.

"All clear," he whispered."Are you right, youth?"

He noticed how haggard the face of his brother appeared in the uncharitable sunlight, and smiled wryly, supposing that his own could look no better after such a long, sleepless night. He longed to rest in his bed once again. They started to crawl forwards, keeping low as they began to lose the cover of the undergrowth. Then a terrifying, blaring sound stopped their hearts. It was the noise of a hunting horn and it was close by. Realising what it meant, they looked at each other in undisguised terror and slowly shrank back into the sparse cover. William Turner put his hand on the butt of his pistol, gripping it as he tried to hold on to his courage. They both quieted their breathing and strained to hear the approaching peril.

The sound of hooves on the road grew louder, until the two frightened men knew that the horses were almost on top of them. Their ears filled with the jangle of harness and the rasping breath of the animals. The voices of the riders were raucous and cocky. Then, there came another noise, one which was harder to identify: a swishing, slashing, strident sound. In another instant a pike blade bit into the ground next to the head of the old soldier, William. Men on foot were slashing the verges to scare out any fugitives.

With a loud roar and a curse, he sprang upwards, bursting through the tangle of weeds and shrubbery above his head. He was a large man, and his angry face was a mask of ferocity. Horses reared in alarm and while their riders struggled to master them. For a long moment the footmen stood stock-still, terrified at this violent apparition leaping up in front of them. He glowered around him, angry as Hell, noting with bitter resignation that he and Edward were totally outnumbered. He shook his head to clear it. Then, on a sudden impulse, he raised the pistol and put its barrel to his own breast. Edward and the others watched in horror, as he yelled in despair, closed his eyes and pulled the trigger.

The hammer fell with a loud click, but the wet powder failed to ignite. A second later, William knew that he had not died, and heaved a resigned sigh. His head tilted back, and he closed his eyes, dropped his pistol and stood open and defenceless. Then one of the riders spurred his horse forward. Edward tried to shriek an alarm, but before he could do so, he saw an upraised riding crop lash down onto the unprotected and unsuspecting brow of his elder brother. William's forehead was split open by the blow, and his knees buckled beneath him. Edward cried out, enraged. As for his brother, the big man's eyes stayed closed. He lay on the ground in a daze. Edward Turner bent to see the blood pouring from the gash, before using the last desperate leavings of his strength to seize the harness of the man who had struck this hideous blow in an effort to unhorse him, but the pike men had recovered from their surprise and two or three of them quickly bore Edward down, tying his hands behind his back as he lay with his face in the wet grass, his struggles growing ever weaker. They kicked him then left him there for a minute or two, until William began to regain consciousness and then they bound him, too. Both prisoners were forced to their feet and made to totter down the road towards Langley Mill, as tragic a pair of defeated men as you would ever see.

The magistrate, Lancelot Rolleston, the rider who had struck the cowardly blow, lagged behind the column, white faced and trembling. He had never been a violent man and he wondered at the power of the anger that had just overcome him. In front of him the pike men shook their heads and muttered, sometimes taking a sideways look at the man with the riding crop. Within half an hour, the hunters and their prisoners reached Langley Mill and hammered on the door of the Junction Navigation Inn, demanding sustenance. They were soon restored by the food and enlivened by the ale. One of the yeomen blew a loud, rasping note on a hunting horn. The rest of the men who were crowded into the parlour of the roadside inn laughed raucously as one of them who stood closest to the horn-blower slapped him heavily between the shoulder blades as he tried to hold a long shrill note. The sound ceased abruptly and was replaced by coughing, spluttering and cursing and a room full of laughter.

By the pantry door, the landlady, Mrs Goodman pulled a face and shook her head angrily. She had had more than enough and her main thought was how to get rid of the carousers and find some peace in her bed. This did not seem likely to happen soon as the unwelcome customers, forty or more, were well-set. As she added up the reckoning in her head she was resolved that they would be made to pay well over the score for all this trouble. The jugs were being drained quickly and she sent her pot boy off to the cellar for more. She would have to be brewing again tomorrow and the revellers would be served the new ale, whether it was ready or not.

On the floor in a corner, without food or drink, the two Turner brothers were seated, tied together, back to back. Their faces and clothes were caked with blood and dirt and their heads slumped forward. One had a fearful gash over his eye and blood was congealed down his cheek. In the midst of the clamour they slept, exhausted. Mrs Goodman noticed that the well-dressed gentleman who had ridden in with the rest was watching the two prisoners closely. As a landlady she was quick to observe that he wasn't taking any drink from the tankard she had filled for him earlier. She was not so pre-occupied with his distaste for her ale to notice how pale and shocked he looked. His fine boots were muddy and his coat and breeches marked from a hard road and a wet night. Before him on the table his expensive hat and elegant riding crop marked him out to be a gentleman, which explained why he shunned the drunken yeomen. Gazing into the middle-distance, he seemed as detached from this world as the two slumbering prisoners he watched so carefully.

Then the hunting horn blared once more as the bleary hunters exited Mrs Goodman's inn, the glare of the sinking sun blinding their bloodshot eyes. Some relieved themselves by the landlady's hedge, but eventually they were all mounted, except William and Edward Turner who were each tethered to a horse and dragged off as the company departed. Mrs Goodman slammed the shutters and bawled at the pot boy as the last sounds of hooves and laughter died away. She retired to her room where she emptied her bulging purse of the coins it contained upon the bed and began to count them.

At the rear of the departing yeomanry, Lancelot Rolleston rode, slumped and exhausted. He soon became detached from the group as he allowed his weary horse to pick its own way slowly back along the road towards Nottingham. He ambled through Eastwood, where every head turned his way and examined him with suspicion, and did not halt until he came to the stream at the hamlet of Giltbrook. It bubbled purposefully, restored from its summer torpor by the heavy rain of the previous night. Except for the sound of running water, this was the quietest place on earth.

Hugh Wolstenholme

Near the end of the rout, the village of Pentrich still clung to its hilltop, drying out from the deluge which had just ended. The squat, stone-built houses gazed westwards over and beyond Ripley, as they had for centuries gone. The tall trees which sheltered St Matthew's Church from the westerly gales waved gently in the breeze and the birds which inhabited them were filling the air with their goodbye songs to the rain. The church door was ajar. It opened out onto a well-kept lawn, part of a small garden which was afforded seclusion by the tall hedge which separated it from the graveyard. In front of his well-appointed house, the curate of Pentrich, Hugh Wolstenholme, breviary in hand, walked, consumed with desperate thoughts.

The day promised to be a fine one, but he knew that it portended more trouble tor him and the parish than any dawn before it. The inevitable retribution would begin soon. Last night, he had knelt in prayer and risen to hear the loud, harsh voices of angry men and the recriminations of alarmed women. Doors that should have long been closed had slammed in the darkness. The name of God had been invoked and words that ought never to have been uttered sounded loudly.

Several times, Wolstenholme had been on the verge of going outside to face up to the men who were setting themselves on a desperate course, but on each occasion the doubts which he felt had unmade his mind. All of Hugh's sympathies lay with his parishioners who were suffering in awful poverty after the weather of the previous summer, the worst in living memory, had destroyed crops and led to soaring food prices. Many families in the area were framework knitters who made high quality stockings that were suddenly no longer fashionable, resulting in widespread unemployment. Violence had grown against the hosiers who had switched from paying a fair price for top-quality garments made by skilled workers to employing children and women to produce cheap rubbish made of old recycled wool. Frames had been smashed by masked raiders who invaded the factories after dark and threatened their owners. Many among his congregation were proud to be Luddites – followers of the mythical General Ludd. Wolstenholme knew it was just a matter of time before the huge rewards, the spies and informers would lead many of his flock to the gallows.

The whole Wolstenholme clan firmly believed in the equal society advocated by thinkers like Thomas Paine and radical journalists such as William Cobbett whose ideas were openly debated by many of the unhappy people in his Parish. Hugh's own father, William, was a leader of radical opinion twenty miles north in Sheffield. Last night, most of the men from Pentrich and nearby South Wingfield had marched off to join with others from the North and Midlands to violently overthrow the government that oppressed them. Hugh sympathised, but knew in his heart that the government would not fall so easily and was apprehensive about the retribution his people might suffer if their rebellion failed. His mind was tormented all night, but he had not gone out to his people.

The cock's crow had sounded the end of the long night. As the sun bleached its way through the un-curtained windows of the church, he had abandoned all ideas of rest. Now he paced in his church yard, weaving among the gravestones, blurry-eyed from facing the nightmares in the darkness. The rain had stopped and there was an opaque mist in the valley to the east, the direction in which the men of his parish had departed. He looked for signs of their return, but none came. Peace shrouded the unstirred valley farms as the silent fog followed the night's heavy rain.

Birds were hopping innocently on the grass, and he recognised his blackbirds and thrushes among a plague of house martins. They seemed so jaunty and innocent, the curate reflected, as they hunted the heads of the unsuspecting worms that surfaced onto the wet lawn.

Isaac and William Ludlam

A mile or two beyond Pentrich in the direction of Matlock, the two Ludlam brothers were completing their flight back to their family home. Young men in their twenties, their clothes and faces showed the signs of the hasty journey. Their dark jackets and long trousers were muddied. Both had set out with caps, but one had lost his in the mad dash when the cavalry appeared. They had followed the green track, scampering down the hill behind Pentrich Church to where it crossed the valley of the River Amber. There was no one awake as the brothers sneaked by the Weir Mill Farm They hurried along, sensing the nearness of home and, eager for its secure familiarity, taking the lane that led to the little hamlet of Wingfield Park, before it continued on to join the road from Crich, close by the ruins of Wingfield Manor.

At the minor promontory called Colburn Hill, they dived off the track to the left, ascending some steps which took them into the concealment of a little quarry. On familiar territory, they followed each other up the bank to the right of the workings, and clambered to the top of the mound. Here, they halted and leaned against the trees, looking down into the small group of houses, which huddled together about two hundred yards away.

Their way had been soft and boggy from the rain, and they were muddy to their knees. They squinted at one another in the sunlight.

"It seems safe enough," said one. This was Isaac Ludlam, called "the younger", because he shared his father's given name. His brother nodded in agreement.

"Shall we go down, then?" he continued. Neither of them moved.

"Cud he 'ah got home ahead of us?" said William, youngest of the brothers.

Isaac shook his head. "There's no way he 'as. He's twenty five years on me and ah 'm beaten. He's either taken or dead."

He had voiced a fear which both shared.

"Is that what you are going t' tell her, Isaac? He's maybe dead or a prisoner?" It was William who spoke.

Isaac shook his head sadly. "Ah don't know what to tell her," he muttered. "She'll have to be told summat, though."

They could see that a middle-aged woman had emerged from one of the houses and was now looking down the way they should have come. Her hand shielded her eyes from the increasing glare.

"She'll want to know why we're safe and father is not come back wi' us. If you can think of owt to tell her, ah can't."

As they watched her, they remembered that their mother was a formidable woman, and a feeling of apprehension began to overcome them.

After a while, the stout, white-aproned figure went back into the Ludlam family house. The two sons stood quietly within the protection of the trees, less eager now to move down to the place they had striven so hard to reach. For them and their waiting mother Life was never going to resume its ordered course. They lingered, finding it difficult to comprehend how circumstances were changing and terrified at what their fate might be.

Thomas and John Bacon

It was midday before John Bacon strode through the gate that admitted him to the house of James Booth. He was a man of fifty four years, but strong and sprightly. The road had taken toll on his clothes, but his reddened eyes were bright and determined.

To call this hovel a house was to flatter it. Muck was part of most people's lives but Booth was avoided by his neighbours in Pentrich for the filth and stench that clung to him and his abode. Bacon entered beneath the porous roof and squelched across the earth floor that was turned to mud by last night's rain. The furnishings were sparse and mildewed and the scratching of rats was company to Booth and any who visited him.

John Bacon and his brother, Tommy, had known Booth for many years. This simple old man enjoyed their company and they were the only neighbours who ever visited his dwelling. It was a logical place to seek concealment for anyone on the run from trouble.

"Tom! Tom! Are you here?" hissed John.

"John? Is that you? Are you alive, man?"

"Yes youth! But not for long if we don't run. The Hussars are close behind me!"

The brothers shook hands and embraced one another.

"Ah know where we can go", replied Tommy. "It's a long walk. Are you up to it?"

John Bacon had just walked forty miles through a wet and sleepless night.

He grinned. "Ah can walk the legs off you any day!"

Tommy, ten years his senior, laughed as he pulled on his coat and picked up his stick. Saying their goodbyes to Booth, they hurried up the hill to Pentrich and into their respective houses – they lived near each other, but each led an independent bachelor life. Within five minutes they emerged with bundles on their shoulders and headed swiftly down the road followed earlier by the Ludlam brothers and descended into the valley of the River Amber. They travelled through Buckland Hollow and on to Ambergate, only once glancing back towards Pentrich on its hill top. They would never see their home parish again.

George Weightman

A big, sandy-haired young man named George Weightman sat wearily on the milestone at the bottom of the south side of the hill below Pentrich. He was tired and hot, and he did not know what he should do next. Though nearly home now, there was no sense of elation or relief. Instead, he felt guilty and disgraced at his cowardice. All the way back from Eastwood, he had dawdled, pulled strongly towards home, but still torn by the desire to keep his promise to Jeremiah. The neighing of horses jarred him and he uncoiled his body from its slouched posture and jumped to his feet. There was no time for lethargy now. Athletically, he bounded up the hill, his great chest rising and falling with the exertion and his big feet flapping on the muddy track. He ran up behind the familiar houses of his childhood, still undecided where he should hide.

He could not risk his own house, or his mother's inn, The White Horse, because of the danger it would bring his family. The hunters would search every house, and if he took to open country in the daylight, they would see him from far off, and ride him down. He hunted the hedges breathlessly for any place of concealment, but none suggested itself. The noise of pursuit grew and any second now the hunters would sight him. With only a few seconds left, George Weightman burst through a gap in the foliage and sprinted towards the centre of the village.

Nanny and Rebecca Weightman

George had been right to avoid The White Horse. An hour after he had passed by his mother was counting the cost of a visit from the yeomanry. Leaving her young grand children in her living room, Nanny Weightman, George's mother, joined her daughter in law, Rebecca, in the parlour. She stomped in through the doorway, cursing the world and its woes. Nanny was renowned for two major accomplishments: brewing ale and cursing. Now she demonstrated her facility with the latter with great gusto and style, invoking the direst of consequences upon those who had ridden into Pentrich, wrecked her home and her living and galloped away laughing. Rebecca was a strong, slim woman in her twenties with dark hair and striking eyes and was married to Nanny's eldest son, George.

They began to clear up the debris. Three strong tables were little worse for wear and these were soon righted, but half a dozen stools had broken legs and would probably go for kindling. A bench that

Rebecca had to separate from a wooden wall panel could be mended, but the panel would need replacing. Dents could be hammered out of some of the abused pewter, but clay jugs and dishes were smashed beyond repair.

The wreckers had tried to topple the big ale barrel, but it was there that Nanny had made her stand, wielding a butcher's cleaver. Nanny was as strong as most men and when she was in a rage she could do damage. Her brothers and children stood well clear when her temper was up and "bees were swarming". They had turned the air blue with their obscenities but had stayed well clear of the swipes she made at anyone who got too close. None had. The ale barrel remained un-broached and intact. Instead the Yeomanry had vented their aggression on the furniture and fittings and left to go hunting for fugitives who might be hidden elsewhere in the village. As they departed they called Nanny a foul old crone and threatened to return by night, torch her inn and burn her for the witch they knew her to be.

Half an hour's industry restored the parlour to a dented version of its former glory, but chairs were few and pottery even scarcer. Rubbing her bruised knuckles, Nanny followed Rebecca back into the living quarters. The children were playing happily. The only sign of the unwelcome visitors were the holes in the ceiling where pikes had been thrust to skewer anyone hiding in the attics above. The two women sat down and each took a deep breath before joining in animated and increasingly emotional conversation about the previous night's shattering events.

George Goodwin

With a white shirt sleeve to shield his eyes against the glare George Goodwin supervised the casting operation. The men had the look of armoured knights quenching the fiery breath of some medieval dragon, as their lances and gauntlets glowed in the light of the furnace flames. Goodwin scrutinised the quality of ironwork produced at the Butterley works to the point of obsession. His workers were experienced and diligent. They had never let him down, but he still felt compelled to observe every step of the process in person.

When casting was finished most of the men took the chance to stroll outside to breath the fresh air and chat. They chewed tobacco and let the light breeze dry the sweat which poured out of them in the heat of their workplace. Goodwin reached out a muscular arm for his coat and went outside to join the men.

"Well boys! That was good morning's work! When you consider all the upset, I am proud of you!"

The workmen nodded their appreciation of his remark. They were looking at him in a different light today.

"I hope we can settle down again now all this trouble seems to be over", Goodwin continued.

"I'm glad none of you had the bad sense to take up with those fools. There would be no place here for any man who did!"

A few minutes later he watched his workers file back inside and remained in the fresh air. He found himself alone with old George Jepson. The old man was fretting and agitated and began to stammer.

"Might ay have a word wi' yeh, Mr Goodwin, Sir?"

Goodwin nodded.

"Sir, it's about what you said where there'd be no place for any who joined the rebels. Ah didn't want to go with them, ah didn't, but they made me. Wock us up in the middle o' t' neet and scared t' life out of us. Told me to get my clothes on and go with them or there'd be trouble. They had pikes and hayforks and slashers, and one had a gun and said he'd shut me if ah didn't go! They gave me a fork but ah said ah wouldn't bear arms against the King! Told me they'd toss me on the fork! Ah had to go, but it was dark and raining and when we got to Langley Mill ah took off and came home ...."

Goodwin's hand on his bony shoulder reassured the shaking Jepson. "Calm yourself, George! I know you are an honest man. You did well to get away. Your job is safe. Now take few deep breaths and go and join your mates. We'll hear no more of this."

Goodwin remained outside, loaded his pipe and tasted the tobacco's bite in the summer air. Today was inevitably a short one as he only had a skeleton crew. Most of the workers had been commandeered and were occupied in the hunt to round up last night's rebels. He stood for a time, looking upwards in the direction of the little village which had suddenly become so significant. Perplexed, he shook his head, tapped out his pipe and went back inside to keep an eye on proceedings.

Ann Brandreth

It would be a long time before the day penetrated the shadowy gloom of Cross Court. Here, in the middle of Nottingham's festering sprawl of precarious tenements, built into haphazard, cramped squares and pierced by narrow, fouled lanes, the sun was often too weary to cast any light. It was always dismal in this empty little room where a fair-haired young woman nursed a baby on her lap. Ann Brandreth had tried to make herself carry out the routines of the day, made plans, but somehow she could not leave the chair and her darkening thoughts. All around her – above, below and all sides - were the sounds of her neighbours. The snores and coughs, the whimpering and screaming of infants and the voices raised in argument were always there. At certain times of day sounds from the bustling streets took prominence, but when night fell the neighbours grew loud again. She had never known silence since she and her husband, Jeremiah, came to Nottingham.

Now it was time to leave once more, she decided: she must go today, straight back to her father's house in Sutton. She had waited in Nottingham to welcome her husband as he marched in triumph at the head of his army. Then the news had come that the Derby men had run away before the soldiers and were being hunted. The next she knew, Ann's tenement world had been shattered as half-a dozen constables forced the door claiming to have come for her husband. It took but moments to search and trash their little room. They found an old rusty sword under the bed and took it with them when they left. As she quieted her crying children, Ann wondered how it was they knew Jeremiah's name.

He would never come now and she must pack up the last of their few belongings and go. She doubted whether she would ever return to this place of bad memories and despair. Suddenly she was crying and could not stop. Sensing the distress, her little daughter Elizabeth, and the baby on her lap were soon crying, too. The sounds of their grief merged into the multitude of groans and sighs that seemed to emanate from the throat of the city itself.

Chapter 2: Lancelot Rolleston

It was mid afternoon on the tenth of June. On the previous evening Lancelot Rolleston was so consumed by nervous energy he had been unable to sit still. Now slumped on his tired horse, listening to the sound of the running water, he was too weary to move. As the stream flowed from a mysterious hiding place somewhere deep among the green bushes, so memories of last night and this morning passed through his mind from their own concealed source.

Thirty-one year old Rolleston was a well-respected and well-connected magistrate who lived at his family home of Watnall Hall which lay about six miles east of the centre of Nottingham. His first wife, Eleanor, had died and he re-married to Caroline, who was a year younger than he. Their children were Caroline, who was eight years old, Louisa who was six and Lancelot who was five. An energetic and committed magistrate, Rolleston was a rising star in Conservative politics.

The drawing room was furnished to the liking of his wife and there, on the evening of the ninth of June, he had paced to and fro impatiently, while his wife sat at her embroidery. She looked up from time to time, to smile at her over-active husband as he strode around the room, hands behind his back clenching and unclenching. Every short while, he would draw a silver watch from his fob pocket, examine its face as he held it in his palm, and check the time against the cabinet clock in the corner. The tick of the latter seemed somehow to click more slowly. Despite its tasteful decoration, the room lacked warmth, even though the setting sun was now painting its walls with golden light.

"Do you think it will rain, my dear?" asked Mrs Rolleston in desperation. As if in answer, a cloud passed over the declining sun and the room darkened. "It has been so hot," she continued, "I think we need some rain to cool everything down".

Rolleston cleared his throat by way of an answer and resumed his pacing. His wife continued the interminable embroidering. The clock clicked even more slowly. Moments later she heard his gasp in exasperation.

"Something must be done!" he exclaimed.

With that and a hurtfully curt nod to his wife, he hurried from the room. She heard the front door slam and went to the window in time to catch him riding purposefully down the long drive. It began to rain as she rang the bell to summon the maid to draw the curtains.

He continued at a cracking pace, oblivious to the worsening weather, until he reached the house of John Worsley. He rapped heavily upon the door. The maid curtsied as she showed him through into a sitting room. He would not let her take his coat. When Worsley entered, he found his old school friend very agitated and wondered for a moment if he had been in any way the cause. His attempts at a polite greeting were brushed aside as his visitor made towards him and seized his arm.

"We must do something, John, now, before it's too late!"

Worsley, shocked by this uncharacteristic disregard for manners and civility, extricated his arm from the fierce grip of the wild-eyed visitor.

"My dear fellow, what has put you into such a state? Have a drink Lance; then you can tell me all about it".

He rang the bell to summon the maid. Rolleston calmed himself with an effort, and feeling suddenly embarrassed, apologized for his behaviour.

"I'm sorry, John," he said. "But I really feel there's not a moment to be lost. What is the point of gathering intelligence if we don't act on it? There's bloody revolution abroad in this city and no one is doing a thing about it!"

"Oh that!" replied Worsley. "That's all been scotched, you know. Byng snared a whole clutch of them up in Yorkshire. Got 'em all under lock and key! The whole thing has blown over. There'll be a few of them hung over this. Mark my words!"

The maid entered before Rolleston could reply and Worsley called for a bottle of port to be brought to them. As the door closed behind her, the visitor remonstrated with his host.

"John! You know it was supposed to be a national rising – the whole country! Just because Byng has caught a few troublemakers in Yorkshire does not mean that we can expect our own rabble-rousers to stay quiet. They've been waiting for this chance for years and I think they could well try to settle a score or two with us anyway."

Worsley looked thoughtfully at his old friend, as though he was considering his words with care.

"Lance," he began. "I have known you most of my life – since our days at Repton - and I admire you greatly. ... Let me finish! More than any other man in Nottingham! It's not like you to get a bee in your bonnet over nothing. So, let us just suppose that your radicals and reformers do manage to put a mob together. What can they do? There are soldiers in the barracks and a couple of hundred of the Yeomanry who could turn out within an hour. Why, we'd scatter 'em in no time! Some good might even come of it! We could hang a couple of dozen of the nastiest and transport a score or two of the rest as a lesson. But it won't get to that. The worst that will happen is that a few dozen of the ugliest will get together, black up their faces and smash a frame or two, like that rogue Towle and his Luddites used to do. By daybreak they will have skulked off somewhere, and the constables will have to root them out of whatever hovel they are stewing in. Now, Lance, sit down here with me, drink some of my port and we'll talk about something more pleasant!"

Rolleston allowed himself to be pushed into a chair as the port arrived, and then played with the glass in his band, still inwardly fuming. He was barely conscious of the beaming face of his friend seated opposite. He was half-persuaded by the logic of what he had heard, but still had doubts.

"John," he said, "I hope you're right. Indeed, you probably are right, but somehow I think that there's more to this than some Luddite vandalism. Every informer told Henry Enfield the same story. Jacobins have travelled the country; plans are set for a national rising this very night! Enfield has even been given the names of the men who have been sent to the different centres to take command, Derby men to Yorkshire and so on. A man from this city called Brandreth has gone to lead in Derbyshire. Yes, I know that you know all this; I know, that Lord Sidmouth knows and has passed the word down that we should all sit tight and let him deal with the matter, but what I am saying is that no-one is dealing with anything! Just two dozen soldiers in the city and they are sitting in the Barracks. The Yeomanry is asleep at home. I mean, suppose there are a few thousand, instead of a few dozen? Sidmouth is safe enough in bed two hundred miles away, but we are right in the melting pot. We should be doing something!"

Worsley refilled his own glass and gestured an offer of more to Rolleston who waved it away, and he looked with an expression of tolerant forbearance at the worried man opposite.

"Let's suppose you are right," he said genially. "What exactly is it that we ought to be doing? Shall we strap on a brace of pistols each and ride out to face the enemy?" He laughed at the thought, scratching his ample waistcoat as he did so.

"Ride out:" cried Rolleston. "Yes, we must ride out and gather intelligence: Then if anything is going on, we can alert the Hussars. Will you come with me, John?"

He leapt to his feet. Worsley had lost his smile all of a sudden and began to look irritated.

"I don't really want to talk about this matter further, thank you, Lance," he said. "I don't know what has come over you, but I'm damned if I like you in this sort of mood."

He was silent and rain slammed up against the window. Rolleston stood up and cleared his throat.

"Well, I'll be off," he said. "Goodbye, John."

"The girl will see you out", said his host sharply without looking up.

Rolleston was soon outside, riding through the wet streets, hastening back towards Watnall. On his arrival, he let himself in and went straight-up to his study. In the corner by his dressing table was his riding crop. He picked it up and made for the door. Pausing, he took a pair of matching pistols from their mountings on the wall and sat down at his desk to load them. He pushed them carefully into the pockets of his coat, along with his pouch of powder and ball and walked along the landing where his wife came out of her bedroom to meet him.

"Back from your ride, Dear?" she asked pleasantly. "You must have been soaked through!"

"I must go out again, Caroline", he replied. "I may not be back until quite late".

Ignoring her remonstrance, he went down the stairs and out of his front door, and rode off at a canter towards the Cavalry Barracks that were situated in the Castle Park.

There was a long delay before Captain Frederick Philipson opened his parlour door and exchanged greetings with his guest.

Rolleston had used the waiting time to peruse the spines of the volumes of military books which lined the shelves, and to pace in front of the prints of obscure, forgotten battles which hung on the walls. This was a comfortable room with a bachelor feel; scuffed leather chairs and the aroma of cigar smoke. He strove to recall what he knew of Philipson, who he had never met. The Crown had posted the Captain to Nottingham quite recently and Rolleston's wife had commented upon his fine manners at some soiree or other. Rolleston himself avoided society evenings like the plague.

Philipson extended a long arm in relaxed fashion. "Very pleased to meet you at last, Sir. Philipson is the name, Mr Rolleston. May I pour you a glass of sack against the weather, Sir?"

He talked in languid, clipped manner and there was a deliberate hint of fop in the way he spoke to which a part of Rolleston took an instant aversion. They exchanged views on the weather, but this was as far as the magistrate was willing to go in the interests of civility.

"Forgive me, Sir," he said. "But, I am amazed to find you here, at your residence on tonight of all nights."

Philipson looked at his visitor in surprise. "You have the advantage of me, Mr Rolleston," he answered. "I am not aware that I am expected elsewhere. I wonder if you can enlighten me."

"Yes Sir, I will enlighten you! I am surprised to find you here drinking Sack when there is armed rebellion abroad!"

Philipson craned towards him eagerly. "Do you have some news, Mr Rolleston? Please, tell me this instant!"

Rolleston hesitated for a moment, but then pushed on. "Captain Philipson," he said slowly. "Tonight is the ninth of June. As I am sure you know, Mr Eaton's informers have told him that an armed rebellion is fixed for tonight! Surely you..."

The soldier's condescending laugh cut him short. "My dear Sir, I think I can relieve your mind. You are probably not aware that my superior, Major General Sir John Byng has rooted out the villains who were planning mischief up in Yorkshire. He has all the self-appointed leaders under lock and key. Absolutely no danger of anything happening now! Of course, my men are keeping their eyes open, watching for any sign of the local disreputables, but if any of them are thinking of trying anything, why, this weather will have dampened their spirits. There is no danger, none whatever. My lads all fought with the Duke at Waterloo. No, my dear sir, you may return to your home easy in your mind."

Rolleston said nothing for a few seconds then spoke firmly. "But there is something going on – I can feel it! It is almost as though you want them to try their revolution!"

Philipson shook his head then laughed loudly!

"Listen, Mr Rolleston," he said. "Did you ride through the city to come here? You did? Well then, were there any signs of rebellion? Come now, were there?"

"Just because I didn't see them doesn't mean they weren't there!" said Rolleston angrily.

"My dear sir, it means everything!" laughed Philipson. "I have experience in these matters and I assure you if anything is going to happen, there'll be plenty to see and hear before it does. The mob has to assemble, and then it has to be whipped up by rabble-rousers and soused with drink before anything gets done. There is always a lot of noise before there is any real trouble, and don't you worry, we will take action if there is any sign of a mob assembling."

"But they wouldn't be in the city," said Rolleston in exasperation. "The intelligence said they would be likely to gather at the Racecourse at dusk. Surely you will send your men out there!"

Philipson bent a little closer to Rolleston, speaking conspiratorially.

"There are things that you don't know. Lord Sidmouth has some very clever plans in place. Why, it might even be to the greater good if a few Jacobins did pop their heads up so we can chop them off and discourage the rest".

The Captain gave what Rolleston supposed to be a knowing look.

"I can say nothing further."

Rolleston could see no more hope of converting the soldier to his way of thinking; he put out his hand in a gesture of farewell. He was escorted to the gate of the Barracks and, having been assured yet again that there was no cause for alarm, rode off again into the night.

Perhaps, he thought to himself, Philipson was right. There seemed little happening and he was probably the only person in Nottingham foolish enough to be out in all this rain. He was surely seeing danger where none existed. Part of his mind however, told him a different story, reminding him that the gentlemen of Paris had disregarded all thoughts of peril right up to the day of their massacre by the mob.

Still in a state of agitation, he knew that if he returned home to the sugary concern of his wife, he would fly into a temper, get a headache and have to endure a sleepless night of self-recrimination. Suddenly resolved, he rode his horse to a nearby livery stable. Dismounting his already flagging bay, he hired a strong-looking grey mare. Bidding good day to the groom, he tugged around the mare's head and guided her out away from the town in the direction of the Race Course.

The park land of Nottingham Forest was a mile north of the city. Within this area of tree, shrub and meadow was the open space of Nottingham Racecourse. Rolleston approached it slowly with apprehension, conscious that it was as likely a place to be robbed as you would find in a long day's ride. Common sense told him to turn back, but he pushed on into the unlit wilderness, his heels ready to spur his horse into flight at any sign of danger.

Danger was closer than he knew. As the mounted gentleman trotted his horse towards them, a dozen men in drab clothes, their faces blackened, pressed in against the bushes on either side of the road. Their hands tightened on an assortment of weapons; muskets and pistols, swords and spears; some lethal-looking iron bars completed the collection. If the rider had seen them, he showed no sign. The gentleman came on, his hat brim down against the rain. Reaching the exact place where the men were hidden, he slowed almost to a standstill. The watchers in the darkness tensed and gripped their weapons as, oblivious to danger, Rolleston nudged the mare's sides enough to stir her, riding away into the gloom.

As the clatter of the departing hooves started to die away, the black-faced men hidden in the hedges climbed warily back on to the road.

"I wonder where he's off to?'" said one. "Probably off to see his lady love," said another.

The grim men around them laughed briefly. They resumed their walk towards the city. After a while, they reached a crossroads, where they halted and held a brief discussion. Finally, one handed his weapons to another and set off on the road towards Eastwood, unarmed and alone. The rest watched him go until his shape disappeared into the night, before turning back to continue towards their homes in Nottingham.

Some minutes later, Rolleston slowed his mount again as he reached the racecourse, for fear of meeting the rebels, but there was no one on this remote piece of common. He made out a small shaft of light which proved to be escaping from a chink in the ill-fitting shutters of a small, lonely house. From the outside the place looked in need of major repairs, although it appeared to be of sound construction and relic from an earlier time, built to keep out unwelcome visitors.

He dismounted, approached the mysterious dwelling cautiously and knocked loudly on the wooden door.

"Gerraway from here!" yelled an annoyed voice from within. "Yer not gerrin' me for no treason!" The last word made Rolleston feel suddenly eager.

"I am Lancelot Rolleston," he cried." I am a magistrate. You are in no danger from me. Open up, in the name of the law".

His words were succeeded by a long silence, and he was on the point of yelling again when the upstairs shutters were flung open sharply. Silhouetted in the lamplight was a long haired, elderly man, whose worried face appeared in the glow as he held out the lantern that it might shine on the visitor.

"Who are yer? What yer want?"

"Sir!" Rolleston cried again. "I am alone, as you can see and I mean you no harm. I am a magistrate. Will you let me in out of all this rain?"

The figure disappeared without answer and the window upstairs darkened once more. Rolleston had two or three more minutes to wait, before the latch was finally lifted and the door opened. The grey face which had looked out at him viewed the muddy boots and stained greatcoat of his late caller with the gravest suspicion.

Rolleston broke the silence. "Rolleston's the name, Sir. To whom do I have the honour of speaking?"

"Roper," the other replied, at last. "William Roper."

"Mr Roper, sir," said Rolleston. "May I invite myself in out of the wet?"

Rolleston was shown into the front room of the house. Roper closed and bolted the door behind them. Rolleston stood in front of the fire, drying his coat and looking earnestly at the old man.

"What was that you said about treason?"

Roper's reply was agitated. "Ah told 'em ye'll not have me for treason! You ain't gerring in this house! But they kicked the door, Sir. Said they'd have it down and then we'd see whether ah would go or not!"

How long ago was this?" asked Rolleston."How many were there?"

Not a half hour ago! Hundreds of 'em, ah'd say"

"Hundreds?" said asked Rolleston incredulous. "I saw nobody. Where did they go?"

"They marched 'round a bit out front then one called for quiet and med a speech. He said there were not enough turned out and what were they to do now they were so few? He wanted to know if they were still for marchin' on t' castle, or wud they wait for t' Derby men as were on their way and t' Northern men. Yes, that's what he said, t' Northern men."

"And?" pressed the eager Rolleston.

"Most on 'em wur for going home and waiting for t' Northern men to come," the old man continued. "Sum ow 'em were asking about t' Derby men. Seemingly these Derby men were on their way and there wur them as didn't want to let 'em down. There wur a lot more talk, but at end they wur for going back home, and if t' Northern men, or t' Derby men, came, they'd turn out again. Then they went. They kicked my door again, though, and said they'd be back for me when they'd took t' castle, or else they'd send t' Northern men for me."

He stopped talking to look at Rolleston. "Do yer think they'll be back, Sir?" he asked apprehensively.

Rolleston shook his head. "No, I don't think they will come back," he said. "Was there anything else that they said? Did you recognise any voices?"

Roper shook his head. He obviously had no more to tell him, and soon Lancelot Rolleston was riding back towards Nottingham, his mind racing. It seemed that the complacency of Worsley and Philipson had been correctly judged as regards the Nottingham reformers, and much that he had feared seemed to have petered out in the rain at the Racecourse.

Rolleston and the other Nottingham magistrates knew what the rebels obviously did not: there were no Northern men on their way. Sidmouth's informers and Major General Byng's soldiers had seen to that two or three days previously when the leaders were arrested. Now the Nottingham men had decided to retreat to their houses, there remained only Roper's 'Derby men'.

At one o'clock in the morning, Rolleston urged his horse along the road out towards the village of Eastwood which stood on the border between Derbyshire and Nottinghamshire. He was on the hunt for the Derbyshire marchers. The rain was, if anything, much heavier.

Twelve hours later found Rolleston sitting still in his saddle near Eastwood and listening for what seemed an age to the gurgling of Gilt Brook He was bone weary after the madcap pursuit of the previous night and the sunshine confirmed that the hired horse was barely able to stand. He was exhausted, but the compass of his mind could not find the direction of sleep. He was so wildly awake that it would be hours his whirring brain shut itself down.

After some time, the animal's snort reminded him where he was; he soothed its loyal neck with a gentle hand. Rolleston clicked his tongue, nudged in his heels, and the sorry beast began to limp towards home. A slow progress took them through the last of the villages before Nottingham itself, through Kimberley and Nuthall. He sensed a barely-repressed hostility in the faces of those village folk they passed. No one seemed to be at work, although people were busy un-boarding their doors and windows now the danger seemed past. Women leaned in their doorways talking to other women, and groups of men lounged here and there conversations stopping as they turned to stare after him in undisguised hostility.

Several times he looked over his shoulder, sensing the malice at his back, afraid a missile might be about to hit him. The only danger, however, was in the stony looks of the men and women who glared at his departing figure as if at the Devil himself. Normally, on an already hot day he would have avoided the steaming stench of the Marsh area of the town, having no need to pass that way to reach Watnall. Nottingham was said to have the worst slums in the British Empire. Today, however, he had to return the hired horse to the stables straight through that most unsavoury quarter. The smells were appalling, and he felt himself near to retching as he rode.

The un-drained, mud-surfaced streets were fouled with nauseating excrement and offal. Amongst it all stood ragged, listless children, who seemed too tired to play. The tall buildings seemed about to totter into the narrow lanes dividing them; it was as if he could hear them creaking as he looked at them.

On the corners were knots of slovenly men, hard-faced and dangerous. They considered him and his possessions with an acquisitive stare and he wondered what it was that prevented them from tearing him from his horse, smashing his skull on the cobbles below, and making off with his fine coat, boots and watch. He realized they were thinking the same thing. After all, what had such men to lose?

It was a relief as he began to emerge from the horrific landscape of that city within a city. He had to steer his horse to the side of the street in order to avoid a young woman who walked in front of him. A small girl, perhaps four years old, plodded at her side; like her mother, she was heavily burdened with a bundle. The woman, trudging slowly along, was carrying an infant on her back.

As he overtook her, Rolleston glanced at her face and was surprised to discover it to be full of character and interest. She was not pretty in the way of the women in his wife's circle and was without make-up or carefully-tended hairstyle. She was obviously ill or exhausted, but her face was strong and even-featured; a look of stoic dignity exuded from within. He found himself raising his hat to her.

If she noticed the gesture, it did not show in any reaction. She marched unstoppably onwards, with determination in her eyes.

As he approached the stables, Rolleston grew conscious of the appalling condition of his hired horse, and began to dread the long, reproachful interview which must result. Old Bentley who owned the stables was a fine man, with a sound business sense, but he had one well-known weakness: he loved his animals. His stable boasted the best horses for hire in the entire Midlands; his clientele included many of the most rich and notable in Nottinghamshire, but he had been known to refuse horses to any, no matter how important, that used too much whip, or indulged in thoughtless play. As they limped into the yard, a groom came out of the stables, with a concerned look on his face for the mare, and a frown for Rolleston. The latter's joints were stiff and his body aching from hard hours of riding; his dismount was painful. The groom took the reins shaking his head angrily as he led the exhausted animal away to its stall. It would be some while till the poor beast was fit to be hired out again. Rolleston mounted his rested bay with an effort and started for home, but old Bentley himself charged out of his office on an interception course. The stables' proprietor had no hair left on his crown, but his magnificent, snow-white eyebrows were twitching in agitation.

"Mr Rolleston, Sir!" he cried.

Rolleston stopped and began to stammer an explanation for the state of the poor mare, prepared as a last resort to use his position as a magistrate to save himself from too much abuse. Old Bentley's reaction bowled him over.

"The mare?" he boomed. "Please don't trouble a thing about it, sir.

Old Amber is a tough old girl. Yes sir, she's proud - we're all proud –
to have been of service to you.

"You're a hero and no mistake. The whole town is talking about what
you did, Sir. You'll be given the freedom of Nottingham, if there's
any justice. You've save us all! None of us would have a stick of
property left if you hadn't kicked those lazy soldiers out to defend
us! My hand, Sir! Take it and my thanks, too! You are a great man,
Mr Rolleston; a great man!"

His mind numbed, Rolleston thanked the beaming Bentley, dug his
heels into his bay and rode in a daze to his own dwelling. He opened
the door as quietly as possible, hoping to reach the bedroom and to
keep, without interruption from the rest of his household, a long
postponed appointment with sleep. It was not to be; he found
himself assailed by a shrieking wife, hysterical children and two
dithering housemaids.

Where had he been? The whole story was needed now, this instant!
Or Mrs Rolleston would swoon. Again. Mobs of murderers all over
the county! Soldiers riding out in the middle of the night! Yeomanry
fighting pitched battles with Jacobins not two miles away from
Watnall Hall! And he had left them defenceless all night! Look at
the state of his clothes!

Dodging the hail of verbal missiles, Rolleston forced his way up the
stairs to the landing. Outside his door he summoned the last
croaking remnants of his voice to obtain silence from the hysterical
jabbering of his family and household.

He spoke firmly, in the manner he used in court to quell protests
against unpopular judicial verdicts. "Mrs Rolleston in a moment I
am going into my room and I am going to sleep. No one – and I
include yourself – is to question me further or disturb my rest. Is
that understood?"

Without pausing for answer he shut the bedroom door behind him and turned the lock from within. Caroline Rolleston gazed briefly at the closed door to his room, thoroughly intimidated by her husband's obduracy. Shushing severely at the two maids she laid a finger to her lips. The three women raised their skirts an inch or two, so that they could see their feet as they tiptoed downstairs.

Sleep came quickly to Lancelot Rolleston, but it did not endure. By seven o'clock, he was awake, but not rested. He struggled out of bed and looked at himself in the glass. He laughed aloud almost when he saw his reflection. The Devil himself, he thought! He pulled the chain to ring the bell for hot water. The maid brought it, tapping timorously at the door curtseying shyly as he accepted it.

"Please Sir", she said. "The mistress says to inform you that Mr Worsley has called and that she has provided a little refreshment for you, if you are well enough to come down and see him."

The news was not pleasant to him.

"Tell her... tell your mistress that I will be down presently." he told the girl.

When he entered the drawing room a little later, John Worsley bounded towards him, his hand outstretched. Rolleston took it, inwardly wincing at the embrace of it and its equally hearty fellow.

"Here he is M'am! Your husband and our hero! The most talked of gentleman in Nottingham", Worsley waffled ecstatically. "My dear fellow, come and join us!"

"Yes, Lance dear", said his beaming wife. "Sit by me and eat something. We must hear everything! Every word!"

He ate and drank, not because he especially wanted anything, but the action of doing so postponed the moment he must talk with these two preposterous people. While he nibbled, Caroline Rolleston and John Worsley sat grinning at one another beaming as though

Lancelot was Odysseus returned to Ithaca. He ate little, lingering over it; eventually he could delay no longer. They perched like carrion, ready to devour his words as he dabbed his mouth with a kerchief. They ushered him to the armchair.

"Well? Let's have it man – or do I have to tell your tale for you?"

"To be truthful" said Rolleston slowly, "last night is all a bit of a blur now. Perhaps if you were to say what you have heard, then I might tell you whether or not you are right"

Mrs Rolleston frowned in disappointment, but Worsley was eager to do as his friend suggested and soon her eyes were dancing with delight as he launched into his tale. After the first few words Worsley had almost forgotten that the real hero of his story was present. The magistrate stayed slumped and unmoving in his armchair, staring at the distant toes of his boots.

"Your husband, Mrs Rolleston, is the toast of the city," said Worsley. "Lance, when you came to me yesterday with your wild talk, I thought you were clearly barking up the wrong tree. I don't mind admitting now that I was wrong, quite wrong, and I hope you will accept an honest apology

"He came to me last night, ma'am, trying to persuade me that there was riot and, saving your presence ma'am, bloody revolution abroad! I wouldn't listen, of course. Told him to go home and put such nonsense out of his mind. But does he go? He does not! Soon he is out alone in the streets, scouring the city for any sign of the murderers, up to the Barracks, telling that lazy Captain to do his duty and get out of his chair and into the saddle. But all he gets is scorn! Told to leave military matters to military men! Am I right, Lance?"

Rolleston nodded abstractedly.
"I am right", continued Worsley. "Does that stop this man? No! He's off out to the Racecourse as fast as his horse will bear him, to see

what these villains are about. But when he arrives, there is nobody there. They have all skulked off back to their hovels, or the inn.

"Is the job done then? Not with this man! The rain is teaming down and he is soaked to the skin, but we see him next on his charger, spurring on towards Eastwood. The village folk tell him that there is an insurrection taking place and an army coming out of Derby to sack Nottingham. He could have ridden back then, and been called a hero, but what does he do? Alone in the dark, he rides the Derby Road in mortal danger, and somewhere on that road, he sees a huge army of desperate men, marching towards him in their hundreds. Only then does he put spurs to his mount and ride away.

"He sounds the alarm at Eastwood and then gallops back to Nottingham Barracks, hammering at the door with a hand like thunder. He had them out of their beds in no time, and soon that idle popinjay in charge is made to see the peril on his doorstep. Away they ride to battle, and where is your husband ma'am? Why, he is there at the head of the troop, like Wellington himself:"

Rolleston gripped the wings of his chair at these last few words, and bit deep into his lip. He had grown hot; he could hear his heart pounding, the noise loud in his ears. Worsley was oblivious to the distress of his host and continued in full flow.

"Of course, a cavalry charge did the trick, and the rabble turned and ran off instantly. It was a brief, but bloody affair."

"Yes! Yes!" cried Caroline, ecstatically. "I found blood on his shirt cuff when I stole in to fetch it out for the girl to wash! I was quite faint, at the sight of it. Fresh blood!"

"Well this man did not faint at the sight of blood," Worsley crowed, pointing at Rolleston. "It is fair to say that he near enough waded through it!

He paused awhile to beam in his host's direction before continuing.

"You would think that by now, with the battle won, and the laurels waiting for his brow, that he would have turned for home to receive them," said the storyteller.

"Any other man, his duty done, would have, you may be sure. But this is a hero of a different stamp to the rest of us, made of rare mettle, rare mettle indeed. He cannot rest until all these marauders are rounded up and confined to jail with a charge of high treason hanging about their necks. So, tired and bloody, he joins up with old Grey, who has brought out a troop of Yeomanry for the sport, and off he goes, leading them in a hunt for the fleeing rabble. Just like a day behind the hounds, old Grey says, and great fun for all.

"Well, the beaters were in action at a ditch near Langley Mill, when they put up this huge and fearsome rebel. He jumped right out of the ground in front of them, with a pistol in his hand and murder in his eye. They are all frightened to death, bar one. Lance spurs his charger forward and drops this villain in the act of shooting, clouts him with his riding crop. Downed him like felling a tree."

Worsley cut short his story here, because Rolleston had jumped to his feet at these last words, knocking over the small table by him as he did so. Glasses and plates went everywhere, and the wine decanter shattered on the floor. Transfixed, they watched the sheet-white hero grope for the door- knob and wrench the door open. In horror they saw a stream of vomit shoot from his mouth onto the wall, the floor, his feet and the bottom steps of the stairs beyond. Still seated, they heard his unsteady legs stumbling up to his bedroom and heard the door slam behind him.

Hopelessly, Worsley saw Caroline Rolleston put her hands together and shape up to scream. She did so, as there he sat eyes wide, mouth opening and closing dumbly.

"His exertions ma' am ", he stammered, taking her soft hand and rubbing it earnestly.
"Dashed odd! Wouldn't have believed it if I hadn't seen it. Calm

yourself Ma'am. Send a girl for the physician. He'll be right in no time."

As Mrs Rolleston succumbed to hysteria a maid arrived to relieve Worsley of responsibility. Unable to comprehend the scene before her eyes she stood gazing stupidly.

"Your mistress, girl," snapped Worsley. "Take her upstairs", he continued waspishly. "When you have done so, call the other girl to clean up this mess!" Pay attention, damn you! Pull yourself together!"

The harsh and angry words had induced the maid to begin her own blubbering; this in turn spurred Mrs Rolleston to even greater upset. Exasperated, Worsley rang the bell continuously, until a second maid came. Tremulously she took notice of his commands, one eye on the two keening women sobbing on the chaise longue, well beyond reach of Worsley's attempts to communicate with them. He retrieved his own hat and cane and left the house with the greatest relief to seek medical aid.

Upstairs, Rolleston had torn off his soiled clothes and sluiced his throbbing head in the wash bowl. The mirror looked at him without forgiveness. His face was white, his eyes red and haunted. There were lines, furrows and ridges of puffy skin. He thought despairingly how old he had become; how far he was now from anything he might ever have hoped to be. Why had he struck the kneeling, helpless man? He had ridden out so full of purpose and certainty, but a different man had limped back. He told himself this was a fever brought on by his exertions, but the self-loathing and anger he felt consumed him more and more.

He turned back to the coolness of his bed, sleeping naked for the first time since his childhood. When the doctor looked in on him later on, with Mrs Rolleston and John Worsley peeping behind him, Rolleston was breathing deeply and easily. The doctor had the sense to let him sleep on. Before he left, he prescribed something harmless and sugary to calm Mrs Rolleston's upset, and then hurried back to the card game which not half an hour previously he had so reluctantly left.

Chapter 3: Telling the Tale

Jeremiah Brandreth

Framed by the sunset, Jeremiah hauled himself painfully up through the trees on the side of the quarry until he reached the top. He gazed into the distance through the gloaming. The worst marks of wear had been wiped from his boots and clothes during his long day in hiding; his face cleansed in the trickle of water which had come down to him from the steep banks. The outward signs of yesterday's flight might have gone, but his eyes were still red vivid with the pain of his remorse. He looked much older than his thirty one years.

He worked out the direction of south west from the sunset. With a last grateful look at the deep sanctuary he was leaving, Jeremiah turned his back on Nottingham. Ahead lay the long road to safety which would take him away from those he loved, as well as those he feared. He was determined to travel by night, concealing himself during the day, until he was well clear of the East Midlands.

Behind him, in the quarry, the fox watched from its concealment until assured of the man's departure. Stretching languidly, it sniffed the air preparatory to its own night time rambling. Soon their shared lair was deserted and abandoned.

George Goodwin

As the evening darkness fell over Ripley, curtains were drawn. The housekeeper took the tray away and left George Goodwin to his sitting room and his own company. He sat, fidgeting as he always did in an unoccupied moment. Reaching for a silver snuff box he slid what remained of a thumbnail into the familiar groove under the lid. From the pile of yellow powder within, carefully he pinched a small amount; this he eased onto the little muscle that popped out when he looped his thumb around the lower joint of his index finger. Raising the hand smoothly to his nostril he inhaled with a snort. Eyes closed, head stiff for a few seconds, he sneezed twice, rapidly. After a short breather, the same action was repeated for the benefit of the other nostril.

The next minute was spent vigorously inhaling and exhaling through his tortured nose. A bachelor's handkerchief was produced from his jacket pocket and a vacant spot selected from the few available. He drew a deep breath into his mouth expelling the air through his nose in a torrent. The handkerchief bulged, but held firm, even when he added two or three smaller supplementary sniffles to clear the last obstructions from his nasal passages.

This agreeable chore accomplished, he turned to a delicate manicuring of his cracked grubby finger nails, picking at the accumulated dirt with a pipe knife and flicking unwanted debris in the general direction of the fireplace. After a minute or two, he stopped to inspect his square strong fingers front and back. In approval he clasped the pristine articles in congratulatory fashion over his solid paunch. Staring into space abstractedly, sucking the last threads of his evening meat from between his teeth, Goodwin snorted in contentment. For a long minute he rested, then shifted to clasp both hands behind his grizzled head, sucking in the straggling corners of his moustache, yellowed by regular snuff taking.

After a while he belched, got to his feet and crossed the carpet to an old oak bureau. Resting his hands on the lid, he turned the key. He brought up a chair, opened the lid of the ink well and reached for paper. Dipping his pen he began a long and laboured letter in which he hoped to give a full account of the events of the previous night.

This would be a long letter. Goodwin did not write prose as elegantly as he accomplished more physical tasks. A man with few close friends, he took no real comfort from female company. The only true empathy he could count upon was with fellow engineers and craftsmen. It was to one such acquaintance that he chose to unburden himself.

Brother to Goodwin's present employer at Butterley and son of one of the ironworks' founders, Josiah Jessop was a fine engineer who would later gain fame as the builder of the Cromford and High Peak Railway.

The letter opened clumsily; its first phrases were inconsequential, but soon Goodwin began to relax. The story of his nocturnal encounters with the rebels, and his attempt to prevent the destruction of the works and equipment which meant so much to him gradually unfolded.

"It was now three o'clock in the morning of Tuesday the 10th. We had just deposited the pikes and the men were separating to go home, when a horseman, George Weightman of Pentrich, son of the woman who keeps the White Horse, rode by. I called on him to stop, but he pushed forward. Another person was then seen on the road from Pentrich near the new shop. Mr Jessop and Mr Wragg ran to see who it was and it was our man Jno Cope. Immediately the main body of the insurgents in number about one hundred appeared marching past Woodhouse's garden in regular order. Rather more than half were armed with guns, the remainder with spears with shafts about twelve or fourteen feet long, or scythes fixed in shafts. One or two had forks and a few were without arms. As we had no guns and did not think it prudent to attack them, I ordered the men to retire to the office where we determined to defend ourselves with the pikes.

"The insurgents came forward in good order, in a line formed two deep opposite the office, extending in a curve to the front of the garden wall to the doors of the foundry yard which were shut. The fellow at their head who acted as chief gave the words "halt to the right, face front!"

"He was a thin little man, apparently not thirty years of age and was dressed in a long brown coat and armed with both a gun and pistols. He knocked with the butt end of his gun against the yard door.

"I went to the office door and asked "What do you want? What's your object here?" He answered "We want your men!"

"I replied "You shall not have them! You are too many already except that your purpose was better. Disperse. The law will be too strong for you. You will all be hanged!"

"No answer whatever was made to us and seeing Isaac Ludlam of Winfield Park (who was armed with a spear), his nephew Jas Taylor (with a gun) and Isaac Moore of Pentrich Lane End, a mason who had worked for us formerly (and carried a fork), all of whom I knew well, l went out among them, expostulating with them and pushing them round by the shoulder bade them get home or they would all get hanged. Ludlam (who is a sort of Methodist parson) appeared much agitated and trembled violently when he said."I am as bad as I can be! I must go on, I cannot go back."

"During the time I was speaking to these men, three young fellows who had been compelled to follow slipped in behind me and got into the Office under our protection, and whether the chief thought us too strong to be attacked, or whether he feared further defections of his men, I know not, but without saying a word or taking notion or what had been passing. He gave word to march and led his men past Woodhouse's house and over the coke hearth, from whence they crossed to the Derby Road at the top of Brick Row and went forward to Ripley. They did not go into the town, fearing, as I believe, to encounter the large body of constables they expected see posted there, but turned left at the Cock, on the road to Codnor. Ten minutes after the first men passed, perhaps fifty more appeared on the road from Pentrich. These did not come near the office but turned likewise up the Derby Road.

"Sometime later a lone horseman appeared: I seized his bridle as he passed and recognized him as William Weightman, George's brother. He has carrying a bag of bullets which he confessed he was taking to the rebels.

"He said his life was threatened if he would not carry them. As we were then expecting an attack from a large body we were told was coming from Heage, we did not detain him prisoner, but allowed him to depart on his promise to remain quiet at home. Instead of doing so, he set off another way, through Swanwick and, so I'm told, informed the insurgents of the capture of their ammunition.

"In less than an hour we had advice from various quarters that a body of them was returning to revenge themselves for its loss. On hearing this addition to the rumours of other bodies advancing on us, we set about fortifying the office, blocking all the windows which command the road with bundles of paper and sacks of flour, leaving only loopholes to fire through.

"We collected about sixteen guns and blunderbusses which we dispersed at the different points with the requisite powder and ball, and the most expert men (old soldiers) were stationed to load and fire them. We also carried a quantity of cannon shot into the upper office to throw through the windows on the heads of our assailants. Here we spent the night until the next morning when, at about eleven o'clock, we had the pleasure to see the High Sheriff and two magistrates Colonel Halton and Mr Lord, arrive, accompanied by the Chesterfield troop of yeomanry.

"By this time we had received advice that the insurgents were dispersing and endeavouring to return home and the cavalry, together with our pike men and those armed with guns, were immediately divided into three detachments to scour the different roads by which they were expected to retreat. One of these is the road from Ripley to Nottingham; another, the road through Butterley Park and the third at Swanwick, towards Riddings. They met the insurgents returning and by three o'clock had taken twenty-eight prisoners who were sent to Derby the same night. Nothing could exceed the zeal and activity shown by the cavalry and pike men in their race after the insurgents, several of whom took refuge in the woods between Butterley and Swanwick. The pike men went in to beat them out and the cavalry stationed on theoutside took them prisoners.

"In the afternoon two troops of yeomanry from Derby arrived and helped take more prisoners and all seems to be quiet tonight. You will be happy to know that none of our workers, apart from some cleaners, took part, and that we managed a good day's work, despite the activity.

"I conclude by hoping that this letter finds you in the best of health and remain your friend and servant."

George Goodwin

Goodwin read over his letter, his pen poised, dipping here and there to correct a sentence or insert a missing punctuation mark. Just before he put down his pen he was struck by a final thought and added a postscript.

"In my view, our men were seduced into this desperate enterprise by the foul words of our former employee. Thomas Bacon. He is the great ringleader."

Satisfied at last and tired enough to sleep, he put down his pen, blotted the papers and folded them up for posting. Opening up his watch he looked at the time, sighed, yawned for a moment or two and proceeded to climb the stairs to his solitary bed.

George Weightman

It was nearly midnight before Hugh Wolstenholme, the curate of Pentrich, had packed off the last of his visitors from his house in Crich. Respectable members of his congregation had turned up in twos and threes to seek his opinion and reassurance on the depredations of the previous night. A hundred questions assailed him and they must hear what he had to say before their fears were finally allayed. What punishment might the authorities mete out to those deluded men? Would the innocent be punished along with the guilty? Was it their fault that they happened to live the neighbourhood of the rebels? When was Wolstenholme going to visit poor Mrs Hepworth whose servant was shot in front of her and her children? Was he going to denounce every heretic and rebel from the pulpit on Sunday? Would he use his influence to make sure the authorities knew that there were still loyal folk in the parish of Pentrich, as well as murderers? To each of the questions he had listened sympathetically, very much conscious of his standing as a man of letters in a simple community.

He had done his best to soothe away worries with kind words and patience. They were only persuaded to depart by the lateness of the hour, and by the fact that he had promised to write to the Duke of Devonshire on their behalf. The Duke was landlord to most local farmers and they looked up to him with a feudal devotion.

A letter to the Duke! That appealed to all and sundry and Wolstenholme must be sure to mention the name of every one of them when he wrote. At this conclusion, the little deputation of Taylors, Hunts and Onions left, parting at the door, to spread the news of the letter next day to relatives and neighbours. Wolstenholme put out the light in the hall with great relief. He barred the door. With a candle in his hand he walked wearily up the creaking wooden stairs. He stopped on the first landing, listening carefully tapping lightly on one of the wooden wall-panels.

There was a little catch at one side; finding it finally, he tugged and an opening appeared in what had seemed to be a solid wall. Had anyone been with the Pentrich curate at that moment, they would have been amazed to see, revealed by the glow from the candle, the legs of a man and a chair appearing from within the cupboard.

"You can step out for a while, George," Hugh Wolstenholme said.

A tall, well-built young man dropped to his knees inside the hidey-hole and peered out, quizzically.

"My visitors outstayed their welcome, but there was much to talk about" said Wolstenholme.

The two men had descended the staircase and seated themselves in the kitchen. George was munching a supper.

"There isn't a deal of room in there for a lad my size" laughed George. "Ah'm not sure how long ah can stick it. No offence intended, Mr Wolstenholme. Please don't think ah'm ungrateful. What ah mean is ah hope ah don't have to stop in there too long. And ah'm putting you in danger! As soon as t' hue and cry dies down, ah'll be off!"

"I think I'd be in greater danger if you left," said Wolstenholme. "You are going to have to get used to your hideaway and stay hidden for a few weeks before its safe for you to leave, but don't worry, you needn't spend all your time in there. You'll be safe enough upstairs, if you're quiet and stay away from the windows. Ah! I think your stew is ready."

Wolstenholme let his dishevelled guest eat his stew, mop the plate clean with bread and wash it all down with a mug of ale. The man obviously had a great hunger upon him and fed himself at great speed.

"Now George," said Wolstenholme. "Into the parlour with you! I want to hear every word of your story, right from the beginning."

They moved into the next room and the clergyman indicated an armchair for his guest to sit in. He produced two pipes, and gave one to George, then passed him the tobacco pouch. They lit up and pulled appreciatively at the stems of their pipes, staring at each other's boots as they lounged in relaxation. George took a moment or two to put his memory in order before beginning to tell his tale.

"Ah was his lieutenant." The pride in his voice was obvious.

"We met up at Hunt's Barn, over South Winfield way. We shared out t' weapons. Isaac Ludlam had a lot of old pikes hidden in his quarry and a few of the Wingfield men had brought these up. They were bragging and saying us Pentrich lot had better be as well provided. When we were all there, there must have been about forty or fifty o' us. The captain called for quiet. He said that t' great revolution had begun and that we were out t' plant t' Tree of Liberty – that's what he called it, t' Tree of Liberty! We started t' give three cheers, but he stopped us and called for silence. He said we were an army now and under strict military orders. He was going t' tell us who t' officers would be. Then there's a lot of shouting about who is t' be officers. All yelling at once!

"Then the Captain quiets us and says there is one Captain and one only and any who don't follow orders are traitors and will be dealt with like traitors. That shut 'em up. He said he'd been in the army and that soldiers had t' obey t' officers. Then he told William Turner and his sister's son with one eye - Manchester Turner, we calls him - to command the front. He had a military word for it that ah don't recollect."

"Vanguard?" suggested Wolstenholme.

"Yes! That's it " said George. "The Turners was t' command t' vanguard and he told owd Isaac Ludlam and his lads to take t' back: the rearguard. Then he put us all into line and told us t' make ready to march But then he walked down t' ranks till he came to me and says "George, youth! You march wi' me, ah've a special job for thee.

"The other lads were jealous and one or two of that Wingfield lot were sneering, but ah took no notice.

"We went to Mr Tomlinson's first, near South Wingfield. He were out in his yard waiting for us, and told the Captain that he shouldn't have him, or take his gun. Then t' Captain put a pistol t' his head and told him if he wanted t' keep it, he had better get into line. Ah felt sorry for t' owd lad, myself, and when ah got t' chance ah tipped him t' wink to run for it and he got clear of us.

"Most places we went, folks were t' same. They all said they wouldn't stir out to commit treason. Only Sam Hunt came because he wanted to. We had t' threaten all t' others. Sam gave us bread, cheese and ale. Then t' Captain said that t' work were too slow and ah should go across t' Pentrich t' my uncle John to ask how they were making out, and hurry them up if need be. So ah started running and found my uncle and t' others. He said that they were waiting in the dry for the Captain to come up and that's what we did.

"When the captain got t' Pentrich he were in a bad mood because we had done nowt. Ah asked him about it, but he got angry and told me t' be quiet. Then Bill Turner said t' Captain had killed a man back at Mrs Hepworth's and that was why he were angry.

"Then he said he had a special job for me and that ah was the only one he could trust. We had a pony off one o' t' farms and he told me t' mount him and ride off t' Nottingham for news of how things were going there. If ah met anyone on t' road, ah was to say 'love' to him. If he answered 'well' then he were a friend wi' a message and ah were t' bring it back.

"If any stopped me and said 'love' ah was to reply 'well' and quick, because if ah didn't they would probably shoot me as a government man! Well off we went – t' pony and me. T' tell t' truth, he was hardly worth riding, poor owd thing. On our way t' bring the news ah had t' walk a lot o' t' time, when he lost his breath.

"Ah were riding past t' ironworks when Mr Goodwin runs out in front o' me waving his hands and shouting. Ah nearly ran him down, but just managed t' go round him. All t' time he was calling out he knew me t' be too honest a man for this business.

"Ah didn't have time t' stop, though, and ah rode on. There were plenty of inns still open along the way but ah didn't go into any of them. We reached Eastwood; t' owd pony panting like his heart was going to burst.

"Just like the Captain said, a man comes out of t' dark and calls on me t' stop. 'Love' he says and ah replied 'well'. Then he knew ah were a friend and he gi' me t' message ah was t' take back. He made me learn it by heart and ah had t' repeat it t' him until ah had it right. The message was: 'Tell t' Captain that Nottingham is taken; t' soldiers will not stir out of their barracks; t' Derbyshire men must come up.' Then he told me t' be off and said he would drink with me later in Nottingham Castle. He wished me 'God speed' and ah set off back.

"Well, t' owd pony nearly died, but we kept going until we found t' Captain at Langley Mill. He were at t' inn there. And everyone was calling for drink. When he saw me he shouted for quiet and made me stand on a table with him t' give the message. When ah told them Nottingham was taken they all cheered. Then he told me t' get myself some ale, but the landlady wouldn't serve me because ah'd no money. The Captain ordered her t' serve me and she'd be paid back later. He said that there were no point in giving her Bank o' England money because it were worthless now.

"Then t' Captain told us all t' be moving. He said Nottingham wasn't far and there was bread and beef waiting for every man who was there by morning, and rum, too. A lot of 'em had too much drink, though, and he had to get t' Turners and Sam Hunt to threaten them.

"The Captain said he'd already killed one man and he'd as soon be hung for two as one. They went, but made him stop at t' Navigationand then again at t' Sun Inn at Eastwood. People were out in t' streets there and they told t' Captain to turn back because a magistrate had gone t' fetch t' Hussars.

"A lot wanted to go home then, but t' Captain told 'em that t' soldiers wouldn't turn out and that t' City were taken. Anyway, old Henry Hole, he said he was off and no one would stop him. He looks our Captain straight in t' eye and walks off. T' Captain points his gun and says he'll shoot him. But Tom Turner tells him it in't worth itand knocks his arm as he fires. T' shot went into t' air and Henry Hole got away. Tom did 'em both a favour!

"Anyhow, we got on out of Eastwood and then what do you think?

James Hill pulls t' trigger on his piece and t' ball went into Charlie Walter's leg. Boot full of blood. We thought we were attacked for a minute and a few of 'em chucked their guns away, and ran off. Well, ah picked him up and put him on t' old pony and told the Captain ah'd tek him back to t' Sun and then come back."

George had told all his story with hardly a break and Wolstenholme had let him do so, listening quietly as he pictured each scene for himself. This pause was a long one, though, and George began looking foolishly at his big strong hands.

"And when you rejoined the Captain, what happened then? What happened when you went back?"

George did not answer immediately and when he did speak, Wolstenholme noticed that his eyes were full of tears.

"Ah didn't go back. Ah just felt bad about things. Ah took Charlie t' inn and folks were looking at me queer and ah just wanted to go home."

"You did well to leave them, George! You are in trouble but others are in deeper than you"

The big man said nothing. Then he blurted out "But he needed me! Ah said ah would come back, but ah left him. He'd have come back for me!"

Jeremiah Brandreth

The plan was not working. By moving at night and concealing himself in the day Jeremiah had hoped to progress toward the south coast without being seen. In the darkness however, he found travel in the strange terrain to be almost impossible. He had to inch his way forward as if blind, with a hand outstretched before him to ward off any branches which might strike him. If he had been able to find a country lane pointing in the right direction, he could have made progress, but none of them seemed to be going the way he wanted. Desperate, he had struck out across country, blundering through hedges and tumbling down mossy slopes until he was bruised, exhausted and in the worst of tempers.

He had given up several times, sitting down to wait for morning amidst beds of waving ferns, but each time he had forced himself up, pushing on further, spurred on by the peril which attended delay. Eventually, he accepted that he was totally lost. He had no idea where he was, or even in which direction he needed to travel He stood: his back against a tree and his heart in despair. The night was dark and he was being hunted far from home. Yesterday they had called him the 'Nottingham Captain;' he had stood at the head of hundreds of men; tonight he was a lonely fugitive and the courage that had kept him going for so long had deserted him as utterly as his comrades. The Captain had once more become Jerry Brandreth from Sutton in Ashfield who missed his wife and children. Every emotion demanded that he set off into the darkness to find them, hold and protect them; common sense and the instinct for self-preservation on the other hand, told him that he must escape and leave England forever.

As he dwelt in this dark mood, a delicious smell of food cooking nearby filled his nostrils. He realized how hungry he was. His belly rumbled and his mouth watered. Jeremiah had experienced hunger plenty of times in his adult life He had often gone a day without food. He would pretend to Ann that he had he had eaten earlier with a friend so there would be enough for her and the children. There was no hiding from the pangs of a few days without sustenance and he began to follow the scent like a primeval hunter. Taut and alert,he picked his way along a hedgerow, climbing carefully through a gap and emerging onto a grassy lane.

The night was very still Even the little breeze that had rustled in the trees and bushes had died away. Jeremiah held his arm up in front of his face and shuffled carefully along the lane towards the origin of the smell. Soon, there was a little fire glowing ahead of him in the near distance, though still no sound or sign of any living creature.

It was so quiet now that he could hear his own breathing and the swish of his coat as it rubbed against his breeches.

It happened in an instant. His heart stopped, as a white owl flew across his path, an inch it seemed, from his face. He felt the wind of its wings thundering past in rage and challenge.

The next second, a horse shrilled loudly. Close by a human voice spat out a warning.

"Stand still or I'll split you in half!"

In his shocked state Jeremiah stood helpless, nerves tight as bowstrings, convinced he was captured and unsure whether to bolt or abide.

Ann Brandreth

In the same room where she had spent the night after her wedding Ann Brandreth lay sleeping, stretched on her front, one leg extended, the other bent away across the bed, forearms resting flat on a level with her head hair spread out along on the pillow hiding her face. She was breathing peacefully.

Her young daughter, Elizabeth, stood gazing at her. Her nightshirt was too big and dragged on the cold floor; she had learned to curl her toes into the extra fold of cloth for warmth. She stared at mother for a long time and felt happy to see her sleeping at last. Since her father had gone, her mother had not laughed; Elizabeth had heard her often in the dark crying, or watched her sitting with her eyes open. She had gone to her in those moments and they had clung together; Ann would smooth her hair and kiss her face softly. Wakening later under her own sheets Elizabeth would see her there, lighting a fire to make oatcakes, her hair tied back in a bunch and her eyes red.

She was standing guard. When her little brother Timothy began to mew in his cot, Elizabeth tiptoed over and shushed him softly back to sleep so that he would not wake their mother. She was standing guard, just as her father had made her promise when he had said goodbye all those weeks ago.

Her mother had put a little bundle of food into his pocket and straightened his collar. She remembered her pushing some unruly curls back behind his ears looking at him reproachfully as she often did. Her father had peered closely at her mother and for a moment it seemed as if they would all start crying again; somehow they had held back the tears.

Then he kissed Elizabeth. "Guard your mother for me, little one until I come home", he said, lifting her up to look into her eyes. Then he bent over the cot to kiss little Tim.

As he turned to go, her mother ran to him; they held one another close for a moment. Her eyes were very tightly closed. As they pulled away she took her little blue scarf from her neck and tied it around his. Then he was gone and she sat still on the bed for a long time, looking into space. Elizabeth cuddled up beside her, holding her hands until she slept, then crept into bed to seek her own dreams.

Jack Johnson

The two men ate together, backs to the wheel of a cart, occasionally glancing over to watch each other's face take on more definition in the slowly increasing light of early morning. In front of them, the little fire danced tiredly under its burden of sticks casting an animated pattern on the four boots stretched out towards it.Jeremiah had tasted his first meal for some days and it had done his nerves good.

"Ah know when somebody's on t' run," said the stranger. " Ah can smell it. Perhaps ah even know why you're on t' run. There in't much Jack don't know."

Jack Johnson was the owner of the cart they were leaning against as well as the grey that stood like a great four legged ghost some yards away down the lane. The rabbit stew was his too, that had lured Jeremiah a few short hours before.

"A man can be on t' run for many reasons", Jack continued. "He might be bound to a tradesman, one that treats him like dirt on t' sole of his shoe and causes him to break his contract, but not you; you're too old.

"You might be a poacher and have t' keepers after you, but you don't move like a country man. Ah heard you coming miles away. No. you're no poacher. You might be a beggar: but you've no pack, and anyway, ah know 'em all, and you're not one of 'em. You look like a gypsy with your curls, but you don't seem at home in t' lanes like a gypsy would be. No, my lad, ah think that there's only one thing that you can be."

Jeremiah studied the man next to him, taking in for the first time the carter's white-whiskered face with its nut-brown clustered wrinkles, fringed with snowy hair and beard. Two narrow, piercing blue eyes glistened and looked deeply wherever their gaze fell. A row of brown freckled knuckles gripped the handle of a purposeful-looking knife resting across the knees of this mysterious traveller.

His hands were big from the tugging of reins and the loading of cargo. He wore a wool cap that seemed to be rooted in his unkempt

white mane.

"What is it ah am, since you know do much? " he asked, quietly.

The old man leaned forward, picked up a stick of wood and began to whittle it intently, with strong strokes of the knife.

"Ah should think you're one of them on the run from the soldiery on account of that business at Eastwood. That's what you are my lad," said Jack, whittling all the while.

Jeremiah thought of laughing off the suggestion and making up a lie. He even began to wonder whether he should overpower this alert old man, steal his horse and cart and use them to aid his escape. He knew he had to say something, otherwise his silence would confirm the truth of the other's estimation.

"Nowt so dangerous" he answered. "Just a skilled man who can't find work. Ah'm off to t' south to see if ah can t get work down there."

Johnson said nothing for a while, but continued whittling. Eventually he stood up, stretching to relieve his stiffness and began to ferret around under the empty sacks that protected his load. His hand emerged clasping the neck of an earthenware jug which he proffered silently to Jeremiah who took it, drew out the cork and sniffed it approvingly. Resting the jug on the back of his hand and tilting it he tasted the ale within.

"Ah don't suppose you'd say no t' some more breakfast stew, neither" said Johnson and he busied himself putting the blackened kettle that contained the meat and vegetables on the campfire. When it was ready the old man used a stick to expertly pluck the pot from the flames and place it by Jeremiah's side. Then he tossed him a battered old spoon and indicated that he should eat. The younger man was glad to obey this silent instruction and was soon greedily wolfing down the delicious stew. It seemed years since he had eaten as well as this, if indeed he ever had.

Johnson had harnessed the old horse and thrown a few scattered items of camping equipment onto the back of his cart. He disappeared behind the hedge for a few minutes. When he returned Jeremiah rose to his feet and offered him the unfinished half of the stew.

"Finish it all, man, said Johnson. "You need it more than me!"

Jeremiah did not argue.

"You'll be heading south, then?" Jeremiah nodded his mouth full.

"Ah'm going that way. You might as well come with me", said Johnson.

Jeremiah nodded again. Johnson clambered on the cart and took the reins. The Nottingham Captain kicked out the little fire which had drawn him to the spot and pulled himself up by the old driver, the pot of stew on his knee. The cart jerked as it moved forwards; Jeremiah looked back with thanks to the little campsite. He pondered why it was that the smoke always grows stronger when the fire goes out.

They rode on together, the two men and the horse, into the brightening day. After a while Johnson began to talk, telling his life story.

"Me father came home one day. Just like in that old song they sing about Spencer the Rover:

> *'And now he is a living in his cottage in the country,*
>
> *With woodbine and ivy growing round the door,*
>
> *He's as happy as those who have thousands of riches;*
>
> *Contented he'll stay and go rambling no more.'*

'Ah'm back,' he says, back to stay.' Poor owd lass wer dumb with shock! Then he looked at me.

"He walks in the house and says good-day to t' mother. She passed out on her legs and we had to pick her up and pour water on her. 'A strong son - ah'm blessed,' he says and he takes me outside. 'This is yours,' he told me pointing at a cart and an old horse, too. Lord Marlborough he was called. T' horse ah mean! 'Ah've give you nowt, all your life, but now ah'm giving you all ah've got, this cart, this horse, and this load - there's all sorts in them sacks. Ah were your age when your old grandfather passed on and he left me his cart.

Ah'm done with t' road now. Ah'm back to stay for what life is left me. Now ah'm leaving you this and plenty of knowledge about trade if you have sense to listen.'

"Then we went inside and she brought him some food and drink and sat with him. They just sat talking there close together and it got dark. Ah fell asleep until he kicked me in t' ribs and says 'You tend your horse, you idle bugger.'

"Well, ah tended that old horse and four more like him, one after another. Ah called them all Lord Marlborough, even t' mares! His old cart lasted a few years, till I had to get another. There was one more after that and now this one. And this will be my last."

Jack Johnson was silent after the long talk; Jeremiah felt he should say something, but wasn't sure what. He had begun to realize how careful someone on the run had to be with words. He envied the carter his simple, uncomplicated life. He decided the best approach would be to ask the old man to tell more of his story.

"I bet you can tell a tale or two'" he said. Johnson let his silence express the merit which he attached to such a question. His only answer was to rattle the reins on Lord Marlborough's back and look intently at the road ahead. Jeremiah was silent, too, for a short time; then he spoke.

"Ah've a son", he said. "Do you have a son t' leave your cart to? "

"Ah've sons, right enough." laughed Johnson. "And daughters! Some ah know about and some ah don't. There's none that ah know well enough t' leave owt to them."

"Ah don't suppose ah'll leave much t' my children," said Jeremiah.

They drove on in silence. Johnson had a route mapped out over the years, one which took him to every friendly house on his road. He would strike off up narrow and almost impassable lanes to find little farmsteads, remote and lonely. Out of the doors would pour happy children, hastily followed by mothers who, like as not, had flour on their red arms, and faces that glowed from the heat of the kitchen.

"What can ah do for thee today, missus?" Johnson would cry.

Usually they would want lace, or salt, buckles, buttons or needles. To the children, the wagon must have seemed like a treasure cave; he produced little toys and gew-gaws to tempt them and they pleaded with their mothers until they were paid for.

From under his hat brim, Jeremiah watched as Johnson charmed the young maidens, turning their cheeks to blushes and their eyes to beacons of joy with his banter. He realized how it might be that the carter had such a large number of unfamiliar sons and daughters. Nowadays, Johnson was still a popular figure wherever he went, but no longer so popular with the young women. Jeremiah, introduced as a nephew learning the trade, saw more than one cheeky pair of eyes gazing in his direction. He was rather glad when the carter concluded his business and waved his goodbyes.

Travelling so openly and obviously was, in one way foolish for a man so keenly sought by the authorities, but in another, it was a wise course. The authorities would assume that he had gone into hiding, and be watching his house, hunting the Nottingham Captain. The tired farmers who came home after a hard day in the fields to heartheir wives and daughters discuss the charms of the tousle-headed little gypsy who was travelling with Jack the carter had no clue they were missing out on a reward that would make them rich.

After two days of travel, Jeremiah was relaxed and quite happy with this easy existence, but he could not help feel a little guilty that he had not confided in Jack. So it was one night in mid-June that the Nottingham Captain sat with his back to the wheel, smoking a pipe to ward off the insects that inhabited the evening air in this part of the long acre, telling the carter the story of his own life.

He trusted the kind old man completely by now and felt he owed him a confession. Jack had the right to know who he had befriended and the danger in which this friendship had placed him.

Chapter 4: The Making of a Rebel

Jeremiah Brandreth

"Ah were born in London, but ah don't remember living there. When ah were a baby we moved t' Barnstaple in Devon. There were me, m' father, mother, three brothers and four sisters. Ah went t' school and learned m' letters, but that stopped when we moved again, t' Exeter. M' father were a stockinger and ah learned t' trade from 'im, but ah were young and didn't want t' settle. Ah didn't just learn m' trade from m' father; he liked his books and he were a follower o' Tom Paine. He didn't see why t' poor who worked hard were poor and t' rich who didn't were rich. Ah've always thought that way myself. Ah found out soon enough that t' army wasn't for me.

"When ah were old enough, ah joined t' 28th Gloucester Regiment o' Foot. We trained at Ottery St Mary, but I didn't take well t' it. One day they sent us up London t' do guard duty at an execution. Them being executed were guardsmen, wi' a lot o' friends in t' army in London, so they needed some country boys who'd be loyal. They were found guilty o' treason, betrayed by an informer that were let off because he told on his friends. He informed on his own brother! T' leader were Colonel Despard, a fine man, a great hero and a friend o' Lord Nelson. Nelson spoke up for him at his trial, but they still found him guilty o' planning t' overthrow t' government. They took 'em down Southwark where 'e was t' be hung - they didn't dare do t' job at Tyburn, or else t' crowd would 'ave saved him. Folk were angry enough as it was, jeering us soldiers and cheering Despard. He looked every inch a gentleman, wi'a brown greatcoat and a white silk shirt underneath. A real fighter! They said when he were in prison he smuggled a message out t' Sir Francis Burdett writ in his own blood, because they wouldn't gi' him pen and ink.

"Well, 'e stood on t' scaffold and t' whole crowd went quiet' nobody in all t' thousands said a word. He thanked us for coming t' see him off and told us 'e was innocent o' t' charges against him, that t' Ministers were sacrificing 'im because he'd dared oppose 'em and that 'e were a friend o' t' poor and oppressed. Then 'e wished us health, happiness and prosperity, and said though 'e wouldn't live t' see it, tyrants would be overthrown and liberty would triumph. Ah thought t' crowd would charge us then, but summat held 'em back.

"Then they 'ung him and t'others, all six. When 'e were dead, they laid his head on a block. Ah remember it well. T' axe didn't tek his head straight off and they had t' tek a knife t' get rid o' t' last bits o' gristle. T' hangman picked up Despard's head by t' hair and cried: 'Behold t' head o' a traitor!' T' crowd were cussin' him, and callin' out 'shame' and t' like. Ah had t' get behind a cart and were sick. Ah've never forgot that day. Ah still see it in my dreams.

"That were enough for me. It were a dirty job and ah wanted no more o' it, so ah deserted. Ah ran north t' Sutton in Ashfield where ah'd family. Uncle Benjamin took me in and ah made m' living as a framework knitter.

"Ah don't know how much you have about t' making o' them Derby Rib stockings you sell. It teks a master knitter t' make 'em. "Shiners" they calls us because t' backsides o' our breeches are shiny from sliding along t' bench in front o' t' frames! Stocking frames are dear t' buy and only a rich man can afford t' price. Most o' us rented out frames at a shilling a week and we were all skilled men, or they wouldn't let us have 'em. We had t' buy our own yarn and needles and there was outwork t' pay for - seaming and fetching and carrying t' yarn and hose t' and from Nottingham. Ah used t' have a bag hosier do mine, one that paid less than full price and did t' travelling for you. You could mek more that way. In my father's time, and when ah started, a skilled man could mek enough in three or four days work t' live on t' rest o' t' week. People bought our hose because they were made t' last, not shoddy.

"All that changed t' year ah got married. Ah'd had my eye on her for months, like all us lads, but she didn't notice me. Ah would dream about her at night and, whenever ah saw her, ah wanted her, but ah never could talk t' her. There were always lads around her and she were always laughing wi' em. Well one Saints Day there were a lot o' us went down Sutton.   There were jugglers and gypsies, fiddlers playing reels, and half t' town drunk. She was there wi' her sister, dancing; she were just beautiful. So slim and nimble, with eyes that could melt you! Ah couldn't take my eyes off her and her dancing, and laughing. T' lads dared me t' get her dancin' wi' me and somehow ah got courage t' ask her. She said she'd like it. After that she said would ah see her and her sister home because they were worried they might be chased by some o' t' lads, but her sister went back first and we took t' long way home.

"Well we were married in 1811 and were happy even though times got hard. Trade began t' go bad a few years before, wi' t' wars and t' blockade, and a lot o' t' merchants began t' up our rents and lower our prices. Ah had t' work twelve hours a day, every day, t' get what ah used t' make in three. Them big merchants ruined us. A few on 'em started using broad looms t' make shoddy hose. They'd make cloth on a broad frame, cut it t' shape and stitch it up t' back. It were cheap enough, so people bought t' damn things, but when you'd had 'em on twice t' seam unthreaded and t' stockings fell t' bits. O' course any fool can use a broad frame, so they brought in untrained men and women t' work 'em, or else thirty or forty apprentices would be taken on, where there might have been three or four skilled men. 'Colting' we called it. And they paid 'em next t' nowt.

"And then there were t' trucking. You had t' buy bread and meat from t' hosier merchant you worked for and he charged a lot for lousy stuff. Or else he'd pay you food instead o' money. Most of us ended up in debt t' one or t' other and then he really had you. If you wouldn't buy from him he'd tell you your work was poor and he wouldn't pay owt for it. They had you all ways.

"Well, once one or two merchants started, they were all at it, though some weren't keen. Us skilled men would have nothing t' do wi' it and we kept mekin' our good hose. But we couldn't sell it against shoddy at half t' price or less. Ah couldn't make a living and ah had a wife and child t' support. Ah 'm not afraid o' hard work, but there were none t' be had.

"Us knitters used t' meet t' see what we could do. Our leader were Gravener Henson. He told us we must unite together, set up a society and persuade t' Government t' listen. Most o' us agreed with him at time, and we paid into his Framework Knitters' Committee. But there were others said we'd starve waiting for t' Government t' do summat for us and that we must take action ourselves right away. That was people like Jem Towle and Bill, his brother. You'll have heard what they did. In t' spring o' t' year we were married, they brought thousands together in t' middle o' Nottingham. All us stockingers were there, and Henson with us. It was supposed t' be peaceful and when it were over, most went home, but a lot o' us set off for Arnold. There was a hosier there that had sixty frames and was colting and making cutups. We smashed all his frames as a lesson. All t' while, there were crowds cheering us on. There were no stoppin' us when we were united!

"Well, it went on from there. All t' summer we went about all over and smashed t' frames o' 'em that were doing cut-ups. We would burn or slash any poor work, but leave anything that was quality. We had a good organisation and all t' names were kept secret. If we wrote a letter t' threaten a hosier, it was always signed 'Ned Ludd', and t' mention o' his name made a lot o' 'em tremble. For a while it seemed that we had done some good, because a lot o' those who had done cut ups were too full o' fear t' keep going, even though there were a lot more soldiers t' guard 'em than before. Wages got higher and though it wasn't as good as it had been we began t' make a bit o' a living. It didn't last but a year or two and then t' bloody hosiers started making us poor again.

"We had tried all we knew and got nowhere, and they were still killing our trade and our livelihoods. Jem's words made more sense t' me because Ann was having our second baby and ah couldn't get enough from work t' feed us. We sold t' furniture and all t' things she had brought with her at t' wedding. Until then, ah had thought it were a crime t' break frames and threaten lives, but them bloody merchants, they knew what they were doing t' us and they didn't care. They thought nowt o' us. All they wanted were profit. Ah started using my time helping organize and travelled round t' villages talking with t' knitters. We'd give 'em a list o' prices under which they mustn't work. Some nights ah went out with Ned Ludd. Ann didn't like me being in danger, but she saw why ah were doing it.

"We would go t' villages, call t' masters and apprentices t' a meeting. We told 'em we were from t' Nottingham Committee and that those who made cut-ups or employed colts t' make shoddy garments were ruining us all. We asked 'em t' keep us informed o' any who did and we'd visit 'em at night. They were t' put papers on t' frames, saying 'let this frame stand, the colts removed', then it weren't t' be touched. They all agreed. Some o' us wanted t' do more and thought we weren't going far enough and we'd never prosper under this government. We should overthrow it and let t' people rule.

"Tom Paine was t' man t' follow and Nedd Ludd was but his servant. My father told me all about Tom Paine's ideas and they made sense t' me. His ideas had united people in America and they beat t' British army and set up a new government. His ideas had got t' French t' chop o' t' heads o' t' French Lords and Ladies, and t' King and Queen.

"For about a year we kept 'em guessing and struck at all those who tried t' ruin our trade. Ah had some narrow escapes. One night in Bulwell ah had t' run on t' a roof t' escape t' guards on this workshop ah was "visiting". Ah could hear 'em in t' street below, so ah climbed in through t' window below me and there were a family sat around t' table. "Good evening", ah said, "Ah'm General Ludd!" They were struck dumb for a moment, food half-way t' their mouths, and then t' father says: 'Good luck t' you, General,' and starts laughing. And that's how ah left 'em all, laughing and saluting, and toasting General Ludd!

"All t' time ah was going out with Jem and his lads, Ann were worried. Ah'd come home early in t' morning, my face all blacked up and she'd be waiting up for me. She didn't say much about it, just kept quiet and brought me food. Ah could tell she'd been crying, though. Then later she began t' ask me where ah'd been and what ah was about. Ah know she were worried what might happen t her and t' children, but she never let me see it and she always supported me.

"There were no work and ah had t go on t' Parish for a time. A skilled man! We got moved t' Wilton which ah told 'em were my birth Parish. That's in Nottingham. We just had a room with no furniture and nowt t' eat. T' children were alwus sick. Ann was thin and me an' all. We used t' get angry with each other. My lass, Elizabeth, always stood up for her mother. She'd run up and beat my chest and tell me t' leave her alone, and her only four! She used t' mek us laugh all t' time and we'd hold each other and her in between us, and Tim on me knee. Ah think at times she kept us together when it was very bad. Christ! Ah would do 'owt t' be holdin' my lass again!

"One day last year, Jem asked me t' go with him t' Loughborough. A merchant down there had chopped wages by a third and t' men had asked General Ludd t' pay a visit. Jem put together a gang. It would have meant leaving Ann for a week while we spied out t' land and waited for t' hue and cry t' stop, so ah didn't go. Anyway, they did t' job and broke up'ards o' fifty frames.

"There were six guards, but five o' 'em were drunk when Jem and his lads arrived. One o' t' lads - not Jem – shot one. He didn't kill him, but he were hurt. Jem was recognized and they hanged him last year. Jem wouldn't tell who were with him and he kept silent t' end. He grinned at me while he waited for t' drop. People in t' crowd there were in rags. Everyone was hungry because t' harvest had failed and nobody had any money anyway. There were no money for soap and t' crowd stank. It was raining an' all. There was no cheer when he dropped. Just quiet. T' magistrates were scared and ordered that there were t' be no hymns or a sermon at his funeral, but we had other ideas and we saw him off in style.

"Bill Towle took over from his brother. He said that he'd show 'em that Jem's men could go on wi' out him. Ah lost interest then. Bill were never meant t' be a leader. They said that when he was on t' Loughborough job he were pocketing lace and had t' be ordered t' burn it. That were Bill: out for Bill first and t' movement after. Anyway, his time as General Ludd didn't last long. One o' t' Loughborough gang were caught poaching and turned informer t' get free. Bill and five more were hanged last year. Ah thought they'd come for me, but no one did.

"So Jem were dead and Henson in jail and we were lost for a while. Ah used t' meet Bill Stevens and John Holmes, men ah'd known for a long time. We would talk o' what we could do, but hadn't much idea. But we read all we could find. There were Cobbett's Political Register and t' Twopenny Trash and t' Black Dwarf, all writing about reform o' Parliament and a better deal for all, not just t' rich. And then there were Tom Paine's Rights o' Man. It was t' new Bible. Ah don't suppose you've read any o' it. Well Tom Paine makes good sense t' me. He wants t' get rid o' t' Poor Laws, give pensions t' old folk and have all t' children schooled for nothing. He would pay for t' needs o' t' poor, by taxing those who can afford t' pay. He would do away wi t' Lords, and have a Parliament that represents all men, not just a few rich bastards. When ah read his ideas, ah knew that he was right. And ah knew it weren't enough just t' read and dream; we must act t' bring in Paine's ideas. We must go much further than Gravener Henson had ever dreamed, and we must be prepared t' fight t' Government, not just smash a frame or two. We must go further than t' Towles, and fight against t' Lords, t' merchants, against any who grind down t' poor. They did in America and in France and so must we!

"We formed our own Hampden Club where we could talk over what we wanted t' do. There were scores o' clubs all over England. We met in secret. Soon, we had a few hundred members, and everyone paid a penny a week as subscription. We used this t' buy forty or fifty copies o' Two-Penny Trash which were full o' t' ideas o' people like us, t' distribute among us' selves. Stevens and Holmes were our leaders.

"Ann and t' children were sick at t' beginning o' t' year. It were a wet autumn, and you remember last winter were very cold. The room were freezing, so in January they went back t' her father's house where they would be warm. She wanted me t' come as well, but ah couldn't take charity, even from Ann's kin and ah had t' stay t' get relief. Ah used t' visit and when spring came, they were back with me. It weren't until ah didn't see 'em that ah knew how much they meant t' me and ah became even more hard-hearted against 'em whose greed had forced us apart.

"One night in spring Bill Stevens introduced a traveller t' us. He were called Mitchell and were coming from Lancashire and on his way t' London. He told us plans were being made all over t' country for a national rising against t' Government. London were going t' gi' a lead, but everywhere else must join in or t' plan would fail. We were t' organize and arm t' men o' Nottingham and Derby and play our part. Then a gentleman came up from London, talking about thousands waiting there t' rise up and how they were in need o' our support. We had been peaceful long enough, he said, and now it was time t' tek a leaf out o' t' Frenchman's book and storm our own Bastille. We must plant t' Tree o' Liberty on English soil! As he talked that night, there weren't a man there that disagreed. We made a secret committee, under Stevens, that was t' plan our part in t' rising that was t' come."

The fire in front o' Jack and Jeremiah had nearly died, so the old carter got up silently t' fetch more sticks for it. Jeremiah stopped talking and occupied his time in putting his pipe t' rights, tapping out the ash on the rim o' the cart wheel behind him, and pressing a new wad into the warm bowl. Jack carried a lot o' tobacco in his goods. Stiff from the long sitting, Jeremiah rose and stood next t' Jack at the fire, joining him in dreaming among the images which played in its flames. They said nothing for a few minutes until Jack stooped and resumed his position by the cart.

"You'd better finish your tale," the old man said.

Jeremiah smelt the wood smoke in his nostrils and looked closely at Johnson. The world seemed completely unreal, and he was not sure whether the old carter existed, or whether they sharing part of a strange dream. He lit a twig in the flames and touched off the tobacco in his pipe. Then he sat down by his wheel and resumed his story, watching the events flicker in the fire in front of him.

Chapter 5: 'Owd' Tommy

Thomas Bacon was an exceptional man, sixty-four years old and still strong. The stoop and the walking stick may have slowed his pace, but his mind and tongue were as nimble as ever. These days they called him "Owd Tommy". He grew his white locks long and with his stick he looked like the reincarnation of an Old Testament prophet and frequently declaimed like one.

He had lived all his life in the village of Pentrich, a small but important centre of the textile trade, overlooking Ripley on its eastern side, and the valley of the Amber to its west. The Bacons had a long history in Pentrich; known as a plain-spoken family, many of them were strong-willed individuals. Tommy had never married and had no children. His sister Ann, called Nanny by her grandchildren and her customers, was a widow, who kept the White Horse Inn in the centre of the village. His brother John, twelve years younger worked as a framework knitter, and was the most popular man in Pentrich.

Tommy had shown unusual ability at reading as a child and this became his life's passion. Having decided at an early period in his manhood, that he would prefer to remain a bachelor, the income he earned at his frame he had spent on books, rather than household items or a wife. His voracious appetite for books had soon led him to the ideas of radical thinkers whose writings fuelled the revolutions in America and France during his youth. He had been twenty three years old when George Washington, inspired by the words of Tom Paine, had defeated the British Army and liberated America from the despotic yoke of its mother country. Bacon had devoured Tom Paine's works and could quote quite freely from them. They furnished the rules by which he tried to live his life.

For most of his working life, a skilled framework knitter could earn decent money, and Tommy had used his wages to travel the country, as well as indulge his passion for books. On his journeys, he became the confidant of radicals from all walks of life and talked to many an educated artisan about the ideas propounded by Paine, and others. His radical views had involved Bacon in several brushes with the authorities in different parts of the country who suspected him of preaching sedition, but could never prove it.

He had observed the French Revolution from a distance, rejoicing in the initial overthrow of the aristocracy and the destruction of distinctions based upon title and property. For a time, it seemed that France would serve as a model for the world envisaged by Tom Paine, but when the National Assembly imprisoned Tom and threatened his life, Bacon fell into disillusion. The rise of the Directory and the emergence of the dictator Napoleon killed the liberal dream of the eighteenth century philosophers.

Tommy Bacon found that his pro-French ideas were not welcomed. He became an object of fun for many, until the pain, misery and suffering, which the long-drawn-out struggle against Napoleon caused, was felt by his fellow villagers. Then, the old frame-work knitter was accepted fully again into the fellowship of his parish as he pointed out the origins and causes of their growing hardships. The very poverty which overwhelmed the Brandreths at Sutton in Ashfield was destroying the livelihood of the families of Pentrich too; so many of the village's households depended upon the income from working frames. Some local folk had, it is true, found employment at the Butterley Ironworks nearby; these soon became the only ones sure of earning a living. After Waterloo, demand for iron fell and even the Butterley Company began to feel the pinch.

In those hard days, in the first two decades of the nineteenth century, some Pentrich men had joined in semi-organised outbreaks of frame-smashing under the mythical Ned Ludd's banner. Tommy Bacon and his siblings were no strangers to the local Luddite leaders. As he grew too old for frame-smashing, Tommy advanced a stage further in thought than the destructive Towle brothers or the patient Henson, and had come to the conclusion that the economic hardships which the knitters faced could not be solved by either man's methods. By the dawn of the year 1817, old Tommy was increasingly convincing those who would listen that the only way forward was a political revolution to establish Paine's ideas. If this were achieved, he insisted, a new economic order could be established, based upon equality, rather than privilege. For a long time, Tommy's views had attracted just a few of his friends and local acquaintances, but the failure of Henson and Towle and their counterparts elsewhere in England, coupled with the poverty which confronted almost every working family north of the Trent after 1811, meant that people were more than willing to talk about overthrowing the government.

After the disastrous harvest of 1816 and the rejection by the Government of moderate petitions, Bacon found it easy to convert local men to his even more radical viewpoint. Elsewhere in the North and Midlands, others were reaching similar conclusions; men such as Bamford and Mitchell in Lancashire; Crabtree, Scholes and Wolstenholme in Yorkshire; Stevens in Nottingham; Hayes in Leicester. After the meeting at the Cock Inn, in Grafton Street, London, at the beginning of that year, Tommy, funded by pennies from supporters, travelled the country helping set up a network of secret contacts drawn from amongst these and many others. By the spring of 1817, they were all agreed; a nation-wide revolution should be attempted. To ensure success each local rising must be made to happen simultaneously, and above all, planned in the utmost secrecy. Organisers were convinced that their revolution needed the support of the workers of London whose substantial masses would be crucial in bringing about the overthrow of the Government and capturing the major institutions of the state. Each local committee began to plan secretly for the rising. Men made pikes in secret, or resurrected old swords, pistols and flintlocks from dusty hiding places. Spinners, weavers, cutlers, joiners and quarrymen, on many a remote moor and heath, drilled, and learned how to counter cavalry tactics from soldiers who had fought with Wellington against Napoleon, in the Peninsula or at Waterloo.

Some of the most fervid of Tommy Bacon's supporters lived to the west of Pentrich in the villages of South Wingfield and Crich, and hamlets like Wingfield Park and Bullbridge. His lieutenant here was William Turner, a tall, strong ex-soldier. William had seen service under the Duke of York and had memories of the Egyptian Campaign but like many a hero before and since, he found his service soon forgotten. He was related to half the folk in the district and his large family centred round the village of South Wingfield. William was a skilled mason. He built a stone house for his parents which he shared with them and they lived quite well. Demand for his work dried up as times grew hard and he did not endure inactivity well. Old Tommy found him a willing recruit as sergeant major for the Pentrich and Wingfield secret army. The quarrymen and knitters of the district, moaned at the military ruthlessness which characterised Turner's training. But like squaddies the world over, rough treatment bound them together in fellowship.

Recruited along with Bill Turner was Edward, his younger brother. The brothers were very close: Bill had taught Edward, twelve years his junior, the craft of the stonemason, helped him build his own home and regaled and bewitched him with tales of his soldiering adventures. Edward was ready for any sort of military escapade, inspired as he was by his brother's campaigns in Egypt and other exotic places, and all the more receptive to old Tommy's stories. The two Turners had their nephew, Joseph, lodging with them in the spring of 1817. With only one eye, Joseph had worked as a clerk in Manchester for a while. The Wingfield men dubbed him 'Manchester Turner', after his time there. In the earlier part of the year, he had been a Blanketeer, one of those who set off to petition London from St Peter's Fields in Manchester. He still bore a grudge against the Government, whose Hussars had ridden him down and arrested him for his part in that peaceful protest. He willingly joined his uncles in supporting Tommy Bacon.

The most respected man in the villages to the west of Pentrich, beyond argument, was Isaac Ludlam the elder; venerable and white-haired, and a deeply religious Methodist lay-preacher. Old at fifty from a life of evangelising and hard work, Isaac was husband to a strong, industrious wife and father to a large family. Together they worked a quarry and a few acres of land at the little hamlet of Wingfield Park. Eking out a living for such a large family was increasingly difficult, particularly when prices rose after the terrible harvest of 1816.

Isaac had known Tommy Bacon for forty years and had always thought him a deluded hot-head. Tommy was not a religious man, but he was a man of principle. Isaac had a deeply etched sense of right and wrong, and as time went on, with his large extended family in hard times, he began to find more and more meaning in the words of his radical neighbour. Regency England was ruled by those whose personal conduct repulsed the puritanical Ludlam. The excesses of the Prince Regent, most particularly his treatment of his wife, were abhorrent to decent people. Rumours of scandal and immorality which surrounded the person of the Regent had shaken belief in the Divine Right of Kings, still deeply ingrained in the minds of country folk. Many Methodists, Isaac included, had turned against the monarchy and although a man of peace, Isaac had become taken with the idea of destroying, with an army of avenging angels, the corruption of the old order.

Soon, Isaac and his sons were drilling zealously elbow-to-elbow with the oathing and blaspheming Turner brothers, steeling themselves to do the Lord's work in eradicating the Gomorrah that was Regency England. Isaac the younger, and William, enjoying each other's company, were accustomed to following their father. Many more decent and law-abiding men joined the secret gatherings because of him, and soon the South Wingfield men formed a small army, eager to fight for the dream which Tommy had laid out for them.

Tommy Bacon himself held sway up the road in Pentrich. He dominated all the councils and nominated his good-natured brother, John, to drill the recruits. It was hardly an inspired choice; John was the most easy-going of men, and more suited to the pipe and glass, than the fife and drum. The Pentrich recruits were a slovenly and slapdash band when compared with the Wingfield men under William Turner, their iron-willed commander.

Pentrich drill meetings were rare, short and only well-attended because of the opportunity they afforded for tactical meetings in the parlour of Nanny Weightman's White Horse Inn. Nanny was Tommy and John's sister. Tommy Bacon made only rare appearances at training. He was frequently away at Ripley's Hampden Club, which he had formed, or at Nottingham, or travelling further afield as a delegate. The four sons of Nanny Weightman, George, William, Thomas and Joseph, were stalwarts of the Pentrich band. Joseph, the youngest, was only fifteen years old, but, like his brothers, he was tall, strong, and eager and possessed of an uncomplicated good nature. The eldest brother, George, at twenty-six was a sawyer by trade. He and his wife, Rebecca had two children. George and Rebecca were well-matched; they were known for helping any neighbour in need. All the brothers had served their time at home under the sway of their redoubtable mother, who still retained the power to make them jump when she spoke.

For some months, Thomas Bacon had been developing contacts with the villages around Pentrich, trying to set up cells similar to those in Ripley and South Wingfield, his own village. Bacon had an agent in Alfreton, German Buxton, a miner, active in recruiting other colliers and knitters for the great rising. Framework knitter John Mackesswick was organising men from his own village, Heanor. Others, in Belper, Heage and Crich had contrived to make contact with Bacon, and through him were in touch with the Nottingham Committee, the rest of the Midlands and towns in the North.

Just down the hill from Bacon's home in Pentrich was the imposing structure of Butterley Ironworks. Built of stone by Benjamin Outram and William Jessop in about 1790, the works had prospered to become the biggest employer in the area; about seven hundred workers at any one time. The Ironworks had long occupied the fertile mind of the Pentrich leader; could he find a way to recruit the men and employ their cannon-making skills for the good of the cause? For a time, he had taken work there himself, as a fettler, using the opportunity to spy out the works, and attempting to recruit Hampden Club members for Ripley and Pentrich. In that period of high unemployment and poverty, however, the ironworkers' jobs were relatively secure and their incomes good: they had no wish, he discovered, to put their livelihoods at risk. Accordingly, Owd Tommy found himself dismissed quickly by the Butterley Company upon which he resumed his old trade of framework knitting. He never forgot the experience however and harboured a long-festering grudge against the owner, Jessop, and Goodwin, the works manager.

As spring turned to summer in 1817 Bacon and Turner travelled to Wakefield together, to a secret meeting at the Joiners Arms, an inn run by Benjamin Scholes; a rough and ready place, overseen casually by Scholes, a man less interested in keeping good ale than in talking radical politics. If his lack of interest in the quality of his drink had lost him custom, then his support for physical force reformers had gained some.

Along with Bacon and Turner that evening in early May, radical delegates assembled from across England; Bamford and the Lancashire men, and a number of Yorkshire delegates including William Wolstenholme of Sheffield. Scholes shut the door to regular trade and the meeting talked in secret about their plans for a national rebellion. The most pressing topic was the news that John Mitchell, the travelling Lancashire delegate was due to bring from London. Amidst the pipe smoke and rhetoric, everyone was eagerly anticipating the word that London was ready to rise. But the men were never to hear this news from Mitchell's lips. At about eight o'clock, there was a knock at the inn door. Scholes went to answer and, in exchange for a password, a stranger was admitted.

Conversation ceased. The newcomer stood uneasily, feeling the hostility and suspicion pervading the room. He was tall and well-dressed, wearing the type of boot made popular by the Duke of Wellington. His breeches and jacket were quality items, if well-worn. The assembly was appraising him with unmasked suspicion and hostility.

He had long side-whiskers, equally as pronounced as Scholes', extending far into a heavily pock-marked face. He introduced himself as William Oliver, a friend from London. He offered apologies for the absence of Mr Mitchell, his colleague and fellow delegate, who had been arrested the previous day at Huddersfield where the two had been changing coaches. This news was greeted with expressions of dismay all around the room.

Oliver was of the opinion that Mitchell, travelling under an assumed name and dressed as a poor weaver, had been betrayed by an informer. He warned everyone to take care. On the suggestion of Scholes, the meeting adjourned to a friendly house on the Leeds Road. Thirty men squeezed into its downstairs rooms a few hours later, and there took a decision which was to have far-reaching effects upon the lives of all present, and many more besides.

Oliver revealed himself as a persuasive speaker. He spoke of the condition of the London poor. He told the northern leaders that London had never before been as ready to take action, but did not dare to act alone. A date must be fixed for London and the rest of the country to rise simultaneously to strike the vital blow.

The hard-bitten delegates murmured in approval when the man from London shared his calculations that there were 70,000 ready and armed in the city, set to turn out at a few hours notice. One after another, delegates began to present estimates of numbers of potential rebels in their own areas. The Birmingham delegation claimed that there were 150,000 from the West Midlands, most well-armed; there were thought to be 10,000 from Sheffield; 8,000 from Huddersfield; 5,000 from Barnsley; 10,000 from Leeds; 2,500 from the Wakefield district. Thomas Bacon held the floor a long time, stressing the need for unity and for an early date for the rising. He concluded by saying that he spoke for at least 30,000 determined and well-armed men from the North East Midlands.

May 27th was agreed as the date when thousands from all over the north and midlands would join their counterparts in London and rise up against the Crown.

Later, Bacon cornered Oliver questioning him a long while about how things stood in London. Before he let him away, Bacon, ever the opportunist, relieved Oliver of 3s 2d as payment for a pair of fine ribbed hose.

Tommy Bacon and Bill Turner returned to Pentrich shortly afterwards, riding on the stagecoach to Ripley and walking back up the hill to their homes. Both men were full of anticipation for the outcomes of the rising and each felt a renewed enthusiasm for inspiring his neighbours into action. A few days later, Turner and Ludlam walked back over to Pentrich, and together with Bacon set off for an evening meeting at Nottingham.

The room at the Punch Bowl was packed with eager men. Jeremiah Brandreth was there, with the leader Stevens and the influential Holmes, all anxious to hear Bacon's report of his meeting in Yorkshire. The old radical made the most of the occasion, going carefully through all the arguments advanced at Wakefield, dwelling long on the depositions of the 'London Delegate', Oliver, before ending the suspense by announcing the date of the rising. Bacon ended his address with a rallying call for unity and resolution in the days ahead, giving emphasis to his words by beating his tankard gently, but rhythmically, on the table before him.

In the days following, Nottingham and the surrounding villages buzzed with secret activity. Each village had its own commander, and each commander had a place on the committee. Nevertheless some confusion ensued when a letter from the Yorkshire delegates arrived, putting back the rising date until June 9th, citing the necessity to prepare more thoroughly. In Pentrich, Bacon's exasperated response was they all could do with a little more time, but the government deserved none. Bill Turner was in agreement, complaining, not for the first time, that although the South

Wingfield men were ready, the Pentrich men remained ill-armed and undisciplined. Perhaps, he suggested, Edward Bacon might use the delay to remedy those deficiencies?

Villagers involved in the rising met frequently at Asherfield's Barn, near Pentrich, a plain wooden building that stood empty, courtesy of the owner. Bacon would call the men out at night and in the light of lanterns they would talk long and earnestly about details that yet needed attention.

Rifts between Wingfield men and the others were growing visibly. The Turners and Ludlams questioned the Weightmans and Bacons incessantly about the preparedness of their neighbours, finding the answers less than satisfactory. The resulting squabbles irritated and annoyed Bacon beyond measure. Bacon's own command of military tactics was palpably questionable and the experienced military campaigner, William Turner began increasingly to hold the floor. A general agreement upon philosophy prevailed; instruction on soldiering remained wanting. The Wingfield men apart, others disliked Turner because of his often-stated low opinion of their military capacity. At some time in those full days Tommy Bacon came to the realisation that a leader from outside was required with the authority to command and unify his men on the night of the rising. He needed someone who was a stranger to most of the Derbyshire villagers, but who at the same time could bring them together, and win their respect. Bacon pondered long and hard; where would he find someone who possessed the ability to command, while not averse to listening to the sage advice of an aged revolutionary?

The answer to his conundrum came after he discussed the problem with William Stevens and John Holmes from the Nottingham Committee. They knew someone perfect for the job; Bacon's band would be commanded by a man named Wain from Nottingham; but it was discovered that he had fallen ill and the Nottingham Committee looked a replacement. At a lunchtime assignation in the Punch Bowl Inn with Stevens and Holmes, Tommy learned the name of the new Captain: Jeremiah Brandreth.

Later that same day, William Oliver arrived in Nottingham. He took a room at the expensive Blackamore's Head and then wandered off to find the Punch Bowl. In the early evening, the Nottingham men had their first sight of the London Delegate. Since his meeting with Bacon and the others at Wakefield, Oliver reported, he had travelled to Sheffield and other cities. From there he had taken the coach to London to report to the council confirming that the date of the rising was fixed and that everything was ready in the provinces. Those present were saddened to hear that while he was in the capital he had visited poor Mitchell their one-time correspondent who was now held in the Cold Bath Fields prison. By contrast later he cheered them all by revealing what had been until then a secret. Eyes around the room shone with pleasure at his revelation that Sir Francis Burdett, Lord Cochrane, Major John Cartwright and Henry Hunt were all party to the rising. Cartwright was to head the new Provisional Government. The first proclamation was printed already, on the same presses used for printing the Black Dwarf. The London men were primed and ready, he assured them. The rising would not, must not fail.

Despite bringing good news, Oliver succeeded in annoying the meeting, declaring Nottingham to be one of the least prepared of all the towns he had visited. Stevens' riposte to their guest was that the Nottingham and Derby men would not be found lacking on the great day. The gathering roared its agreement. Oliver posed a number of informed questions concerning plans and numbers; the visitor appeared well satisfied with their answers. Acknowledging the determination of his hosts, Oliver beamed benignly and slowly withdrew an important- looking paper folded inside his coat. The men who clustered round him eagerly absorbed the plan of campaign devised, said Oliver, by the radical leaders in London.

The document outlined the proposed role of each of the regional armies on the night of the rising. The object of the Nottingham men was to secure their own town. On the successful completion of that action they were to await the arrival of the northern men, who would join them in taking boats down the Trent to capture Newark and then marching south to London. Oliver informed Bacon and Stevens that they were summoned to a meeting of the provincial delegates at Sheffield on June 7th, two days before the rising. At this point they would be allocated districts of their own to command, probably in Yorkshire; it had been resolved that no one should act as a commander in his own town. The Nottingham men expressed incredulity at such apparent lunacy; the obvious issue of newcomers not having any idea of important places, routes, landmarks and so on was as plain as the nose on your face. Oliver explained that the plan had been devised to ensure that no general would demonstrate any undue favour or waste precious time in settling old scores with authorities locally. It was better that way, he said, though it was not without reluctance that their objections were silenced.

The main proceedings of the meeting completed, Oliver was keen to leave; he was anxious to catch a morning coach back north. Before he could depart he was cornered by Tommy Bacon. Tommy was unhappy, in reference to the proposed meeting in Sheffield that all the major leaders should be gathered together in one place, a mere two days before the start of the rising itself. The risks were obvious. Oliver tried to persuade him that it was a necessary meeting and that security would be very strict. The old revolutionary remained unconvinced.

By contrast Bacon's idea that Brandreth should lead the Derbyshire men was warmly embraced as such an arrangement was very much in keeping with the plans voiced by Oliver earlier. Oliver promised to speak in support of Jeremiah at the Sheffield meeting.

One unforeseen problem remained as Jeremiah refused Bacon's request point-blank, looking for support from Holmes and Stevens. The four of them had remained at the Punch Bowl after everyone else had left. Stevens nodded. Holmes's view was that Jeremiah had no choice other than to accept the honour of such a command. He had been selected by the committee because they knew he would do a good job; the London delegate himself had approved the choice, and was taking Brandreth's name with him to the delegates' meeting in Yorkshire. The Derbyshire men had been alerted and were eager for his arrival. There was nothing to be done but accept, and no word could he utter but "yes", if he was truly loyal to the cause. The reluctant general was silent for a moment making no response until Bacon came striding across and grasped Jeremiah's shoulders with his mottled hands.

Holding the younger man at arm's-length he looked him in the eye, his face kindly as ever, and his voice pleading. "Will you come, Jeremiah?" he asked quietly.

The Nottingham Captain

Jeremiah nodded his assent. His companions slapped him on the back, pouring ale into his mug, wheedling away enthusiastically at him until he appeared convinced that the job was within his capacities and that he would be playing a full part in the achievement of a new order in England.

Stevens saw him home leaving him at the door, well after midnight. The children were asleep, but Ann was waiting for him, looking tired and ill. She glanced up when Jeremiah entered, but said nothing. He went over to her kissing her forehead, conscious of the smell of beer on his breath which only served to emphasise the lonely poverty of their little room.

The Nottingham committee had equipped Jeremiah with a map issuing him a long series of instructions to memorize. He had rehearsed his speeches in the long workless afternoons and found impressive phrases in the Rights of Man and the Political Register to impress the thousands he was to command. The committee had armed him, too, with a brace of unmatched pistols and a pouch of powder and ball. Jeremiah secured these in his sack and on the fifth of June set out for Pentrich.

That evening, at the White Horse, Brandreth met with Thomas and John Bacon, George Weightman, Bill, Edward and Manchester Turner, and Isaac Ludlam the elder. He was introduced as the 'Nottingham Captain' and it was agreed that his real name would be kept secret until the rising had succeeded. A dozen or so Pentrich people listened with interest as tactics were discussed.

The Captain questioned each in turn as matters arose. The most crucial issue was to make sure that everyone turned out precisely at the appointed time. A list was made of all those who were committed and, equally as important, those who were not. Brandreth came with clear instructions; every house must be visited and every man must be made to turn out. However effective in the tightly-jammed tenements of Nottingham the plan might have proven, it was not designed to take account of the sparsely populated fringes of East Derbyshire. After much debate, Brandreth decided to cut his force into sections. The Wingfield men would start early, dividing into two groups to scour the lonely farmhouses between that village and Pentrich. Men from Crich and Fritchley would work their way across join them. Those from Pentrich would rouse the immediate vicinity, and meet the Wingfield men at Pentrich Lane End. German Buxton's Alfreton group should between them raise Swanwick, Ripley and Codnor before the arrival of the main body and forces from Belper and Heage. When they were all assembled, the army would move on Nottingham, rousing Langley Mill, Eastwood and the city outskirts. Once within its walls, they would merge into the vast army of Nottingham men, along with those thousands from the North, to march onwards to London and victory.

There was much debate in the little gathering about what should happen to the ironworks. Bacon and others were concerned that Butterley should be considered a prime objective. The works should be soundly secured for making cannon later. Brandreth countered the suggestion, claiming the works were a secondary consideration at the side of ensuring all forces arrived in Nottingham on time. Any potential delay at the ironworks was to be avoided at all costs. The

Butterley Company could wait until they had leisure to take it.

Passions ran high as Brandreth argued out the matter with his lieutenants; finally Thomas Bacon agreed to seek a compromise. They would send someone over to Nottingham for Stevens' opinion. Brandreth agreed to be bound by the decision of the Nottingham Committee and Joseph Weightman, brother in law to Nanny and uncle to her boys, was chosen.

The weapons they had at their disposal were discussed in tortuous detail. Isaac Ludlam produced a paper which catalogued the entirety. It was a short and unimpressive list. The bulk of the men were to be armed with pikes and spears; many forged by Isaac and his sons had been secreted in the family's quarry. One or two had promised to bring guns, but most possessed no firearms. Objects such as guns were of little use, in the ordinary course of things, to skilled men with hungry families. Where an occasional piece did exist, it had often been sold to buy food. The only people certain to have guns in such a rural area were gamekeepers and farmers. Few of either were expected to join the rising willingly. Brandreth emphasized this as another reason for visiting farms around the district, despite the delays such tactics might cause. The men on those farms must be made to march and forced if need be, to fight for their freedom. Any guns in their possession must be taken for the use of willing volunteers.

Ammunition was in even shorter supply than weapons. Even those with guns often had neither powder nor shot. Bill Turner had remedied some of the deficiency in bullets, but there was no obvious way of finding a trustworthy store of powder. They would have to conserve the little they had, as carefully as possible. So confident was Brandreth about the quantities waiting for them at the barracks in Nottingham that even the sceptical Turner seemed satisfied.

Attention was turned to a final timetable for the next few days. Brandreth expressed the hope that his presence would remain a secret until the day of the rising, as the authorities would be eager to know the doings of any stranger in the district. He was assured that security was tight. No man would breathe a word. In conclusion, it was agreed that the Captain needed a guide to show him the lie of the land, and take him to those loyal men he wished to meet personally before the night of the rising. George Weightman promptly volunteered his services; he knew the district better than any poacher and could take him, by the most secret of routes, anywhere he wished to go. It was unanimous. Not only was George the man for this particular mission it was well known that he had room enough to house a temporary guest. The Captain closed the meeting in an impressive manner, reminding those assembled of the sacred nature of their cause. Ludlam interjected. They were doing God's work he intoned, and must proceed with a pure heart, shunning any thoughts of private gain.

Brandreth resumed his theme, saying any opposing them, no matter who, must be dealt with severely. If that meant shooting one's neighbour or kin then so be it. Any who tried to desert or to lay information before the authorities must face the harshest military disciplines. Now they were more than ordinary men; that must not be forgotten; they were commanders of an army, and that army was at war. There would be no prisoners taken; and no quarter would be given or asked for, except that women and children would not be harmed. Any man who stole property or forced a woman would be liable to instant execution, as would any who refused orders.

Bill Turner nodded sagely at this, realising the necessity of such commands, aware though that they were easier to make than to enforce. The gathering ended in a sober mood, hands clasped in resolution. Brandreth was almost asleep on his feet as he trudged behind the long-striding Weightman. The little house was dark and quiet; a candle was lit to show Jeremiah to a pallet on the floor. George furnished a blanket, wished him goodnight and went off to tell his sleeping wife, Rebecca, of their unexpected visitor. Jeremiah squeezed out the last few moments of consciousness to remove his boots and put his coat beneath his head.

He fell into a deep sleep. Darkness and rest were all he knew until the birds began to sing in the early morning light. He began to dream of the wife he had left the previous day. He could see her face, almost feel her looking down on him, and sense her presence in the room with him. He saw himself in their little house in Nottingham and knew that if he opened his eyes she would be standing there. The previous night, with its speeches and conspiring, would be a dream, and they would be together once more, as if he had never left. He stretched, pushed back the cover and awoke to find himself staring into the eyes of Rebecca Weightman.

Chapter 6: Oliver's Travels

A Close Call

William Oliver, who was known to the provincial radicals as the "London Delegate", was quite pleased with the enthusiasm of the Nottingham men. They seemed to be very solid for the cause, and were certain enough to rise on June 9th. He left the city, aboard the northern stagecoach, happy in the knowledge that his presence and encouragement had reinforced their conviction. He sat, humming and drumming his long fingers on his knee, occasionally bracing himself against the side-walls of the coach when they encountered one of the many deep ruts on the way between Nottingham and Sheffield.

He knew the Yorkshire town quite well by now, having spent several days there on his last tour, and he had met many prominent rebels. He soon found his way to the Bluebell Inn, where he asked after William Wolstenholme. He was told that he was expected to arrive at any time and so he took a seat in the corner of the parlour, hiding his gentlemanly appearance behind a large mug of Sheffield ale. As he waited, he went through in his mind what he would tell Wolstenholme, who was a very astute man. A skilled joiner, he had the habit of measuring everything carefully and he would be likely to interrogate Oliver very thoroughly. Birmingham's delegates were not an impressive lot and he knew that the West Midlands would not rise unless action was proving to be successful elsewhere first. The Lancashire radicals were eager enough for action, but they had been frightened by the Blanketeers episode some months before and the arrest of John Mitchell had taken the wind out of their sails. At this stage of the proceedings, it was clear they would be on-lookers, not participants.

Oliver decided that he would suppress the news from Lancashire, and concentrate instead upon the fire and enthusiasm of the

Nottingham group. William Wolstenholme arrived in due course and shook Oliver's smooth hand with one rasped from working with wood. He was soon followed by several other dusty, grimy artisans, who drifted in apparently aimless and separate. When the room had filled, the landlord closed the shutters and barred the door, and Oliver soon found himself beginning yet another ensnaring address to another charged meeting of radicals.

He told them first of the eagerness of the disaffected masses of London. Soon the northern folk were reassured to hear of the size of the London battalions and delighted that Burdett and the other gentlemen radicals were to place themselves at the head of proposed Provisional Government. Animated discussion followed his well-received speech. Wolstenholme thanked him, saying that his encouragement and unflagging loyalty to the cause was an example to set all like minded patriots marching on the ninth. Shortly afterwards, he walked Oliver to the coach which would take him on to Wakefield, the next hotbed of revolution.

His welcome in that fine old town was not as warm as the one he had at Sheffield. His host, Benjamin Scholes, was up in arms about the postponement of the date of the rising, as he maintained that his men were boiling over to get at the government. This delay would give opportunity for informers to penetrate the conspiracy and reveal their plans to the magistrates. Oliver was used to these last minute recriminations and doubts, and he used all his experience to calm down this prickly innkeeper, and to soothe his fears.

The next day, the indefatigable, well-dressed London Delegate took yet another coach that called at Bradford, before proceeding to Manchester and Liverpool. Everywhere he saw signs that the people were ready for action, but confirmed his belief that the Lancashire folk were not prepared to act until they were sure that the rising had been a success elsewhere. He then re-crossed the Pennines and arrived in Leeds on June 2nd. Here, he heard some bad news from his local contacts, so that when on the next day he met Scholes in Wakefield, he was prepared for a savage outburst.

Even with this foreknowledge, however, the bitterness and aggression of the innkeeper's manner was a shock to Oliver. As soon as he walked through the door of the dirty, stale-smelling inn, Scholes had seized his arm violently and dragged him out of the quiet parlour and into his cluttered living quarters at the back. Waiting was one of the Sheffield men, whom Oliver knew by the name of Thomas Bradley.

"Tell him, Bradley," said Scholes, pointing rudely at Oliver. "Tell him!"

Before Bradley could speak, Oliver looked Scholes in the eye and said "If you want to tell me about the arrests in Sheffield I already know!"

"Tha' knows! What did ah tell thee in this room a week ago? If we delayed, ah said, informers would be among us and we'd all be for it. Now t' Sheffield lads are in jail and we'll be next, mark mi words!"

While Scholes spoke, Oliver noticed how rotten the man's teeth were. He didn't seem to have a good one in his head. When he left off shouting, Oliver asked "How many were taken?"

Bradley replied that there were four held, including William Wolstenholme, but that he didn't expect any of them would talk. The Sheffield Committee was in disarray, though, with hardly any of them stirring out of doors for fear of arrest. Scholes was wringing his hands in temper, and now he ventured another attack, more menacing this time, because he managed to keep his voice under control.

"Thomas and me, we've been sat here wunnering who it was that did for 'em. There's an informer somewhere and we can't think who it might be. Ah wonder if tha' can help us find out?"

Oliver went on the defensive. "I don't know the Sheffield men as well as you do. I'm sure I can't think who might have informed, though I think it's likely that someone did," he replied, irritated by Scholes' veiled accusation.

"D' you hear that, Thomas, he thinks someone did inform!" Scholes was mocking now. "Ah'm bloody sure they did and ah'm bloody sure of something else, an' all, ah think that bloody someone is thee! Tha's not one of us, tha' don't talk, dress, look like one of us! Tha's a bloody informer."

"Is that what you think, Thomas?" said Oliver white, but calm.

"Ah suspect everyone, even thee – even Scholes here", replied the Sheffielder, obviously uncomfortable.

"Me?" cried Scholes. "Tha' thinks it's me!?"

"What ah mean is," said Bradley, "there's no point in accusing anyone without evidence and we've none to tell us who t' informer is."

Oliver had found his moment and he leapt to his feet. He was a good six inches taller than the innkeeper and now he towered indignantly over him, speaking firmly and prodding his finger into Scholes' chest forcefully.

"I've stood enough of this. You accuse me of the lowest crime a man can stoop to, that of betraying his friends. In normal times, I would take you outside and thrash you for it. But these are not normal times and there's more important work to do than deflating windbags like you. Be quiet! I've travelled this country from end to end, weeks at a time, always looking over my shoulder for the constables. There's none worked harder or risked more for our cause. You say I don't look like you: well, what better disguise for a traveller than the garb of a gentleman? Don't you understand, you oaf, that if I travelled around looking like an out of work pauper, the authorities would spot me easily? Dressed like this, nobody believes I am associating with the men I do meet. And just because I look, talk and dress differently, and you need a scapegoat, you choose me to be the informer you want to find.

"Well, I'll tell you something, Scholes. If, when this venture is completed, I have the misfortune to meet you again, I shall show you who the informer is and I'll also show you who has the hardest fist between the two of us. By now Oliver was gripping Scholes by the shirt front and glaring at him. Scholes was red and speechless. Bradley asked them to calm themselves and sit down and discuss matters like the comrades they were. He excused Scholes' outburst, blaming the anxiety which he felt about the arrests, but said that Mr Oliver had every right to his anger at being accused of such treachery. Gradually, Bradley's words began to reduce the tension and the three of them sat down together. On Bradley's suggestion, Scholes brought some ale for them and the Londoner told them what he had learned from his travels in Manchester. The afternoon passed drinking sour ale and the three went their separate ways: Scholes to attend to his empty inn; Bradley to return to Sheffield and Oliver to his lodgings, and a night's sleep that he badly needed after all his exertions.

The next morning Oliver rose in time to catch the coach to Leeds. Scholes arose late with a thick head and began to souse the plates and mugs of the previous night under the pump in his back yard. He was still convinced that Oliver was the informer. He would have been most surprised, therefore, to have seen Thomas Bradley sneaking through the back garden of a house in one of the better areas of Sheffield, looking furtively over his shoulder, before gaining admittance through a side door. He was ushered into a reception room and here he stood, holding his hat, until Hugh Parker, one of the senior Sheffield magistrates, entered.

They conversed together for the space of about fifteen minutes, Parker making extensive notes with his quill, and stopping Bradley when his tongue ran on too quickly. Then the Magistrate rose and opened a bureau, drew out a guinea and handed them to Bradley, who long familiar with the procedure, made his mark on the receipt which bound him to his most lucrative employment. Then he left as cautiously as he had come. Parker closed the door after him and opened a French window to freshen the air. Over the next half an hour he wrote a letter to the Home Secretary, Lord Sidmouth, in which he enclosed Bradley's description of Oliver and details of his onward journey. Parker was enjoying his role as spy master. It was he who had ordered the recent arrests of the Sheffield leaders on Bradley's information. After he had finished his lines to Sidmouth, be wrote a second letter to the Mayor of Leeds, informing him of the imminent arrival of Oliver in that city and expressing the hope that this man, whom Bradley described as the most important of the plotters, would be apprehended before he caused even more mischief.

Totally unaware of this, Oliver journeyed to Leeds and booked lodgings. He was becoming well-known to landlords throughout the north who believed him to be a very active commercial representative. He maintained the façade by tipping pot boys and chambermaids handsomely, and jawing away in the friendliest way possible, with landlord and landlady alike. That was how he spent the evening of June 4th. The next morning he strolled in leisurely fashion through the centre of the wool-rich town and. entered its burgeoning slum area, visiting the houses of two or three that he knew to be active in the cause he was doing so much to promote.

On June 6th, he travelled through Wakefield yet again, on his way to Dewsbury, reaching his destination in the early part of a fine morning and sought out Thomas Murray, a flax-weaver from Leeds, at the inn where they were appointed to meet. Murray, a blunt and morose man, was appointed as Oliver's guide to a final meeting of the Yorkshire delegates that had been summoned to sort out the last minute problems caused by the arrest of the Sheffield men. It was after midday and they were toiling up the hill towards the village of Thornhill Lees, near to Dewsbury. Oliver was not much used to walking, and was complaining to an unsympathetic Murray of a pain in his back, which he attributed to the roughness of the stagecoach travel.

Suddenly, their hearts jumped as they heard a loud cry of "Halt or you are dead!" A second or two later a squad of red-coated dragoons, their guns trained on the two bewildered travellers emerged from behind the trees on both sides of the road. Despite the protestations of Oliver, they were marched briskly, up the hill and into the village inn that had been their original destination. Outside the door of the inn sat a portly looking gentleman in the uniform of a Major General. His face was red with the sun, his profuse whiskers were white, and he was drinking a mug of the ale for which the Sportsman's Arms was renowned throughout the area.

Oliver blustered forward. "What is the meaning of this, Sir? How dare your men arrest me like a common felon and drag me up here? What is your name, sir, that I may take this complaint further?"

The object of his invective looked him square in the face, put down his tankard and said imperiously: "My name sir, is Byng: Major General Sir John Byng, Commander of the Northern Division. As to what my men are about, why sir, they are arresting a clutch of rebels, with which base fellowship, Sir, I have information that you and this rascal with you have the closest possible links. I would advise you, Sir, to say no more at this juncture, but to save your breath to plead for mercy at your trial for treason."

At Byng's curt nod, their captors pushed the two prisoners through the door and into the inn and slammed it shut behind them. There were nine or ten others there, in the dim interior and Oliver knew most of them. They looked thoroughly miserable sitting slumped at tables amidst the remains of a struggle. There was beer and broken crockery on the floor and most had bruises and gashes to their heads and faces. They clustered round Oliver. Thomas Bradley was among the men already taken.

"Ah'm ashamed to say that ah' believed what Scholes was saying about thee, but, well, if tha's here, then that proves tha' aren't t' informer."

Oliver smiled weakly at Bradley's words, and sat hunched, sharing in the general atmosphere of low spirits and despair. Suddenly he got up and went to the shuttered window at the back of the room. He peeped through the crack in the middle where the two hinged, wooden boards failed to meet truly. Outside he could see a rough field which descended into a large wood that stretched as far as he could see there was no sign of soldiers on this side.

"I'm going to make a run for it," he said quietly.

Bradley took his arm.

"We thought of that an' all," he said. Tha' d not get ten yards before tha' were shot. There's no cover. We reckon that if we stay here and deny all, there's little we can be charged with. We have no weapons and we can swear that we are just met here for drink and fellowship."

The others nodded and he continued: "Perhaps they may lock us up for a while, but it might not be for long. At any rate, we'd still be alive."

Oliver glared at him. "That might do alright for you, but what do I say? How do I explain what I'm doing here? Someone has betrayed us, laid information against us. I'm not chancing staying. If you won't come, just pull that window open when I say."

Bradley shook his head at Oliver's words, but two of the others went over to the window and seized a shutter each. Oliver peeped through, then stepped back and nodded. The men tugged, the shutters creaked open, and he leapt through the open window. He stumbled as he landed, but ran, ducking and weaving, down the hill. The men inside the room saw a soldier raise his gun to his shoulder and watched him follow his target from side to side, taking careful aim before he fired. There was a loud noise as the powder ignited, projecting the ball up the long barrel. The prisoners groaned, but then cheered when Murray, at the window, cried: "He's missed!

Bastard missed!"

Oliver ran and ran. Deeper into the belt of woodland he went, until he struck a path that seemed to follow the direction he wanted. He listened for sounds of pursuit, but heard none. Following the path, he eventually found himself on the Wakefield road.

News of the arrests had gotten to Wakefield some minutes ahead of Oliver, through those who had escaped Byng's net up at the Sportsman's Arms. One of those fortunate enough to get away, John Dickenson, recognised the London delegate as he saw him preparing to board the southbound coach, and the two had had a quiet and hurried conversation as they awaited the driver. Dickenson was amazed at Oliver's daring escape and congratulated him. Neither of them had a clue as to who might have betrayed them. Oliver excused his hurried departure, but said that he knew now that he was a marked man in Yorkshire and that he must get south. Dickenson agreed and left for his own hiding place: a room in a nearby inn which overlooked this very street. Oliver relaxed as the stagecoach took him speedily beyond the boundaries of the town of Wakefield. It had been narrow escape and he was lucky to still be free to carry on his vital mission.

As the stagecoach lurched southwards, he took stock of his current situation. From his travels in Lancashire, he reflected, very little could be expected from that county on the 9th of June. As for Yorkshire, the arrest of Wolstenholme and the Sheffield leadership, followed so closely by the arrest of the ten at Thornhill Lees made him doubt that anything would induce those still free to join in the rising. Birmingham and the West Midlands would follow, but not lead, so the only hope of success for the insurrection in the north rested fairly and squarely upon the shoulders of the men of Derby and Nottingham. Oliver was so exhausted that slept soundly on the fast-moving coach that jolted over every stone and bounced in and out of every rut on the way to its terminus at Nottingham.

Back in Nottingham, preparations for the rising were advancing.

Brandreth had departed for Pentrich to organise the Derbyshire villagers. Stevens and Holmes were in regular contact with him and with South Nottingham and Leicester. Brandreth's friend, Henry Sampson, was doing his best to rouse the villages to the north of Nottingham.

Sampson and Brandreth had got to know each other quite well in the months he had been living in Cross Court. They recognized qualities in one another that made them enjoy meeting together. As Jeremiah had become more and more involved in the work of the Nottingham Committee, Henry's enthusiasm for the cause had grown. He would sit and listen to Stevens, Holmes, Brandreth, Bacon and the numerous visiting delegates, and amaze them all later with his exceptional ability to recall exactly who said what to who. Sampson was popular with most of the Nottingham reformers, because he was a good listener and was interested in even the tiniest details of their activities.

Thus no one had objected when Brandreth proposed that his friend, who lived at Bulwell, should be appointed the delegate for that village, and have responsibility for recruiting delegates from the nearby settlements of Hucknall, Kimberley and Arnold. Sampson had accepted his promotion proudly and had set about the dangerous and thankless task of trying to attract men he hardly knew into the cause.

After a week of hard work, he had little to show by way of success. He had, it was true, received the reluctant promise of a couple of men in Arnold and Kimberley that they would put the word around that the rising was imminent and find out who would join, but they neither were interested in the added danger of being members of the Secret Committee. To add to his disappointment, Sampson was told that during his fruitless absence, the London Delegate had visited the town on his way to Sheffield, and that he had brought the splendid news with him of the participation of Burdett and Cartwright in the projected rising. Henry greatly wished he had been able to meet the London delegate and hear the words from his own mouth.

The night before Jerry Brandreth's departure for Pentrich, Sampson had called upon his friend to say goodbye. As he entered the pokey little room, he greeted Ann and Jerry. Sampson was a little bewildered about Jerry's sudden and soon departure and wanted to straighten out the facts out in his enquiring mind. Jeremiah explained the reasoning behind the decision and poured out his worries about assuming command, and leaving his family for so long. As they parted for the night and Henry promised to call back the next day to bid a last goodbye before Jerry left. Unfortunately, he was delayed on the next morning and did not arrive at Cross Court until after Jerry had left. He chatted to Ann who was clearly very worried and had no idea of when Jeremiah would return. Then she had closed the door and he turned to pick his way through the unpleasant streets to meet with William Stevens.

The committee members were belatedly tightening up their security on the eve of the rising grew nearer and Sampson had walked all the way to the Golden Fleece, before he remembered that the meeting had been switched to the Sir Isaac Newton. Here he learned that the Sheffield leaders had been arrested. Holmes and Stevens were in a fierce debate. The former was forcefully demanding that the rising should be postponed until it was found out how far informers had penetrated other groups; the latter claiming that the few thousand from Sheffield did not matter, and their plan must be adhered to. Stevens won the argument, but there were many who remembered Holmes' words over the next few crucial days.

It was at this stormy meeting that Sampson received the timetable for the rising on the ninth of June which had been kept secret until it was absolutely necessary to give out the information. Sampson, himself, was to bring on his Bulwell men at 10 pm. Groups from Mansfield and Sutton in Ashfield would have reached him by then, having started at 8 o'clock.

The Leicester men were to come in from the south, Brandreth and the Derby men from the west, and everyone would converge on Nottingham Racecourse 11 p.m. This information and the prospect, finally, of action, made those present leave the meeting in a much more optimistic frame of mind than had seemed likely when the news from Sheffield had been broken to them. There was to be a final gathering at Punch Bowl at 9 o'clock on June 7th, to hear of any last-minute alterations, and receive the report of the travelling delegate from London, Mr William Oliver, who was calling in on his way from the north to the capital.

Nottingham festered in the June midday, and the dirty streets seemed to melt under a remorseless sun. The smells were intolerable in the poorer areas and even the rich districts had an unwholesome stench about them. Flies clustered on the dung-heaps at the end of the streets, buzzing and pestering, and driving the sweating people mad with their presence. Many sought the shade of the trees and a lucky few found places to bathe in the Trent or in little tributary streams. In the evening, the midges turned out in incalculable millions to bite any who remained outdoors without a lighted pipe in their mouths. The exhausted sun began to set and the men who were to finalise the timetable for Nottingham's part in the great revolution, began to cram into an upstairs room at the Punch Bowl Inn.

William Oliver's diary told him it was June 7th. He stood hoping for air, at the window of the inn, but not a breath seemed to have entered Barkergate, where the Punch Bowl stood. The heat and the stench of the men in this tiny and absurdly crowded room, where bodies squeezed into every available space made Oliver's head swim. He would have loved to faint and force his hosts to carry him to the cooler street. Perhaps he should pretend to do so, and when he got outside, he would jump to his feet and run off, as he had done when he escaped the troopers at Thornhill-Lees. Inwardly he vowed that he would never ride on the inside of a stagecoach again, but would always ride in the cool air, in the summer at least. But Oliver had more to worry his mind than the heat, because a good part of the oppression in the atmosphere was due to the hostility which his former friends were now showing towards him.

As he had arrived, Stevens had taken him aside. Oliver would know, he suggested, that as well as the capture of Wolstenholme's men at Sheffield, the authorities had now netted many of the other Yorkshire leaders at Thornhill Lees. Oliver said that he did know, and outlined briefly how fortunate he had been in own escape. Stevens congratulated him, but warned that there were a good many at the meeting who had begun to believe that he, Oliver, was a spy. Stevens told him that he, personally, had no doubt that Oliver was true to the cause, and that he could count on the support of many there, but that he should be most careful.

As the meeting began, Oliver sat tensely on the right hand of William Stevens, while the latter called for order, Silence prevailed almost immediately. Stevens began by welcoming all who had come and wishing good luck to their designs. He said that this was probably the last meeting of all the delegates before the grand affair was completed and that before each man left, he must know for certain what his own part was, and what those he represented must do. However, he knew that John Holmes had a matter to raise before they heard the final dispositions. Holmes stood up, tall but stooping, a very unfortunate-looking man, with a lined, morose face. He looked briefly around the room, hoping that the moment of silence the gesture created would build tension, and then swung round to look at Oliver.

"Informer!" he yelled, his finger pointing. Many men in the room voiced their agreement at the charge. Oliver sat, straight-backed, looking full at Holmes. He said nothing, but the disdainful look on his mottled face spoke for him. "Have you no answer? Don't you want to deny the charge?" rasped Holmes after a moment.

Oliver was silent a while longer and then said evenly: "Charge? What charge?"

"The charge that you're a spy! A blasted informer! You've done for 'em in Yorkshire and you will do for us, next" snarled Holmes.

"That is not a charge," said Oliver, with a mirthless smile. "It is a load of false claptrap, without a single jot of evidence to support it. Charge?!"

Not everyone liked the cynical, mithering Holmes, and even his supporters were beginning to feel unsure about Oliver's guilt. Holmes made a brave attempt to rally.

"You're a spy, and that's easy enough to prove," he said. "First, where were you when t' Sheffield men were arrested? You were just leaving Sheffield. And when they took the others near Wakefield, where were you?"

"I was with them," said Oliver. "And while the rest of them sat there and waited to be taken off to jail, I escaped through the window, dodged bullets and got clear. And then I came here to persuade my loyal friends, if there are any here still loyal, that we owe it to those brave men to rise and overthrow the tyrants who would imprison them."

"That sounds likely, ah must say," laughed Holmes. "Ah know some of them lads. They are twice t' men you are. Twice t' men! Look at you with your silk neckerchief and your silk gloves!" Here he jerked Oliver's necktie clear of its home in his shirt.

"Tell me t' answer to this," continued Holmes, in full stride now. Where does t' money come from to pay for your good clothes and t' best rooms at the inn? What sort of a job must you do, I wonder, that permits all this? And London! All we know about London is from you. I want to know exactly how many are persuaded to our cause there. Now you take as much time as you like, but make sure that you answer us t' our liking."

Oliver looked full of indignation. His face poured with sweat and his eyes stared ferociously at this ignorant man who dared to importune his motives.

"I have told you more than I should already. It is madness to bandy about the names of those who are risking their lives for our movement. Those famous and dedicated men who have risked everything to speak for reform in the heart of reactionary Westminster, they trust me; you apparently do not. As for my own occupation, I was a builder but failed because of a fall in trade.

"As to the numbers of those loyal in London, I must tell you that it is hard to be certain. Being so close to the seat of oppression, our security must be strong, so that the exact numbers are kept in but few hands. All I will say on that point is what Mitchell said, who now languishes in the Cold Bath prison awaiting our rescue. That is all I have to say, save only this: I have laboured long and hard and risked all in the cause and beg that no matter what you do with me, keep faith with those others throughout the land who depend upon you to rise with them on the 9th."

Oliver fell silent. As usual his words and delivery of his speech had given his audience much to think about. There was much muttering and whispering before Holmes spoke again.

"Stevens says you don't want t' stay here and play the part of a man, but you're off to London, away from t' danger."

"That is easy to answer," said Oliver. "I must go to London in order to inform our leaders that you are ready and that all is set for the rising. It will shake their confidence if I do not return before the 9th."

The London Gentleman might have thought that the compelling logic of his argument was enough to have convinced even these hostile listeners, but he sensed that this was not so. He thought for a moment, looking around the massed, hard faces and then said: "Might I suggest a solution that could satisfy us all? I will remain here as Mr Holmes suggests if you will send another in my place.

Surely that would confirm my good faith?"

Stevens, who had observed the events of the previous few minutes in some discomfort, seized on the point.

"I do not think that will serve," Mr Oliver. "To my mind, the offer is so generous that surely none now can believe ill of you. No, you must go t' London as you planned. None of us can replace you there."

Holmes snorted at this, and the men, many of whom still had doubts, looked for him to object. Instead he said, unexpectedly, "Yes, perhaps that is the best thing." He looked at Oliver.

Many of the men seemed about to interject, but went Holmes continued. "If he's going, let it be now, I don't want him staying t' hear more of our plans so he can betray more of us. But just remember, we're not so fond of being hung in Nottingham as they Yorkshire. If thou art a spy we'll find you wherever thee runs and gut you!"

Holmes lowered his stabbing finger and did not speak further. Oliver, in response to a nod from Stevens, rose with as much dignity as his nerves would allow him, and offered his hand. Stevens shook it and Oliver departed, his knees shaking on the narrow staircase as he went down to the street. He breathed deeply of the evening air and set off at a brisk pace for the Blackamore's Head where he was lodging.

Once or twice he heard, or thought he heard, a footfall behind him, and looking round, imagined shadows down the criss crossed alleys which intersected the unlit lanes he was taking. Reaching his inn at a sprint, he pushed hastily past the customers in the parlour, and galloped up the stairs to his room. He looked around the edge of the window into the street below, where he could make out three men who seemed familiar to him, though he could not recognise them. They loitered menacingly outside the building for a few seconds, and then disappeared from his sight.

He backed into the room and sat on the bed. He wished the door would lock, but it had nothing but a latch. He improvised as much of a barricade as possible with his two travelling bags. He closed the shutters, checking the catch on the inside, and then lay down to smoke his pipe, and think deeply about the escape he had just managed.

Back at the Punch Bowl, the meeting had ended in a less than triumphant fashion, and Stevens had seen his commanders leave looking distinctly down in the mouth, despite his attempts to rally them. The episode with Oliver and the arrests up in Yorkshire had left clouds of doubt over all their actions. Holmes had stormed off in a huff immediately the meeting concluded and it was Henry Sampson who walked back with Stevens. Walking along, they went over the business of the next few days to see if the Bulwell man had it fixed in his mind. They parted in friendship, and Stevens was grateful for the reassurance of at least one trusted adviser.

Oliver slept patchily that night and rose red-eyed. He sent the pot boy to confirm the time of the London coach and packed his bags behind the closed doors of his room. At the appointed time, he went down into the parlour of the inn to settle his bill. The landlord was attending to a well-dressed, portly man who, it turned out, was bound for the London coach. Oliver immediately introduced himself to his fellow traveller, Mr Robinson of Tamworth, and in his substantial company walked watchfully to his coach. The streets seemed much less dangerous than on the previous night, but Oliver was much relieved to feel the coach jerk into motion and to let the turning of his wheels convey him out of this perilous city.

Chapter 7: The Days Before

Jeremiah and George

Those few precious days were memorable.

George Wightman's huge strides, as he loped up and down the hillsides he had known all his life had Jeremiah breathless in pursuit. Together the two young men roamed the green land around Pentrich, down into the valley of the River Amber, up onto the grassy ridges at Wingfield and Crich. They called in at a dozen hamlets and villages, with names like Whatstandwell, Ambergate, Nether Heage, Hartshay, Buckland Hollow, Ridgeway, Bullbridge, Wingfield Park and Fritchley. Everywhere folk smiled at them, despite the hard times. Jeremiah found out early that his plea to have his presence in the locality kept secret had not been heeded. He was welcomed everywhere as the Nottingham Captain. Old soldiers saluted him as they stood amidst scuttling chickens. Children peeped shyly out at him, hiding coy faces in the ample skirts of the sun burnt women, who shaded their eyes from the sun, to get a clear look at this famous stranger. With his dark curls and dark eyes, he cut a romantic figure and many likened him to a pirate.

At cottage after cottage there was an invitation to enter and drink a little of the brew which the woman of the house would put before them as she watched her husband forget the indignity of poverty for a few moments as he bragged of his military prowess, sharing the company of this shabby little general and his young aide. The same woman would marvel inwardly at the dreams of men and at their unyielding unwillingness to sit and accept the bad times along with the good. And she would soon be sitting late into a dark, wet night and dread each succeeding minute as she waited for her soldier to return.

At the inns which dotted the area, Jeremiah would rest and muse, while the tireless George Weightman gathered him a small audience. The courtesy shown to him, the feeling of hope which he seemed to engender when men spoke, and the enormous generosity of the village folk made him giddy with pleasure. In a life of monotonous, unvarying toil, in an existence haunted by the spectre of poverty, he had clutched at what little joy life had offered and clung to it even after it had disappeared. In those long weeks when he had abandoned his trade and lived on the paltry hand-outs from the parish, he had known the scarring enervation of idleness. Now in this marvellous June, in a landscape bright with colour and shining with promise, he holidayed for a brief while, free, for once, from the shackles which had encumbered him all his days since leaving his boyhood behind.

The men would come and he would explain the plans, and expand upon the hopes their actions would fulfill. Some were plainly cynical, but others caught the fire in Jeremiah's words and were consumed by a desire to join and strike a blow against the old order. George would stare at his Captain in rapture, frowning on those who attempted to gainsay his arguments and smiling hugely at those who accepted the words that so charmed his own ears.

As the evening came on the two friends would realise how worn out they were as they climbed up the hill, towards Pentrich across the course of the old Roman Rykneld Street, summoned by the bells of St Matthew's. George would open the door to let Jeremiah into the little house and Rebecca would look up to appraise the two hot, dusty men that she must feed from a scanty larder. They would sit for a time later as the light dimmed and chatter quietly about the day. Jeremiah would relax with his pipe in the benign presence of these two wholesome people and pat the head of their little girl when she shyly showed him the little rag doll that her mother had sewn for her. And then he might play with the little scarf he always wore round his neck.

Ann

Over at Sutton in Ashfield, Ann was also sitting, letting the day ebb away from her. Her father nodded in the armchair opposite, his face a mass of dark creases from the mine, and his big hands, with their blue scars, clasped comfortably in his lap. George Bridget had done the same every evening as long as she could remember. A big strong man, he would walk to his work before the sun was awake enough to rise and before any woman was about. He shared the miner's chauvinistic superstition that it was bad luck to see women while on the way to work. Then he would toil, cramped up in the dark for twelve, or perhaps fourteen hours. Then he would return home to soap off the worst of the day's dust, before dressing to eat a huge meal. After that, without sitting down a moment longer than was necessary, he would walk the few yards down the row to the inn. He would stay drinking for two hours and then come home to fall asleep in the chair, his hands clasped in his lap.

Ann's mother's job had been to keep his strong body stocked with food, heat water for his return home, see that there was always a stick of tobacco and a tin of bread and cheese for him to take in the morning, bear his children, and wake him from his chair in order to get him to bed. In return, George Bridget had been a loyal and generous husband and a loving father. Ann's mother had died two years previously, and her sister Agnes, married, and living a few doors away, had made sure that he was bathed and fed. His grandchildren had taken away most of his loneliness.

Ann sat while her father snored peacefully. She tried to picture Jerry, but had long discovered that the more someone loves another, the harder it is to see his face in one's mind. Time slipped away until it reached the point where Ann must wake her father.

George Goodwin

Ripley's bustling market place was ideal for the purposes of George

Goodwin and John Fletcher. Fletcher was a portly, red-faced, bull-necked little man, with small podgy hands and a squeaky, nervous voice. He was the local brewer and presently felt, not surprisingly, that his brewery would be a prime target if anything were to come of the growing rumours of insurrection. Goodwin had been delegated by his employer, Jessop, to go with Fletcher to the Cock Inn at Ripley to help Colonel Wingfield Halton, the South Wingfield magistrate, sign on some special constables to protect both the brewery and the ironworks.

Over in the market place, several hundred people were assembled to hear a visiting quack give out his patter and peddle his wares. A travelling salesman was a prime target for the local wags and much fun and sport was expected. The quack was a well-dressed man, who looked exceptionally sprightly and fit for someone nearing the end of middle age. He had stretched a substantial wooden board across two ale barrels and was dancing a little jig to music which he provided himself on a fiddle, pulling the most hilarious faces as he drew raucous laughter from the merry crowd. He finished to cheers and applause, plucked a stone bottle of his patent medicine from the hand of his boy assistant, and gestured for silence.

"Naaah then!" he cried. "Good gentlemen and fine ladies, get your elixir, here! It has cured the Prince, cured Lord Liverpool, Lord Sidmouth and Lord Castlereagh...

"It's a pity it didn't poison 'em!" yelled a man in the crowd, and many there cheered him.

"Clear off and peddle your sugar water to them 'as has money t' waste on it," yelled someone else. A few of the younger men began to think of upsetting the barrels, but the quack thrived on the attention heckling afforded and continued his patter.

"Naah then, good folk, don't be led astray by the opinions of men paid by my rivals: This bottle contains magic liquor which is widely famed as a most efficacious boon to all who are possessed of a troubled constitution!"

"A troubled constitution!" cried one on whom Tommy Bacon's tuition had not been wasted.

"Aye we have one of them right enough: And while that constitution is writ by lords and administered by thieves, we'll keep our troubled constitution! But there's a rough wind blowing in this country that will......."

"Aaah! The wind? This will cure your wind, Sir," laughed the quack and the audience laughed with him.

"A pity tha don't drink more o' it yourself," another interjected. "You might blow less hot air out yer arse!"

In the midst of the laughing, good-humoured crowd Shirley Asbury and Anthony Martin, two Butterley ironworkers, threaded their way to the door of the Cock Inn. There was a thin line of men, queuing in front of them and they bore the few minutes waiting patiently, their heads bowed, saying nothing to one another. As the line ahead grew shorter, others joined behind them and soon they were standing before the table where Wingfield Halton sat, flanked by Goodwin and Fletcher. A few questions were asked; heads nodded or shaken; Goodwin vouched for the integrity of his two employees and said they were fine, dependable young men. They made their marks and money was put onto the table for them to pick up. Asbury and Martin were now enrolled as temporary special constables and went out, blinking, into the sunlight and mingled back with the crowd.

The magisterial trio enrolled a hundred and twenty men that day, before deciding that they had done enough. They were sitting back after a fine lunch of game and claret, in the privacy of a small room upstairs at the inn, when they received an important guest. Considering his grandiose title, Mr Hallowes, the High Sheriff of Derbyshire, presented a rather dismal appearance. He was below average height and his clothes, though well-made, looked slightly too large for him. His pinched, disappointing features, made him seem much more likely to be the puppet than the puppeteer. The High Sheriff was a creature of ceremony and not a man of action.

Goodwin, Fletcher and Halton stood to welcome their guest who was riding with an armed escort from Alfreton to Derby. He sat down with them and accepted their hospitality, and the group began to talk about the rumours of insurrection that were abroad, and the dangers to property and life that attended them. Fletcher went downstairs at one point to relieve himself and returned in great agitation closely followed by a roughly dressed fellow whose appearance set him out to be a farmer.

"This is Henry Hole," said Fletcher. "He lives up at Pentrich and he has news. Tell them what you told me, Henry."

Hole gripped his hat-brim and peered hard at the legs of the table in front of him. "There's a big meeting up at t' White Horse, Mrs Weightman's house," he said haltingly, and waved his arm in the rough direction of the place to which he was referring.

"There are many up there. The captain from Nottingham is there. There's a lot of folk coming and going. I thought it my duty t come an' tell thee."

Hole's speech petered out. Fletcher looked at the faces of the three men who sat at the table.

"Well?" he said in a voice shriller than ever. "What are we waiting for? There's a hundred special constables outside. We could be up at Pentrich in ten minutes, net the whole bag of them, and nip this rioting in the bud."

Goodwin nodded furiously obviously agreeing with Fletcher, but the two senior men stayed seated and looked at one another gravely.

"That will be all, Hole, thank you," said Halton, and the farmer backed out of the presence of his betters, bowing respectfully. Goodwin closed the door.

"I don't think," said Hallowes, measuring words, "that your plan is very discreet, Mr Fletcher."

"Discreet?" the brewer gulped, amazed at the words.

"Yes, discreet." Hallowes continued from his chair, "You see when one deals with the mob, one must employ discretion; you must not be precipitate. If we were to go rashly into that village, there is no telling what might happen. Such an assignment is best left to the soldiery. Why who knows what the rabble might do in such a situation? No this sounds like a military matter to me, and not one for the civil authorities to meddle in."

Goodwin made a vain plea for the High Sheriff to reconsider, pointing out that it would be worth any risk if they were able to secure the leaders of the disaffected, before they could actually cause damage, but it became clear that Hallowes was not a man of action. He brushed Goodwin's remarks away politely, and then declared that the solution was for him to continue to Derby, where he would ask the commander of the dragoons there to take a force to Pentrich immediately. He would go that very minute. Halton expressed a desire to accompany him, so he might travel back and help direct the soldiers, and then the two of them bade their good days and set off on their mission.

Goodwin and Fletcher resumed their seats, marvelling at the smug complacency of the officials who had just left them.

The White Horse

Nanny Weightman was running low on everything. There weren't enough tankards, mugs or beakers for men to drink from and quite soon, she expected, there wouldn't be enough ale unless her worthless son got back with the cart from Fletcher's with some more. Even then, it would take time to settle.

The main body of the men were inside her parlour, but there were several dozen more peeping in through the windows or lounging about outside. Jeremiah sat against the far wall. Above him, to the left, now pasted on a table-top, was the map he had drawn. In front of him on the long, thin table were official-looking papers. Turner and Ludlam sat to one side of him; John Bacon on the other. George Weightman stood behind his right shoulder, cramped for space, but reluctant to be excluded from any of the events which were taking place.

Men queued in groups up to the table and stood in front of it, questioning Jeremiah once more on the part which their village must play, where to meet and when, and advancing a host of other queries for their leader to answer. He felt buoyant, and handled each question with flair and gravity. He radiated confidence and many doubters made up their minds on the spot to follow him, no matter what befell.

On the instructions of Stevens, Jeremiah informed them all that once they reached Nottingham, they would all be given money to send back to their families to keep them while their breadwinners proceeded south. When Nanny asked about food on the way, he had soothed their worries with promises of bakeries being seized and forced to make bread; of butchers yielding up their beef on the point of a sword; and of rich city innkeepers donating beer, ale and rum to the cause. For those who could write, Jeremiah had a pen and paper for them to copy down the following poem, which he had composed with the aid of Rebecca Weightman. They were to take it back to their villages and read it out to inspire any who still doubted and learn it to sing on the march:

"Every man his skill must try,
He must turn out and not deny;

No bloody soldier must he dread;
He must turn out and fight for bread;
The time has come you plainly see,
The government opposed must be."

Copies of the poem were transferred outside the inn, where men waiting their turn to see the Captain began to learn and chant it delightedly. Other verses emerged during the day and soldiers' songs from the war with Napoleon were adapted for the cause.

The day was cheered even further when Joseph Weightman (not Nanny's son, but her husband's brother of the same name) returned during the afternoon from a mission he had been dispatched upon the previous day to see Stevens and the Committee and find out how things stood with them. Old Joe had found the company of the Nottingham folk most convivial, had drunk himself asleep and delayed his return. He now felt much recovered, he said, and yes, all was well in Nottingham. The plan was unfolding just as it ought. The old man's news, and the manner in which he had come by it made him an instant celebrity, and he was pressed by the good-humoured meeting to try a little of the local ale, and tell how it compared with the Nottingham brew.

By now, Shirley Asbury and Anthony Martin had returned from Ripley Market and joined the throng. Some of those who had been in Ripley that morning had seen them going into the Cock Inn and one of them informed Bill Turner. He jumped up at the news, interrupting the Captain and ordering the two constables to be seized. No one laid a hand on the frightened interlopers, but those men by the door stepped menacingly across its opening, in case they tried to leave. Jeremiah questioned them.

"Why are you here? Are you come as spies t' betray us?"

It was Asbury who answered. "Sir," he said "we've lived in t' village all our lives. We're here t' drink some ale with our neighbours because it's a hot day and we are out t' betray no one."

Turner stepped away from his seat and stood in front of Asbury, his eyes blazing. He really was an imposing man when angry.

"You signed on as constables this morning, both of you! You're Government men now, and we are pledged t' destroy t' Government!"

The two constables blanched at Turner's threat, but Martin found his voice quickly.

"Bill, just because we took t' Government's money doesn't mean we would betray our own folk! You know all Butterley men were told to sign up," he said.

"Look sir," and here he appealed to Jeremiah, "our families live here, do you think we would betray anyone?"

Nanny Weightman had no doubts about what to do.

"Captain," she cried. "If you would take my advice, you'd not chance these two betraying you. Why not put t' buggers up my chimney and set someone t' guard 'em until they can do no harm?"

Jeremiah joined the laughter, and then gave his decision.

"If any here think our movements are still secret," he said, "they are much mistaken. Look outside this inn: there are scores o' men waiting, each with a family to gabble his secrets to. No, we are out in the open now and even if we're betrayed, what of it? They might as well try to stop t' tide! Let no man forget that we here are just a small part o' a huge army and when we reach Nottingham, we'll be swallowed up by t' Northern Clouds as they stream in their thousands from Yorkshire and Lancashire, rushing t' break over London. No, ah believe this man here and his friend, t' be honest enough, though neither should have enrolled. Even if they are spies, well, what does it matter?"

Jeremiah's speech saved the two constables who soon squeezed themselves nervously into a corner, to sip ale and glance appreciatively at the one who had spoken with such eloquence on their behalf.

As the number of men outside the inn began to dwindle in the late afternoon, and the road finally cleared, The Captain and those twenty or thirty who remained sat in a more relaxed fashion, eating some of the bread and cheese that young Weightman had brought back from Ripley, along with the extra ale.

All now appeared set for the rising in two days time, and they all felt curiously light-hearted about it.

Bill Turner spoke. "Ah don't know whether the Captain has heard, but the rest of you have, about George Booth, John King, John Brown and Tom Jackson."

The men about him nodded, and Jeremiah remembered Weightman sitting on a tree stump near South Wingfield, telling him how in February, a band of local men had burned the ricks of the local landlord, Colonel Wingfield Halton, because he had evicted several families in the depths of winter for not paying their rent. Subsequently, four of the group had been discovered and were now awaiting trial in Derby. Turner's mention of the four doomed men cast a gloom on the gathering for a few moments, as the men reflected that the imprisoned arsonists would almost certainly be hanged at the next assizes.

"Well," continued Turner, "it seems t' me we should strike a blow for them lads on Monday night. We should draw t' badger. It would not take long t' set a fire at Halton's door and when he came out we could shoot him and settle a score for our friends."

Jeremiah considered his lieutenant's request carefully, especially as many of the others seemed enthusiastic for it, but then replied, "Our orders are clear Bill, and we can't change 'em now. We must get on t'

Nottingham wi' t' greatest speed we can manage. We would do them lads a better turn if we overthrow t' government that has them jailed, and remember, there'll be plenty o' time to take care of t' likes of Halton when our objects are achieved."

As Brandreth was making this speech, Wingfield Halton himself was riding home alone from Derby. When he and Hallowes had reached the town, they found that the dragoons had been marched off southwards. Hallowes had decided that, by the time they were summoned, the conspirators of Pentrich would have dispersed, and that there was consequently little point in any further action. The Wingfield magistrate had reluctantly agreed, and the two had parted to transact their respective business dealings in the town. Then Halton had ridden home, passing within a few miles of the men who were plotting his murder.

Tommy Bacon

Tommy Bacon sat under a tree near to James Booth's little lean to. He was skimming through his worn copy of the Rights of Man. Frequently he would put the book to one side and gaze off into the middle-distance. He had a strong feeling that something was wrong, although he was not sure what it was. He had ridden over to see Stevens a few days previously, in the best of spirits. Plans he had worked on for so long and with such industry, seemed to be on the very verge of success. From being a lone voice, crying in a very dangerous wilderness, he now found himself the revered elder figure and philosopher of a vast movement. He was able to report to Stevens that the Derbyshire villagers had taken Jeremiah Brandreth to their hearts in a manner which he would not have believed possible, and that, in consequence, Derbyshire would turn out in tremendous force on the ninth.

Stevens had taken this news well, but seemed much preoccupied. He had curtly refused Bacon's request that the plans should be altered to permit Brandreth to take the ironworks, saying that it was no time for Tommy to start settling grudges. Bacon had felt affronted at the bluntness of his one-time acolyte and been saddened to see how unimportant this committee seemed to be regarding him now that the time for action was come.

A few moments later, however, Bacon had forgotten his own pique when Stevens had told him of the Sheffield arrests. Bacon knew Wolstenholme well and also knew of the effect that such news would have upon morale of the Yorkshiremen. He advised Stevens to send instantly to Yorkshire - he would go himself - to talk to the remaining leaders and have their opinions first-hand. Stevens had said that there was no need, as the London Delegate was due in Nottingham, and would bring with him the latest intelligences from the north. If he said to call a halt, then they would do so, but Stevens hoped that he would not, as delay could do great damage to the men's spirits.

Tommy walked home the next morning, full of doubts which he could not frame words to explain. His lifetime of experience as a plotter and conspirator had sharpened the instincts that now told him that there was great danger near. He returned to Pentrich and thought long and hard in his sober little house, before wandering along to George and Rebecca's home, the epitome of an old gentleman on an evening's stroll. Once inside the parlour, Bacon told Jeremiah that Stevens wanted the plan to proceed, that the ironworks should be let be if there was any resistance and that there had been a little trouble in Yorkshire, but nothing to affect the rising. He also told Brandreth that he had heard that the authorities had sworn out a warrant for the arrest of one Thomas Bacon of Pentrich and that, accordingly, he was going into hiding for the time being. This would avoid causing problems for the Captain in these busy days. His co-conspirators were most understanding when they heard his last suggestion, and said that it was for the best. He had left the house very slowly, burdened with the best wishes of his friend and his friend's uncle.

Jeremiah and Rebecca

Sunday passed in a fever of last minute preparations. In many a little stone house excited men brought out makeshift weapons and hefted them from one hand to another. The inns were much too full for a Sunday, although, on balance, the churches and chapels were much better attended than usual. There was an atmosphere of expectation in the air. Towards night, the rumour spread abroad that London was already beset by armed rebellion and that the north was now stirring.

Monday dragged on slowly for most, and Jerry Brandreth was no exception. He had slept fitfully and the ever protective George, who had risen fresh as usual, told Rebecca that she was to let the Captain sleep on. He had then hoisted his oldest daughter on his broad shoulders, and left the house, whistling as he went.

Jerry awoke some minutes later, his eyes full of sleep. Rebecca brought him a cup of water which he drained in one, grateful for the relief which it gave to his stone-dry mouth. He began to push his curly hair into place, conscious that he must look like a scarecrow and, as he did so, caught Rebecca laughing at him. He smiled at her. She went outside to fetch a pitcher of water for him, poured it into the bowl, found a piece of soap and a soft cloth so that he could wash himself. He thanked her and sluiced his face.

"Do you want summat t' eat?" she asked him.

He replied that he was not hungry.

"Don't you feel well, Captain?" she taunted playfully. "If your brave men could see what you looked like first thing in t' morning, they might not be so eager t' follow you!"

"They follow me because ah'm one of 'em," he said, a little later.

"One of 'em'!" she laughed. "You're nuthin' like 'em!"

"In what way?" he asked, puzzled.

"It's hard to put into words, really. You have caught them like you were snaring rabbits. Take that great oaf of a husband of mine: he looks at you like you were t' king or something. He never misses a word you say, and he puts me to sleep every night with tales of what you've done."

"There's nowt special about me," he protested. "I'm poorer than any of 'em. Turner knows about soldiering. Owd Tommy has t' gift o' words. Folk should follow them, not me. T' be honest, ah thought they wouldn't accept me and ah'd be packed off back to Nottingham as soon as ah arrived!"

"You really don't know do you?" she said. "Look, the difference between you and Old Tommy - Turner, Ludlam, George - is that they would like to believe in all this, but you really do believe. It shines out of your eyes. While you believe in it, they can."

"Ah don't understand you, Rebecca," he said. "Tommy has been preaching rebellion for years; it was him persuaded t' lads in Nottingham. How can you say he doesn't believe in it?"

"Ah'm not too sure that he does believe now that it's so close. Ah don't think he'll turn out on t' night."

"Ah'm sure he will," Jerry protested. "But if he doesn't, it will be because he's an old man, not because he doesn't believe."

Rebecca shook her head and went to tend a crying baby. Brandreth sat on a stool, watching her.

"You know what you remind me of?" she said a little later?"

"No, What?"

"Toy soldiers! All this marching and drilling; all these speeches, plans. You can't really think you will overthrow t' King and t' government? This is just play. Ah just pray you will all come home safe."

Brandreth looked at her, shocked at what she had said. "It's not a game! We are part of a huge army! The whole country."

Rebecca interrupted him. "A game! That's all it is. You'll go out and make a lot of noise. Some of you'll get arrested and t' lucky ones will have a narrow escape. Then it'll be harvest time and men's minds will be occupied. All this'll be forgotten. The rich will still be rich and the poor will be poor."

"You're wrong, Rebecca. This is no game! It is more than breaking frames because we've no work! This is about turning the world upside down! They think they are better born than us, but you, me, George, Ann, we're as good as any o' them. Better! Any who set themselves above t' rest and make others poor so they can have much more than they will ever need must be knocked down. Ah started in this because ah wanted work and food for my family, but it's about more than that now; we have a right t' more than just bread and work. We have a right t' combine together; a right t' vote for t' Parliament that rules us and a right t' say and write what we think. Those are t' things ah 'm fighting for now and for t' rest of my life! Ah've walked in t' shade, but now there is a chance t' do summat that might change everything."

"Another speech!" she said sadly. "Fine words, but they are nothing t' do wi' t' likes of me and George. We don't understand that sort of talk. It doesn't really matter to us who t' government is, or whether we can vote for it or not. We wouldn't know who t' vote for, even if we had chance. And men will never let women vote anyway. All these men who follow you are t' same. They just want food and money, and t' belong, that's all. Ideas won't change t' way t' world is. Can you make t' harvest better than t' bloody Prince can?"

He was exasperated with her, because he had believed that Rebecca understood. Now she talked like all the doubters he had ever met who could only see failure; the ones who had shaken their heads at his words and gone home rather than be associated with his treasonable utterances. He had hoped for so much more from Rebecca.

"But you were all for t' rising," he told her. "You helped me write that poem. Ah thought you believed in us."

"What does it matter what a woman believes?" she retorted. "When has what we thought made any difference t' what men do? Whatever ah say, you'll do what you want anyway!"

He has not wanted to upset her. "Ah'd rather ah went wi' your blessing," he said, less angry now. "George needs you to back him, an' all."

"Oh, yes, ah'll back him," she was crying now. "Ah'll stand by him and wait for him t' come home. Ah'll look after t' children while he's gone, and gi' him a shoulder to cry on if he comes back after they beat you. Ah'll do all that, just like all us women with husbands, just like your wife will do for you. We'll wait and get on wi' living, while you play your games."

He said nothing at her outburst, finding no words which would serve to dispel her doubts and worries. She went to the window and looked out so he wouldn't see the tears. As the sun ducked behind the clouds in the western sky, those with a nose for the weather predicted rain. Before the sun rose again and the rain stopped, the lives of George, Rebecca and the folk of Pentrich and South Wingfield would be irretrievably altered.

Gathering

George Goodwin commuted on horseback between the ironworks and Ripley Market Place, never stopping more than a few minutes at either location, and rushing the three-quarters of a mile in between at a fast pace. His watch was very much in evidence, showing seven, eight, nine, ten o'clock and all the minutes in between. Fifty constables were ensconced in the ironworks, while Fletcher had a further seventy disposed about his brewery and Ripley Market. The men waited in silent anticipation, often fancying that they heard shouts or shots, or the clatter of hooves in the distance, but always being disappointed. There was talk of sending an armed group out to reconnoitre Pentrich, but Fletcher would not spare any from the brewery, and Jessop was anxious not to weaken the defences of the Ironworks.

George Goodwin hated the boredom of inactivity and inwardly cursed at the caution of those who had had the capacity to take active steps to prevent the rising, but had preferred to sit and do nothing instead. A fine amount of work he'd get done at the ironworks he reflected if he adopted that attitude! As if in a deliberate attempt to ruin what remained of his good temper, the Almighty chose the hour of ten o'clock to unleash the heavy rain which had been threatening Ripley and the villages around it since early evening. Goodwin found himself marooned by the weather at the house of the jittery Fletcher and soon cursed himself into silence as they waited together for the action to begin.

It began to rain heavily on William Stevens too, as he led his reluctant group of about twenty men out towards the Nottingham racecourse.

"That's about all we need," said the man at his side, shifting his heavy hammer to his other hand so that he might pull up his collar.

The rain worried Stevens. Such weather would convince any waverers to stay snug and warm and forget their promises to turn out. Apart from Tommy Bacon's enthusiastic reports about Brandreth and the Derbyshire men, the news over the last few days had been relentlessly grim. One by one, the Nottingham committee delegates had reported an atmosphere of despondency spreading among their men. Most put it down to the fears sparked by the arrests in Yorkshire, and the consensus was that Oliver had betrayed them, and if they went on with the rising, the authorities would be waiting to trap them.

Sampson, normally a tower of strength, had reported weakly that he would hardly be able to raise a dozen or two from the villages to the north, so apathetic or hostile were the men now. Stevens had tried to maintain his optimism, clinging secretly to the hope that if Brandreth could get his forces up to the centre of Nottingham, then the city folk who were now so reluctant would turn out in support. They reached the racecourse just before eleven. A few groups of men, wet through, were milling around, waiting for orders. Holmes was there already and shook his head as he saw Stevens.

"Look, there's not three score here. We'll have t' call it off!"

Stevens glared at him, and angrily told him to have some faith, that it was early yet and the weather would slow men who had a distance to travel. The numbers did increase as Stevens had maintained, and for a while it began to look as though there would be enough for the job. At half past eleven, Henry Sampson appeared with four or five more with him. Stevens recognised the voice of his friend in the darkness and moved over to him.

"Henry, how many are with you?" he asked.

"Only six of us," Sampson replied. "We waited for t' Sutton men and t' Mansfield men, but none came, so we came on ahead."

Holmes seized Stevens' arm and whispered, "We must call it off. If we start things with so few, t' rest will desert us."

Stevens began reluctantly to agree with him. The Derby men were the last hope, but they were late.

At nine o'clock, Rebecca Weightman kissed her husband on the lips and Jeremiah on the forehead, then turned away so that she would not see them leave. They went out into the lane, and walked over the brow of the hill and looked across towards the west. The sun was sinking behind Crich Stand after its long day as they walked downwards, past The Weir Mill farm and along the lane which led to South Wingfield. At Ludlam's quarry about a mile further on, George shrilled a whistle and old Isaac came out from under the trees in answer. Soon the Ludlams, Brandreth and Weightman, each encumbered with three or four large pikes were climbing out of the valley and up to the road between Crich and Wingfield. They marched a little way towards the latter village, before turning off to the left and making for a little building shielded by some trees, a hundred yards away.

Bill Turner was already waiting at Hunt's Barn and with him his brother Edward and the rest of the South Wingfield men. The Captain, George and the Ludlams deposited their pikes, and Manchester Turner was told off by his brother to distribute them among the men. The Wingfield party was well armed already, but the pikes would come in useful to equip any later recruits who needed a weapon. The Turners were eager and active, putting the men into line, with the Ludlams as the rearguard and themselves in the van.

Another party appeared from the direction of Crich, and ambled up towards the barn. Turner swore at them in a soldierly fashion and told them to fall in and mind that they did their duty. Then he went towards Jeremiah, who stood lost in thought, looking reflectively at a gap in the hedge.

"What's these, Bill?" he asked.

"Halton's keeper hangs 'em up t' scare off others," he replied.

Jeremiah looked up sharply at him, and then turned his attention back to the hedgerow, where three dead, decaying weasels were suspended from a bough. The faces of the dead little animals were contorted and full of pain, like those of the men whom Jeremiah remembered from two executions he had witnessed. Isaac Ludlam joined to say that the men were ready. Then the Nottingham Captain took a deep breath of Derbyshire air and turned towards the waiting men who were the vanguard of his army of redressers. As they walked away, the wind stirred the three little bodies in the hedge and they danced in the last pathetic moments of daylight.

Chapter 8: The March

The Advance

The farmers around Pentrich and South Wingfield had too much to lose to become involved in any activity as hazardous as a treasonable rising against the Crown. Likewise, there were those amongst the farm labourers who were too fearful, or too set in their ways to join a violent insurrection. Many had been worried for weeks by persistent talk that a great rising was in the offing, in which they would be compelled to participate. Some had already been threatened that should they try to stay at home when the rebels arrived, they would be forced at gun-point to march away. In market places and taverns, they had caught the glances of neighbours and strangers, sensing their whispered conversations threatened menace. To those reluctant ones, the Nottingham Captain did not appear as a messiah come to liberate them from poverty; he was more the Angel of Death. Cowering behind their bolted doors in the lonely night, families huddled about them, they waited in dread for the sound of insurgents, wondering whether to fight or capitulate.

They came first to the house of Henry Hardwick. The timid old man quietly passed his gun across the threshold to his neighbour Edward Turner. The old man was too infirm to join the train; he was left to watch as his visitors walked from the yard down the lane. Closing the door against the darkness, Hardwick went to sit by his frightened wife. Henry Tomlinson, owner of the next house, was neither old nor infirm. In addition, he was owner, rather than tenant, of his small farm, and was not about to leave it to go out and commit treason. He locked his door at ten o'clock that evening. He and his wife had taken up a position in the fold yard, from where they could see the house clearly. The two of them spent the next hour listening hard in the rain for the sounds of marching men,

Henry holding his gun, resolutely. Soon a lantern flashed in the lane and there were voices. Breathless, they watched the rebels take up positions by the windows of their empty house, and heard hammering on the door.

"What dost tha' want here?" cried Tomlinson from behind them. The men turned at his words, and one held up a lantern that Tomlinson's face might be seen. The little man who had banged on the door advanced.

"We will have that gun off thee," he said, sharply.

"Tha won't," replied the farmer. He pointed his weapon at his unwanted visitors.

"You are one man with one gun. You've but one round to fire. If you try t' shoot, it will cost your life. If you injure me, my men will kill you and burn your house as an example t' others who may seek t' prove as foolish."

After a brief period of thought, Tomlinson sadly lowered his gun, and presented it, butt first, to the rebel leader. One of his followers took it.

"There!" cried the farmer. "Tek t' bloody gun and leave us be!"

"You must come wi' us," said the little man.

"Like Hell ah will!" Tomlinson cried, his anger getting the better of him. He looked straight into the stranger's darkened face.

Ah"ll not budge and tha'll not mek me!"

In reply, his protagonist produced a pistol from his belt and cocked it. He put the barrel to Tomlinson's head. "Unless you fall in line and march wi' us to Nottingham, ah'll kill you. Those who are not with us are against us. You must decide now; we've no time t' argue."

The farmer knew that he was beaten. Muttering about leaving a wife alone in such a remote place, he reluctantly found a place in the line. The marchers moved down the lane. Mrs Tomlinson began wailing. They prodded Tomlinson forward, through the gateway of his little farm. Twenty yards further on, while they waited to cross a stile he found himself in the company of one he knew.

"George Weightman!" he said. " Th'art never part o' this lot??"

George replied that he was.

"Then th'art not t' man I took thee for! Forcing innocent folk t' leave their women in t' middle o' t' night in such a lonely spot!"

George was obviously not happy about Tomlinson's recruitment either. This was a man he had known and liked all his life.

He paused then whispered "Come along wi' us a bit, but when I give you t' nudge, drop out to t' side."

Tomlinson nodded, and a mile or so further on, as the group approached yet another farmhouse, he took the signal and faded away gratefully into the trees. House after house was assailed. Some folk resisted a while behind locked doors, but the men outside invariably gained admittance. Elijah Hall, who had hidden his guns and his sons from the insurgents, was beaten by their Captain until he revealed their whereabouts. Then he and his lads were given pikes to carry, and forced into line. Isaac Walker, a widower at the next house, was relieved of a fine brass-barrelled pistol by the Captain himself; after firing a shot from Walker's doorway to test it, Brandreth thrust it securely into his belt. Walker was shoved into line with the rest and they marched onwards.

Out of all the householders visited that night, there was but one went willingly with them; Samuel Hunt a young man, with a wild streak in him, which had frequently irritated his staid, respectable neighbours. The adventure of an armed march on Nottingham appealed to him and he eagerly awaited the arrival of the column. When they arrived at his door, Samuel was standing on the step with a cup of ale for the Captain, and a table full of bread and cheese set for all to share. While the rest ate and drank Hunt pulled on his coat against the rain, and he and his servant Daniel took their places near the front of the march, with a gun apiece, and the thanks of the captain to sustain them.

Not much distant from Hunt's now deserted farm was the house of Mary Hepworth. Widow of Joseph Hepworth, whose family had occupied the fine old building for several generations, she had two grown up sons, Francis and William. Francis had come to his mother some days before, having visited South Wingfield to buy some goods. He told her how at the inn he had been accosted by the Turners. They had warned him that he must join the rising when they came to the farm for guns. Francis had refused to have anything to do with this suggestion, and had threatened to report them to Colonel Halton. The Turners had taken exception to this, and Bill had promised that when the rebels called upon the mother, he personally would kill the son. Mrs Hepworth immediately packed Francis off to relatives who lived at Melbourne in the south of the county. He was to remain with them until the trouble was over.

At about midnight heavy knocking shook the door of the farmhouse. Mary Hepworth gathered her other son William and her two labourers, Robert Fox and Robert Walters, along with her daughter Emma. They battened themselves in the kitchen and refused to open up. Frightening noises terrified the shaken inmates, as those outside battered the kitchen door, with what sounded like huge stones. Some of the rebels went around to the side windows and succeeded in smashing an opening through them. William Hepworth pushed his sister and his mother through into the next room, while Fox put his weight against the door.

Someone yelled: "Surrender your men and your guns, or you all die!"

A moment later, a shot was fired. The inmates screamed. There was a moment of ghastly silence; Robert Walters fell backwards over the bench he had been sitting on. He was mortally wounded. Those within heard the men outside remonstrating with their Captain.

"Tha's no need to shoot people, Captain!" someone cried.

Others voiced their approval.

"It s my duty t' shoot them opposing us," the leader shouted back. "And I'll be damned if I'll put up with any more insolence. Get back in line or you'll get the same as him bleeding inside!"

Mrs Hepworth was convinced that her son had been shot. Finding him unhurt, coupled with her anger at the severe wound inflicted on her servant, her resolution stiffened, and she abused the rebels who were climbing into the room.

Beating her fists on Isaac Ludlam's chest, she berated each man, while they ransacked her home in search of hidden weapons. After a few minutes, they were gone; two guns, her reluctant son and the other servant went along with them. A little later, Robert Walters died of his wound, a weeping woman on either side of him, in mourning for his soul.

Hugh Wolstenholme

Hugh Wolstenholme, the Pentrich curate, sat up long after midnight. He had tried prayer, tried reading, tried port wine, tried any and every means he could think of to settle his mind, and failed. Wolstenholme was fully aware of what was happening in his parish that night. Enough local folk had been in to tell him. As a member of the Established Church, and its local representative, his duty was clear enough; to condemn the lawless behaviour of the reformers. Vicars and curates in recent months, throughout the Midlands and

North had done so repeatedly. Wolstenholme had been nurtured at the breast of the English Establishment, having entered the Church from a solid, middle-class family, after a period reading Theology at Cambridge University. There was, however, more than one branch of the Wolstenholme family, and the house of his father, William, at Sheffield, was a radical one. By now, Hugh knew of the arrest of his father and other Sheffield reformers, and resented it strongly. Close to his cousins since boyhood, he had always felt more in common with them than with his Church of England colleagues and Cambridge fellows. More than that, this tall, energetic man had formed great sympathy for the radical cause his family had espoused.

The curate of Pentrich confused many of his folk by refusing to condemn the reformers from the pulpit. Neither had he attempted action against those who talked of violence, conspiring in the parlour of the little inn, just across the road from his fine, stone church. His sermons had dwelled long upon the blindness of the Pharisees and Sadducees and had praised the virtues of community and fellowship of the early Church. Pentrich was a working village and the farmers, labourers and craftsmen, who predominated in the pews of its church, found much in what he said relevant to their own lives. It was easy to recognize the modern-day oppressors of the poor as Pharisees, when there was very little Christian charity exhibited by landlords and propertied folk in the area.

It was just after midnight. June 9th was become June 10th. Wolstenholme was standing wearily in the church porch, looking out into the rain. His wife and children were safe at the house they kept at Crich, three miles away across the fields. There was nothing to see beyond a light or two burning in the houses of some of his neighbours. He was in great turmoil as to how to respond to the rising he knew was taking place at this very moment. He could not condone violence, but equally he was driven to support the ideals of those who were risking all to make a better world. Hearing the sounds of men in the road outside Hugh turned down the lamp and peered into the night.

Delay

Jeremiah led his men into Pentrich in order to find John Bacon's contingent, which had failed to turn up at the set rendezvous. By now, the Nottingham Captain was a figure almost unrecognizable, buckling visibly under the burden of command. Every minor decision that needed to be taken was referred to him by men who acted like so many sheep following their shepherd. After the shooting of Walters they had become wary of him and many now were sullen when he voiced his commands. Bill Turner was in a dudgeon over the indiscipline of the column and raging over John Bacon's failure to show. Isaac Ludlam was tagging along wearily in the rearguard, anonymous, wrestling with his conscience.

Brandreth had sent Weightman ahead to gather the Pentrich men and he turned up eventually with good natured John Bacon and several dozen others. He was staggered to find the party had done nothing beyond stand around in Asherfields Barn. He had given the clearest orders that this group was to scour the village for reluctant volunteers before the Wingfield men came up, but now the job had to be done by the whole band, which would cause more delay. The watch John Bacon carried showed the time was well after twelve. Brandreth was battling to control his growing anger.

Not until two hours later did the splintered parties re-assemble after scouring the village and nearby farms. Many of the men took the chance to steal back into their own houses to seek shelter from the rain. It was left to Turner and his angry Wingfield recruits to shake out the reticent men of the village. Many petty outrages were visited on the householders of Pentrich before Brandreth was able to form a column of just over a hundred men and give the order to march. The Captain grew more and more impatient at any attempt at delay, becoming increasingly belligerent in his manner.

George Weightman was dispatched to bring back news from Nottingham. Mounted on an old and inadequate pony, George dodged past Goodwin's restraining arms at Butterley, and nursed his steed along the road towards the distant city.

The Men from Nottingham

After Holmes had convinced him that the only sensible course for the Nottingham men to take was to go home and wait to see if the Derbyshire villagers got through, William Stevens made a bad speech to those assembled. Holmes and the others filtered back despondently, towards their abodes. They nearly ambushed magistrate Lancelot Rolleston as he rode past them on his lonely mission, but let him through, failing to realise that that in doing so, they were dashing the last faint hope of success. Stevens his mind in torment, walked alone and weaponless towards Eastwood. He was still convinced there was an outside chance of success if Brandreth could bring his Derbyshire villagers through, and long before he heard the clattering hooves of George Weightman's pony on the lonely road he had made up his mind what to tell him. He made George repeat the message until he had it by heart: "the town is taken, the soldiers will not stir out of the barracks and the Derbyshire men must come up." Stevens had watched him go, shaking his head at the retreating, mounted figure. Deciding he had better get out of the rain for the few hours remaining, he plodded back into Eastwood to seek shelter.

Slow Progress on the Road

Brandreth approached the Butterley Ironworks at the head of his men with great reluctance. It had never been his wish to attack the place, and the Nottingham committee had instructed him to avoid delay at all costs. He was already hopelessly late and desperate to get to Nottingham with all possible speed. The Turners and John Bacon, however, were anxious for some real action and so it was that he found himself in uneven confrontation with Goodwin.

If the truth were told, Jerry Brandreth had been badly shaken by the shooting of Walters. He was not sure in his own mind whether the gun bad gone off of its own accord, or whether he had actually pulled the trigger. All he did know was that no one, except poor Walters, was more shocked than he when the pistol fired. From that moment he had forced himself to shout commands and brow-beat those who delayed him into action, but in his heart he was convinced he never wanted to kill again.

When Goodwin sallied out of his office at the ironworks unarmed into the mass of hostile men, oblivious to his own danger, Jeremiah and most of the others felt admiration for him. It would have taken a harder man than Jerry Brandreth ever could be to shoot such an assailant; the order to march on was inevitable. As his creaking army crept quietly and secretly through the back streets of Ripley, Jeremiah could feel the confidence of his men ebbing away, fast as the rain water trickling along the road beneath him. Ringing in his ears were the parting words of George Goodwin: *"You are going with halters round your necks!"*

In an attempt to raise morale he allowed the marchers a brief stop at the three inns around Codnor. He took one third of the force into The Glass House; another group invaded The French Horn and a Third the New Inn. There were now about a hundred and fifty in the party, all told. The three innkeepers were roused from their beds in the middle of the night and forced to unbar their doors. As the men pushed in out of the rain, with pikes, pistols, swords and guns before them, their hosts and hostesses recoiled with horror. Their shock turned to disgust when it transpired that the ruffians who entered did not intend to pay for what they drank. After downing a quart of ale, the men at the French Horn tested their guns and raised their spirits by loosing off a few rounds through the window. Manchester Turner, who never could hold his beer, was regaling the laughing occupants of The New Inn with tales of his derring-do so far on the march, complete with pistol noises and high-pitched impressions of hysterical wives and daughters pleading that their men folk should not be pressed.

At The Glass House Inn, Jeremiah's mood lifted briefly when German Buxton with twenty miners and stockingers caught them up. A large group from Heage and Belper came up soon afterwards. These new arrivals wanted their share of free ale and food too and it was well over an hour before the column could be persuaded to resume. As he left Brandreth called for the reckoning. Mrs Thorp, the landlady told him he owed twenty eight shillings. Brandreth informed her that she would be compensated by the Provisional Government in a few days. She laughed bitterly in his face.

"Tha'll pay me never! Tha's a thief!" she cried.

Brandreth lost his temper.

"The Hell ah won't," he cried. "If ah offered you Bank of England money, it would be of no use t' you after tonight."

With that they proceeded, advancing more and more slowly; tiredness, the effects of the ale, and the fact that the pressed men were deliberately dragging their feet to delay the march slowed them further. When she saw how distressed old Isaac Ludlam was, Mrs Thorp whispered to him to hide in her cellar, but he refused and moved off sadly.

Dawn was approaching as they reached the Junction Navigation Inn at Langley Mill. Without waiting for a command the rebels started hammering on the door, crying out for ale. The shaken landlady, Mrs Goodman, dressed and came down to find her inn packed with a press of thirsty men; her pot-boy overwhelmed, and the whole building in danger of collapse if the walls inside received any more pressure. She did her best to serve those nearest the ale barrel, but it was a hopeless task, till a big tall man of about forty fired a shot to get silence; this achieved, a little dark-haired man, their commander, began to speak.

"Men! We have wasted enough time already! Now hold your tongues and listen. George Weightman has returned from

Nottingham and he has a message which you must all hear. Up you come, George!"

He pulled the big man on to the table top beside him. "George has spoken with our friends", he continued. "They have sent us a message Tell everyone George."

George screwed up his face in embarrassment and made the only speech of his life.

"The town is taken," he began. "The soldiers will not stir out of the barracks! The Derbyshire men must come up"

There were a couple of silent seconds while they digested his news. Then Bill Turner called for cheers and the other men hurrahed enthusiastically. On the table, a proud Weightman found that his captain had clasped his arm in a comradely fashion; he felt incredibly happy. With Nottingham taken even more bullying and effort was required to get the men out of the inn, and back on the march. Isaac Ludlam, who disliked drunkenness, and Bill Turner, who despised indiscipline, bullied and cajoled; George Weightman frowned and looked sour. Brandreth reached for his pistol, but it was still many minutes before the inn was empty, and Mrs Goodman was able to leave her room to right the furniture.

Many of the men could no longer see the need for hurry now that Nottingham was captured. More than a few began to drift away from the rearguard fearful that the protection night had afforded their faces was beginning to disappear. The main body of marchers, footsore and extremely tired, continued along the road, pressing on into the village of Eastwood. The border between Derbyshire and Nottingham was safely crossed, and the journey was more than half over. Though it was only six in the morning, most villagers seemed to be out and about. For a few moments, Brandreth believed it to be his first contact with a village in the hands of the Nottingham rebels. Sadly, the people of Eastwood were merely curious observers. The rebel rank and file demanded another halt, and their Captain was obliged to allow them a stop at the Sun Inn.

While he sat there in council with Turner and Weightman, a thin, nervous little man approached the table. He was from the village, he said, and wanted to warn the Captain that soldiers were on the way. He told how one of the Nottingham magistrates had come to the village earlier and informed all who were then in the tavern that the rising was not going to take place. The Nottingham rebels had gone home, he told them, and only a few dozen from Derbyshire were still intent on trouble.

The gentleman had ridden off towards Langley Mill to spy out the land. He returned an hour later with news that the Derbyshire insurgents were on their way and then ridden off towards Nottingham, with the avowed intention of fetching the military. Other Eastwood folk were passing on a similar message to Brandreth's rank and file. Many began to debate, in the light of such menacing information, whether they should continue with their mission. Thoroughly tired and disillusioned, Jeremiah shouldered a path through the packed inn out through the door to the road. The rain was teeming down upon clusters of depressed men, over whom the loyal Ludlams exercised a precarious guard. Bill Turner and George Weightman browbeat those inside to follow. The last of the forces of the great rising shuffled disconsolately for all Jeremiah tried to rouse them with promises of bread, beef and rum.

The lanterns would not be much longer needed, but the one George Weightman held for his Captain glowed yellow in the rain. The men were wet, they were tired, Brandreth cajoled them, but the hardest part was behind them. Having come this far they could not turn back. The moment they had left their homes and set their faces towards Tom Paine's distant jail, they had cast aside the old life and habitual subservient ways. They were rebels now, and their only salvation was in the success of their rebellion. What were a few soldiers against so many? Why Bill Turner and his Wingfield lads would see them off on their own! Brandreth doubted that the Hussars would come anyway. If they had sense, they would stay in their barracks, and not venture out to certain death and defeat.

As they always did the words of the Captain swayed the minds of those who heard and onwards the army passed, out to the edge of Eastwood in the increasingly light morning. At this point, the most reluctant of many forced marchers, old Henry Hole, took a decision which was likely to have dire consequences. He broke ranks and marched back against the flow of the column, towards home. The rest of the procession stopped to watch what would happen.

George Weightman blocked Hole's way, until the Captain came up and brusquely ordered the farmer to join ranks once more. He reinforced the instruction by levelling his gun at Hole's head. Hole pushed the barrel aside, trembling with fear and rage. He held a wicked looking paring knife in his hand.

Point that bloody gun at me again and ah'll split thee!"

Brandreth's men saw their leader's face whiten.

"Get back into line now, or you'll be shot!" he cried.

The men were silent, watching the two protagonists duel with eyes that contested hatred against resolution. Hole must have seen something in Brandreth's look which the others had not; after a few moments, he stepped past him with a bitter smile and continued to walk away.

The army began to mutter; the other leaders realised that unless Hole was stopped, his action could be the signal for wholesale desertion. Bill Turner and George Weightman looked at Brandreth for a lead. They saw him raise his gun once more pointing it at the retreating farmer's back as he walked on regardless. The Captain's face was screwed up to a squint along the barrel of his weapon.

He pulled the trigger. The pistol fired.

In that very instant Thomas Turner, a distant relative of the Turner brothers, leapt from the ranks in time to knock Brandreth's arm upwards. The shot rang out, and the ball soared harmlessly skywards. Turner backed off, wondering what his insubordination might bring. Jeremiah glared at him. Hole looked around, an expression of disbelief on his colourless face. Grasping quickly that he owed his life to Turner, he nodded his thanks. His saviour stepped back into the anonymity of the line, and those nearest him began to quietly congratulate him upon his action. Hole gave Brandreth a look of sheer contempt, before turning his back upon him once more and walking doggedly away. Jeremiah watched him for a long second, and then spun around on his heel, shouting the order to march.

Unused to marching at speed, several of the undrilled and tired men collided with each other as the train started forward. Having already happened many times during the night, this provoked much laughter and occasioned copious cursing. Unfortunately, the consequences of this particular collision were much more serious as one of the clumsy recruits managed to discharge his gun as he fell over. The ball took him in the lower leg and he lay bleeding, screaming with pain.

At the sound of what they took to be an attack, some of the more nervous began to scatter and run. The Turners and other steadfast souls tried to stop them, but two or three score in all probability had deserted the Derbyshire ranks before order was restored.

The injured man needed immediate attention. Since he was no further use George Weightman offered to carry him back to the Sun aboard the ubiquitous pony.

As they departed Jeremiah resumed his place at the head of his jaded army. Secretly, he was immensely glad that Turner had intervened.

The Hussars

Lancelot Rolleston had ridden as if all the fiends in hell pursued him, abusing the horse in such a way as he could not help but be ashamed of his conduct later. The sentry at the barracks at Nottingham Castle had no opportunity to initiate the formalities attending any well-dressed visitor's arrival. The agitated magistrate pushed past him and dashed across the square to Philipson' quarters, bawling out the officer's name at the top of his voice. A mere eighteen privates of the 18th Hussars, along with one NCO and Captain Philipson himself were available for duty at the barracks. Rolleston tried unsuccessfully to badger the officer to lead out his men. A final threat to expose the incompetence of a soldier to Sidmouth himself proved successful. The troop mounted. Riding out of the gates, they were reinforced by two other magistrates, Mundy and Kirkby. The addition of these two worthies brought the total number representing the interests of law and order up to twenty-three. As they galloped westwards, the small numbers at his command worried Captain Philipson a great deal.

As the Hussars approached Giltbrook from the east, so Brandreth and his force came in from the west. After Hole's desertion, about eighty fresh volunteers had appeared on the road: men who had missed their original rallying times, but had stuck on the track of Brandreth, until finally catching up. These eighty had not, however, made up entirely for the numbers lost through desertion and the Derbyshire army probably numbered less than two hundred as they were about to meet the Hussars near the Giltbrook stream.

It was over in seconds. At the first sight of the cavalry galloping towards them in the distance, at least three-quarters of the men ran back towards Eastwood. William Turner's commanding voice rallied his South Wingfield troop for a few brave seconds and they began to form a line. Then they, too, broke in panic and fled at the first sound of gunfire from the soldiers. Edward Turner seized his brother's arm and dragged him away to cover. The two Ludlam brothers sprinted away together, forgetting their old father, who limped off as best he could. Jeremiah found he was alone screaming impotent orders to hold the line and immediately caught the fear of panic. He raced away, leaping over the discarded weapons which cluttered the ground before him. He ran without conscious thought, overtaking those others who had chosen, as he did, to run to the south.

As he flew past little pairs and trios of breathless men, who had slowed to a walk, exhausted, he looked for folk he might recognise. However, the people he was most familiar with, the Wingfield and Pentrich men, instinctively raced west towards their own home villages. Brandreth was running south, away from them, and the thought came to his mind that if there was any place he dared not visit it was that green land where he had spent those few very happy days.

Rolleston and half a dozen troopers rode to the west on the track of several score of the routed insurgents. The Hussars gleefully cut out individual stragglers and rode close behind them, deliberately frightening the already desperate men, before riding them down. Rolleston, too, found this pursuit invigorating, and when the man he was chasing fell to his knees and gave up running, the magistrate felt disappointed and resentful that the hunt was over.

During the course of that deadly morning, about forty of the marchers were rounded up and forced off, hands bound, to the prisons of Derby and Nottingham. The Turners were cornered in their ditch near Langley Mill where William received a nasty gash in the forehead from Lancelot Rolleston's riding crop. Alone of all those who had run, the old soldier had held on to his weapon throughout the flight. Isaac Ludlam had somehow managed to evade the troopers and found himself a temporary sanctuary at the Glass House, where he lay ill and listening for the voices of the men who pursued him. George Weightman, who had run home ahead of all the others, sought sanctuary with the sympathetic clergyman, Hugh Wolstenholme. John Bacon roused his brother and the two of them set off together into hiding. William Stevens trudged back to Nottingham to confirm the final failure of that black night.

The revolution was over. The Northern Clouds had not come. Nottingham remained undisturbed. The Derbyshire villagers had risen alone. It would be their fate to suffer the wrath of a government that was determined to be severe. Back in the villages, women waited for husbands who were either arrested or remained on the run, afraid to return home. Rebecca and Nanny Weightman, Mrs Ludlam and dozens of mothers, wives and children waited as the day wore on. The only news that came to them was bad.

On the Run

Jeremiah Brandreth ran south as far as his legs would take him. The direction he had chosen, opposite to most that fled, turned out to be the only one that, in the excitement of their easy victory, the Hussars failed to pursue. When he could no longer run, Brandreth walked. Tired out, he finally slipped into a thick bank of woodland. There were no visible tracks and the undergrowth made his progress difficult. Branches pulled at his breeches and coat, and scraped his face, but he pushed on blindly, preferring to struggle against obstacles, rather than risk being seen. At the far side of the wood, when he reached it, he saw a large expanse of open land in front of him, stretching away to the south. He noted figures in the distance. They were probably men working the land, he decided, not soldiers in pursuit; even so, he dared not risk being spotted by them or by anyone else who might be witness to his escape.

He walked along the edge of the trees, keeping just within their shadow, and stopped to look at his clothes. The brown coat and dirty breeches would blend in with his cover, he decided; his black hat would not stand out, but Ann's scarf must go from his neck, into his pocket. At the end of the wood he came to a depression in the land in front of him; a natural feature possibly, but he doubted it. Most probably it was a disused quarry. Brandreth looked into its depths, and noted that there seemed to be no obvious track down. The bottom was flat with a grassy clearing. The thickly wooded sides were steep and difficult. He realised that anyone descending those slopes could not easily avoid making a great deal of noise, enough certainly to wake him in time to take action to evade capture. His mind mulled over all the alternatives, finally dismissing the temptation to put more miles between him and those hunting furiously for the Nottingham Captain and seek a safe place to rest.

Nottingham Captain! He laughed quietly, but out loud, remembering the title. He hadn't gotten within ten miles of Nottingham! He wondered what had gone wrong. Even if his part in the rising had failed, the Derbyshire presence was only a small addition to a great army; perhaps, he hoped, the rising had succeeded. But why had the cavalry come if Nottingham had been taken and the soldiers were staying in their barracks? The thought gnawed at him and he decided that he must think through the possibilities for an explanation. Those thoughts must wait, though, until he had made himself secure.

He lowered himself gingerly down the first part of the slope, digging his heels into soil that was soft after the rain. He grasped at branches to lower himself wherever he could, but slipped several times and had to suppress a curse. Jeremiah eventually reached the bottom and looked around for a hiding place. No one, he thought, had visited the place for months; the undergrowth was thick and just as capable of concealment as had seemed from above. Jeremiah shuffled himself down into the wet undergrowth and sank helplessly into his own thoughts. He felt weak and helpless as his tension faded and the adrenalin that had supported him so long drained away. In a little while, despite the wet and his own despair, he began to doze.

Chapter 9: Spy Master and Spy

Henry Addington was the son of the Earl of Chatham's doctor. A medical man, he was valued by his patron not least because he prescribed port as a specific for gout. Born in 1757, young Henry's strong connection with one of most politically powerful families in England was thus established. Both the Earl of Chatham (known later as Pitt the elder) and his son, Pitt the Younger, were Prime Ministers of Britain. Henry Addington profited much more from the patronage of this very influential family than from any of his own personal qualities. Despite being a poor orator and a shallow thinker on many political issues, he was nevertheless, hard-working and well thought of among the Whig faction in British politics.

As the Speaker of the House of Commons for twelve years, and Prime Minister for four, Henry had gathered wealth and honours. He took on the latter office at the personal request of George III himself, when his former schoolmate, Pitt the Younger fell slightly out of favour. Addington's lack-lustre performance however, made the House pine once again for Pitt, whereupon he gratefully and eagerly subordinated himself once more to his protector. For his services, the King gave Addington the present of a fine house in Richmond Park, and seven cows from the royal herd.

Also bestowed upon him was the title Viscount Sidmouth, a rare honour for one of middle-class origins. His period of premiership behind him, Henry Addington settled down to faithfully serve a number of other Prime Ministers. By 1817 he was Home Secretary in the Ministry of Lord Liverpool, facing a period of severe domestic unrest almost without parallel in British history.

At the beginning of the year discontent caused by the Napoleonic wars and consequent hardships for the poor, had bubbled over. Maintenance of Law and Order became the prime political issue.

The widely unpopular Prince Regent narrowly escaped injury when two missiles smashed the windows of the royal coach. Clearly not a serious assassination attempt, this incident polarized political extremes in the country and hastened what Sidmouth regarded as the inevitable confrontation. Petitions of loyalty flooded in from the royalist middle classes; the aristocracy snorted in fury, sensing revolution in the air, and radicals began to agitate as never before. In every part of the country magistrates noted disaffection on the increase, and meetings in support of reform increasingly widespread. Trouble on a major scale was likely. The real problem at first was not the opposition and Sidmouth had no real fear of scattered radical opinion, but how to deal with the growing civil disobedience was another matter.

Parliament was still a long way from admitting that the country needed an organised police force. Public order was maintained on a variety of levels by unlinked and uncoordinated departments. Each town had its own watchmen. These worthies were usually old soldiers or retainers, put out to pasture, rarely up to the rigours of a dangerous job. The Town Clerk and the magistrate in each urban area usually had constables at his disposal. These men worked rather like bounty hunters and were much more efficient with a reward in the offing. Rewards would also be paid to people prepared to lay information against any who had broken the law. Many local officials maintained their own informers on a fairly regular basis. Magistrates had the power to enroll special constables if circumstances demanded. As a last resort, the standing army, much reduced in the years after Waterloo, could be called upon to combat civil disorder. In addition most areas had their own militia, 'the yeomanry,' armed and mounted, usually maintained at the expense of some rich local worthy.

Such a haphazard system was less than ideal for fighting a war against secret societies that organised on a national basis. Moreover, it was plainly useless for providing the sort of detailed information the Home Secretary needed to deal adequately with a concerted attempt at a general insurrection. A Parliamentary Committee set up to investigate the extent of secret anti-government activity in January 1817, reported back in March. It concluded that covert political organisation was widespread and rooted in the Hampden Clubs. These were political debating societies set up some years earlier. Now they served as forums for those who advocated sweeping and violent political changes. Agitation was strongest in the Midlands and the North, where there was much talk of revolution. In London, famous radicals, like Burdett, Hunt, Cobbett and Cartwright, egged on huge assemblies at the Spa Fields, which ended inevitably in violence.

Propertied people in the capital became firmly convinced that severe measures were needed to control the situation. In response, Sidmouth suggested, and his colleagues readily agreed, that combative legislation was required in order to protect the country from the disorder threatening. Thus it was, that a government which in recent years had refused petitions and made frame-breaking a capital offence, introduced a whole series of even more repressive acts, which later generations would decry. The Habeas Corpus Act was repealed. Henceforward, the authorities would have the power to hold suspected criminals without trial; the freedom of the Press was severely curtailed; the law against sedition was tightened. Powers granted under this legislation would be exploited frequently in subsequent months. The most effective tactic however, which Sidmouth decided to employ, did not have the substance of legal backing and breached many people's sense of fair play. The Home Secretary deemed it necessary to recruit a network of spies and paid informers to infiltrate the secret societies. Coincidentally in March 1817, he received a letter. It was unsigned; the writer emphasised need for secrecy. When what appeared to be correspondence from a crank landed on his desk, Sidmouth made a mental note to upbraid his assistant Beckett, for allowing it through. But something in the way the missive was written made him agree to its request for a meeting.

William Oliver was the name of Sidmouth's secret correspondent, but it was made clear he was writing under an alias. Such was the man Beckett announced some days later into the presence of the Home Secretary. Addington felt at ease behind a large oaken desk. It reminded him of his rooms at Brasenose and formed a physical barrier between him and those who visited on business. The Home Secretary gestured his guest into one of several chairs. Oliver settled on the nearest one. The flat surface of the desk between them was uncluttered. An orderly pile of papers stood sentry on each side. There were pens and ink close to hand. Occupying the central place of importance was Oliver's letter; underneath it a few sides of notes, which Beckett had prepared, outlining their guest's recent history pieced together from the Department's investigations.

The obligatory moment or two of silence held as Sidmouth shuffled the papers, absorbing their contents. Then he looked up to see a tall, straight limbed person, probably aged about forty. The hair was sandy in colour, grey mingling in the long side-whiskers, indicating that Oliver's beard, if he ever should wear one, would be a salt and pepper affair. He was dressed as he probably imagined a man of fashion should be; brushed light brown coat atop of a rather gaudy waistcoat, over a white shirt; breeches of a dark brown mixture, and the sort of boots that the Duke of Wellington was making famous. His face had never been handsome and the effects of smallpox had further reduced its beauty; not a face to look on for long, with its pitted cheeks and light-coloured little eyes.

Oliver sat legs crossed, his gloves inside the inverted crown of the hat he held upon his knee. He looked at Sidmouth's mouth, which hardly seemed to open as the Home Secretary thanked him quietly for his letter.

"You mention that you may have some important information to impart to me, Mr Oliver. Perhaps you will acquaint me with-" Sidmouth searched for the word - "it?"

"Certainly, my Lord."

Oliver's obsequious Cockney voice was as ingratiating and irritating as his letter had promised it would be, and as his appearance suggested. Sidmouth began to regret the impulse which had persuaded him to grant this interview.

"I have recently made the acquaintance of a man named Charles Pendrill my Lord," Oliver continued. "I wonder if you are familiar with that name?"

Sidmouth nodded. He was indeed, and very interested in any information he could find about Pendrill, a well-known agitator. An associate of Colonel Edward Despard who had a led a gang that plotted to kill King George, Pendrill was a known leader of the London Jacobins.

"Well, sir, Mr Pendrill is a boot maker by trade, a Jacobin by profession and a nasty piece of work by breeding. I became acquainted with him through mutual friends and professed to have some sympathy with the dangerous views he holds, in order to see that he wasn't going to do anything which might put the country in danger. He seems to have taken to me and he admitted me into his confidence very quickly. He told me that there is to be an armed insurrection, and soon. Soon, mark you sir!

"We visited the Cock Inn in Grafton Street together, and he introduced me to some of his cronies. Villains they are sir, true villains with no shred of patriotism. I have the names sir, if you wish them."

Sidmouth looked at the informer as he stopped talking. Oliver noted that he did not seem shocked or even impressed by this important information of his. He looked bland and imperturbable. Oliver shifted position in his chair, feeling suddenly uncomfortable.

"Mr Oliver," said Sidmouth quietly. "I have had an underling check upon your bona fides. It would appear Mr Oliver that you are not an entirely trustworthy character."

Oliver began to speak, but Sidmouth's arched eyebrows told him to remain silent while the older man continued.

"You have tried a number of different ways to earn a living: most of your attempts have been via the building trade. You have called yourself a carpenter, represented yourself as a surveyor, and most recently you have masqueraded as a master-builder. You have maintained your rather extravagant life-style by borrowing money widely. There is evidence that you have a wife living in Shrewsbury whom you have deserted and that there may well be another in White Chapel, similarly robbed and destitute, and under the mistaken impression that she is Mrs Oliver. Your luck ran against you in May last year when you were seized as a debtor and placed in the Fleet prison for five months until such friends as you possess raised sufficient funds to rescue you, and set you at liberty to defraud once more.

"Now you come before one of the King's ministers and claim patriotic intent in order to wheedle money out of the Government! I wonder, sir, why I ought to trust the words which I heard you uttering such a short while ago:"

Oliver had shown surprisingly little reaction to what was said, after his first attempts at denial, and now he sat passively until Sidmouth concluded his charges.

"What you choose to listen to, my Lord, is not for me to try to influence," he said. "I have come to you today in good faith. Yes, it is obvious that you suspect that in my case, financial gain may come before patriotic duty, but I must tell you that no amount of money would make me endanger my country"

He finished at this. The Home Secretary was considering whether or not to go through with a plan that he had had at the back of his mind for some time.

"I'm surprised that the likes of Pendrill would take a man like you into his confidence," he said. "You hardly look like a Jacobin yourself The haunts he frequents are not the sort to be visited by anyone contriving to look like a gentleman as you obviously seem to be trying to do."

Oliver ignored the insult implied in Sidmouth's words; "I think that is why I am in their confidence. Pendrill and his sort need gentlemen to become involved in their movement. They need orators, need tacticians and need respectability if they are going to get the support they require. I am very good with words my Lord, I can make as radical a speech as any in England and, what is more, I can persuade people that I believe in what I'm saying, even though I don't. They love flowery words and that is my true trade."

Oliver's ability to speak well under pressure interested Lord Sidmouth more than the expression on his pinched patrician face indicated.

"Mr Oliver," he asked. "I wonder whether it would be possible that your patriotism is sufficient for you to consider engaging yourself in a slightly more thorough investigation of the activities of these disreputable acquaintances of yours? You see, I am very keen to study their actions and form an idea of their plans, in order to prevent any possibility of a threat to the security of the realm."

Oliver did not take long to reply. "May I assure you my Lord, that for the love of my country I would be willing to put my own life at risk. I will acquaint your Lordship with all the information that I can gather."

Sidmouth looked at his man closely. "Of course, I need hardly tell you that any such gathering of information would have to be on an entirely unofficial basis. You would have to appear at all times to be acting upon your own initiative, and dealings with this office would be in secret. I might also add that in the interests of security, I would personally be prepared to swear that this meeting, and any subsequent ones, did not take place. Do I make myself clear to you?"

"Yes, my Lord, you do," replied the spy. Oliver had left shortly afterwards to spend some time in an antechamber awaiting Beckett, who was now summoned to talk with Sidmouth. When the official returned, he gave the department's new employee instruction on how to address important mail, and how to claim expenses. Oliver was then given a cash payment of four guineas and told to leave the premises as discreetly as possible, and to communicate any information which he should come by as it became necessary, to Beckett.

Oliver left the building, hat set at a jaunty angle and a twinkle in his eye. Sidmouth summoned Beckett once more.

"What was your impression of our visitor?" he asked the civil servant

"To be blunt my Lord, I thought him a shifty and untrustworthy type and I must say that I resented paying him any money," he replied.

"Yes, I resent it too, but I fear that it may be necessary to employ more of his kind if we are to ferret out the rogues behind this plotting. Comfort yourself with one thought, Beckett. If he gives himself away, and is silenced forever, we will hardly feel guilt that such a wretch has departed this earth."

Beckett nodded and withdrew, not entirely convinced of the ethic of employing one Englishman to betray another. He left Lord Sidmouth still seated behind his ludicrously large desk, musing over Oliver's letter.

The London Delegate

In the days that followed, Oliver threw himself into his new profession with an energy which had not characterised previous periods of employment. Pendrill who had introduced him to the London reformers conveniently decided to evade arrest by travelling to Liverpool to emigrate to America. Oliver found his absence from the secret meetings he himself now attended very much in his interests. Sidmouth was impressed by the quality of information his agent quickly procured and was delighted to receive a letter announcing that Oliver was to join Joseph Mitchell, a well-known travelling agitator, on a secret tour to meet plotters in the Midlands and North. He made immediate arrangements to have Beckett supply Oliver with a good deal of money as advance expenses, and sat back to await each mail eagerly.

In his guise as a gentleman, Oliver travelled north with well-known Lancashire radical Joseph Mitchell, the latter going under an assumed name, and purporting to be a weaver. He wrote copious notes back to Sidmouth in London, from Birmingham, Derby, Sheffield and Chesterfield. The Home Secretary became acquainted with characters like Wolstenholme and Scholes, and back in his office in London, the ageing Lord shuffled Oliver's letters trying to picture the faces of the men he was meeting. Oliver arranged for Mitchell, who was proving a risky travelling companion for the spy, to be arrested as the stagecoach halted at Huddersfield. As a result, his hands were much freer, and he quickly became, for the men of the North, their only contact with the thousands of Londoners eager to rise up and overthrow the government.

The ubiquitous Oliver was soon sending other names back to Sidmouth, including that of Thomas Bacon who he met at Wakefield. This meeting was a severe test for the informer, but he passed it well. The delegates, suspicious at first of a man who came to them straight after the arrest of Joseph Mitchell, were won over by the Londoner's stirring speeches and his obvious devotion to the cause. Besides that, he was now their only link with the London thousands who were crucial to the success of the rising.

When, in the third week in May, his agent returned to the capital, Sidmouth was eager to see him. Beckett showed the traveller into the office and closed the doors discreetly. Oliver accepted a glass of wine from his host and seated himself in comfort to drink it.

"May I offer my congratulations on your work so far, Mr Oliver?" said Sidmouth. "I am exceptionally pleased with what you have managed to achieve in so short a time."

Oliver basked contentedly in the warmth of Sidmouth's praise. Thanking him, the spy dismissed it as of little account; there was, he said, no praise as great as the knowledge that one was serving the interests of one's King and country. The formal courtesy concluded Sidmouth was eager to get down to the real business of the meeting; the need to persuade Oliver to take his spying role a little further. Standing up, he walked around his chair to gaze for a few moments out of the window.

"Mr Oliver," he said at last."I want you to undertake another tour of the areas from which you have just returned."

There is a service that I would like you to perform. Oliver listened carefully, while Sidmouth advanced a very devious plan. His reasoning was that as a rising in the near future seemed inevitable, it was a dangerous enough circumstance to require desperate counter measures. Accordingly, Oliver would travel this time to the North and Midlands, under the protection of a note from Sidmouth himself revealing his identity, and obtaining the co-operation of the authorities on the spot. Oliver would furnish such details as were necessary to enable the arrest of as many of the major delegates as possible in advance of the date of the rising. Right up to the moment of the arrests, Oliver was to continue in the part of reformer. He must do his utmost to ensure that others would continue to organise the rising.

If plans for the overthrow of the government were postponed and meetings of conspirators were suspended, the whole exercise would have to be repeated. Oliver must make sure the conspiracy continued long enough for its perpetrators to be arrested red-handed. The spy agreed readily and left to book his passage northwards. Beckett was instructed to contact the magistrates of the North as well as Major General Sir John Byng, in command of the army stationed in Yorkshire. Beckett was normally scrupulously thorough, but in his letter writing on this occasion he failed to include on his mailing list the Sheffield magistrate, Hugh Parker.

When Oliver returned to Yorkshire, he had an uncomfortably close brush with the authorities when Parker, acting on his own initiative and information courtesy of his informer, Thomas Bradley, ordered the arrests, on the evening after Oliver had left the city, of Wolstenholme and the rest of the Sheffield leadership. Sidmouth received a letter from Parker a few days later, informing him of the capture, and describing how a delegate from London had narrowly eluded the authorities' trap.

Beckett came apprehensively into Sidmouth's office, well acquainted with the reason for his summons, having read Parker's letter before passing it along to his master. When the Home Secretary was angry, he resembled nothing so much as a buzzing wasp and his voice had a sharp, threatening lisp which Beckett had come to fear. The official was soundly berated for his inefficiency, and in much the same vein, Sidmouth was damning about Parker's meddling initiative, which had nearly cost him his whole plan. Dismissed at last from the oppressive presence of his master, Beckett in some disgust began to write up a fair copy of a letter from Sidmouth to Parker. The Home Secretary congratulated the magistrate for his zeal, but asked that no more arrests should be made in case the Government agent's delicate mission should be revealed.

The later incident at the Sportsman's Arms where Oliver had made his spectacular escape was not the result of official lines becoming tangled. This was, in fact, a scheme which the spy himself had suggested to Byng, when he visited the Major General at Camps Mount, shortly before the meeting. Oliver's presence was the reason why Byng himself had taken part in the operation. The ruse had worked well. Eight key conspirators had been arrested, as well as Thomas Bradley and unknown to Byng, and Oliver. The Major General had ensured that a trusty soldier was placed at the rear of the inn, with orders to fire and miss if the gentleman tried to escape, but to make sure to hit anyone else. Oliver had played his part well, secure in the knowledge that his escape would not meet with any serious resistance.

When Sidmouth was made aware of this joint initiative between his agent and the army commander he was even more annoyed than he had been by Parker's independent actions. The Home Secretary had concluded that the rising's organisation was so ramshackle and naive, it might on balance be best if he allowed it to happen in order to visit spectacular punishments upon its perpetrators. Sidmouth hoped that Oliver had grasped this line of thought; it was not of course politic for a Home Secretary to directly suggest such villainy to a man as devious as his agent was proving to be.

Sidmouth spent many hours alone in his office, ordering the papers Oliver sent; making plans; conscious all the time of his own remoteness from events two hundred miles to the north. There seemed little doubt that effective command of those who would have risen in Yorkshire was now completely scuppered. Both Byng and Oliver informed Sidmouth that they suspected nothing major would happen on the ninth, in the industrial towns of the Pennines. It was increasingly obvious that any rising now would be in the area around Nottingham and Derby where the indomitable rogue Thomas Bacon had laboured long and diligently to promote it.

In addition to regular bulletins from Oliver, Sidmouth was receiving other intelligence from the Nottingham area, from the Town Clerk Thomas Enfield who employed his own informers, in the manner of Parker at Sheffield, and other magistrates throughout the country. They had regularly furnished him with details of the extent of radical feeling in the city and Enfield was well acquainted with the names and doings of Bacon, Stevens, Holmes and other active conspirators. During May, the informers began to give precedence to the name of Jeremiah Brandreth and emphasised his increasingly important role in the councils of the rebels. Enfield forwarded to Sidmouth in London letters from his informers adding words of his own. He pleaded for more troops to be stationed at Nottingham to discourage the disorder which threatened. Sidmouth added Enfield's information to the increasingly large pile on his desk, and continued to watch the situation. He wrote back thanking Enfield with the news that he would send some Hussars presently.

He was also in communication with the Duke of Newcastle, a man who, despite his title, was Lord Lieutenant of Nottinghamshire. Sidmouth knew the ultra-Tory Duke well and cautiously suggested to him that the trouble expected be allowed to occur. Minimal damage would be inflicted, but it would be worth the cost if the persistent and troublesome reformers in the area were caught red-handed committing treason. Newcastle received Sidmouth's suggestion in the manner the Home Secretary had hoped. Soon Enfield and the local magistrates were being quietly informed that there was nothing to fear, as Sidmouth had everything under control.

Oliver returned to Nottingham. At the stormy meeting in the Punch Bowl where his life was threatened, he played the very role his master in London had suggested. Oliver's enthusiasm for the cause, together with his ability to make the Nottingham men feel they would be betraying all the other radicals in the country if they abandoned the plan, was sufficient. He was able to persuade them to go on with a rising that now had no chance of success.

He then made his escape by the side of his new acquaintance, Robinson, the fat Tamworth businessman, on June 7th. Uncharacteristically, Oliver over-did the claret and bragged to his companion of his mission from Lord Sidmouth. As they sat at dinner in their inn at Tamworth Robinson was impressed by his travelling companion's ability to spin a good yarn, but he listened tongue in cheek to such a wild, improbable tale.

The idiot claimed to have visited every known part of the north and midlands at least twice in a month and persuaded a vast conspiracy of villains to take part in a spurious and treasonous rebellion on a date he had suggested to them. He had even persuaded them to send their leaders to places they did not know, just to sow confusion. Most leaders had been arrested, with just a few left at large so they could embark on a hopeless attempt to bring down the government. These would be hung to frighten off any other would-be rebels. This man Oliver even claimed to know Lord Sidmouth who was behind the government's plans!

They parted in Tamworth, Robinson to sell his wares, while the informer carried on to London to wait in the capital for news of June 9th and the outcomes in the East Midland counties.

Sidmouth had a map of the Nottingham district in his office and even more papers on his desk. He examined the area closely, finding the places identified by Oliver and Enfield's informers, paying special attention to a remote area, twenty miles west of Nottingham. He puzzled long and late over the potential threat presented by an isolated rising in the obscure villages of South Wingfield, Pentrich, Alfreton and Swanwick. It appeared from the detailed information before him, that the Nottingham Captain, sent to organise the rebellion in those villages, was pivotal to the success of the plan. It was essential that Brandreth should attempt a rising so that treason could be proved against him and his followers. The punishment meted out would be enough to terrify would-be revolutionaries for a generation.

For all his middle-class origins, this thin, stooping little man pacing his office late in the night was first and always a practical politician of the old aristocratic school. His dearest ambition was to restore the country to an ordered state. This required the outbreak of a small rising creating enough commotion to justify to the people of Britain the wholesale rooting-out operation he felt to be necessary. Sidmouth believed he would be able to purge the land of the disaffected and dangerous Luddites, Jacobins and Liberals, who threatened the peace of the realm. In purely political terms, such success would also pave the way to a personal victory against those in Parliament who taunted him as a parvenu, laughing at him as a small man whose enjoyment of rank, title and privilege, could be put down purely to the Earl of Chatham's gout and his liking for port wine.

Chapter 10: Picking Up Pieces

Nottingham

Hidden by the crowd in a room full of pipe smoke and loud men, John Holmes, Henry Sampson and William Stevens sat huddled in talk. Holmes looked as morose as ever. If anything, as he moaned on and on at the other two, his skin was more blotchy and his hair stragglier than ever.

Employing poor Sampson as a go between in order to attack the former chairman of the defunct Nottingham Committee, he refused to talk directly to or even to look at Stevens,

"Of course," he railed, "If people would have listened to good advice, we'd none of us be frightened of us shadows now. Ah knew that slimy toad were a spy! Ah said it often enough. Well now it's proved for anyone to see. But he's not t' only one to blame. What about that man that led Jerry Brandreth and his men into t' bloody ambush? What about t' blood on his hands?"

Stevens butted in here, to fight back against Holmes' attack.

"Some ambush!" he exclaimed. "Two score troopers and a couple of magistrates! That's all that stood between Brandreth and Nottingham, and he turns tail and runs! If they had stood firm there, we could have taken t' city; t' doubters would have eaten their words then! No, there's no blood on my hands! 'Course, if t' same doubters hadn't turned cold on t' issue when we assembled at t' racecourse, t' soldiers could've been fully occupied wi' t' Nottingham men, and t' Derby men could have strolled into town. Who knows what might have happened when t' country heard we'd got Nottingham taken?"

Holmes snorted in disgust and Stevens concluded his speech by tossing back a mouthful of ale. Henry Sampson stared into space, unwilling to risk taking sides. Like the other two, he was terrified he might be arrested. All of a sudden he looked much older than his thirty three years.

"Where would Jerry go?" he asked, changing the subject, hoping the argument might cease."Ah don't think he'd stray too far from his wife and children; he dotes on 'em."

Holmes shook his head, plunging his top lip into his drink. Stevens looked thoughtful; "If he's any sense, he'll get well away. If ah were him, ah'd head for one o' t' ports. Getting out o' England is t' only hope for him now. He might be able t send for his wife and bairns in a year or two."

All three looked reflectively at the table, at their ale, the men around them.

"Hang on, though," said Stevens after a minute. "Hang on, he has a sister somewhere down in t' south. Ah were asking him about his people once and he told me. She's living somewhere famous. Brighton! That's t' place! Now if ah were him, that's where ah'd be going. Why, you can nearly swim t' France from there! That's what he'll do, ah bet."

"Never mind him," said Holmes. "He's safe away. What do you think we should do? Ah don't think it's safe here. There's other informers about - apart from Oliver - and ah don't fancy a long spell in jail."

"Ah reckon we're safe enough," said Stevens. "What did we do? Went out on the ninth t' meet a few friends, and then most of us came home early. There's not much they can charge us with."

The three of them relapsed into a self-recriminating silence.

Later, Sampson and Stevens walked back towards their homes together. They talked quietly about what might have come to pass if people had proceeded with just a little more resolution.

"You mean t' remain in Nottingham, then?" Sampson asked. "We'll be able t' meet?"

"Yes," Stevens replied. "I'm staying. There's t' wife and babies. Ah'll bet Jerry Brandreth is missing his family."

They exchanged goodnights. Sampson strolled off, deep in thought, towards his home in Bulwell.

Stevens was brooding, too, as he neared his own house. He stopped to piss in the street and noticed a light ahead, as a pipe briefly flared. His ears caught the sound of men whispering near his front door. His head cleared and his senses sharpened as he realized the danger; he pressed against the wall next to him. He spent a minute or two in anxious contemplation, before tiptoeing down the little lane at the back of his cottage. Hardly daring to breathe, Stevens crept along until he came to the back wall of his house. There appeared to be no one watching this side. He felt in the corner for a familiar loose brick and quietly eased it out of its place in the wall. There in a little space behind it he had hidden a cloth purse full of money.

Stevens had received the weekly contributions of the members of the Nottingham Hampden Club, prudently keeping a proportion to act as a fighting fund. He had also used a little, like many a club treasurer before and since, to pay his own expenses. Now he planned to use the remainder to save himself from prison. Pushing the little cloth purse down into his coat, he fastened the buttons, debating briefly whether to bid farewell to his wife and children. He decided it too perilous a course. Patting the cornerstone of the tiny cottage, instead, he stepped on his silent way into the anonymity of the night.

When, some months later, he finally wrote to his destitute family, William Stevens was safe in America, a temporary guest of the exiled radical journalist, William Cobbett. The latter was already publishing Stevens' bitter denunciation of the man by now infamous as "Oliver the Spy", part of a campaign against the government's rascally behaviour.

George Weightman

Hugh Wolstenholme kept George Weightman in hiding for some weeks, hoping to find a chance to move him to a safer refuge outside the district. Hugh's wife and children had been sent away to Denby where Hugh was also the curate. This left Hugh free to hide George at Crich and to take food to a group of young men, hiding in a nearby hay loft, who had managed to escape the hussars. A month after the disastrous events the curate made a journey to his cousin's house in Eccleston, near Sheffield, where he arranged that George should move preparatory to journeying to Hull. From there a boat passage to safety could be found for him.

Wolstenholme returned the next day to share the plan. His secret guest thanked him, but there was little real enthusiasm in his words of gratitude. Hating his confinement, George despised even more the idea of leaving England. Pentrich was his home, and he wanted no other. He missed Rebecca badly and was often on the verge of leaving his hiding in the vicarage to sneak out to see her. Sensing the danger in such an expedition, Wolstenholme lectured him sternly, urging him to think of both their necks, and the danger to Rebecca if a wanted man was caught at her home.

George remained unconvinced, but promised not to risk anything. Wolstenholme sought a moment alone with the dark-haired woman. He was able to whisper to her that her husband was safe; that he hoped to escape abroad, and that George would send for her and the children. Hugh carried Rebecca's love back to her husband.

George made the curate promise that before he left for the north, he would arrange a meeting between himself and Rebecca. One night at the beginning of July, Wolstenholme led a small figure, features concealed by a dark shawl, through a side door. For two hours, the two young people tried hard to renew their love, knowing they faced months, years or perhaps a lifetime of separation. Rebecca began by reproving her husband, but her gentle scolding melted away almost immediately at the sight of his hound-sad eyes. She held him close to her breast, stroking his head with her long hands. Later, they stretched side by side in the softness of the bed, mingling joy with sorrow. Many words were left unsaid as they clung to the last moments of happiness.

As the first light of day began to show, Hugh Wolstenholme knocked at the door reluctantly. Their time together was over. For an unforgettable aching moment, Rebecca and George held on to one another, before rising tearfully from the bed to dress themselves. Wolstenholme waited for them at the foot of the stairs; they descended sheepishly like children about to face a disapproving father. The shepherd of Christ looked on them with kindness, assuring them that God would not desert them if they kept faith always with Him and with each other. After Rebecca had gone and the door bolted behind her, George sat morosely, hands spread to hold his face, elbows braced against the kitchen table.

When the light of dawn had almost subdued the glow of the lantern, Wolstenholme came back, yawning, to lead the burly giant back up to the room that served as his hiding place. George saying nothing, sat down on the bed, before stretching himself out slowly on the side where Rebecca had lain. The curate wisely left him there.

Isaac Ludlam

Isaac Ludlam, the elder, fled surprisingly quickly from the scene of the Giltbrook ambush. The remorse which had overtaken him in the early part of the rebellion overcame him completely, rendering him oblivious to bodily pain. He ran all the way back to Eastwood, and hammered fiercely at the door of the Sun Inn. The landlady, still frightened from the earlier depredations, peered through a window at the top of the building. Her trepidation disappeared when she recognised the old man below, reassuring herself he was alone. She hurried down to let him in. For a full ten minutes she berated him for his despicable conduct; his ears rang with her reproaches, until his shoulders slumped and his head throbbed. Why had he become bound to such rough people? Why had he not accepted her earlier offer of sanctuary? She had known immediately that he could not belong with the others. From the instant she had seen him leaning on his ridiculous spear, piously praying standing apart from the loud group clamouring for ale in the early hours, she knew he should have no place in such company. So ill he looked, and harmless; she had plucked his tattered sleeve, offering to hide him in her cellar while the others marched on to their doom. He had looked at her kindly, assuring her that he must stay and finish what he had started.

Besides, his sons were with him; he could not dream of deserting them, even if he wished to forsake his duty. She could see herself again shaking her head at his attitude, unable to comprehend such obduracy, annoyed beyond measure. Leaving him to his own devices on the fringes of the unruly crowd, she had set herself to clear her house of such uncouth custom, demanding payment of the grubby little man leading the villains. All the same, she had felt her face flush a little watching old Isaac, a forced smile on his grim face, marching out proudly to command the rearguard.

After her tirade was over, she put food and ale in front of him, but he was too tired and tense to take anything. She ushered him to her cellar towards a paliasse on the floor. Here, among refuse and barrels of ale, he had lain, within feet of the yeomanry who would dearly have loved to have put hands upon him. He stayed for three days and nights. Through thin walls he had strained to hear the customers; he picked up snippets of conversation, later amplified by his voluble hostess. From these sources he learned how many of his friends, including the Turners, were taken and lodged in Derby Jail to await trial. His heart broke to hear of his sons taken, captured at the family house at Wingfield Park in front of their mother. Rewards were offered for George Weightman, the Bacons, Brandreth and himself.

Two days after his enforced concealment he had developed a rasping cough which tore his chest and made his head ache. Several times the good landlady came with hot rum pleading for him to be quiet lest he should betray them both. The old man had done his best, but by the third evening he knew he must do right by his saviour and leave the inn without delay. His cough was too difficult to control and besides, he was nearly mad with his dark imprisonment, and increasing feelings of guilt and remorse. A desire to do penance on the road came upon him, to journey like a pilgrim until his sin of treason, and his trespasses against the will of God, were shriven.

The landlady did not try hard to dissuade him; her own nerves were weakening. With a bellyful of hot rum and a parcel of bread and cheese, Isaac Ludlam took the road back towards Ripley. It was night. He walked slowly, but without any attempt at concealment. Revellers leaving the inns at Langley Mill and Codnor took no notice of a harmless old man who shuffled and coughed past them. In disregarding him of course, they missed the chance of acquiring a small fortune in reward money.

The next day Ludlam dozed near Bullbridge, despite the attention of some children who thought him an old tramp and fair game. Something about the sadness in his eyes seemed to spoil their fun, and they left him to his rest. In the late afternoon, he turned his watery eyes away from the tempting road up the hill to Crich and beyond to his home at Wingfield Park. Isaac had fathered many children upon that hill and buried as many more in their infancy. His children's children cheered his days and made the disappointments of his increasing poverty bearable.

He was well aware that it would be long months before he could be safe there again' if ever he could. With tears in his eyes Isaac crossed the coach road near Ambergate and walked down towards Belper. As night fell he continued some way beyond the little village, renowned both for its violent nail makers and its hostility towards travellers.

It was some distance higher up on the Ashbourne Road, near Turnditch, before he paused to rest.

A Parting of Friends

Jeremiah felt much easier after his confession to the carter. Jack had long since ceased to be shocked by the doings of men; he had done plenty of mischief himself in his time on the road, and thought no harm of Brandreth for his tale. The pair continued southwards from the village of Sawley, near where they had met. They meandered slowly through many tiny settlements. Johnson told Jeremiah the names; Kegworth, Shepshed, Ibstock, Market Bosworth, and many more. They struck off the road regularly to little isolated farms and hamlets. For the people in such places the ancient merchant traveller was a source of everything they had run out of and could not get to market to buy. He also functioned as a travelling postman, taking bits of news, gossip and letters from one farm to another. Jack Johnson and his sort flowed like blood in the veins of the land's extremities. While there were carters like him, isolated country folk felt less remote from the mainstream of the nation. Bosworth was the most southerly part of Johnson's route and it was time for his passenger to disembark.

They sat outside a little inn, drinking some ale at midday. Jeremiah fingered a purse of money left still from the Nottingham Committee which should have helped him buy arms for his little army. He had enough, he calculated, not to worry for the foreseeable future, and bought dinner and drink for Jack and himself. He felt much easier after his confession to the carter.

Jack had carefully inquired of his customers about the happenings of the ninth of June. Jeremiah sat silently when he heard how only the Derbyshire men had marched, that Nottingham had been quiet and that he had been betrayed.

"There's a lot of folk will call you villain, right now," said Jack. "If your plans go well and you escape, and the men who were with you hang, then they'll always remember you as one. You'll be a living villain, though.

"But if you somehow get caught and they take you back and hang you, why, women will weep, men will make ballads for you, and those who refused to turn out that night will be bragging about how they stood at your side. They'll make a saint out of you if you hang, but if you get away, and others suffer in your place, why, you'll be the Devil. No one will remember you, or your rising; and if they do, it will not be a fond memory. That's what I have to say: please God, you'll get away, and if you do you'll be forgotten; if you don't escape, why, its death for you - but at least folk will remember your name."

"Ah won't be remembered, then, " replied Jeremiah. "They'll not take me alive. Ah've seen men hung."

They finished their ale in sombre silence. Then Johnson stood up, slapped a packet of tobacco down on the table, and dusted the breadcrumbs from his coat.

"Ah'm off," he said. "Give a thought t' me as long as that tobacco lasts, but after that, forget me."

He turned away during his speech, and Brandreth rose also. He put one hand on Johnson's shoulder and grasped his old paw with the other.

"Thank you for all, my friend," he said quietly.

Smiling at these words, Johnson nodded, walked to the cart, patted Lord Marlborough, and took his seat. He rattled the reins on the horse's back and the two of them moved off sedately. Brandreth sat down again losing himself in his thoughts. The serving girl came and filled his mug; he barely noticed her. What would it matter, he asked himself, whether or not folk heard of him or his rising? What would it signify to him, safe in America, to be called "villain"?

He had to admit it to himself, though, the idea of a heroic end was an attractive one: to stand up there in the centre of a huge crowd, voices stilled to hear his valedictory oration; his denunciation of those who had wrought his doom. He had been energized by the fear and excitement that took over his being as he rallied his forces back in Pentrich, and now, in his mind, he was feeling precisely the same thrill as he imagined confronting the execution crowd.

Then he thought of George Weightman, Bill Turner and the rest. What must they be thinking now? That their Captain had betrayed them?

Two noisy men came to occupy the bench a little way along from him. His wandering thoughts reverted to the immediate future.

Travelling with the amiable carter had brought him away from the centre of the troubles threatening him still, but he was no nearer the sea and escape from England. He pulled the little purse from inside the coat on the bench next to him, and emptied out the coins which it contained; money entrusted to him that now must be spent to secure an escape.

South

Jeremiah caught a coach from Market Bosworth to Leicester. There he bought a passage on the outside of a stagecoach to London. Stagecoaches travelled at the rate of about seven miles an hour; companies and drivers vied with one another to be fastest. Travel was quicker on the firmer roads of summer. He found the fast movement on the rutted summer roads quite exhilarating. Gripping tight to the rails on the coach roof, prevented him being launched into space, though he found his arms soon became painfully sore. The coach driver allowed only a twenty minute stop for dinner at Bedford, before the coach careered off again. The passengers found themselves bolting down their mutton and potatoes with indigestible haste. This well suited Jeremiah Brandreth, who faced danger every time the coach came to a settlement.

At each stop, the passengers changed and Jeremiah ingratiated himself with the driver, throwing down bundles and boxes, helping women and children up to the roof of the coach. The latter's screaming and giggling at the furious pace, and the excitement of it all, had the merciful effect of making conversation difficult. Brandreth found himself spared the task of having to talk to curious strangers. London was full and dangerous, just as he remembered. Jeremiah found a cheap inn and flopped down for the night on a smelly doss which had served many sleepers before him. The noises of men in the steaming hot room, made sleep almost impossible.

He lay, unhappy, through most of the short night, stiff from the stagecoach journey, his depleted purse, wrapped in Ann's little scarf, held next to his heart. Fifty years earlier, it would have taken a full twenty four hours to go from London to Brighton; in this age of high-speed travel, it took a mere seven.

As the coach rattled out of London, Brandreth had been amazed at the beauty of the countryside surrounding the capital city. He wondered at the relative prosperity of the area to the south when compared with the north and midlands. Little cottages by the roadside were well kept, and beautifully thatched. The sight of many impressive and stately mansions enlivened his journey. The folk he saw at the roadside, avoiding the juggernaut in which he now travelled, seemed happy, ruddy-faced, well fed. Beside them, the thin little man from Nottinghamshire looked insignificant and harmless.

In 1817 Brighton was arguably the most prosperous town in the Kingdom. The Prince Regent had taken a liking for the seaside, and most particularly to Brighton. He was especially concerned to improve the amenities of his favourite resort, having embarked, some years earlier, upon a scheme to convert the old Pavilion into a grandiose pleasure palace. The Pavilion had been built in the 1780's by Henry Holland, in the Greco-Roman style; the Prince Regent hired John Nash to reconstruct it in a mixture of Indian and Chinese design. Financial impecunity left little money available to the Prince for his project; Sidmouth and others were so concerned that the Cabinet took the unprecedented step of writing to him the Prince to ask him to exercise some economy.

By 1817 however, more funds had become available, and there was an influx of European tradesmen into Brighton who were kept busy dealing with requirements from both architect and interior designers.

The hungry little frame-work knitter from Sutton in Ashfield gazed at this garish extravagance with a mixture of awe and disgust. The recent gaudy developments were certainly spectacular, but the sight of the Regent's Grand Pavilion had little appeal for Jeremiah. When he arrived in the town for his first ever glimpse of the sea upon which he hoped to sail to freedom, the Pavilion was on its way to completion: the low original building had been extended on its north south axis, and oriental windows installed; there were sharply pointed battlements and a series of Indian domes, dominated by one huge onion-shape in the very centre.

Ellen was older than her brother Jeremiah. When they married, her husband worked for a hosiery merchant in Nottingham. By luck, industry and good business acumen Alfred Marshall had prospered in trade. A move to London supported by his industrious wife, followed soon afterwards by the birth of the first of several children, had paid off handsomely.

In 1814, the Marshalls had moved again; this time to Brighton. High-class hosiery was in great demand from the top echelons of society, who patronized the town in the wake of Britain's next king. The family's first small house had been quickly bettered, and now Brandreth's kin enjoyed a most comfortable standard of living, in a pleasant and busy little street.

Ellen Marshall bade her brother a cordial enough welcome. Family bonds among the poor of Nottinghamshire were unbreakable and, if the truth were known, Ellen missed her own folk a great deal. She would have willingly sacrificed her own recent prosperity for the security of the proximity of brothers, sisters and parents. He arrived unannounced during the afternoon; the babies were sleeping and her husband working. They had time to chatter and exchange news of their respective families.

Brandreth inspected the four young Marshalls with great concern, and announced his fine opinion of them. Ellen introduced him as their 'Uncle Jeremiah' and he gave each a penny from his diminishing store.

They avoided any talk of the reason for his visit. Ellen knew from her husband's newspapers that her brother was a wanted man. She had tried to pretend that it might have been another of the same name leading the treason, but in her heart she knew this was not remotely a possibility. She was further aware that there was little help she would be permitted to give her brother, however desperate his need. To Marshall's credit, he did not display the emotions possibly expected when he arrived home to find a dirty, dishevelled criminal with a price of 100 guineas on his head sitting with his wife.

He clasped the hand of his brother-in-law firmly enough murmuring how good it was to see him. Then silence.

"I'm afraid you'll have to go tomorrow morning," said Alfred. "It isn't safe for any of us if you stay longer."

Jeremiah nodded; Ellen turned away to hide the tears in her eyes.

"Ah understand," said the unwelcome guest. Ah've no wish to put you in danger."

"And I wish you had come in better times," replied Marshall. "I have no understanding at all of what you and those with you were about. I find it impossible to believe that you have killed a man and tried to capture a city: the whole thing is beyond me. That's as may be. All I know now is that you are Ellen's brother, and that I will not betray you. But you must go from here tomorrow."

They sat down to a meal. Jeremiah found his plate heaped. Ellen heated water and he soaped away an incredible amount of dirt. Alfred Marshall put out a shirt of his own and a pair of breeches.

Ellen mended some of the worst rents in his coat and, while he was washing, found his purse, secretly slipped two guinea pieces into it. Wrapping it in the scarf again she put it back into the coat pocket.

He slept that night in a real bed that smelt of lavender, and slumbered long after daybreak. Marshall awoke his guest to bid him farewell.

"I have work to go to Jeremiah," he said. "I wish you God Speed, and hope that you go to a better life for yourself. I want you to take this to help you on your journey, and to make up in some way for the hospitality which I am unable to show you."

He put a small purse of money onto the white coverlet. They shook hands again, Marshall in his fine coat and trousers and Jeremiah naked and thin between the sheets. The door closed behind him, and the guest was left to the last of his slumbers. Before he left the house, Marshall took his wife into his arms. Holding her close for a second or two she clung to him, tears coursing down her cheeks.

Stowaway

The inn had four floors, though the building was not especially tall. On each level, the beamed ceilings were low enough for anyone of more than average height to bash his head on. It was crowded with seafaring men, swarthy and dangerous, each with an earring and hands big from hauling on ropes.

A blind fiddler provided music; a one-eyed innkeeper served ale and rum, and two or three whores brightened the place and lightened the pockets of the patrons.

Enjoyment for those who had finished the long Atlantic crossing amounted to a belly full of drink and a roll with the women.

Consolation for the ones whose money was spent and whose next voyage was due was little else but ale on credit. Smoke filled the air; sawdust carpeted the floor; the tabletops were sticky with drink.

"Ah'm looking for a ship," said Jeremiah.

He was talking to a scrawny, tattooed man who was unmistakably a sailor. They leaned across their table to talk in hushed voices.

"Ah'd like t' work my passage to America," he continued.

"You ain't a seaman, though, are you?" replied his companion. "No call for any that's not a seaman now. There's hundreds wanting a ship now that Boney is on St Helena and the wars are over. No chance for you, mate."

"Ah could make it worth a man's while t' help me find one, or maybe get aboard as a stowaway," said Jeremiah.

"Hah!" laughed the other. "A stowaway! They'd work you half to death and dump you in New York without a penny of pay!"

"Ah wouldn't mind," said Brandreth, doggedly.

"On the run, are you?" questioned the other. "Deserter are you?"

"No," he replied, in a voice which gave him away. "It's just there's no work. Look, there's a guinea if you can get me aboard a ship for America."

The sailor peered at him closely.

"If I was caught helping a stowaway," he said slowly. "If I was caught I'd lose me berth, be stuck here just like you. For a guinea, it's not worth it. Now were you to offer me two guineas, I might just take the risk."

They sneaked up the gangway in the early hours of the morning. The docks had been dark, except for the odd ship's lantern, and their movements had been further cloaked by the noise of the ship itself as it creaked in the swell. Watchers would have thought them shipmates returning to the ship to sleep off the drink: there were many such about the docks of a night.

Brandreth knew nothing at all about the vessel he was hiding in. The sailor who had taken his money had assured him that it was due to sail for America on the morning tide. He was to stay hidden for a couple of days before making himself known.

Everything had happened so swiftly, that he had not thought to ask more. This, he regretted almost as much as not purchasing food to see him through the two days he must stay concealed. He was equally unsure as to exactly which part of the ship he was on. His companion had rushed him up the gangway, barefoot, making him carry his boots. From his hiding place in a sail locker, Brandreth heard noisy preparations for the ship's departure. Instructions whose meanings he did not understand were yelled; rippling sounds of sails being unfurled, men hurling farewells; the shrill calls of women on the quayside. He was bound for America. His long pilgrimage through an England he could never return to was over.

He snuggled down into his far from uncomfortable berth. As always, at momentous times in these days, he found Ann's scarf in his pocket, slipping it between his hands. It caused him new anguish to think of her and how she must be feeling. It would be a long time until he could send for her and the children; indeed, something in his heart told him it might well be never. He tried to force the thought from his mind. He found himself thinking of Jack Johnson's words, reminding him that if he escaped and others died in his place, he would be castigated a villain. He thought of Marshall's incapacity to understand the rising; he remembered Ellen's red eyes as she closed the door upon him. He brought to mind those few days in the Weightman's house and the brief beautiful fellowship of that time preceding the rising. He saw again the eyes which looked towards him eagerly for a lead, and a twinge of happiness came to him as he recalled being accepted by the men at Asherfield's Barn. His memories swung full circle and the sad face of his lonely wife appeared came to him as the ship began to weigh anchor. Then he remembered Rebecca looking sadly into his eyes and saying that he was just playing a game soldiers and he laughed inwardly. For the time being he would have to play a game of sailors.

Outside, on the deck, the crew strained at the capstan, and grunted their responses to the shanty man as he sang:

"Did you ever see a Wild Goose sailing o'er the ocean?

Ranzo, Ranzo, away, hey,

It's just like them young girls when they take a notion,

Ranzo, Ranzo, away."

Chapter 11: Hue and Cry

George Weightman

In the first week of July, the fine weather which had characterised the second half of the previous month broke suddenly. Rain hurtled through the western sky, rattling fiercely on the window of Wolstenholme's study, but gazing out into the wet afternoon he was far from miserable in himself. Convincing himself that the rain had settled in for the day, he went upstairs and stood outside the attic room door. George Weightman opened to his knock. Only twenty three years old, George was looking older, worn down by his depressing and lethargic existence over the past four weeks. Smiling, as ever when his solitude was disturbed, grateful for the company of Wolstenholme, his expression even more eager than usual, he too, had noticed the rain, and was equally aware of its significance.

"Tonight, George," said Hugh Wolstenholme. "We'll go tonight. The weather is filthy and there won't be a soul out to see us."

They chatted together a short time, before Wolstenholme descended the stairs. He remained mindful; despite the inclement weather, there might be visitors to receive. George Weightman stood back a discreet distance from the window, gazing out in the direction of South Wingfield and Crich at the advancing weather. Long-tailed clouds brushed the hilltops behind them. He knew they signified a dark and damp night to follow. There would be no moon; no one to watch the long-planned departure of the two to the north. George was looking forward to the ending of his long confinement, which was beginning to become intolerable. The knowledge that Hugh Wolstenholme had risked all to shelter him and that his continued stay at the vicarage worried his host a great deal, made George eager to leave. Confined indoors during the recent beautiful weather, his own prison-like existence was another reason why he wanted to depart. The most pressing reason, however, was his fear of remaining any longer near Rebecca and the children; that he might risk all and sacrifice his freedom just to visit them; to be with them once more, as before the Captain came.

He would have given anything to sit quietly with his wife at home again. Night after night he remained in his little cell, pacing around, staring out of the window, thinking he would rather be dead than away from them, forever on the verge of leaving his sanctuary to sneak away to his own house. He could almost sense Rebecca lying awake in their bed waiting for him. Morning always found him caged still in Wolstenholme's garret, looking tired beyond measure, his spirit devastated. He owed it to them all, wife, children and Wolstenholme too, to remain in hiding, and he had vowed to do his duty.

George's Good Samaritan brought him food and conversation to while away some of the lonely hours of the evening. Wolstenholme inspired hope in the future; a vision of the Weightman family ensconced together once more in America, blissfully happy. Wolstenholme would bring news, too, of the continued success of Brandreth, the Bacons and Ludlam, eluding pursuit, and evading the clutches of the authorities. Clergyman and guest both looked forward to the simple talks which enlivened their lonely days.

It was a little after eleven o'clock, and the night was a foul one. Two dark-cloaked figures hurried out of the rain-lashed vicarage garden dropping down the hill, eastwards, towards the road between Derby and Chesterfield. They approached Broadoaks Farm. Wolstenholme had made an arrangement with old Taylor, the householder, to have two horses stabled. The story was that Wolstenholme was expecting his brother to call at Pentrich. From there the two of them were planning to dash northwards to the bedside of an ill relative. Old Taylor accepted Wolstenholme's payment and explanation without the smallest vestige of suspicion. He was, after all, dealing with a clergyman. The horses had been hired in Nottingham from a Mr Bradley's stables and Taylor's son had ridden them back to Broadoaks, two days earlier; fine animals that went by the names of

Samuel and Robin. Hustled along the lane by the gale at their backs, George Weightman had no time for any farewell to his home village. They walked as quietly as possible towards Taylor's stable and tried the latch. At the moment the door swung open, the horses inside whinnied and the dog which Taylor, kept chained at night, started to bark in furious excitement.

Within thirty seconds old Taylor appeared at his door, a lantern in one hand, a gun in the other. The light from his parlour flooded the stable yard illuminating the two dark-shrouded men who stood in the rain. Hugh Wolstenholme walked quickly towards him.

"Only my brother and me, Mr Taylor, come for the horses," he said. "We must dash to Sheffield. No need to come out, it's a filthy night."

Taylor had no intention of venturing out if he could help it. He doubted the wisdom of any who would make a journey on a night like this, but supposed it took all kinds of people to make a world. He shouted at the dog. Retreating into the little shelter that kept it dry, the hound continued to regard the scene with undisguised suspicion. Weightman remained by the stable, swathed in the black of his cloak. Wolstenholme joined him, and the two saddled up the horses leading them unwillingly into the rain. Mounting up, they dug their heels into the poor animals' sides, heading out of the yard to the accompaniment of more barking. Within five minutes, they struck the coach road starting north, looking for the entire world like a pair of highwaymen, cloaks billowing in the wind.

They pushed onwards, galloping through Alfreton, Higham, Clay Cross and Tupton, passing not a soul on the way. By the time they reached Chesterfield, the town was deep in slumber. They clattered through cobbled streets as quickly as they could. The road took them up through Dronfield into Sheffield itself. The city was noisy, lights burning and smoke rising, even in the dead of a wet night. No sign, however, of anyone being out and about. They passed through the noisy centre of industry and headed further north. By now men and horses were worn out by their exertions and the harshness of the weather. Wolstenholme was anxious for journey's end. Dawn was battling its way through the gloom as they trotted out of the little settlement of Shiregreen on the last lap of their ride.

The radical Wolstenholmes, a popular and respected family, hailed from Ecclesfield, about eight miles to the north of Sheffield. Even though the insurrection was well buried by now William Wolstenholme and his sons, James and Thomas, were still being held on magistrate Parker's orders. His brother, who was also called Thomas, was still free. Luckily for him, the informers had failed to connect him with the Sheffield conspiracy. He was eager to help George Weightman.

The rap on the door came about half-past six in the morning. Hearing their feet in the street outside, Thomas had the door open in an instant. The two gaunt, wet men felt the Sheffield iron worker's firm handshake as they entered. Hugh threw off his wet cloak. He approached the fire which his cousin had kindled against their coming. George joined him, as Thomas donned the curate's cloak to lead the horses to the barn of a sympathetic friend.

Hugh and George slumped, breathing deeply. After some moments, the curate picked up a piece of bread and cut a lump of cheese. He indicated that George, too, should eat. The two tired men sat quietly in that strange little kitchen, munching their bread and cheese, ruminating on the future. Within half an hour, Thomas returned having accomplished his mission. He had to wake his guests.

"Them horses were in a proper lather," he said. "We gave 'em a good rub down and a bit of a feed, and put 'em in the warm. They'll be reet." The two travellers thanked him.

"Well, so tha's Mr Weightman?" Wolstenholme continued. "Don't worry lad, tha's safe enough here and welcome to what ah have. Ah've met your uncle, owd Tommy, a rare bird he is! Still leading them a dance from what ah hear. Still that's him, what about thee?"

George saw that he was expected to answer Thomas' question.

"Well," he said. "Ah'm hoping to lie low for a while if tha'll let me, and then try and get a boat out o' Hull. Ah've a little bit of money, maybe enough t' get me a passage t' America."

"Right lad," said Thomas "Tha can keep thi' head down here for a bit, and ah'll find out what ah can about boats out o' Hull. Don't fret lad, you're safe enough here and welcome to what ah've got."

George nodded gratefully. A little later, Hugh suggested that they stretch out and get some sleep. Thomas showed them where. He left them removing their boots, while he jogged through the damp steaming streets on his way to his job at the ironworks a few hundred yards away.

Isaac Ludlam

Isaac Ludlam turned over on the little cot where he had been coughing for the past three days. The old lady looked over from by the fire. The kettle was boiling on the hob; she took a cloth and lifted it clear of the flames. She poured boiling water into a bowl on the little table. A spicy smell pervaded the room as the water infused herb-leaves that lay shredded in the bowl. She stirred the liquid awhile, strained it into a beaker and took it across for Isaac to drink. He raised himself up, leaning upon one elbow while he sipped the liquid. She looked at him, at his dazed eyes and pallid complexion. The hot drink had, at any rate, soothed his cough.

"That will make you sleep," she said. "Sleep is what you need now and plenty of warmth."

Isaac sank back into his pillow and fought to control his cough.

"Thank you," he said. "Ah owe you a great deal, more than ah can ever repay."

He lay down again in the comfort of the two blankets around him and soon fell asleep. It was her husband who, taking him for dead, had found this stranger lying by the roadside. At first the old man thought he had been the victim of a robbery; a closer look revealed a man too poor to be robbed. Standing over the prostrate form, he saw the eyes open, and the mouth plead for aid. Unable to pass by someone in trouble, her husband had carried the tramp home for a bite to eat to put his strength back. She in turn perceived that this white-whiskered stranger needed more than food and began to apply her skill with herbs to soothe the cough tearing apart his chest. The remedies she applied made her patient sleep through most of the day and the whole of the night. She refused to let him up, even when he woke. Her husband had let her get on with her ministrations, knowing better than to interfere in any way with her medicine.

Sleeping his illness away, Ludlam experienced the most vivid dreams imaginable. His deeply religious mind was so visited by demons that his nurse had to soothe their flames with a cold cloth held to his brow. On other occasions, angels would transport him away to lie on golden clouds. His healer welcomed the smile on his face as he slept easily. Intermittently he would dream and in babbling gave away his identity. She soon knew he was the same Isaac Ludlam, whose part in the recent disastrous rising had earned him a price upon his head. Names such as Bacon and Turner, and Brandreth, on handbills read out to her by friends in Uttoxeter market, she now heard repeated from his fluttering lips. She peered at him closely. How little like a villain this mild old man looked! In his lucid moments, she saw the haunted look in his eyes and wondered even more, sensing the deep feeling of guilt which lay behind them.

The Derbyshire rising meant nothing whatever, to this couple in their lonely little house above the town of Uttoxeter. The husband laboured on the land of a local farmer. This brought enough in cash and kind to eke out a simple existence and they bothered no one. Though Pentrich was probably only a matter of twenty five miles distant, she had never heard of the place. For all the difference to her the actions of Brandreth and others could have as well taken place on the next planet. She did not share with her husband the information which her patient had divulged in his delirium. This would pose a dilemma for her spouse, once he became aware of the identity of his uninvited guest with a price on his head.

After a week of expert ministration, Isaac Ludlam recovered most of his health. Under the woman's knowing care, his constitution reasserted itself. In return for her nursing, he made himself useful by aiding her in a variety of household chores, repairing for instance, minor defects on the outside of the building. The man of the house was grateful and pleased to see him recovered. He was less happy, however, with the response his visitor provided to questions about himself. Where was he bound for? Where did he hail from? What was his trade? Where was his family? To these queries, the aged traveller would only respond in the vaguest of terms, and the householder grew suspicious at this reluctance to reveal himself.

As for Isaac, such questioning put him into a dilemma. He hated deception and despised having to conceal his identity behind an alias. For a day or two, resting in the dying embers of his fever, he had been able to put his troubles aside and allow his mind to become whole once more. Now his guilt awoke anew. He could neither reveal his true name to those who had aided him, nor could he bear to keep it a secret. The lies with which he deflected the probing of the old labourer, were loathsome to him, and unconvincing in consequence. It did not take him long to decide that in order to avoid the mounting danger of exposure, he must leave almost immediately.

He would not leave such a calm haven without reluctance. When the old couple awoke next morning, they found the house swept, the fire set and their visitor's pallet tidied and empty. The departed pilgrim had written a short note thanking them for their hospitality, and signing himself as, "A Weary Pilgrim." The old lady seemed about to say something to her husband who stood shaking his head at the stranger's departure. Biting her lip, she kept her information secret. Isaac Ludlam was on his way to visit the house of an old friend to ask sanctuary. He needed to clear the doubts from his mind and decide what to do next. So it was that in the dawn of late June day, he knocked at the door of a house just off the Uttoxeter High Street. Failing to gain a response he was about to try again when he realised it was still early. The household, like most of the others in this sleepy place, was probably still at rest. He laughed at himself, realising just how far outside normal society his flight had moved him. Sitting himself down on the step, he waited for the householder to arise.

That evening, he sat at the table of his host, John Glynn, and did the family the honour of saying Grace. It was a plain meal, served on a spotless white table cloth. The six scrupulously clean and perfectly behaved children sat respectfully among their elders. Their mother smiled modestly at her husband and his guest, and the meal was partaken of in a dignified silence. When it was over, Ludlam thanked Mrs Glynn for the fine meal, bidding goodnight to the younger children. Then he and John Glynn adjourned to the tiny study with its score or so bound volumes of religious tracts lying tidily at rest on a shelf. A big bible was open on the angled lectern which stood where it could receive the light entering through a little window.

They sat without words for ten, perhaps fifteen, minutes, after the fashion of this unruffled Methodist household, before Glynn broke the silence.

"We have much to talk over, friend Isaac," he said.

"My dear friend," replied his visitor. "Ah have so much ah wish to say. Will you listen and ease the burden which weighs so heavily upon my mind?"

Glynn nodded, separating his hands from their benign clasping on his chest, to indicate with one of them that Isaac should begin. Isaac started to talk. His confession lasted well beyond sunset.

At the little stone house where Ludlam's body had been healed, the old woman was binding, with a piece of white linen, a long gash in her husband's leg. She could mix up an ointment to heal the wound within a few days, but she could do nothing about the crushed foot that was causing the old man such agony. A heavy stone had done him a great deal of damage as it fell. It would be long before he would walk on it again. Her husband thought of nothing but the pain he was experiencing; the old woman was already feeling the pain of hungry days ahead now he was unable to work. Without his labour they would have no income and her thoughts, not unnaturally, began to stray to the reward money offered for information about the recently departed Isaac Ludlam. She reproached herself bitterly for a missed opportunity. Someone else would pocket the reward now, someone whose need would be nowhere near as great as her and her crippled husband's.

Tommy Bacon

Tommy Bacon had prepared for his departure from Pentrich some weeks before he left, by writing a number of letters to friends whom he could trust, in various parts of the country. He had also mapped out in his mind the best route to take to bring himself and his brother John safely to refuge across the Atlantic Ocean. The two had journeyed without stopping to Ashbourne, where lived an eccentric old bachelor named Cockayne. This man of books and letters was descended from a noble family of the same name who had been Lords in the town of Ashbourne from the reign of Edward the First. A Cokaine, William, had been Lord Mayor of London in 1619; others had been poets, playwrights and noted hunters of the fox and hare. This old man had inherited little from his ancestors, except his name, and enough of a dwindled estate to keep him above the poverty line. He and Bacon, through their common literary activities, had been acquainted for years, and Bacon had lodged on a number of occasions in Cockayne's dirty, dusty, rambling old house. Old Cockayne kept no servant. He begrudged the expense. Consequently Bacon spent considerable hours there cleaning and tidying for the old man. Recently, Old Tommy's active involvement in the preparations for the rising had kept him from Ashbourne for more than a year. Few if any by this time remembered he had ever been there. For his part, Cockayne had no interest in politics: he was an antiquarian who pored over volumes of archaic literature. He wrote copious notes, but had never published. Bacon was confident that John and he could remain in safe hiding in the old man's house while their trail grew cold.

Tommy's letters reached his friends in different parts of the country. The request was simple enough and soon his friends were delighting in instigating rumours that the old rascal was in their locality. One hundred pounds reward was offered for Tommy's capture. This lent excitement to the rumours. There were literally dozens of reported sightings of the Bacons in the next few weeks. Henry Enfield in Nottingham dispatched constables to Manchester on the basis of strong reports; then to Leicester, then Liverpool. Each time the mission failed, and the expenses began to mount steadily. Enfield's letters to Sidmouth became less and less optimistic, the replies more acerbic. A strong rumour circulated that Bacon had, in fact, got clear of the country; that he was settling in America with his brother. Henry Enfield was not listening to rumour by then. He believed this one no more than any of the others.

The Bacons remained in anonymity among the antiquities of old Cockayne's house. Their host was quite amenable to their visit: he had been so diverted by his studies that he had only heard vague rumours of the rising. He knew nothing of the involvement of his old colleague, or of the reward offered for his capture. John Bacon, affable and relaxed as always, cheerfully endured his stay with these two literary eccentrics. He reasoned that if he could not go back to Pentrich, this place would do as well as any until they made it to America. He grew his beard by way of disguise and took the scissors to Tommy's wild locks. When he had finished, Tommy had the look of a dapper old gentleman.

Isaac Ludlam

Ludlam felt relief after his confession. Glynn listened with patience to the long monologue. His response was simply that they had both better sleep on the issue and discuss matters on the next night. In the meantime, Isaac was welcome to stay, provided he kept to the house, until his course of action was decided upon. Ludlam spent several long relaxing days in the spotless, white-washed house. Glynn's deep religious convictions did not forbid laughter, and it was a happy family that played host to the elderly fugitive. He especially rejoiced in the presence of children. They made up in part for the separation from his grandchildren. In the evenings, Glynn and he would retire to the little retreat; there amid the books they discoursed calmly, dwelling at length upon the dubious morality of Isaac's conduct in associating himself with the rising.

Ludlam admitted early on that he had been unhappy at the use of firearms. He did not carry one on the march and neither did his sons. He had carried a spear, but was not sure if he had ever meant to use it. The others on the rising were Ludlam's neighbours and he had agreed to take part, mainly out of loyalty to them. Glynn and he were in agreement that many of the objects of the rising were laudable. As non-conformists, both objected strongly to the dominance over them of the established church, and disliked a political system they had no share in. Both agreed that political change was necessary and inevitable, but Glynn said he could not countenance any violent attempt to induce it. Ludlam agreed. The death of Walters he now realised had been a grave sin. The Captain had been entirely wrong to fire the fatal shot. Equally, the Captain, Turner and the others had been wrong to force unwilling men from their homes to join the desperate venture. Isaac admitted his faults freely: his most humane of hosts listened and forgave him. That forgiveness breathed new life into Ludlam's troubled soul.

One afternoon, Isaac felt he must leave the confines of the house. It seemed so long since he had been amongst hustle and bustle and he found it hard to resist the lure of the sounds of the market. He reasoned he would be safe enough in the crowd, filled, as was usual for a market day, with strangers from far afield. He left the empty house and joined the throng. A profoundly simple man Isaac had a child's fascination for trinkets and baubles, and the loud and raucous patter of the market men and women. He revelled in the gaiety of families holidaying happily in the convivial atmosphere. John Glynn spotting his sparkling, innocent eyes as he stood in the crowd, hurried across to hiss angrily in his ear to get himself home. Isaac nodded; sad to have annoyed his host, he took himself off dispiritedly. By evening, Glynn regretted his anger and family and guest ate in a relaxed and pleasant atmosphere once more.

Isaac Ludlam was arrested at Glynn's house the next day, taken by Fletcher and Booth, two constables from Pentrich parish. Wingfield Halton dispatched them as soon as he heard from the Uttoxeter magistrates of Ludlam's whereabouts. Apparently the magistrates in Uttoxeter gained the information from an old woman who recognised Ludlam at the market.

George Weightman

George Weightman took quickly to Thomas Wolstenholme, a true Yorkshireman who insulted most those he liked best and said nothing to those he disliked. He and George soon began to banter with one another, despite the difference in their years. The Derbyshire man was young, naturally honest and perennially cheerful; impossible to dislike. Thomas was a carefree bachelor; even though harbouring George was risking a jail sentence, he appreciated such forthright company.

But Wolstenholme was frequently sought out by Thomas Bradley, Hugh Parker's spy. Wolstenholme resented Bradley instinctively. He felt along with many that it was a pity after the arrests at the Sportsman's Arms, that Bradley, rather than some of the other delegates, had been freed by General Byng. Three of the more popular leaders were still held, including William Wolstenholme, but Bradley had returned to his old haunts, bragging of how he had talked himself free. Thomas tried to avoid his company, but found him more and more evident at the pubs he himself frequented. Bradley was still all for conspiracy and a rising, but Wolstenholme, and those other reformers still free, were badly shaken by Oliver's betrayal and the disaster in Derbyshire. They had no further interest in planning any more rebellions. Accordingly, little was said to Parker's man and it was a full week before Bradley became aware that his reluctant drinking companion was housing the fugitive George Weightman. Even then it took an unfortunate accident for him to come by the information.

Wolstenholme carried a jug of brown ale back to his house one night and he and his guest sat down to drink it. Their talk was convivial as ever. The ale disappeared much too quickly, with both men ready for more. Thomas thought for a moment or two; he went to his pantry, returning soon with a formidable looking brown bottle; this poured forth, when corked and tilted, a dark, strong-smelling concoction, which he introduced as finest Jamaica Rum. Wolstenholme had acquired the distillation some six months before, and failed to find courage to drink it. After two terrible mouthfuls, he decided he would stick to ale. This time, he made a better attempt to tackle the bottle; soon, George and he were beginning to feel its benign influence.

Wolstenholme's body woke itself with an effort the next morning. He had to rush unsteadily off to work to avoid being late. In doing so, he failed to close the house door. George slept on through the morning and failed to hear the footsteps as a friend of Wolstenholme's wandered in to check why the door had been left open all the morning. The man saw George Weightman sleeping in peace, and allowed him to continue without interruption. He closed the door as he left. After work, this same friend saw Wolstenholme at the local inn, downing a well-earned quart of ale to put back the sweat lost during a day next to the furnace.

"I'll tell thee what Tom, that's a trusting' soul," he said. "Tha goes off t' work and leaves tha door wide open for any bugger to walk in."

Wolstenholme looked up with a start and Thomas Bradley, observant at his elbow saw the expression of alarm which briefly crossed his brow.

"Who's yon sleepy sod staying' with thee? He never as much as looked up when ah went in to say 'how do' to him at dinner time," continued Wolstenholme's helpful neighbour.

"He's a pal of mine from Doncaster," said Wolstenholme. "We had a bit too much last eve. Ah'd still have been sleeping at dinner time if ah could have. Sithee, he weren't dead were he?"

The neighbour laughed. "No bugger who snores that loud is dead."

They all joined in the laughter.

Later that day, Thomas Bradley strolled round to Thomas Wolstenholme's dwelling. He went down the side of the little house and looked in through the window. The two men inside were in animated conversation, and did not notice him. Bradley walked quietly away to inform his employer Parker the magistrate that he suspected the guest prone to sleeping so late was probably none other than George Weightman, whose description had been so widely circulated.

Weightman joined the Turners, Ludlam and many more that he knew in the jail at Derby. The men who were responsible for arresting him, Fletcher and Booth, knew George well enough and he had gone along with them shocked and quiet when they had entered Wolstenholme's house. The same neighbour who had inadvertently betrayed him to Bradley tried to atone somewhat by intercepting Thomas with the news, before he arrived home to be met by Parker's reception committee. Thomas escaped northwards to the house of a relative and was never questioned about harbouring the Pentrich fugitive.

Tommy Bacon

The last of the Pentrich fugitives to be captured were the ubiquitous Bacons. John and Tommy had lain hidden at Cockayne's house for some weeks. John had grown his beard in the first ten days, and chanced his freedom going to shop in the market He was not averse, during these sallies, to calling at the local inn and enjoying a pint of ale with the landlord. He was able to keep up to date with the news from the garrulous innkeeper, informing Tommy later what was happening in the world outside the narrow confines of Cockayne's house. Through John's excursions they learned the sad news that the Ludlam brothers, old Isaac himself, and finally George Weightman had been taken and were being held in Derby Jail.

Sir William Boothby, J.P. occupied Ashbourne Hall, the former seat of the Cockayne family before its scions had dwindled into poverty and impotence. Boothby himself could trace his ancestry back to before the conquest to a family originating in Boothby in Lincolnshire. His own father and mother had been driven from the hall in 1745, by Prince Charles Edward, who had occupied the town. This ingrained memory made him all the more determined to hold on to it. He despised any who disturbed the status quo; thus, in the early part of 1817, when the six weary survivors of the Blanketeer march limped towards Ashbourne, they found the old Hanging Bridge defended by the magistrate himself, along with his yeomanry and every male in the town sworn in as special constables. The fiery old Justice arrested all six and held them in the town jail, before being persuaded to release them, to return to their distant homes.

This same man had been outraged by Derbyshire rising. He had circulated the town of Ashbourne with descriptions of the men wanted by the authorities. Moreover, he had put about orders that the presence of any stranger was to be reported to him at once. There were of course many people in the town with better things to do than to hunt for non-existent rebels. A few even had sympathy with the lost cause of the Pentrich and South Wingfield men, but someone started to ask questions about the two guests staying up at old Cockayne's house.

The innkeeper had alerted the man he knew as Mr Spencer to the interest being shown in him and his literary brother. The affable bearded newcomer had laughed the news off lightly. Nevertheless, the innkeeper later recalled to his regulars, neither Spencer nor his brother was seen in the town after that.

The Bacons continued their route across the country. Even though Tommy had to put money by for their passage to America, enough remained for travel on the outside of stagecoaches and accommodation at cheaper inns. Tommy planned an itinerary which avoided the most obvious route to the south coast ports. Instead of taking the traditional way to London, through Northampton and Bedford, he decided to cross to Cambridge, reasoning that the quiet, agricultural paths of East Anglia would be less likely watched than the more frequented main roads to the capital. They travelled short distances, hopping off each coach before it had fully completed its journey, staying overnight at Melton Mowbray, Stamford, Peterborough and Huntingdon and, with other poor travellers, sleeping in crowded inn bedrooms.

Their downfall came at Huntingdon. Tommy had never been to the place though he had travelled as a radical delegate to nearby Peterborough where he had addressed a meeting of tradesmen on the subject of reform, about twelve months previously. Many indeed throughout the country were sympathetic to reform, but the meeting at Peterborough had not been well attended. However, among the few present was one Mark Chapman, a local builder. Unsuccessful in trade he blamed the government and society in general for his own shortcomings as a businessman. At that time he was considering leaping upon the reform bandwagon, but one look at the sparse collection of shabby workmen, present that July night in 1816, persuaded Chapman there was little profit to be made out of any association with reformers. He drifted away long before the meeting's end.

Thinking little about that night, he read, nearly a year later in the columns of the Huntingdon, Bedford and Peterborough Gazette an account of the rising. Spotting the name Thomas Bacon with a hundred pounds reward upon his head, Chapman immediately recognised the old man at the meeting at Peterborough. Having bought into a partnership, and now living in Huntingdon, Chapman was sitting drinking at the town's Black Horse Inn when the coach arrived from Peterborough. He nearly choked on his ale at seeing the two old men coming in through the door. He did not recognise the one with the full white beard but the other was Thomas Bacon, unmistakable though shorn of his distinctive locks. Chapman finished his ale and sauntered out of the inn in a casual and unruffled manner. Reaching the door, he scooted off as fast as his fat legs could carry him to the house of Mr Wigston, the magistrate. Chapman's loud hammering at the door set that particular gentleman against the perspiring interloper and he was not at all disposed to receive his information warmly.

Despite Chapman's repeated insistence that he do something at once, Wigston was not going to move immediately. He thanked Chapman coldly, informing him that he would initiate the requisite action. If some reward was due, and the miscreants apprehended within the parish boundary, Chapman would be duly contacted. Meanwhile he should avail himself of the opportunity the door afforded him to leave the house. When the fat man departed, Wigston summoned his constables. They talked quietly and a plan was agreed.

Unaware of all this, the Bacons had eaten quite well, spending a reasonably pleasant night. Before retiring, they booked a next morning passage on the coach to Cambridge. The landlord was agent for the coach company. He also acted on occasions as Wigston's informant. He was happy to supply the constables with the information that the two men they were interested in were travelling the following day.

At about ten o'clock next morning, the Cambridge coach left

Huntingdon setting out towards St Ives on the first leg of the journey. It was another hot sunny day. John and Tommy Bacon were pleased enough to get down from their conveyance at St Ives to stretch their legs. The five constables waiting at the inn formed a wide circle around the brothers who viewed them with mounting suspicion. A brief fight ensued, during which John Bacon landed a haymaker in the face of one constable and saw him crash to the cobblestones, before two other assailants overwhelmed him. They were taken to Huntingdon to be held until identified.

On the same day as he wrote asking for the assistance of Mr Enfield in Nottingham, to convey the prisoners, Wigston undertook the pleasant task of explaining to Mark Chapman, that since, on information received from another quarter, the fugitives had been seized outside the town, the builder was not entitled to any reward for his public spirited behaviour, beyond the satisfaction of having done his duty.

Chapter 12: Return and Betrayal

Nottingham

Henry Sampson was drunk. He had spent his money too freely all night, trying to find some consolation among the men at the inn. Although they drank, there was little good fellowship in the Punch Bowl this evening and he had grown bitter and depressed as the night became more and more of a disappointment to him. He had tried singing to liven up his spirits, striking up the old Luddite song normally a certain winner:

"No more chant your old rhymes of bold Robin Hood,
His feats I do little admire;
I'll sing the achievements of General Ludd,
That hero of Nottinghamshire,"

His voice was rasping and hoarse and the crowd at the inn was not in a singing mood. He reluctantly let the ballad die and consoled himself with a little more ale.

"They're all gone," he said to a toper supping next to him. "All gone! Stevens is gone, Holmes is gone and Jerry Brandreth is gone. There's only me left now; only poor old Henry."

"Ay, Jerry Brandreth is gone, alright," said the man fiercely. "He's out of it, but there's plenty who followed him that aren't. He'll be in America now. How many weeks is it? Six He'll be in Boston Harbour by now, him and bloody Stevens."

"Don't talk about Jerry Brandreth like that!" cried Sampson, in a voice that was supposed to be threatening. "He's a friend o' mine; o' all o' us!"

The other drinker looked at him in disgust, swore nastily and moved away to talk to men in another corner of the room. A few minutes later, Sampson went out and started on his long way home. He had five or six miles to walk to his house and the night air began to sober him up. At least his wife wouldn't be waiting when he got home, as she had taken the children away with her to Bingham, to help nurse her old mother. The noise of those six brats would be certain to see the old lady off, thought Sampson, and he sniggered at the idea. It was very late when he reached Bulwell and padded up to his door. He was sober now, but very tired and ready for a long sleep. He lit the lamp and sat down to take his boots off. There was a knock at the door. Henry jumped up and went to the window, pressing his face to the very edge of its glass to see who it was at the door He could make out the ends of a dark coat, but nothing else.

"Who is there?" he called.

The only answer was another knock.

"Clear off, no one means any good at this time of night!"

Whoever it was outside tried the latch. Sampson attempted to hold it down, but failed to do so. The man outside pushed the door inwards until there was a six inch opening and a voice that he thought never to hear again whispered to him.

"Henry, let me in. It's me, Jerry!"

Jeremiah Brandreth had lost weight and his gaunt, hollow face in the lamplight looked a hundred years older than when Henry had last seen him. He didn't appear to have slept for days and his clothes were shabby and bedraggled. He looked to be a beaten man. Sampson was completely sober now and recovering quickly from the shock, let the fugitive in and told him not to worry, because his wife and children were away for the week. Jerry made straight for the chair and flopped down while Henry found some cold stew in a pot. He offered it to his guest who began to eat eagerly.

"Why did you come back? Everyone was sure you were away safe, t'

America," Sampson talked while his friend ate. "Where've you been hiding? There's a hundred pounds reward out for you - a hundred pounds! You're mad t' come back t' where folk know you. Whatever possessed you, man?"

Brandreth took a break from his meal to answer. "Ah worked my way down towards the South Coast," he said. "Ah thought my sister there might ....well, no matter. Then ah got t' Bristol, waited around t' docks and managed t' smuggle myself aboard ships bound for America. Twice ah thought we were away, but they found me both times and kicked me ashore. Ah had nothing left. No money, no work, no friends, just enough left for coach fare t' Leicester, so that's what ah did, ah took t' coach. That was yesterday, no, t' day before. Ah walked up here from Leicester, thinking who ah could trust. It had t' be you, Henry; you're t' only one ah can depend on."

Sampson told Jeremiah he could stay until the family came back and the refugee's eyes watered as he grasped the hands of his most loyal friend. Then they decided that they were both exhausted. Sampson showed him to the big bed which four children normally occupied, before sinking tiredly into his own. Sleep came to Sampson quickly, but not before he had had time to plan what to do. As for Jeremiah Brandreth, he rested better than for many weeks, relieved of the worry of solitude for the first time since he had parted from Jack Johnson, five weeks previously, in Market Bosworth.

Sutton in Ashfield

The next day, protected by his new growth of beard, some of Sampson's clothes and a very large hat, Jeremiah walked quickly out of Bulwell and on to Hucknall, where he joined a northbound stage. He travelled outside behind the driver, feeling very vulnerable, worrying every time the bored old coachman posed him a question to eat away the time. At length, the horses were pulled up at Sutton in Ashfield and he quickly dismounted to thread his way through the less crowded alleyways. The fugitive affected a limp and a stoop as disguise, because he was so well known here, and hobbled through the familiar byways to the house of Ann's father.

He trod very carefully as he neared the house, and looked back over his shoulder many times. Standing in the shelter of a garden wall Jeremiah peered down towards the group of houses in one of which were his wife and children. Even now, it would not be too late for him to pull the hat further down over his brow, and go back the way he had come, but he hardly gave this thought a second before dismissing it from his mind. He limped down the street like a stranger; everything was quiet and deserted in the middle of the day. The men were at work and any children were indoors, eating whatever scraps their mothers could find for a midday meal. He speeded up as he neared George Bridget's house, then opened the latch and went in.

Ann didn't faint or burst into tears when she saw him. She stood up slowly, her eyes fixed on his. He looked at her in wonder and disbelief before walking across to embrace her.

"Don't squeeze so hard!" she whispered. "Jerry, you've lost so much weight," she said as she fingered his ribs and pushed him back gently. "Your face is really thin an' all, and ah don't care much for t' beard."

He laughed happily. "You look well," he sighed, holding her at arm's length. You've put on a bit of weight."

"Ah usually do when ah'm wi' child," she replied quietly. This remark stopped Jerry in his tracks. Ann was in the fourth month of her third pregnancy. He gulped, unable to say anything coherent, and then pulled her to him again, holding her gently and stroking her hair.

He still could not find any words. In a while they sat down and Ann called Elizabeth in. Brandreth's daughter came into the room shyly, finger in her mouth. She barely glanced at the stranger, but dashed over to her mother and clung to her skirt.

"You know who this is Lizzie, don't you?" said his mother. "Its t'
beard that's frightening her, Jerry."

Jeremiah cooed, cajoled and coaxed Elizabeth for a minute or two,
until the youngster overcame her nerves and came over to him. A
few moments later, Ann was watching delightedly while the two of
them rolled around together on the mat, Jerry hooting and laughing
like a boy. She moved into the other room so that they wouldn't see
the tears that were beginning to fill her eyes. Ann sat by the little cot
where Tim slept, stroking his head.

She closed her eyes, and once again sank into one of the memories
which had sustained her through the long period of his absence.
They had slipped out of the house, first thing having filled his
pockets with bread, and tiptoed into the street, closing the latch
carefully so as not to wake anyone. They walked briskly for a while,
until the sun had cleared the trees and it was warm enough for him
to take off his coat, so that they could sit and listen to the morning.
Ann picked a single buttercup and looked at the yellow reflecting
onto her finger in the sunlight. Her hair shone in the light and Jerry
gently pushed this shining veil from her face and become part of her
dream as he bent to kiss her.

The day was perfect and they roamed strange tracks, clambered to
hilltops and quenched their thirst amidst the deep oaks of fairy
glades. They shared bread and kisses. To her he was everything. His
black curls and dark skin made him look like Romany, but his eyes
had none of that wildness and there was no hint of guile about them.
Nobody had eyes as gentle as her Jeremiah, nor lashes as long, and
no man seemed as much like a little boy or as innocent. She watched
him as he tossed pebbles into the stillness of the pond, dreaming
among the ripples he created, and she put her arm around him
resting her face on his shoulder and dreamed on with him into the
afternoon.

They were making their way home, their thoughts returning to the reality awaiting them. As they reached a bend in the lane, a man trotted towards them on horseback and they moved into the side to allow him past. Ann noticed how well the rider sat on his horse and what a noble figure he made. The mount was clipped and gleaming; it bore a Walsall saddle of the best leather. The man wore a shiny top hat and his clothes were new and fine. As he approached, Ann dropped instinctively into a courtesy, bowing her head. The rider stared ahead in haughty indifference, not altering his course from the centre of the track and coming dangerously close to her. Jeremiah grasped her upper arm and moved her firmly but gently into the side, glaring at the rider. Ann saw her husband's head raised haughtily, returning the aristocratic indifference of his adversary, and was worried what danger such defiance might produce. The rider spurred his horse past them, as though they had not been there, and she clung to Jeremiah's tense body as he gazed in hatred at the departing figure until the bend in the track took it from his sight.

"Bastard," said Jeremiah. Ann stood away from him.

"You shunt 'ave looked at him like that," she said.

"Like what?" said her husband still angered. "Like ah 'm as good as him?"

"Like you were going t' kill him, or something. He looked like a Lord. You shud 'ave touched your cap, shown respect."

Jeremiah was angry now. "Respect? What is there t' respect? Listen, we're as good as anyone. God created us all in his own image; Jesus was a carpenter's son. Ah'll touch my hat to nobody, and you shun't bow down before t' likes o' him. You look t' bastard in t' eye!"

She had heard such speeches from him before and been afraid of their meaning, but she had spirit and a temper too, and spoke up when she knew she was right.

"What have we got t' be proud of?" she demanded.

He cut her words short, glaring at her furiously, and pointing down the track after the horseman.

"He doesn't work either," he cried. "He's no job, but plenty of money. That's t' only difference between us: his father give him money. Well, there's enough for everyone in this world if it was shared properly. Doesn't t' Bible say it's easier for a camel to go through t' eye of a needle than for a rich man t' reach Heaven? He should share out his riches, and then ah might touch my hat t' him."

Ann shook her head and felt her anger dying away.

"Those are fine words, but there's always been rich and poor. He's not going to share his money wi' us, no matter how poor we are. There's always going t' be rich and poor, and there's no way you or anyone will change that."

Jeremiah quietly replied, "Ah don't believe that."

They continued their walk in silence, but within a few minutes he reached for her hand and held her close.

"Whatever ah say, whatever ah do, it's because ah want more for you and t' children we're going to have. Ah love you and can't stand t' see you hungry and crying"

"While ah've got you, nothing is more than enough," Ann whispered. "We'll manage somehow until times get better."

Ann came out of her reverie as Tim stirred in his cot. She picked him up and walked through to the other room, where Jerry was holding Lizzie under the arms and swinging her to and fro. He looked up as the new arrival bawled his welcome, put Lizzie down, and went over to his wife and son. He looked at the little face, and when he saw his father, Tim stopped crying and began to giggle in delight.

"Well he remembers you, anyway," said Ann, as she shifted the little pink burden into the arms of her husband.

She found Jerry something to eat and while he ate, he inquired about how she was managing. Father was generous, she told him. Jerry felt inadequate; he had nothing to give them.

Tim played happily on the floor and Lizzie, exhausted by the excitement, lay dozing next door. They sat together on two chairs, holding hands.

"You can't stay here – t' place is watched. What will you do?" Ann said.

"Ah know it's not safe," he replied. "Ah must be off soon. T' only thing that ah can think of is for me t' head up north, one o' t' big towns. Ah can use a false name, find work somewhere and send something back t' you. After a month or two, they won't be looking as hard for me, and you and t' children could come up. We could make a fresh start."

He stopped talking and found her looking away. "Ann, you will come, won't you?" he asked.

"Of course ah will. You know ah will," she said sadly. "But we are going to be apart again, for a long time this time. Perhaps we'll never see each other again."

They held each other again and he told her that bad pennies always turned up, that she wouldn't be rid of him as easily as that, and in a while she was smiling and noticing how gentle his eyes still were, and how innocent he still looked even after all that had happened to him.

Tightening the Snare

Back in Nottingham, a hastily summoned meeting was taking place in the office of the Town Clerk, Henry Enfield. Little Enfield was exceptionally excited and was already composing his letter of triumph to Lord Sidmouth in his mind. Mr Mundy, one of the heroes of June the ninth, was also in high spirits, rejoicing at the thought of the imminent capture of the "general of the insurgents", as the newspapers now called Jeremiah Brandreth. Lancelot Rolleston was also in the room. He was not a healthy man these days; his face was surely as pallid as that of William Turner, who by now had spent six weeks in the darkness of Derby's old jail. The three were met to discuss the best way to capture Brandreth. There was a fourth man in the room, and his name was Henry Sampson.

Sampson had been Enfield's paid informer for nearly three years, having worked in a similar capacity for his predecessor as Town Clerk, Mr Coldham, since 1812. He was paid a retainer each week to report on Luddites like Towle and trade unionists like Henson, to Enfield, who then passed the information along to his hosier friends. Sampson had worked diligently to infiltrate the Secret Committee in 1817, and had achieved results which, if they were not as spectacular as William Oliver's, were at least as hard-earned. It was a measure of his ability as an agent that he had been trusted by all the committee, even after the failure of the rising, though he had been peddling information about some of its members for five years. The fact that Brandreth regarded him as a friend, even though it was Sampson's letters alone which had brought his name to the attention of Sidmouth, bore testimony to devious character.

Now Sampson was here with these men, who came from another class: men who despised him, and the morality which would permit him to behave in like this. He was here, playing the part of Judas in the betrayal of a man who was supposed to be his best friend.

"If you'll be guided by me," said Sampson. "You will wait for him t' return t' me house and then seal it off front and back wi' constables. He's a little man, and lost a lot o' weight, so they should be able to tek him wi' out much of a struggle."

"You don't think we ought to have the Hussars handy, just in case?" asked Mundy.

"Oh no," said Enfield. "Not the soldiery. The sight of them tramping about the streets would cause a great deal of alarm. It might frighten him off. Is that not so, Mr Rolleston?" Rolleston nodded by way of reply, and the other two looked kindly back at him. They knew that he was still unwell. Indeed, if anything, he seemed to be wasting away.

They settled it as Sampson had suggested. Mundy insisted on staying while Enfield called in the constables and briefed them, but Rolleston, his duty done, took his leave and set off to ride slowly and thoughtfully home. Sampson set off for the Punch Bowl Inn, to gain himself an alibi by drinking with one or two of the remaining radicals, while Brandreth was taken.

In Sutton, Jeremiah was about to take his leave. Elizabeth was re-appointed to the task of guarding her little brother and persuaded that her father would be back to see them soon. Jeremiah kissed both his children, and then went to join Ann by the door.

"Ah'll be back for you. You'll see me again," he said. "Ah'd write you, but you know they'll be reading t' letters."

"Just think of us instead. Think of us every day," Ann pleaded.

"There won't be a moment until the end of my life, when ah don't think of you," he whispered, taking her to him again.

They stood there, leaning together, their arms around one another for a long time, neither wishing to ever break the spell. Then Jerry whispered "Look, ah have something to keep me safe always."

Ann moved back and looked at the little blue scarf she had given him all that time ago, when Pentrich was still a mere point on a map, and her husband was not a fugitive. She took the scarf from him, kissed it and then knotted it tenderly around his neck. She straightened his hair with the little frown she always had when she did so. He opened the door and closed it immediately behind him and moved off limping and hunched up towards the old barn at the end of the street. Ann ran to join Elizabeth at the window tearfully watching Jeremiah disappearing from sight.

He returned to Bulwell in a similar manner to his outward journey, riding the coach to Hucknall, his eyes watering in the wind, and approached Sampson's house on foot at about eight o'clock in the evening. He looked around carefully. There was no one about, so he went inside the little dwelling. His host was not there to answer his shouts, but Henry had said that he might well be late, so there was nothing to worry about. He sat down, removed his boots and closed his eyes.

Almost straight away he was awakened from his dozing by a knock at the door. There were two men outside: he could see them through the window He put his boots back on and opened up They told him that they were constables looking for rabbit snares and that he must let them in. He replied that there were no snares or poachers there, but they could look if they wished. They went to the far side of the room, cutting him off from the door through to the back yard. Then two more men marched up to the front door and through it. He heard the words of arrest as if he had been expecting them all his life. For a moment, he instinctively tensed himself for a struggle, but then, to the surprise of his captors, he shrugged his shoulders and offered no resistance. A fifth constable came in through the back, carrying the cords with which they bound the Nottingham Captain.

In Barkergate, Henry Sampson was drinking too heavily for his own good. Some at the Punch Bowl wondered how this out-of-work knitter with six children and a wife to support had money for ale.
The next day, when news of Brandreth's capture leaked out, and

someone would recall that Sampson's house where he was taken was full of furniture, while those near it were bare, it became even more obvious to the mistrustful patrons that he was a paid informer. From that day onwards, Henry Sampson would never be without the feeling that there was a shadow on his shoulder.

After an interview with the triumphant Enfield and Mundy, Jeremiah Brandreth spent the first night of his captivity sleepless in solitary confinement at Nottingham Castle. In the light of early morning he was surprised to see a white face peering through the bars at him; a haunted, ill face. Later on, his guard had mentioned that this had been Mr Rolleston, the magistrate. He was very ill, the man had confided.

That morning, Brandreth met his five constables of the previous night once more. They were to convey him in a cart to Derby where his old followers waited, unaware that they were to be reunited with their captain. He was not at all sure how well they would receive him.

Hugh Wolstenholme

It was one of the finest places on earth to be. There were many magnificent views in England, but Hugh Wolstenholme was sure that although other places might have claims to equality the view from the hilltop above Crich village had no superior anywhere in the land. The sun shone out of a clear summer sky and the breeze in this high place brought a welcome coolness, which those who toiled in the valleys below him would envy. He had ridden out today in the dual hope of escaping the burdens of his pastor-ship which had lately pressed him severely, and that the exercise would tire him sufficiently to make him sleep for a full night. The hill seemed the ideal place to think and to put his world in perspective, and he had tethered his horse and trudged to this high point for the solitude, and for the symbolic nearness of this point to heaven.

He looked to the north and followed the Derwent Valley, wooded and spectacular as it swept past Cromford through the savage gorge at Matlock, on its way into the hazy distance. Here the trees obscured the mill which Richard Arkwright and Jedediah Strutt had built over fifty years earlier that had revolutionised the cotton industry. Down the valley southwards he could make out further evidence of Strutt's ambition in the new mills that stood at Belper. Further down along the Derwent, invisible in the heat-haze, would be the town of Derby, with its many spires and its castle and jail. Here Weightman and the others, the Nottingham Captain among them, languished in chains, waiting for their trials to take place.

To the south east, in the immediate foreground, was the lovely church of Crich, which watched paternally over the elongated cluster of stone cottages peppering the ridge to Fritchley and Bullbridge. As he turned round, he noted the curious ridge, with its bare rocks by a stone wall, behind which the ruined towers of Wingfield Manor destroyed on the orders of the regicide, Cromwell, stood defiantly. Next to the remains of the Manor, he could see the houses of South Wingfield, now missing the sixteen men were now pining away in the prisons of Derby and Nottingham.

Beyond, Alfreton and Swanwick dreamed in the heat and his eye was led towards the ironworks at Butterley where the day's activity was signalled by the column of smoke which drifted lazily above. It would be as hot as Hell in there today, he thought to himself. He could see the roofs of Ripley and thought that on the far side of the bustling market town he could, perhaps, see the satellite village of Codnor. Further east in the haze, the road to Nottingham ran through Langley Mill, Eastwood, Giltbrook, Kimberley and Bulwell before it reached the city, nearly twenty miles away from the spot he now occupied. Reluctantly, he brought his eyes back and saw the little church-topped hill where stood the village of Pentrich. St Matthews was obscured by the trees that served as a windbreak, but he knew that the solid little church would be there to return to and the thought was not entirely comfortable.

Pentrich itself was a depressed place now. Nanny Weightman's licence to sell ale was withdrawn, and anyway, she was missing many customers Twenty-one local men were now in jail and those who remained free were unwilling to risk associating at the house of a woman whose two brothers, brother in law, and four sons were under lock and key. No doubt many of these prisoners would never be at liberty to walk up the steps of the churchyard again, or duck in through the low doorway of the White Horse.

As he mused, Wolstenholme realised that, if it had been about anything for the people of his parish the rising had been concerned with demanding the right to pursue one's own trade from one's own house and be self-sufficient. The deeper dreams of a truly fair and equal society that Tommy Bacon and Wolstenholme's own family had promoted may have stirred something in the hearts of the disenfranchised and marginalized villagers, but ultimately their aspirations were mainly concerned with a bigger loaf. Already, men were taking it for granted that they must toil exhausting hours in huge industrial concerns like the mills of Strutt and Arkwright, or the ironworks of Jessop and Outram.

A generation before, it would have seemed strange for a man to have worked from anywhere except his own home, and without his family to aid him. Now all was changing and he foresaw that the villages with their antique customs and their extended family structures must fade away, and the men and women whose forefathers had dwelt in quiet security must be uprooted. Families would immure themselves in the urban sprawls that were already spreading out around towns like Nottingham, Sheffield, Leeds and Manchester. His own parish must shrink and Pentrich would dwindle. Within a few years it would be no more than a cluster of houses looking remotely down from its hilltop perch, a monument to a futile attempt to stem the tide of change.

Chapter 13: Derby Jail

The jail where the thirty one Pentrich captives found themselves had been built sixty years earlier in the part of Derby known as Nun's Green, which stood to the north and west of the town proper. From the front, the outside of the building looked impressive enough with a strong, plain design, brick-built, with tall Doric columns supporting the pediment above the main entrance and round towers at either end. Both male and female prisoners were confined here, and there were three small rooms for debtors to occupy, separate from the cells of the felons.

For the latter, there was a day room, and seven night cells, each of which had a floor area of seven feet square, and stood eight feet high. Each cell was ventilated at the top of its door by a grill which opened onto the passage outside it. The jail was quite adequate to contain twenty prisoners in fairly humane conditions. Unfortunately, while the Pentrich rebels were incarcerated there, the total number was in excess of sixty, and the overcrowding meant that the men were sleeping in a seated position, six or seven to a cell at night. The day room could not physically hold all those who were supposed to frequent it, and on all but the most inclement days, the inmates had to spend their time in the prison yard.

Sanitary arrangements under such overcrowded conditions were poor and the prisoners were frequently ill. Health was not improved by the standard prison fare, which consisted of the traditional bread and water for most, but those with money enough were able to send out for extra food. The Pentrich and South Wingfield folk, with one or two exceptions, were all reliant for help on their destitute dependents and thus condemned to the bread and water from the outset. Poor food, poor sanitation and overcrowding combined to debilitate the prisoners and lower their already despondent spirits.

Jeremiah Brandreth arrived in Derby jail on July 23rd, 1817. He had been on the run for a little over six weeks, and his followers had used this time to condemn him for being lucky enough to make his escape, while they lingered in their festering cells, waiting for the law to punish them.

William Turner had been in prison as long as any, and had suffered more than most from regret and remorse at the failure of the rising. He was pained more than the others in the early stages of his captivity, because he was the only one of the principal leaders to have been captured straight away. He had sat against the dirty wall of his cell and brooded, night after night, envying Brandreth, Bacon, Ludlam and Weightman their freedom, half hating them for it.

Bacon he despised because it had been his months of persuasive argument and encouragement that had stirred the South Wingfield and Pentrich men into their resolution to rise. Then, on the night of the rising, old Tommy was nowhere to be seen. Bill believed Tommy had probably planned his escape before the rising even started. In Bill's bitterness he regarded Isaac's conduct with contempt. He had cracked at the first sign of violent action, refused to carry a decent weapon, even though he was marching off to war, and proven to be totally useless when it came to preventing the desertions. George Weightman, the proud young puppy, had been the Captain's favourite, promoted above those more experienced and reliable to be closest to his councils. A fine loyal aide Weightman had been when it came to it. When the troopers charged, the trusty lieutenant was nowhere to be seen, he was probably running back as fast as his legs could go to tell his Uncle Tom to get ready to flee.

In his first week at the jail, Turner, recovering slowly from the concussion which Rolleston had caused him, had felt pleased that Brandreth had escaped. His last sight of the Captain in the confusion at Giltbrook was of a man standing his ground and trying to rally those who were running away. He had not liked the Nottingham interloper much until then. But, as time passed and he began: to review the events of June the ninth in his head, Turner's mind turned more and more against his erstwhile leader. Brandreth had failed to deal firmly with the Pentrich group who had delayed them all so much; he had behaved in a cowardly and inexcusable manner in not attacking the ironworks; he had failed to shoot Henry Hole, whose desertion had led to imitative action by so many more; above all, he had failed to take the advice of Turner himself, their only really experienced soldier, on at least a dozen occasions. Was it The Captain himself who had misinformed and betrayed them? More and more, in his depressed mind, Bill Turner gradually came to hate the man who was now rumoured to be travelling to America.

George Weightman was next of the principals of the rising to arrive at the jail He was looking well, and waved and smiled at the prisoners in the yard who included his three brothers. He took to prison life, as to everything else, in a cheerful manner, and soon was regaling the men, who were dulled by the daily routine of the jail, with tales of his escape and capture. He took care to leave out the names of the Wolstenholmes in his enthusiastic narrative. The prison was a happier place for George being there.

Isaac Ludlam was brought in a week later, and presented a total contrast to George. He was weeping copiously as he reached the prison yard, and his sons and friends were aware, even from the outset of the sad change in his personality. He took no comfort from being surrounded by those who were concerned for him, talking only briefly of his period of freedom, and declaring himself repeatedly to be penitent, and asking the forgiveness of the uncomfortable men who began to drift away from his depressing presence. Soon, even his sons tired of his melancholy and morbid religious mutterings, and he was left to the solitude which he needed in order to communicate more closely with his hysterical God.

Then, a day or so after Ludlam's arrival, the bored Derbyshire villagers were amazed to see the Nottingham Captain, now bearded and wasted, walk into the prison yard. He stood, hands in pockets, sheepish and apprehensive, his former followers waiting in knots of open-mouthed shock, staring at him. Even the felons who had never seen him before remained silent and quizzical with the rest. It was good-natured George Weightman who broke the tension as he hurried over to stand smiling in front of Brandreth. He looked down on the new arrival, and held out his big hand. Brandreth looked sadly into George's open face and clasped the proffered hand with both of his. The prisoners began to talk quietly, while George put his arm around Jerry's shoulders and led him over to a spot by the wall to talk to him. Most of the Pentrich men came over to him in the next few minutes, being less prone to animosity towards him than Turner's South Wingfield group. They told him of the prison routine and of their fears and hopes, and suddenly he was the Captain again. He began to feel a sense of belonging and identity which he had never known in his days on the run. Despite the hopelessness of it all, despite the inevitability of the ending to come, he was happy to belong to a fellowship once more.

The jailer, Mr Richard Eaton, was much less happy. He was being asked to keep secure over sixty male prisoners in a jail built for twenty. Quite clearly, the trials of the rebels would not take place for some time, probably not until the end of the harvest, so Eaton was extremely worried that now the man whom they regarded as their leader had come, those who had rebelled once might well be considering doing so again. What, would to happen to himself, his wife and the two deputy jailors if sixty desperate men decided that they had nothing to lose and tried to escape?

He made an appointment with Mr Lockett, the local solicitor who would be acting for the Government until the prisoners were tried and sentences carried out. William Jeffrey Locket had become a pillar of Derby society, since his move there from his Cheshire birthplace. A staunch monarchist, he was a firm opponent of reform. Any slight sympathy he might have felt for the Pentrich and South Wingfield people was obscured by the fact that their confinement in Derby was causing him horrendous administrative problems. Eaton had already been to see him about the overcrowding, the sanitation and the food allowance, and he was becoming heartily sick of the whole affair.

As for Eaton, he disliked little Mr Lockett a great deal. Whenever Eaton suggested some improvement for his unfortunate inmates, it was Lockett, and his bureaucracy he had to overcome.

"What can I do for you Sir?" Lockett peered pompously at the Derby jailer, motioning him to a chair.

"It is about the prisoners," Eaton replied, steadily. We may be facing a serious problem."

"Mr Eaton," Lockett interjected. "Your problems are always serious ones. Before you proceed further, I must inform you that there is no possibility of my agreeing to incur any further expenditure."

Eaton rose angrily to his feet. "In that case, Mr Lockett, I will bid you good day and not presume to waste your time further!" said the jailer, icily.

With that, he turned, opened the door and started homewards.

"Eaton!" Lockett twittered, anxiously. "Where are you going, man? I beg of you, wait a moment!"

"I don't believe I will," replied Eaton. He continued on his way, but not before pausing for one last observation.

"I tell you Lockett," he said, steadily. "The consequences of your refusal to take the advice of an official of this County will be entirely upon your own head!"

An hour later, with his pride in his pocket, Lockett stood together with Eaton gazing through the window of the jailer's house which overlooked the exercise yard. A light rain was falling upon the dispirited felons huddled below.

"There are sixty three men out there, Lockett," said Eaton. "About ten of them are really nasty ones: three murderers and two highwaymen; there are four rick burners, a few petty thieves and one lunatic caught at bestiality up in the north of the county. As well as all these, there are thirty men who, not six weeks past, took up arms against the King and were only stopped from bloody revolution by the presence of the Hussars. Sixty three in my jail built for twenty. The stench and the sheer misery of being crowded all night in an eight foot cell, seven or eight to each, would drive a saint mad. It wouldn't surprise me in the least if these villagers decided that they had nothing to lose by trying to escape, especially now that they've their Captain with them.

"To keep these prisoners penned in, I have the assistance of two deputies, my brother and my wife. What chance would we have against a determined escape bid? I have been governor here for enough years now and my father was governor before me. Many times, I have felt danger in my job, but never as keenly as I do at this moment; these men are desperate, they have nothing to lose, and they have an undisputed leader in this Jeremiah Brandreth.

"You have employed four special constables to alternate watches at the prison. That means that there are but two at any time available as a second line of defence. What then? There are some soldiers, true, but only half a company billeted all over the town, it would take half a day to muster them in the event of an escape. There is no cavalry within half a day's ride of the place, and any prisoner who got clear of Derby would have a good chance of eluding pursuit and making good his escape. Can you imagine the consequences if we were to permit such a thing to happen? I doubt if you and I would be treated with sympathy by our employers."

In reply to Eaton's long assessment of the dangers of the situation, Lockett spoke dismissively. "I am sure that you are exaggerating, but I agree that we ought to do something," he said. "I will dispatch another letter to Lord Sidmouth asking for more soldiers, including cavalry, to be sent. In the meantime we'll put Brandreth and the other leaders of these mutinous men in irons! The leaders will not be too keen to devise an escape plan if they are ironed and unable to run themselves. It will not prove too expensive, either."

Despite Eaton pointing out that none of them had been found guilty on any charge, the next day, first Brandreth, then Turner, then Weightman and five or six of the others identified as ring leaders, were taken to the entrance of the prison. They were each, individually led to the nearby smithy of Mr Bamford. Jeremiah went first, unsure of what was going on. Though he questioned the special constables, they would not tell him where he was going, and it was not until he reached the premises of the blacksmith that he understood.

The smell of scorched hooves of shod horses still pervaded the air in the noisy shop, where Bamford and his assistant stood bare-armed and leather-aproned to execute their special commission. They had assembled sets of chains which would permit the unfortunate men to move around with difficulty, while preventing all prospect of escape. First, two shackles were put onto Brandreth's wrists and riveted into place. They were already joined by a chain which was threaded through a thick leather loop which was attached at its other end to two metal loops which led to similar shackles for his ankles. The smith hammered the bolts home to complete his work, and Brandreth found that his stride was now shortened, and his arms would neither reach further upwards than his face, nor further apart than a couple of feet. He grew pale, despite the heat of the smithy.

The effect upon his men, of seeing their captain so fettered, and Turner and the other principals, too, was to markedly depress their morale, and the inconvenience the chains caused those now wearing them was almost beyond enduring.

Tommy and John Bacon arrived at the jail two days after the irons had been put on their erstwhile comrades. Soon, they also would share this painful inconvenience. The bad luck which had marked their capture in such circumstances had annoyed the elder brother considerably, and it had taken all of John's patience to humour him on the way back. They had been transported by cart through Leicester and Nottingham, and the short tempered Tommy had traded violent abuse with those who came to gawp at the famous fugitives' progress towards Derby. The old radical leader violently objected to being made a public exhibition of, in this way, by the ruling class he so much despised. So was in an exceptionally foul mood when the folk of Derby turned out in hundreds to witness his well-publicized arrival at the town's jail.

The prisoners who knew Tommy had lost respect for him during the long weeks in which they had been incarcerated, while he roamed free. They remembered his persuasive words and fine speeches now with bitterness and regret, recalling that although he had been so eager to have them rise, he had failed to join them on the appointed night. His neighbours remembered that he had always been a bit above himself, isolated from them by his books, journeying and plotting. He had never really belonged to the fellowship of the villages around Pentrich whose councils he had so obviously dominated.

So it was that apart from his good-natured nephews, there were few who had rushed to welcome the elder of the Bacon brothers to his new abode, although there were many who had come to shake the hand of the happy go lucky John, and asked him how he fared. A day or two later, when the Bacons joined the select band which wore irons, Tommy had won favour for himself by volubly protesting the violation of even the limited rights which were normally afforded an untried prisoner. The constables and the smith laughed at this peppery old man, and the muscular Mr Bamford had warned him not to further offend the only man in Derbyshire capable of unfettering him again. Bacon returned disgustedly from the smithy, soldered into his chains, and prickled by the discomfort which they were causing him. The sight of him so inconvenienced made many sympathetic to the old man and he soon found a few willing to listen to his increasingly vitriolic speeches in condemnation of the despots who had them imprisoned.

Even the cynical and unforgiving William Turner grudgingly allowed himself to be drawn into the fellowship which enveloped all those of the prisoners who had taken part in the rising. There was a pride in the fact that they had all taken a stand, Thomas Bacon excepted, when the folk in other places had stayed safe at home. Old Tommy had likened them to the liberating army of George Washington at Valley Forge: they too had been a small group of men, most of them not soldiers, who had stood firm against all the odds. They likewise, had been inspired by Tom Paine, and Bacon was of the opinion that if Washington had been betrayed as they were, he, too, would have been defeated and have lingered long in a British jail.

The Pentrich and Wingfield men liked the grandiose comparison, and were even happier when Bacon compared Jeremiah Brandreth with George Washington and himself with the inspirational Tom Paine. The men were proud of their Captain now he was again amongst them: he had kept faith. George Weightman was of the opinion that Brandreth had leapt voluntarily from the ship which was to take him to America. Instead of being ejected as he claimed, the Captain had returned to his men of his own free will, despite the inevitable consequences of such action. It was just the sort of rumour the other rebels would take to and they accepted the story as part of building a larger than life persona for Jeremiah.

Even Bill Turner and Tommy Bacon came to believe the tale, and they looked on Brandreth as did the rest, as someone beyond the common order, somehow above them all. The Captain denied George's story, of course, but then, they reasoned, he would, wouldn't he? He kept silent for most of the time, replying easily enough when someone instigated conversation with him, but happy enough to sit alone, calmly smoking his pipe and dreaming of times past. They passed the dreary month of August in boredom and discomfort. The flies buzzed around their sweaty and unwashed bodies and they awoke every few minutes in the night, suffocating in the heat of their absurdly cramped cells. They could only lie down properly in the courtyard during the day, and many did, to try and stretch out the cramps and kinks caused by a night spent in a seated position in the cells. The bread and water diet made them weak and listless, until Eaton forced Lockett to authorize him to provide meat and fruit on alternate days. This was a great comfort to the enervated prisoners, and their spirits were buoyed up a little by it. There were many moments of despair, though, chiefly when memories of friends and families would be too real to bear.

Then the tears fell, and their pain was no longer a dull-edged gnawing, but an agonising stab, as the enormity of the consequences of their actions began to dawn once more. None of them spoke much about the fearful future if it could be helped. Outside, the summer proceeded gloriously towards the harvest. Ironically, after all the shortages and sufferings caused by the disaster of the 1816 harvest, that of 1817 was promising to be one of the most bounteous ever.

A Spy Unmasked

The days following the rising of the ninth had been unique in Lord Sidmouth's long political memory. He received the congratulations of his colleagues on the defeat of a national rebellion with great satisfaction. The news was good, with letters from a number of official sources in Derby and Nottingham painting just the sort of picture that Sidmouth hoped to see. There had been a short, spectacular and noisy rising which had been quelled in heroic fashion by two dozen loyal men. Many prisoners had been taken and conveyed to the county jails, but only one servant had been killed and there was negligible damage to property. In addition to the Derbyshire event a similar noisy gathering near Huddersfield had also been dispersed successfully that same night, and half a dozen rioters arrested. The rebel leadership was in total disarray, with the Yorkshire delegates still held in the northern prisons and the Midlands' figureheads either on the run or in jail. Informers aplenty were in evidence now, and magistrates were beginning to forward letters from dozens of loyal citizens eager to betray neighbours who had been connected in some way with the subversion.

He repeatedly read a letter of congratulation received from the Duke of Newcastle, Lord Lieutenant of Nottinghamshire.

"As your Lordship is aware the plot had been hatching for some time, which we knew, and were prepared accordingly. We thought it much more desirable to let the matter come to a Crisis than to endeavour to crush it before the Designs were openly disclosed. I am very glad that we adopted this mode, as we have now not only become acquainted with what the bad People will do, but we have ascertained that the Country People are not of their way of thinking."

All in all, Sidmouth had been able to reflect, the operation had gone off exactly as hoped, and what was now needed was for the courts to sentence those who had committed high treason to the severest punishment possible.

He particularly congratulated himself on his judgment and boldness in commissioning William Oliver, now in hiding, to infiltrate and destroy the radical opposition. For a few days, therefore, Sidmouth was buoyant, and Beckett found him in the best of humours each day in the oak-panelled office. But one morning, four days after the news of the defeat of the rising, Beckett was obliged to bring distasteful news. He knocked at Sidmouth's door, entered, and showed his master the newspaper that had arrived on the mail coach a few minutes earlier. It was a copy of the Leeds Mercury and it contained an account of the doings of one William Oliver who had been exposed as a spy by the Yorkshire radical, John Dickenson.

Dickenson, it will be remembered, had encountered Oliver after his miraculous escape from the ambush at Thornhill-Lees. After saying goodbye to Sidmouth's agent, Dickenson had retired to his inn window to watch the coach depart, with a feeling that there was something not quite right about Oliver's story. Just before the coach departed, Dickenson had noticed his target alight to talk with a man in the uniform of a servant. After Oliver had left on the coach, Dickenson chatted to the man and learned that he was the personal servant of Sir John Byng, commander of the Northern District. Pressed further, the liveried footman told Dickenson that he had seen Oliver in his master's coach a few days earlier. Dickenson was in a fury, but undecided what to do. He was on the run himself and dare not make his own whereabouts too public, so he sat down in his room overlooking the street and composed a long letter to the editor of the Leeds Mercury.

The newspaper had radical tendencies of its own and sources among the radical leadership, and journalist Edward Baines had soon been able to put together an account of Oliver's travels and the way he had promoted the rising. Sidmouth was white and shaking before he had the report half read. The implication was clear that he himself had instructed Oliver to provoke a rising. Baines was especially hostile to Oliver, calling him the *"prototype of Lucifer, whose distinguishing characteristic is, first to tempt and then to destroy."* The political capital that his numerous opponents would make out of such an accusation was obvious, and Sidmouth's mind dwelled much upon the ex-debtor and failed builder who was currently hiding in a safe house in London. In succeeding days, Parliament was in uproar about the idea that the King's government might have been as un-British as to stoop to spying and provoking the illiterate and naive villagers. Lord Castlereagh was compelled to make a statement in Parliament, when Sir Francis Burdett asked the Government whether it had given Oliver authority to attempt to provoke a rising.

Castlereagh had denied that such authority had been given and avowed the employment of Oliver had been necessary to protect the security of the realm. In the House of Commons, Hiley Addington, Sidmouth's brother, rose to make a statement amidst hostile looks and catcalls:

"Mr Oliver had taken no part in any plots. He came to the Home Office at the beginning of April and offered information which he considered beneficial to the country, but which he had not obtained by being implicated in any conspiracy. He asked no reward and

never received a shilling from the Government, except what served to defray his travelling expenses."

Throughout the country, Englishmen refused point blank to believe that Oliver, a past debtor, had put his life at risk purely through altruistic motives. Sidmouth began to realise that the tide of public opinion was turning in favour of the rebels, who began to be portrayed as innocent dupes, rather than scheming revolutionaries. At the end of July, the half-dozen rioters who had been arrested at Huddersfield on June the ninth were brought to trial. To Sidmouth's disgust, the jury refused to convict them, and there was no doubt that the hostility to the Government, provoked by the participation of Oliver, was the prime reason. The upright Yorkshire farmers who reached their verdict had no sympathy for violent rebellion, but shared a well developed sense of fair play, and they were outraged. The irony for Sidmouth was that for years, the Home Office, the Town Clerks, the Magistrates had been using informers as the only possible means of preventative police action available to them in a land without its own law- keeping body. Oliver had almost single-handedly broken up a massive conspiracy against the entire fabric of society, and those he had protected were now in full cry against him. His deceptions had managed to unite the physical-force and moderate wings of the radical movement as never before, when the actions of Bacon and Brandreth should have driven a massive wedge in between them.

Sidmouth summoned Oliver to him at the Home Office in late July to discuss his future in the light of recent events. Oliver was very keen to be got well away from the country, as he expected, quite rightly, that were he to be recognised in almost any part of England, his death would not be far away. Sidmouth was inclined to agree with him, but he was not really worried that Oliver might be silenced by violence; his real concern was the damage which Oliver might do were he to speak out publicly about his role in recent events. When the meeting concluded, he gave his agent a purse of money promised him a new life outside England. In return, Oliver, by now hiding under the alias "William Richards", agreed to travel in disguise to Derby for the trials, in order to testify against the rebels, once they were apprehended.

Sidmouth's temper improved somewhat in later weeks when Brandreth and the other principal fugitives fell into his hands. He was particularly delighted when Thomas Bacon was apprehended after so many years of fomenting revolution. His demeanour was so improved that he sanctioned payment for the extra food Lockett had requested for the prisoners. After all, the Opposition would be able to make great capital out of the situation if any of the Pentrich rebels were to be so inconsiderate as to die in captivity before their trials. As an afterthought, Sidmouth made a condition that Rev Pickering, the Chaplain who met with the prisoners should find out all he could about what they knew of Oliver and what they might say about him.

Pentrich

In the quiet village of Pentrich, people kept very much to themselves and the normal social run of the place was suspended. Hugh Wolstenholme did the rounds of the old and sick as usual, comforting those who were worried about the men in Derby. But his thoughts were elsewhere. He returned, one afternoon, to see Rebecca Weightman attending him upon his doorstep. She had brought her daughter who favoured her mother in looks. Rebecca always maintained that her little girl had inherited her father's good humour, while her boys had their father's appetite.

"Will they 'ang him, Mr Wolstenholme?" Rebecca asked.

Wolstenholme thought of the jolly, healthy young man he had tried so hard to save. "I pray that they won't," he replied, in a tone which he had employed to impart comfort to so many folk in the recent past.

"But you think they will?" she said.

"He was not there at the final confrontation," rejoined Wolstenholme. "And do not forget, he aided Henry Tomlinson's escape: that will stand him in good stead. Also, his age is in his favour and may stay the Judge from a death sentence if George is found guilty."

His voice ended on an optimistic note, but Rebecca was not cheered.

"Then, at best, he'll be transported and ah'll never see him again," she said sadly. "He might as well be dead t' us."

"While there's life, there's hope," he concluded, hating the words as he uttered them.

After a little further conversation, Rebecca murmured her thanks and led her daughter away. He watched them go, exchanging waves with the little girl until they passed through the garden gate. He retired to his parlour and occupied himself in thought. His first thought was for Rebecca and her children. She was a fine, able young woman who had borne the recent suffering with courage and dignity. She was a great support to many of the other women, especially the heart-broken Nanny Weightman who was missing her two brothers and four sons, and who could no longer support herself through trade. In a fair society, Rebecca would flourish. Now she faced a future of poverty and regret.

He was extremely troubled about his own attitude towards the rising even now. In part he was proud of the prisoners and how they had risked all to make a better world. They were much braver than he. But his main concern was the damage to men's souls which violence must engender. More immediately, the pastor was most concerned about the spiritual harm which enforced, separation from the men folk, was doing to the wives and children of his parish. If the consequence of the Pentrich rising was that families were fragmented and suffering and despair resulted, how could any humanitarian justify it? He had made a point of visiting all those families concerned and had seen the real horror of destitution and despondency, reflected in the faces of those whom he sought to comfort. It took a tremendous effort of will for him to return time and again to those hopeless homes on his doomed mission to provide comfort, yet, even so, he could not bring himself to condemn the gesture which the men had made.

Though the wives and mothers railed at Brandreth and Bacon, and cursed the names of Turner and, of course, Oliver, he suspected that underneath all their anger and frustration, there was a vestige of pride and support for the dashed aspirations of those who now waited for trial and sentence. As the shadows of evening began to dull the light in his parlour, Wolstenholme rose to his feet and perused the bookshelves which held the many works which he had read and studied. He took down his well-worn copy of Thomas Paine's writings, and thumbed through the pages until he arrived at the extract he sought.

He read out loud to himself:

"When it shall be said in any country in the world, 'My poor are happy; neither ignorance nor distress is to be found among them; my jails are empty of prisoners; my streets of beggars; the aged are not in want; the taxes are not oppressive'." There was a long list here which he skipped through, before continuing *"When these things can be said, then may that country boast of its constitution and its government."*

Ann

Ann heard the news of Jeremiah's capture on the day it happened. Constables pushed in the door at Cross Court and searched her almost empty home, frightening the children. They had sworn at her and made threats, before finding an old sword that Jerry had hidden. It was blunt and had no handle, but they had seemed delighted to find it. She cried when they left. After that Ann had kept indoors for a week or so, shunning the gossipy company of the women she knew, but she had to go to the market in Sutton for soap and buttons, which were both necessary for the daily maintenance of her father. Inevitably, she was recognised as the Nottingham Captain's wife, and soon a woman she had known all her life, and avoided as much as possible, had cornered her by a stall in the market place. Ann stood resolutely, stoically enduring her neighbour's interminable felicitations.

She had heard what a fine man her husband was, despite what many folk were saying about him; how much the speaker wished that Jeremiah should be spared the full weight of the law; how badly Sutton folk thought of the traitorous Henry Sampson who had sold his friend for gain. This Oliver seemed to be the villain who had caused all the trouble. She had made agreeable noises when questioned about her circumstances, her pregnancy and her future intentions, before finally escaping on grounds that her infant must be fed. After the oppression of the woman's company, it was a positive pleasure to sit alone with her children in George Bridget's little parlour, where Jerry had wrestled with Timothy only a short time before.

Ann found herself thinking back over their lives together. How she'd dreamed about him asking her to dance, long before he did; scheming with her sister to find a way to get him alone; making her friends jealous that she should have his arm to cling to, and going with him everywhere proud and happy.

He was never rough with her, like so many of the colliers seemed to be with their wives, and she, in her turn, had kept her tongue and used her patience at times when others would have flown into a temper. The children were beautiful and took after their lively, gentle father, and their family life was happy. She hated poverty and sometimes they had quarrelled when hunger made them tense and irritable, but somehow, they had always just managed.

Jerry was always proud, though, and would never accept help, even from her father. When they had been forced onto Parish Relief, he had become a different person and their marriage had suffered. She was deeply hurt that he distanced himself from her, and was often reproachful. She always regretted it, because she knew how hurt he was that his skills were no longer needed. She lay sleepless alongside him, worrying at his unspoken worries as poverty began to overwhelm them. In those terrible days when he had begun to follow General Ludd, and had condemned her to endless, wakeful nights while he ranged, black-faced, with Jem Towle and the others, Ann had often thought of leaving him and taking the children back to her father's house.

She dozed a while in her chair, dreaming of a day back in those anxious times. She had gotten out of bed, though it was barely light, not having slept at all, and seeing no point in making any further effort to do so. She bent to the hearth, and busied herself there, so that soon a little fire was blazing. Ann fetched up a stool and huddled up near the fledgling flames, hoping for some heat on this chilly day. By now, she was a bride of one year, and there was a little baby nestling in the retreating warmth of the bed which his mother had recently vacated.

She got up to check that the blankets were allowing baby Timothy to breathe, before going back to her stool and her thoughts. Ann did not look up as Jeremiah hovered by the door he had just closed He came over by her and stood waiting upon an answer to his greeting. Receiving none, Jerry turned and walked towards Timothy.

"Get away from him with all that black on your face!" she hissed. "He'll think you are the Devil!"

Jeremiah seemed about to answer, but thought better of it and went to the pitcher and bowl at the other end of the little room. He occupied some moments in washing his face, dabbing at it with an old piece of cloth.

"There, is it all gone?" he asked. She nodded. He began to undress, quietly so as not to disturb the baby.

"Are you coming back to bed?" he asked.

Ann did not answer so he shook his head at her back, sighed hugely, and sank into the bed. Baby Timothy began to stir and was soon bawling as loudly as his infant lungs would permit.

"Leave him," said Ann, severely. She picked Timothy up. "He's wet! You're all wet, aren't you?"

When George Bridget came home, his face blackened with coal dust, he found that his daughter had heated up the water and there was soap ready for him to use. She greeted him cheerfully, and helped him wash. There was a good, heavy meal waiting when he had dried himself, and he ate it solidly, pulling faces at his two grandchildren throughout. Then he stood up and pulled on his coat and went out whistling, in the direction of the inn. Ann sat with her daughter in her arms and chattered to her young son until it was time for them to sleep.

Chapter 14: The Trials

Wives and Mothers

The financial resources open to the British Government enabled the deployment of a large team of lawyers who set about preparing prosecution briefs against the imprisoned rebels. Back in Derbyshire, the relatives of the languishing men were too devastated by the rising and its aftermath to even begin to think of a defence. Some leadership was required, and when it came, it was Hugh Wolstenholme inevitably who set the wheels in motion. The clergyman had been frightened at the potential implications of George Weightman's capture; common sense required that, in order to avoid the risk of losing the living of Pentrich, he now completely disassociate himself from the radical cause which had affected so many of his parishioners. His heart told him however, that his only course was to act to save from the gallows as many of the unfortunates as possible. In early August he called together representatives of the families of all those held in Derby and Nottingham jails and set them down in the pews of St Matthew's. He spoke with brevity, pointing out that whereas the prosecutors were well prepared for the impending trials, nothing had been arranged for their own men. Clearly no money was available to pay the expenses of defence counsel or witnesses, even though it was rumoured that some London radicals had begun a collection. Wolstenholme hoped that Burdett, Cartwright, Hunt and the like would have assured generous support, but apart from the latter these voluble reformers seemed to be distancing themselves from those who had followed their words. Wolstenholme's conclusion was stark; they should muster every ounce of urgency to think what, if anything, they could achieve by their own efforts in support of their husbands, fathers and sons.

The largely female congregation began to talk quietly. To most sitting in those wooden pews in the house of their God prayer seemed the only course pursuable. No more pragmatic alternative seemed to be available. It was Nanny Weightman who put across the view of the majority.

"We've all thought for weeks what can be done," she said. "We've sat together many a night, but t' truth is there in't a thing we can do. Its money we need, right enough; summat we've none of. There aren't but three or four here not receiving alms from t' Parish, where can we get money t' pay for lawyers?"

It was evident that the majority of women present were in reluctant agreement.

Then Rebecca Weightman spoke. "They didn't just do this for 'emselves and us," she argued. "They were trying t' help all t' poor families. Surely, there's many would remember that? Then there were all them who ran away or stood by and did nowt. They owe our men summat. We should get out in t' villages and collect money - beg in t' streets if we have to."

Mrs Ludlam made herself heard above the clamour at this suggestion.

"That is all very well Mrs Weightman, but none of us is prepared to beg," she said. "Our husbands, sons, they wouldn't want it. No matter how bad things get, I know Isaac won't let me beg."

"Isaac in't here to stop you," said Rebecca firmly. "None of 'em is here. We make our own decisions now. Our men went out t' fight for justice. Right or wrong, what they did, that don't matter. What matters is my man needs me, and there isn't a thing ah wouldn't do to help him. And if there's a woman in this room who'll follow pride before her wifely duty, I turn my back on her."

The women, even Mrs Ludlam, were silent at the sense of determination they heard in Rebecca's voice. Wolstenholme looked at her, tears of pride beginning to well up inside him.

"Tell us a little more about what you propose should be done, Rebecca," he said.

She blushed. "Ah have no plan," she said softly. "Ah just thought if we women - and the children too - if we give ourselves set places t' go to, we could shame folk into helping us."

Nanny Weightman butted in. "They wouldn't let us do that. They'd arrest us as beggars! Next thing we'd know, we'd be in prison with 'em!"

"I don't think so," said Wolstenholme. "I don't think they would dare to interfere were you to beg money for your husbands' cause. There is not too much sympathy for the men, but there is much felt for their families. Rebecca is right: this is your only chance of raising money to furnish an adequate defence."

Wolstenholme's words helped to remove doubts. While the men had drilled and schemed, the Derbyshire women had minded the children and fought the battle against hunger from their own kitchen tables. If the men had felt the hopelessness and frustration of unemployment and poverty, it was the women who had suffered the consequences. Even strong-willed and brave wives, like Rebecca Weightman had taken a back seat, while the men had started on the path to the rebellion, condemning their families to destitution. Women had not been admitted to the secret councils or invited in any way to participate in the rising, but now, at last, there was a way to try their own strength through taking direct action.

In the weeks following the meeting at the church, husbandless women took their orphans with them and went begging. The proud and reluctant Mrs Ludlam, urged on by her sons' wives, led a family group to hold out bowls on the street corners of Ripley. The Turner women walked to Derby, and many more Wingfield wives along with them. Nanny and Rebecca persuaded an old man to ferry them along with three or four others in a horse- drawn cart, to and from Nottingham. For each of the collectors, Wolstenholme had printed a placard that read: THE DERBYSHIRE WIDOWS. HELP US DEFEND OUR HUSBANDS. Despite the logical contradiction contained in the two phrases, the message they broadcast was clear enough.

At first the campaign did not go well. In market places women just as poor as they stalked haughtily past, while rough men shouted abuse. Some collectors were so assailed that they ran for home weeping in frustration, having earned nothing but insults. But every day, they bore themselves with dignity and gradually began to notice a change in people's attitudes. Something about the women's proud bearing and determined faces transformed the anger of the townspeople into sympathy and admiration. In a few days, the atmosphere had changed. The women became a popular feature; stallholders and shopkeepers brought them food; even the better off contributed.

George Goodwin sent a guinea. Not daring to put money directly into Mrs Ludlam's bowl, he commissioned a boy to do so in his stead. Poor folk, knitters and their wives, near destitute themselves, pressed pennies into their children's hands so that they too could give little contributions to the cause. When the womenfolk met at Mr Wolstenholme's each evening, they were a happy and proud gathering, feeling that at last they were part of the fight, and proud of their success.

"Ah met t' strangest man in Nottingham," said Rebecca, one evening. "He were well-dressed, but so thin. His clothes were falling off him and he looked, well, he looked like he were dying. His eyes were really sunken, like he was haunted. He talked t' me for a few minutes, asking where ah were from and whether ah had a man in t' prison. He wanted t' know how well we were doing and how George fared and so on. He looked at little Sarah, here, and said he hoped she'd see her father soon. And then he said he hoped she would forgive those whose blindness had made her father desperate enough t' risk losing such a beautiful child. She must forgive him, he said. Then he raised his hat t' us, and was gone. Oh, he asked who were keeping t' money safe for us, as he might give us some. Ah told him it were you. Did I do right?"

"Yes, Rebecca, you did right," replied Wolstenholme. "You see, we have even managed to touch the hearts of the rich now."

The next day, Wolstenholme received a visitor, who gave him a purse of money. He was the servant he said, of a gentleman from Nottingham, who would not like his name mentioned, but wished good luck to the cause. After the man had gone, Wolstenholme counted out thirty guineas from the purse. He stared at the money shining on the table in front of him, musing long at the significance of the amount, and wondering as to the identity of that mysterious stranger who had sympathised with Rebecca.

After two weeks, the amounts raised by the collectors dwindled to such an extent that it was hardly worth the women making the journey to the towns. Nevertheless, nearly one hundred guineas had been raised and the women were proud, if not happy. There was news as well; one of the radical leaders in London, Henry Hunt, had finally started a collection and some money from that quarter could be counted on. Another surprise was when Mrs Ludlam, one of the most reluctant at the outset, came up with an idea which they all found moving.

"Isaac and my sons are sleeping sitting up on pallets o' dirty straw, eight t' a cell," she said. "Ah'm sleeping in a comfortable bed. That no longer seems right to me. Tomorrow, ah'm going to sell that bed and any other bit o' furniture that might raise anything, and put t' money in't fund."

She sat down amidst the admiring stares of her friends. She carried out her plan the next day, and many of the women imitated her shortly afterwards. At the beginning of September, Wolstenholme found that he had a hundred and forty six guineas and a few shillings at his disposal. His parish was as united and Christian as it had ever been, and his people, though poor in material possessions, were rich in spiritual peace. He said his prayers of thanks with a sincerity rarely achieved before in conversation with his God.

The trials were set for October. It was important that defence lawyers be appointed without further delay. Wolstenholme took up his pen one evening after the women had left, and wrote to two men who had been recommended to him: Robert Bond of Leicester and Thomas Wragg of Belper. He invited both to act as solicitors for the men and asked them to suggest someone who might be approached to appear as counsel. In a few days he received the assent of both. The two legal officers conferred before proposing that Mr John Cross from Manchester should be requested to act as counsel for the defence. Shortly afterwards, Wolstenholme received a letter from Robert Bond with the news that Thomas Denman, a notable lawyer from Nottingham, had contacted him, offering his aid to the Pentrich and South Wingfield prisoners. He was prepared to forego his fee if necessary. Bond added that he knew Denman to be a most capable lawyer; as a defender of Luddites in recent trials, he had gained both fame and notoriety. Despite his background at Eton and St John's Cambridge, Thomas Denman had always held liberal views. As an Eton fag he had been branded with a poker for refusing to make a speech to amuse the older boys. Recognising a kindred spirit, Wolstenholme at once wrote back to Bond and instructed him to accept Denman's offer. Hopes were beginning to rise for the men in jail. He passed the news on to the women and they waited impatiently for the trials to begin and for the fate of the men –good or bad- to be decided.

Hugh Wolstenholme

Lord Sidmouth was shaken that several juries, where an informer's evidence was admitted, had refused to convict those charged with High Treason. The name of 'Oliver' was despised throughout the land. It seemed clear that his involvement in any legal case would be bad both for the Government, and for Sidmouth personally; furthermore it would weaken the chances of a successful conviction. The Home Secretary was still determined to visit upon the

Derbyshire rebels the severest retribution so that any further ideas of revolution would be discouraged by the gruesome spectacle of a bloody execution. Within Liverpool's inner Cabinet, none of whose members was either liberal or squeamish, the experienced voice of Sidmouth carried sufficient weight to persuade those present to concur with his plan.

Sidmouth, keenly eager for the trials to come on, was irritated beyond measure at the delay in commencing them, but he had to remain patient. As the glorious summer of 1817 mellowed into a golden and fruitful autumn the farmers of Derbyshire were rubbing their hands in anticipation of an abundant harvest. It was quite impossible, Beckett assured his master, to call in the several hundred jurymen needed for the trials, before the harvest was gathered in. If they were to do so, the chances of gaining a guilty verdict out of dozens of disgruntled farmers herded together in Derby whilst their crops were still in the field would be remote. Reluctantly, the spy-master acquiesced. He took to pacing interminably around his office, sucking in his drawn cheeks, and gazing far away. The only work that interested him, Beckett observed, was reading over the briefs the prosecution was painstakingly preparing for the trials that were finally set for October.

In Derby itself, Lockett was under the severest pressure. It was his task to organise every detail of the trials to come. His problems were major. No one could remember such a large trial ever taking place in a provincial town. The enormity of its scale frightened Lockett. He was required for instance to write to the three hundred throughout the shire whose ownership of property qualified them for jury service. For each of these jurors, as well as for the judges and the ten prosecution officials, accommodation had to be arranged. Derby was a bustling town, but there were simply not enough suitable premises to cope with such an influx. As well as all these details, and the reams of paperwork involved, Lockett had the normal business of the administration of justice to attend to. At this time that included the erection of a scaffold in order that the death sentence, recently imposed upon the four convicted of firing Colonel Halton's ricks, could be carried out. Lockett could feel himself going grey under the weight of the worries he was obliged to carry.

The four rick burners were executed in front of Derby Jail on a wet afternoon. Wolstenholme had travelled over to stand in the crowd. Halton was back in his house at South Wingfield. The four were led out of the jail during a lull in the rain, and brought onto the scaffold. They were in tolerable health, Wolstenholme noted, and in fairly good condition. He remembered that they had all protested their innocence of the crime. Only one of the four, George Booth, was a member of his parish. At twenty one years old he was one of the two youngest; Thomas Jackson from Matlock was a few months his junior. As they stood quietly on the scaffold, there was a sudden squall of rain and Wolstenholme saw the four who were about to die trying to shelter their heads and bodies from the shower. The crowd laughed at the irony; this rough and unsympathetic behaviour disgusted him. The throng had come to witness a spectacle that no one should see. He recalled execution tales which the newspapers and journals always printed for their readers to gawk at: tales of bravado and horror on the scaffold. He remembered that when Towle's brother and his gang had been hanged in Nottingham but a year before, they had spent their last few minutes on earth throwing oranges to the vast crowd come to see them swing, in keeping with a long, macabre tradition, which required the victim to play a full part in the barbaric pageant.

Wolstenholme left before the men were killed. As he rode his horse back out of Derby, he heard the gasp of the crowd as the drop launched the poor men into the bottomless space. He muttered a prayer, feeling useless and impotent, and returned home in the worst of moods. Clergymen, he knew, were ruled by the stricture that convicted felons might be buried in the cemeteries of their home parish if the curate agreed, but under no circumstances was a sermon to be preached at the burial ceremony. Wolstenholme was quite aware of this edict, and in normal times would have respected it. But the parish of Pentrich was no longer ordinary. Wolstenholme knew that he owed the dignity of a decent burial not just to Booth, but to his parents, and the whole of the Pentrich folk too.

They gathered at the graveside in that grey afternoon watching the meagre coffin of George Booth being borne to its final destination. Over a hundred had turned out, mainly women and children, with a sprinkling of older men. After a short prayer Wolstenholme began his delivery of the words that placed him in a peril of his own:

"I know that most of you today expect me to inter the body of this young man with the greatest expedition possible. It is customary on the occasion of the execution of a man convicted of a felony, for the minister to either forbid his burial, or else rush his body into the ground with obscene haste. That is not the way of a Christian. This man is the child of God as much as any in this congregation. It is a forgiving God who looks down upon us today, and I am sure that he has already forgiven our deceased brother, George Booth.

"This young man was wrong to fire his landlord's ricks, although he denied it to the last. He was young and misguided but his crime injured no one. His execution was nothing less than murder. At this moment, many of our friends, husbands, fathers and sons await trial in Derby. There is little evidence against most, but they are in danger from the false testimony of their friends and neighbours who have been called to bear witness against them. I pray that the hearts of those called to speak will soften; otherwise I fear that the same murderous fate will befall our loved ones.

"I am equally sure that unless we often our hearts and announce our forgiveness of this man, then we can hardly expect our own transgressions to be remitted upon the day of our own judgment. The following reading is taken from the Book of Matthew, Chapter five, verses three to twenty:"

And he began to read from the beautiful verses:

"Blessed are the poor in spirit: for theirs is the Kingdom of Heaven.

Blessed are they that mourn: for they shall be comforted.
Blessed are the meek: for they shall inherit the earth.
Blessed are they which do hunger and thirst after righteousness:
for they shall be filled.
Blessed are the merciful: for they shall obtain mercy.
Blessed are the pure in heart: for they shall see God.
Blessed are the peacemakers: for they shall be called the children of
God.
Blessed are they which are persecuted for righteousness' sake:
for theirs is the Kingdom of Heaven.
Blessed are ye, when men shall revile you, and persecute you, and
shall say all manner of evil against you falsely, for my sake.

Indictment

It was Wednesday, October 15th, 1817. Derby was full to bursting with crowds of people from all over the county who had come to watch the commencement of the trials. The first sight of consequence for the happy revellers outside Derby Jail in the mild morning was a military train acting as escort to those insurgents imprisoned at Nottingham. The crowd cheered the newcomers loudly and some of the apprehensive men did manage a wave and a smile to the folk of Derby. They were ushered into the courtyard of the prison and were soon all smiles and delight. German Buxton clasped the hand of the Captain but noted in his mind how shrunken he'd become. He was disgusted that Brandreth and the others were ironed; disgusted and angry. Upstairs, Eaton watched the happy reunion in the courtyard, wondering how his packed jail was going to cope with a dozen more criminals. Outside the County Hall, where the trials were to take place, those watching buzzed with interest at the sight of a post-chaise filled with pikes, spears and other assorted weapons. These, they decided correctly, would be produced as evidence against the defendants. The next episode to stir the crowd was the sight of the High Sheriff, Thomas Hallowes, leading the three Judges and many local dignitaries to a service in All Saints Church. The band of worthies retired to the George Inn for lunch before setting the crowd going once more by their arrival at half-past two at the County Hall in time for the commencement of proceedings. It would be hard to imagine a scene which so clearly illustrated the gap between rich and poor. The gentry of Derbyshire sat with their distinguished visitors from London clad in the best and most expensive of clothes: silk gloves and handkerchiefs, golden chains, watches of silver, all of these and many more adornments.

The prisoners occupied the dock in tens and twelves; the courtroom was not large enough for them all to be accommodated at once. It was all smocks and patches with them, and dirty, ragged jackets and breeches. Only Samuel Hunt had managed to procure himself clothes different from those he had worn for the last five months in jail. Bacon, Brandreth, Weightman, the three Turners and the three Ludlams, together with Samuel Hunt and young Robert Turner, were brought into the dock as the first batch. Brandreth stood in the centre at the front, through no design of his own. He was now stooping from the weight of his chains all those weeks; his eyes, however, were clear. The others held their heads bowed, but Bacon and Brandreth stared straight at the Clerk as he commenced reading a long indictment, declaring that "moved and seduced by the instigation of the Devil ...they,... together with a great multitude of false traitors ...unlawfully, maliciously and traitorously assembled ... did march in a hostile manner through diverse villages ... and did then and there ... endeavour by force and arms, to subvert and destroy the Government and Constitution of this realm."

It took ten minutes to read out the complete indictment with its several dozen names and precise but complex and archaic legal language. At the end of it all, they each in turn pleaded "not guilty" and were led away, back to their crowded cells. The first day of the trial was ended, and the Derbyshire rebels were thoroughly perplexed and tangled by the legal jungle in which they now found themselves trapped. Right up until the beginning of the trial, Sidmouth insisted that the prisoners be all charged with High Treason. Most of the legal men on both sides involved in the trial were of the opinion that only the leaders of the insurrection should be so charged. The others might be better indicted for riotous assembly. Sidmouth, however, was adamant. The prosecution team had therefore assembled a case according to his instructions, and worked an appropriate strategy.

Thomas Bacon would come to trial first, followed by Brandreth and the other leaders in descending order of importance. The old radical would be easy to convict upon the evidence of many who had heard his seditious speeches in the preceding months; Oliver's testimony would not be needed. Even though he had not actually taken part in the rising, Old Tommy would hang for inspiring it. As for Brandreth, Turner, Weightman, Ludlam and the others, they had risen against the Crown and there were any amount of witnesses to prove it. Oliver, again, would not be required to testify, as there were many outraged householders who would provide all the evidence a jury could need.

The plan was put to Sidmouth by Sir Samuel Shepherd, the Attorney General, on the eve of the prosecution delegation's departure for Derby. Shepherd was the same age as Sidmouth but he had indulged himself more in life's temptations. Although he had enjoyed his years much more, he wore them less well, than the Home Secretary. He was also very deaf and frequently had to resort to an ear trumpet, in the courtroom.

"I'm pleased with the work of your department, Shepherd," said Sidmouth. "It's a thorough job and I know that you will see it through in Derby. I cannot however let you go without reminding you once again of the need to keep Mr Oliver's name out of the proceedings."

Shepherd was astute enough to comprehend Sidmouth's anxiety and his answer reassured his fellow minister.

"I understand perfectly the embarrassment that might be caused if Mr Oliver's doings were to be brought to the attention of the jury, Sidmouth. Have no misgivings, we'll keep him well out of it."

Sidmouth thanked him. "As you requested, Oliver will be transported up to Derby in case there is an urgent need for him," he said. "He will be at the George Inn, under the name of Maule, George Maule. He will be disguised."

"Maule?" said Shepherd. "I know that name, where have I heard it before?"

"George Maule is an official at the Treasury," said Sidmouth. "I have given him a few weeks leave."

"Damned clever," laughed Shepherd. "Really though, you must leave it to us legal lads now. I've a trick or two lined up to pressure the defence counsel into falling in with our plans."

Shepherd left, leaving Sidmouth a little happier, though with some serious misgivings still, fuming indeed that he could not himself prosecute and for that matter, carry out the executions into the bargain.

Lawyers for the Defence

John Cross and Thomas Denman were possessed of different types of characters. Suffice it to say, they did not get on. The first cause of rancour was the fact that Cross, the brash Mancunian, demanded a hundred pounds from the fighting fund in advance of the trials, refusing to set foot in court if he was not paid. Wolstenholme had no alternative but to hand over the money increasingly apprehensive that there would be insufficient left to pay the expenses of witnesses. The patrician Denman found the conduct of Cross almost impossible to understand and had told him so as they lunched unhappily together at the Talbot Inn a few days before the trial

"I'm not as naively altruistic as you are, Denman. If the fee isn't paid before the trial, I'm certain that it won't be afterwards, and that won't do for me," Cross said as he attacked the leg of his roast chicken.

"Yes," replied Denman. "But with respect, your action has prejudiced our chance of winning this case."

"Winning?" Cross nearly choked in amazement. "How on earth can you believe that we might win this case!? They are all guilty as Hell!"

"The obvious way to win is to play up the part of Oliver as the agent provocateur who incited these poor misguided men to ..."

Denman had no chance to finish before his, luncheon companion interrupted.

"No! Absolutely not!" cried Cross. "We must advance the idea that they have been misled alright, but by the likes of Cobbett and Burdett, not Oliver."

"But why not?" demanded Denman. Other cases have been thrown out at the very mention of an informer's evidence. I'm confused. Don't you want to win this case?"

Denman was genuinely unable to understand his colleague. Cross did not reply, but continued to pick at the food on his plate. Denman did the same until Cross decided to answer.

"I have been in communication with Sir Samuel Shepherd," said Cross.

"He - we had long and frank discussions and well .... to cut the story short, he made me an offer which I have decided to take."

"What is the nature of this offer?" Denman inquired, coolly.

"Simply that if the name of Oliver is not called then the Government would not press for the death sentence for more than a dozen," Cross said, engrossed with the food on his plate. "It would agree that the rest be tried on a lesser charge. Damn it man, don't look at me like that. They have committed treason you know!"

Denman shook his head. "There's more than one way of committing treason," he said, in a low voice.

On the night before the trial commenced, Shepherd and his nine assistants were dining in comfort. One of the government solicitors noticed that Thomas Denman was putting up at the same inn and called him over. They had been up at Cambridge together, and had friends in common. The lawyers spoke convivially and joked about the trial ahead, and Denman joined in until they all thought him a good fellow.

Thus, when the Nottingham advocate craved a few moments of Shepherd's time in private, the old barrister was ready enough to give it to him. They adjourned with bottle and glasses to the Attorney General's private room, Shepherd pointing his ear trumpet in Denman's direction, asking him to speak up. The Attorney General was notably hard of hearing and approaching the day when he would become completely deaf.

"I intend to call Mr Oliver as a witness in the trial of Thomas Bacon," said Denman after the initial pleasantries had been exchanged.

Shepherd was startled. "I thought we had an arrangement!" he snapped.

"Not one that I am party to", replied Denman "You will have read something of the character of Thomas Bacon. You will know that he is not some illiterate pauper. I have spoken to the man and know him to be intelligent, devious and defiant. You should know also, that more than a dozen leading radicals have written to volunteer to testify against Oliver and the part he played in the insurrection. If you push the charge of High Treason against him, I shall advise him to claim that he was duped by Oliver."

"That won't save him," Shepherd replied, annoyed by Denman's argument.

"Possibly not, but we must remember that the jury might follow those in other recent cases and acquit. Besides, if Oliver's part was revealed under oath, I would imagine that it would cause acute embarrassment in high places."

Shepherd sat stony-faced. "What exactly is it that you want, Denman?" he demanded.

"Ideally, I would like all my clients to walk free, but I realise that is not possible," Denman replied. "I admit that even if I can prove that Oliver actively provoked the rising, it does not constitute a legal defence against a charge of Treason. I am not forgetting, either, that an innocent man was killed on the ninth of June. Accordingly, I would like to suggest this compromise to you: Jeremiah Brandreth killed a man; he was the undoubted leader of this insurrection; him I cannot save from conviction. With the others, however, the case is different. Some of them are almost as guilty as Brandreth to be sure, but others are harmless innocent victims of the rash words of others and have surely been punished sufficiently over these last few weeks."

Shepherd and Denman came to no real conclusions that evening and did not part on friendly terms. Shepherd was extremely irritated that his pleasant evening had been thus troubled, and irked that his relaxed mind must now, on the eve of the trial, be made to consider a change of tactics. Before the morning dawned and his cavalcade was ready to start, Shepherd had informed his puzzled aides that the plans made so long before were now to be altered. His new course was to put Brandreth on trial first, then to follow him with the most active leaders of the rising, like Turner, Weightman and Ludlam, singly. Thomas Bacon, whose likely antics might distract the jury, was to come lower on the list of those to be tried. Shepherd also indicated that a number of those least active in the insurrection should eventually be allowed to go free, without evidence being offered. During that long night, the Attorney General dictated two letters to inform others of the new strategy: one had gone to Sidmouth in London; the other had been slid underneath the door of Denman's room by a chambermaid.

Jeremiah's Trial

There are millions of words spoken in law courts every week, but the only two a defendant wants to hear are "not guilty." Jeremiah Brandreth stood in court from ten thirty in the morning on the first day of the trials until six o'clock that night; on the succeeding two days, he occupied the same space, while strange men argued his life away in complicated language he could not always follow.

In the beginning, he concentrated his mind upon the proceedings, marvelling at the oratory of Sir Samuel Shepherd as he opened the case for the prosecution. When he began to talk of statutes proclaimed in the reign of Edward the Third and to read extracts from them, Jeremiah and probably most people in the court room began to lose the thread of his argument, but the old gentleman with the ear trumpet was soon talking of more familiar events. He cited the assembly at the White Horse, the map Brandreth had used, the promises that Stevens had told him to make, the gathering at Hunt's Barn, and all the subsequent events of June the ninth. Everything seemed so far away that Jeremiah saw it all as a dream and not as a reality he had instigated and led.

Those watching him marvelled at his calmness and his lack of response as the most serious charges were levelled against him. In truth, the whole scene of bewigged judges and advocates, long legal gowns and thick books recording forgotten details of past trials, seemed little more to him than an extension of the same bizarre dream. He continued to gaze with unnerving serenity at all that took place, the gentle eyes which had so charmed Ann, fixed on some point that no other could see.

Witnesses were being called, many of them only vaguely familiar to him like Anthony Martin and Shirley Asbury who recalled Brandreth and Rebecca's poem being read and sung. He remembered Thomas Turner of course, and the moment the young man had prevented him from shooting Henry Hole in the back. Tom had turned King's evidence to escape punishment. Mr Tomlinson told his story, and Brandreth learned, for the first time, of George Weightman's helpful action on behalf of the old man. He remembered Mary Hepworth too, although he would not have recognised this prim and neat little widow had he not heard the spite in her voice as she offered her damning evidence against him. He felt the old tremble of remorse at the name of Robert Walters; he wondered again why the gun had fired, and whether his finger had really pulled the trigger. Henry Hole was stood before the court and told his tale bitterly. George Goodwin was next to take the stand. Brandreth was keen to set eyes again on the man who had faced his army so bravely that night. In the daylight, in that courtroom, he looked much less imposing; he told his story in stilted, halting language, unhappy and uncomfortable with so many eyes upon him. Several householders were called whom Brandreth did not know and could not remember. They could remember him well enough it seemed, as their evidence was added to that of so many others hostile to him.

At the end, came three from Nottingham who were complete strangers. He listened with great interest to their tales, because he had not yet truly understood why Stevens and the Nottingham men had failed to turn out on the ninth. The answer was supplied first of all by old William Roper who coughed and blinked all the way through the tale he had told Lancelot Rolleston as the rain fell on that dark June night. Rolleston came next. As he recounted his part in the movements of the night, Jeremiah realised how crucial the stubbornness of this individual had been in preventing him from reaching Nottingham. If he had not roused the soldiers, the Derby men would have got into the city and linked up with Stevens and the others. What might then have happened if news spread that the Castle had fallen! Rolleston, as a material witness for the Crown, had been excluded from the court proceedings; during his testimony his answers had been brief and non-judgmental. As the questioning ended, he had a brief opportunity to appraise the prisoner in the dock; for a moment their eyes locked, before Rolleston departed to be replaced by the final witness, Captain Phillips. The soldier described the confrontation at Giltbrook and the hunting down of the fleeing rebels, ordering the incidents in precise and military language.

Mr Cross, a man whom Brandreth had not taken to in their brief consultations before the trial, led the case for the defence. He countered Shepherd's legal arguments with skill and dexterity and a completely confused jury, composed entirely of yeoman farmers, was treated to a resume of legal changes to Edward the Third's statutes enacted during the reigns of Mary, Edward the Sixth and Henry the Eighth. He went on to make a succession of more comprehensible points towards the end of his two hour long speech. Making light of the Prosecution's claim that the rising was highly organised and desperate, he made great play of the fact that Brandreth needed to show some men how to fire a gun on the very night of the rising.

"What weapons did the men have with them to effect such a bloody revolution?" he wondered.

"The infantry? That formidable body of infantry was armed with a dozen fowling pieces and two score of pikes. And what was the extent of their cavalry? They had provided themselves with a pony. That was the entirety of their cavalry. As to ammunition, a single parcel of bullets was all that had been exhibited, and one man, a pauper from Nottingham, had been styled their 'Generalissimo'."

Cross stuck to his plan; he blamed Cobbett and other radical leaders for circulating the sedition which had so obviously deluded his client and those who had followed him. What measures had the magistrates taken to prevent such literature being passed freely throughout the land? In Cross's compelling opinion, very little had been done.

The impoverished defence called only a single witness and he was of little value. Denman looked on bitterly while Cross asked the Parish Overseer from Wilford, John Hayward, what he could tell the court about Brandreth. Hayward confirmed that Brandreth was an out of work framework knitter who had received relief from his Parish. At this point Denman rose to give the final speech; his fine oratory however, could not counter the weight of evidence and the whole court, including Brandreth himself, knew that the case was lost. The Prosecution's summing up followed, taking up the latter end of the day's proceedings. At a quarter past six, on Friday, October the seventeenth, the court adjourned.

The next morning, Hugh Wolstenholme rose at five o'clock and rode over to Derby, in the hope of gaining his seat in the courtroom. Unfortunately, there were hundreds of people in the town with the same idea; as a consequence, the Pentrich curate found he was unable to beat the crush that swept into the room at eight o'clock when the doors opened. He was compelled therefore, to stand outside with the masses waiting for the conclusion. Those inside heard from the Chief Baron, long-serving and distinguished judge Sir Richard Richards, a summary of the evidence. By ten past ten, the summation was complete and the twelve men of the jury left the court. They remained in secret deliberation for twenty three minutes, before returning to their box. Half in this world and half in his dreams Jeremiah heard the foreman pronounce: "guilty of high treason".

The court was immediately adjourned for the day. The jailer, Richard Eaton, prepared to lead Jeremiah away from where he sat in mesmerized silence. A number of spectators crowded near to him, observing that someone had done him the favour of washing his face and hands that morning. They also noticed that there was a faint trace of perspiration on his prison-wasted face. They pestered him with questions, at a moment that cried out for peace and solitude; he returned a smile as answer to each, not wishing to speak. Someone proffered a pipe and lit it for him. It was a little clay pipe and soon he was puffing upon it, seemingly happy. There were some women in the little crowd, rough, kindly court servants who offered him a drink of Negus, port wine and lemon juice, spiced with cloves. He accepted this, too, gratefully, but without a word. Eaton informed by one of the military that the cart, which was to take his prisoner back to the prison, was not yet come, let him accept these comforts. Brandreth sat smoking in the midst of concerned stares from the humble folk about him. For a fleeting moment that old feeling he had experienced tentatively in early June in Pentrich returned, the sensation of fellowship and friendship.

A journalist, anxious for something for his London editor, asked Jeremiah for a statement. The guilty prisoner ignored the question when first asked; faced however with the persistence of his interrogator, Jeremiah eyed him unkindly and referred him to Mr Bond the solicitor. "Any statement I make will be through him," said Brandreth, observing the reporter's efficient nod before adding, "However, I do not intend to make any." The crowd laughed at this and their hero sipped his Negus quietly. It was time to go. Eaton cleared the crowd, but one young woman pressed forward with a parcel of sandwiches for Brandreth. Accepting the gift he thanked her and tried to put it inside his hat. The sandwiches would not all fit, so he took the little blue scarf from his pocket and wrapped up the rest carefully inside. Supping down the rest of his drink he permitted himself to be escorted from the courtroom.

As the little procession emerged into the open air, blinking and walking slowly because of Jeremiah's chains, the crowd for a moment went wild with cheers then stopped as if on a signal. Eaton looked up in alarm, and the javelin men with him as escort, tightened their fingers on their weapons. The prisoner sat impassive in the cart. The driver stirred his horses into action and the little cavalcade moved off nervously. In his many years of conducting the condemned through crowds swollen in a bid to see, Eaton had never experienced anything like that feeling.

There was complete silence, even though heads poked from every window. Onlookers were packed ten deep on either side of the road, all silent out of respect for the quiet man in the shabby, dirty clothes, unlit pipe in the corner of his mouth, a parcel of sandwiches upon his lap, sitting at Eaton's side. The silence continued until the doors of the jail closed behind them.

The other folk in the courtyard, from Pentrich, South Wingfield and Alfreton ran forward to surround Brandreth as his escort released him. From every mouth came the question etched into the worried lines on each concerned face. The response to his friends was the one word: "Guilty". For a minute, shoulders drooped and eyes misted over.

Then George Weightman cried, "Cheer up lads! Let's show them we're men!"

It was hardly profound, but it was all that they needed. The hard-pressed and hopeless prisoners clustered round Brandreth once more, shaking his hand and patting his shoulders till he smiled.

"You shall all have a piece of my sandwiches!" he cried.

They completed this saddest of days in a happy fellowship which, had either been informed of events, would have bemused the beleaguered William Lockett and further angered an irate Lord Sidmouth.

Chapter 15: Judgment

Letters

On the evening of the day he was convicted, Jeremiah was approached in the courtyard by Richard Eaton. The kindly jailer told his charge that since he had now been tried and found guilty he was permitted at last to receive visitors if there were any he wished to see. He offered Brandreth the use of his office and pen and paper if there was a letter he wished to write. Brandreth nodded at this, and Eaton showed him to his office. Brandreth thanked him for the suggestion that Eaton should write at his dictation, but took the pen into his own hand. Eaton left the room to give him privacy.

Derby Jail,

October 18, 1817

My dear beloved wife

At last I thought it my duty to write a few lines to you, which I am sure will affect you very much, to inform you of my dreadful situation; but I hope God will be your friend - and if you will by prayer appeal to God, you will undoubtedly find great consolation and relief for your distress, and as a husband and father let me entreat you, that you will act a motherly part to the poor fatherless children, and bring them up in the fear of God, which is my sincere desire, and likewise conduct yourself in an undeniable manner, as an example to the children to the love and fear of God, in the faith of Jesus Christ, so that you may never depart from that faith in Christ.

And I wish for the convincing of all the souls in the house, that they may be at the arrival of this, and that we may all meet in heaven, where trouble ceases, and all is joy and glory.

And I pray to God may this fatal stroke be joy to all that belong to me, instead of sorrow. Oh, that I may be the cause of their holy salvation. May it penetrate each wounded heart, so as to be their sole conversion to God.

My dear, you may suppose my feelings are not easily to be described. At this time the sentence is not passed, but I am found guilty by the jury this day.

My dear wife, it would give me great consolation if I could see you before I depart from this life, but my dear, as you are enceinte, I would have you advise with some older woman whether it would be proper or not; and if she thinks it would not be of serious consequences, I should be very glad, but let it be well considered before you come to me, and if you do not come, let your father (if he thinks it would be not more than he could bear). If neither come, I shall write again, so God permit me.

So, my beloved wife, I hope you will excuse my short letter at this time. You may inform all friends that God gave me great fortitude to bear up my spirits on trial.

So I hope the blessings of God will be with you all, and most especially with you and our little babes.

So I conclude.
        Your most affectionate husband.

        Jeremiah Brandreth.

For Ann Brandreth,
George Bridget's,
Bedlam Court,
Sutton in Ashfield.

Later, when Eaton read the letter and made the obligatory copy, he found himself in a mood half-way between sadness and anger. He had not come to know Jeremiah Brandreth up to now and from a distance had observed him to be a morose and surly man. His impassive expression throughout the trial and lack of reaction to his sentence, bespoke him as a cynical and hard person. Now this tender and religious letter revealed a deeper character and his command of pen and language suggested an intelligence and ability wasted in an unemployed man who was about to be sentenced to a gruesome death.

Richard Eaton made sure that the letter was posted to Sutton and sent the copy over to Mr Lockett.

Ann's written reply came a week later:

Sutton, Octr 26, 1817

Dear Husband

I received your letter (or rather the unwelcome tidings that it contains) on the 25th Inst. And it is in vain for me to attempt to describe my feelings on the arrival of such unwelcome tidings it contains. I leave you to judge my feelings, yet distressing as my situation is it is nothing in comparison to yours (I mean as to the situation I am left in) but I shall forbear saying much at this time as I intend, if God permit, to see you in the course of one week, if I can by any mean get conveyance. In the meantime I hope that God which is more merciful than man will give you comfort and consolation, and if you have (which is the general opinion) been drawn in by that wretch Oliver, forgive him, and leave him to God and his own conscience. That God who will give to every man his reward, though when I call him a human being I scarcely think him so (though in the shape of one). Oh that I could atone for all and save your life. But I forebear saying any more. Praying that God will be with you to strengthen and comfort you, and should you suffer, bring you through Christ to eternal glory, which is the prayer of your unhappy wife, Ann Brandreth.

Eaton asked Lockett's permission to give Jeremiah the letter, but this was denied. Lockett frowned upon the accusations against Oliver and sent the letter to Sidmouth asking for direction. No reply ever came.

William, Isaac and George

A week previously, on Monday, October the twentieth, a dejected William Turner was brought into court. The long months of imprisonment had left their marks upon both his body and his mind. He had lost much hair, and his face had grown lined and thin manifesting none of that strength and vitality it formerly possessed. His eyes had no light to them, and expressed only mournful resignation.

Before the jury could be sworn in, Thomas Denman rose and asked leave of the Chief Baron to bring the attention of the court to a serious matter that prejudiced the interests of his client. He held up a newspaper for all to see: it was a copy of the Courier, a London publication.

"The paper which I hold in my hand," he began, "gives a statement of the proceedings in this Court in direct violation of the prohibitions of your Lordships. It is not a full statement, but a partial and garbled representation which has prejudiced many people against my clients. I submit that because of this barefaced attempt to elude the prohibitions of this court, it is now impossible to obtain an unprejudiced jury or uncoloured witness testimony. I find it unthinkable that such a gross act be permitted to occur, especially as the paper concerned is well known to be under the influence of the Government."

Mr Justice Abbott, one of the Judges, pointed out that no newspaper was, at that time, under the influence of the Government. To this, Denman responded with a weak smile and an apology for making the suggestion, but proceeded to inquire as to what punishment precisely the Court intended to mete out to the proprietors of the

Courier. Sir Samuel Shepherd was most upset by Denman's insinuation that the Government had deliberately influenced the Courier into publishing an account of the proceedings, with a view to turning the jurors against the remaining prisoners. He could not allow Mr Denman's suggestion. The matter was not resolved in any satisfactory way.

The trial continued. In order to decide William Turner's fate, another jury consisting wholly of farmers was sworn in. Cross and Denman based their defence upon the argument that Turner had been deluded and led into the rebellion by their erstwhile client, Jeremiah Brandreth. According to them, Turner was not even present at the murder of Walters; it was totally out of character for him to be in any way hostile to the Government. He had fought for his country as a soldier and was an upright, honourable character, as a number of witnesses came to testify.

Denman, especially, played up the idea that Brandreth was the prime mover of the rising.

"Did anyone ever see a man with a more commanding eye, or aspect?" he demanded. "Even his beard, far from disguising him, is only in accord with his general character. He looks exactly like the Captain of an armed banditti."

For all the skillful pleading of the two defence advocates, the jury returned a verdict of guilty of High Treason on William Turner. Two days later, Isaac Ludlam was delivered of the same verdict.

George Weightman came to trial next. Despite his long confinement, he looked strong and healthy and made a good impression on those in court. He was found guilty but one of the jurors, John Endsor of Parwich, was difficult to persuade. As verdicts had to be unanimous, George was unlucky not to walk free. This showed how disgusted even a loyal farmer could be about the role of government spies in the rising.

It was officially recorded that: '*the Jury found the prisoner Guilty; that he had no lands &c. to their knowledge; and that they strongly recommended him to Mercy, in consideration of his former character.*'

Saving the Rest

That evening, Denman and Cross went to see those prisoners who remained as yet untried. The two lawyers had a long and painful conversation with them in the courtyard. Later Denman went to the George Inn and had himself shown into Shepherd's room. The two men looked at one another with mutual respect. Shepherd now knew Denman to be an especially skillful lawyer, whose eloquent appeals to the emotions of the countrymen jurors had caused the prosecution lawyers much concern. For his part, Denman admired the elegant way in which the Attorney General had controlled the case. Shepherd had half-expected Denman's visit; the prisoner due for trial the next day was Thomas Bacon. Both men knew that if Bacon testified, the name of William Oliver would not be withheld from the attention of the Jury; and Lord Sidmouth's spy was the most hated man in England.

Oliver had been summoned to Sidmouth's office on the day before the trials began at Derby. Beckett made him wait for several minutes in the outer room, while he consulted with his employer. Then Beckett re-emerged.

"Lord Sidmouth instructs me to tell you that you are to proceed to Derby for the trials," he said in a haughty fashion. "It is dangerous for you to go there except in disguise, so you must take the appropriate steps to alter your appearance. You will travel under the name of 'Maule', and be accompanied by Mr Raven. I will inform you of where to meet him presently."

"I was called here to see Lord Sidmouth," Oliver interrupted. "Please tell him I am here." "His Lordship knows that," replied Beckett coolly. "He has no wish to see you personally. I have some money here for you, enough to cover expenses and no more. When you and Raven reach Derby, you will go directly to the George Inn, find your room, and stay there until you are instructed either to give testimony, or return.

"It should not be necessary to warn you that your testimony should in no way imply that you have been in the employ of this office. If you were to make such an assertion, then you would be prosecuted vigorously. You may say only that you undertook this action on your own initiative and received no instructions, from this office. Is all that clear?"

Oliver had no alternative but to do as he was ordered. He arrived quietly in Derby, sporting a newly-grown beard. His minder, Raven, imprisoned him at the inn, and he sat fuming while Brandreth and the others went through their ordeal.

"You will have seen today's newspapers, Sir Samuel?" said Denman.

The two legal men were seated in comfortable armchairs relaxing with some rather good brandy. Shepherd had indeed seen the newspapers.

"I wonder how much credence you give to these reports that Mr Oliver is in Derby, in this very inn, under the alias of 'George Maule'?" Denman was enjoying this part of the conversation.

"Oh, you know how exaggerated newspaper stories can be," replied Shepherd dismissively.

"I have heard a rumour that Mr Maule took a southbound stage earlier this evening, just after the newspapers appeared," said Denman. "This whole country is rife with rumours."

He took a sip of brandy and rolled it appreciatively around his tongue, before continuing.

"You know, Sir Samuel, that my client, Thomas Bacon, will make very serious allegations against Mr Maule, I mean Oliver, during his trial. I have seen him this very evening, and he is of the opinion that it is his only chance of avoiding a guilty verdict. I will be honest with you: I told him that the only way he can cheat the hangman is to change his plea to guilty, and look for mercy from the court. When I gave him this advice, however, he replied that he didn't think that the Government would stop at hanging only four and he is determined to proceed with his plan."

Shepherd had listened closely straining to catch each word with the help of an ear trumpet. He offered Denman more drink, before replying. "This Maule or Oliver business is most... discomforting," he said presently. "I would be most reluctant to pander to the popular press and have Oliver's character and activities bandied about in court: it would tend to cloud the real issues. This man Bacon is undoubtedly guilty of Treason, to my mind, and obviously deserves punishment, but you must not think that my office wishes to exact an unending revenge upon these miscreants. Quite possibly, if Bacon and the other remaining principals were to offer to alter their pleas, then I might be able to allow it without objection. In that situation, I would think it unlikely that the court would pronounce sentence of death upon them."

"I see," said Denman, thoughtfully. "Of course there are a large number of prisoners as yet untried who are obviously mere pawns. It hardly seems fair that each one of them should receive severe punishment. Apart from anything else, it would prolong the trials, and until they are over, I do not think the country will settle."

"Oh, I quite agree," replied Shepherd. "Of course, even though some of them are as innocent as you imply, not all of them fall into that category. But, I do concede the general principle that it might be better if we can in some way shorten the proceedings."

"In that case," said Denman briskly, "I will accept a little more of your excellent brandy, and then I suggest we give some attention to the details of the remaining trials."

On the morning of Saturday, October the eleventh, all the remaining
prisoners were brought to court. There was a large crowd outside.
It was a cold, wet morning and they were thoroughly soaked. The
Bacon brothers, Samuel Hunt, Edward and Manchester Turner,
German Buxton and three others were first to be led into the
courtroom. Their clothes stank with the wet of the rain and the heat
of the room. Hunt, wearing a black suit was the only one to be neatly
dressed.

Denman rose and announced that all the prisoners wished to alter
their pleas to guilty. Shepherd confirmed that the Prosecution had
no objection. As Thomas Bacon was led forward to plead formally,
he looked straight at the Attorney General, his face expressing
something of the triumph which he felt.

Ten more prisoners were led into the courtroom after the first batch
had pleaded; Denman announced that they had similar intentions.
The remaining twelve prisoners including Ludlam's three sons and
James, Thomas and Joseph Weightman the younger were called in.

Shepherd rose and addressed the Court gravely.

"It is not my intention to offer any evidence against the prisoners at
the bar," he said. "It is one of the ends and causes of human
punishment that the example of those convicted should deter others
from committing the same crime."

The twelve men, most of them young, looked around in amazement,
not really sure of what they heard. Then the Chief Baron rose to
admonish them, and give them their discharge. He concluded with
severe words.

"Take warning by what you have seen and thank God that you are
spared," he intoned. "Endeavour to, live sober and religious lives,
and strive day and night to reform yourselves, so that you may

become a credit to society, so that your days may be passed in comfort here and be followed by a happy eternity. Go home, thank God, and sin no more."

At the conclusion of these words, the court was silent. The young men stood, unsure of what to do, until Sam Ludlam pushed his young brother Isaac from the dock. They began to walk towards the door of the court, the rest following; as they did so, there was uproar among those watching. They went outside into the packed streets, their own tears of joy falling as they were overwhelmed by the cheering of the populace. Soon they were being borne shoulder-high through the streets and feasted in the local public houses, hardly able to grasp the fact that they were free.

Sentences

Back in the courtroom, Jeremiah Brandreth stepped slowly into the Dock; George Weightman, tall and ruddy-cheeked despite his imprisonment, was a step behind. William Turner and Isaac Ludlam followed, to stand heads bowed in the direction of the Chief Baron. Denman sat staring sadly into space. Shepherd looked over towards his young rival, feeling admiration for the determined and inexperienced lawyer who had fought him so hard.

Brandreth looked up at the sound of his name. He was reminded he had been convicted of High Treason, and asked whether he had anything to say why the sentence of death should not be pronounced upon him.

His eyes flashed for a second as he looked at the Chief Baron, and then he said "Let me address you in the words of our Saviour - 'If it be possible, let this cup pass from me', but not my will, but your Lordship's be done."

Turner, when asked the same question, said that he hoped for mercy. Isaac Ludlam shook violently as he begged for his life. "May it please your Lordships to show mercy? Ah hope your Lordships will. If ah may be spared, my life hereafter shall be in such conformity with laws of God and man that no one shall repent that my prayer was attended to."

George Weightman could think of nothing to say.

Those in Court waited in expectation for the inevitable next step, but it was some time in coming. Denman, Shepherd and everyone else stared at the Chief Baron, as he wiped his eyes with a handkerchief, obviously overcome with emotion at the thought of what he now must do. He regained his composure with difficulty, and placed the black cap upon his head.

"Prisoners at the bar," he began. "In the unhappy situation in which you now stand, it becomes my duty to pass upon you the sentence of the Law, which you have incurred by the violation of the laws of your country. It must be some consolation, however, that you have had every assistance and advantage that men in your situation should have. You have been defended by Counsel of your own selection, who, without any interruption from any quarter, used every exertion in your favour which their experience, their learning, and great abilities suggested to them.

"You were tried by several juries, whose respectability was undoubted. During the whole of the investigation on this most important and solemn occasion, every attention has been paid to every side of the question; and yet those juries found themselves compelled by the most irresistible evidence, to find you guilty of High Treason. Your insurrection, thank God, did not last long, but while it continued, it was marked with violence and with the murder of an innocent man, who did not offer the least provocation. That conduct has shown the ferocity of your hearts.

"Your object was to wade through the blood of your countrymen, to extinguish the Law and Constitution of your country, and to substitute for the liberty of your fellow-subjects, anarchy, and the most complete ruin. God be praised, your purpose failed! It is not my intention to dwell upon this dreadful picture, but I may be allowed to express my sincere hopes, and sincere wishes that the example which you furnish on this important day, may deter others from yielding to the wild and frantic delusions of rapacious spirits, and warn others, if others there be, from being made instruments in the hands of hellish agitators.

"Let me beseech you to weigh well your condition: your lives have become forfeited to the violated laws of your country. Make the most of the small portion of that life which is left, and endeavour to make some compensation to society by repentance. May your example serve to teach that great lesson that Mr Goodwin read to you. You did go with halters round your necks, and the laws, thank God were too strong for you."

The Chief Baron paused here. Sir Richard Richards had presided throughout the trials. He was not an inhumane man, and had, as the legal arguments ran their course, let his colleagues on the bench direct most of the proceedings. Now he was called upon to administer a terrible sentence of punishment upon the four wretched men who stood before him. He wiped his eyes once more.

"I do not trust myself to say any more," he continued, his throat betraying him.

"I must now pass upon you the awful sentence of the law, which is, that you, and each of you be taken from the jail from whence you came, from whence you must be drawn on a hurdle to the place of execution, and be there severally hanged by the neck, until you are dead; your heads must then be severed from your bodies, which are to be divided into four quarters, and to be at his Majesty's disposal."

The Chief Baron was in tears when he concluded his speech. The courtroom was totally silent, everyone looking at the four doomed men in the dock Brandreth and Weightman stood still, their features not betraying much of their emotions. William Turner hid his head in his hands.

Isaac Ludlam did not appear to have heard the sentence.

"I entreat your Lordships to spare a man who is father to a large family," he babbled. "I solemnly swear that I will in no way transgress against the Lord's holy laws and will strive and endeavour to lead a life free from all blame..."

He continued to talk in this vein, until Mr Eaton took his arm and compelled him to follow the others out of the courtroom. When the door was closed behind them, Ludlam came suddenly to a true realisation of his position; his hysterical protests were loud enough to reach and distress those who remained in the chamber.

Lancelot Rolleston

Lancelot Rolleston was riding old Amber again.

For three desperate months, he had felt himself sinking deeper and deeper into melancholy. He had not known why, and he did not really care. Through half-closed doors he would hear Caroline whispering instructions to the maids and quieting the children; it brought back memories of how his mother had acted when his own father had gone into his long decline.

His only contentment had been in the times he could sit alone in his chair; other people, especially the gregarious Worsley and the fussy Mrs Rolleston, annoyed him beyond measure. He neglected his body spitefully, allowing it to become dirty and undernourished. Soon, he had begun to walk with a stoop; he took to sleeping through the whole day, rising only at night. The women would hear his restless pacing. When they arose in the morning they would find dishes full of hardly-touched food littering the kitchen.

At first, his friends visited him out of duty, relishing his company no more than he enjoyed their presence. After a few weeks, they came no longer. The Town Clerk, Henry Enfield, despaired of him, for

Rolleston neglected his magisterial duties as he did everything else in his life. Still, the magistrate's exhibition of daring on June the ninth had endowed him with a popular heroism which was slow to die among the conversations of the propertied classes of Nottingham. In the light of this Enfield decided to ask Rolleston to perform a duty for him. The five constables who had arrested Brandreth had not received the hundred pounds reward which the Government had offered: Lord Sidmouth seemed to have forgotten about Enfield's letter on the topic. Henry Enfield hoped that a written request from the hero, Rolleston, might expedite matters; for that reason he had asked him to write to Lord Sidmouth on the constables' behalf.

The Town Clerk was shocked at the deterioration in the magistrate's appearance in the few months since the rising. He appeared unshaven and dressed in a filthy, ash-stained dressing gown. His eyes were red and sunken; one side of his face twitched nervously. They sat in the Rolleston's parlour while Enfield told his host the reason for his visit. When he had finished, Rolleston was silent and stared at him intently, as though Enfield were still talking. The Town Clerk nervously asked once again whether or not Rolleston would write the letter.

Rolleston began nodding his head furiously, intoning "Oh yes! Oh yes!" in a most disturbing fashion.

Enfield left quickly, with little optimism, but the letter had indeed been written and the constables received their money within the week.

A few days after Enfield's visit, Rolleston began to feel better. The thought of food suddenly seemed appealing, and he amazed the maid servants by rising in time for breakfast one morning and eating heartily.

Life had begun to appeal to him once more. He started to exercise, attend to his family, keep regular hours and resume his place in society. He had always enjoyed riding, and he spent the splendid autumn of 1817 in the saddle. Before too long, he hardly remembered his illness, although the memory of previous events was clear enough. Rolleston was no longer concerned with his past; he was too happy in his present. Old Bradley rented his wealthy customer gladly the very mare which had served so well on June the ninth. Old Amber seemed to bear Rolleston no grudges from the hard use he had been put to; rider and steed struck up a friendly partnership during the course of several pleasurable excursions. On October 29th, they were trotting briskly through the countryside near Alfreton in the gorgeous afternoon.

Rolleston was riding the very road which had once taken him into his madness; it no longer held any terror for him. Old Amber bore him along through Langley Mill and Codnor to Butterley. They passed on through Swanwick heading towards Alfreton, where Rolleston hoped to call in upon the High Sheriff of Derbyshire, Mr Hallowes. As he rode on, the hero of June saw a woman on the road, travelling towards him. She seemed somehow familiar as they neared each other; he saw she was pregnant. He wondered what a lone woman in her condition was doing on the road. As they passed he urged Amber into a little faster pace in order to reach his destination in good time.

Ann's Journey

Ann Brandreth arrived in Derby in the early evening of the same day, having walked alone all the way from Sutton in Ashfield. The good people of Sutton had collected enough for her fare, but she knew the money would be better spent on food. After twenty miles, she was exhausted. She knocked determinedly on the door of the jail to gain admittance. When the guard heard who she was he called Eaton; seeing her condition, and in order that she might rest herself, he conveyed Ann straight to his own rooms, where Jerry had written his letter a few days before. Mrs Eaton came in and sat with Ann, offering her some bread and a drink. Moments later Eaton returned.

Jerry was with him. The jailer and his wife left immediately.

So shocked was she by the change in his face Ann did not notice at first the chains that bound him. He was pale and scrawny, much thinner than when she had last seen him at Sutton. His eyes had dark rings beneath them, and his brow was furrowed. His hair was much too long. Eaton had washed him while his wife had acted hostess, and had cleaned up his clothes as best he could, but Jeremiah still looked like a beggar.

Ann said nothing; she ran straight her husband, tried to hold him, and found the chains prevented her. She cried out in her frustration, but bit back her tears and was quickly calm again. Jeremiah stood, devastated and ashamed. He could think of nothing to say.

"How did you come here?" he asked, at last. "By coach?'

"No, ah walked," she replied.

"What, all the way?" he exclaimed in disbelief.

"Ah'm well enough," she replied. "You know me, ah love walking."

Jeremiah shook his head, his eyes closed, realising why it was that she must walk. He had nothing to give her.

"How are t' children?" he asked.

"They 're well. Tim had a cold, but he's better now. They ask about you."

"What do you tell them?"

"I say that you have gone t' America," she answered. "I tell 'em you'll send for us one day and we will all be together again across t' sea."

"And we will," said Jeremiah, eagerly.

Eventually, much too soon, came the jailer's knock at the door. "Kiss t' children for me," he said.

Ann nodded. "We never 'ad much, but while we were together, it were enough for me," she said, sadly. "Ah don't think ah ever really understood why you did them things, and ah can't help but regret you did 'em. We will pray for you, my beloved, and ah hope you don't have t' wait long for me in Heaven."

They kissed for the last time. He wanted to hold her close, but the chains prevented it.

A few hours later, the Eatons were together in their sitting room. It was dark outside. They had been very quiet for some time.

"How much did you give to her?" he asked.

"Not much," she replied. "Enough for the fare and food for her and the children. I just couldn't bear to think of her walking back all that way, feeling as she must, and in her condition. Fifty one shillings, husband. Did I do wrong?"

"You did not do wrong, Mrs Eaton," he replied.

"She refused the money several times," she added. "I persuaded her that women from the town had given it to me unasked. They wouldn't take 'No' for an answer, I said, and me neither."

"They are both so proud," said Mr Eaton. "I can't work him out at all; never had a prisoner like him. He shows no fear at what must happen to him, and just bears it all quietly. Neither Pickering nor I can persuade him to talk much about himself, nor how he came to be involved in such a business."

They reflected in silence for some minutes, thinking upon their condemned prisoner and those others who were to share his fate.

"I hope that he bears himself in this proud manner to the end. I hope his dignity carries him through and that he doesn't break down and disgrace himself on the scaffold," concluded Eaton, as they went off to their bed.

Ann walked all the way back to her father's house in Sutton. It was well after midnight when she arrived, worn out and in near despair. The light still burned downstairs; her father had waited up for her. This night, he had forsaken the ale house, dandled the children upon his knee, put them to bed and waited up by the lamp.

When his daughter came back he held her tenderly for the first time since she was a small child. Ann let all her tears come out and clung to her father for a long time. She relived her short life over in her mind; it felt that she might never know happiness again.

The Condemned Cell

Jeremiah sat propped up against his wall in the cell he shared with George, Bill and Isaac. Bill dozed, waking every now and then to shuffle position and groan. George was sleeping soundly. Isaac was awake, but in one of the quiet phases of his disturbed behaviour. The lay preacher's mind had snapped at the pronouncement of his sentence, and nothing he said made real sense. It was hard to be sure whether he had understood the news that his three sons, at least, were to be spared transportation to which the Bacons, the two other Turners, Hunt, Buxton and others had been sentenced. They and many of the younger and least prominent were given short prison sentences.

Jeremiah lay awake, thankful that Isaac was at last silent. The small cell was completely dark. He found night time best for reflection. He felt lucky in many ways that he had been given a long time to prepare for his end. He thought through his past life slowly, dwelling upon those incidents about which he felt guilt, saying prayers, inwardly, to atone for them. The death of Robert Walters caused him a great deal of sadness; he prayed daily for the man's soul, and for his own forgiveness. He had made tactical mistakes that had delayed his men, but he had been given too little time to organise and arm them. Otherwise, he had no regrets about the rising, beyond the fact that it had not succeeded.

For Ann and his two children he experienced inconsolable sorrow; he felt his failure to provide for them much more deeply than any other pain. In his mind, he forgave those who had failed him: Tommy Bacon, who had fomented the rising and yet escaped the gallows; William Stevens who had sent the false message that led to the ambush; William Oliver who had lured them on; Henry Sampson, his friend, who had sold him to the constables.

It took him a long time to forgive Oliver, and many days of mental turmoil before he could honestly say he felt no more animosity towards Sampson. The night wore on and Brandreth realised that he must sleep, no matter how reluctant he might be to waste any of the brief time left to him.

William Turner had asked Eaton to write a letter on his behalf to his old commander, the Duke of York. Mr Pickering, the Chaplain, had recommended it. William waited daily for an answer, by turns optimistic and despairing that his old general would not forget a loyal soldier, and would intercede to have him spared the gallows. The letter so fervently hoped for never arrived. As the days before his death diminished, so Turner felt closer to his new Captain, who had, at the end, stood with his lieutenants. There is no doubt that he would have cheerfully killed Brandreth with his bare hands when the latter first returned to the prison. In the days leading up to the trial however the Nottingham Captain had been a quiet tower of strength and an example to the others. He accepted the sadness and squalor with dignified fortitude, never mourning his luck, or cruel destiny. Had Brandreth escaped to America, as was planned, Turner would have cursed his name with his last breath, but now they were fast friends once more. In those rare moments Brandreth was prepared to talk, they reminisced about the campaign and lamented the betrayals of Oliver, without which, they believed success would have been theirs.

George Weightman's loyalty to his Captain never wavered. When Brandreth first returned to his imprisoned men, it was George who persuaded the others that he had come voluntarily, having leapt from the ship which was bearing him to freedom because he would not leave his men to suffer without him. Brandreth, of course, maintained that he had been discovered, beaten, and thrown off the ship, but the honest George knew better. Soon everyone was persuaded by the Weightman version of the story, and there was no way the Captain could gainsay it. George did not much fancy the idea of being hanged, so he did not give it a great deal of thought. He was pleased in a way that he was to share the same fate as his Captain. When Rebecca had visited him, she had first berated him for being such a great big fool as to get himself caught; nevertheless, before she left, she touched his hand through the bars of the cell and told him that she would marry no other until the day she died. His last sight of her dear eyes was when they were shining with tears.

Isaac Ludlam responded to Pickering's chaplaincy, becoming much calmer in the initial few days after his sentence. He consoled himself by reading religious tracts and with the preparation of an oration; this, he intended to deliver from the gallows, in which he would call upon all to repent and to be warned by the example of his own ignoble fate.

As he watched the four condemned men walking the prison yard in the one hour a day permitted them for exercise, Eaton shook his head sadly. On his desk was a formal dispatch, written on parchment, and signed by Sidmouth himself. It read:

In the name and on the behalf of His Majesty George P.R.

Whereas at a special Sessions of Oyer and Terminer and Jail Delivery holden at Derby, in and for the County of Derby,

Jeremiah Brandreth, otherwise called the Nottingham Captain, William Turner and Isaac Ludlam, the elder, have been convicted of High Treason, and had sentence passed upon them to be drawn upon a hurdle to the place of execution, and there to be hanged by their necks until they be severally dead, and afterwards their heads severed from their bodies and divided into four quarters, and to be disposed as we should direct. And whereas we have thought fit to remit part of the sentence, viz: dividing the bodies of the said Jeremiah Brandreth, William Turner and Isaac Ludlam, the elder, severally into four parts, our will and pleasure is that the execution be done upon the said Jeremiah Brandreth, William Turner and Isaac Ludlam, the elder, by their being drawn and hanged, and having their heads severally severed from their bodies according to the said sentence only, at the usual place of execution, on Friday next, the seventh day of this instant November. And for so doing this shall be your warrant.

Given at our Court at Carlton House, the first day of November, 1817, in the fifty-eighth year of our reign.

By command of his Royal Highness the Prince Regent, in the name and on behalf of His Majesty.

SIDMOUTH

To our trusty and well-beloved High Sheriff of the County of Derby, and all others whom it may concern.

Eaton summoned Pickering and asked him to communicate to Brandreth, Turner and Ludlam that they were to die on Friday, November 7th. Their bodies were not to be cut into quarters, but they would be beheaded after being hanged. George Weightman was to be separated from them before being told that his sentence had not yet been confirmed.

Eaton sat down at his desk as the parson departed on his sorry errand. He began to watch the rain, as it swilled down from the harsh November sky. When the executions were over, he reflected, life would get back to normal. Then the thought struck him that for him, at any rate, nothing would ever again be like it was. The certainties that governed how he lived had been shaken; good and evil had inter-twined like brambles and blocked the path ahead. He shivered, feeling the chill of approaching winter.

Chapter 16: Redemption

Preparing for the End

During those last few days, Brandreth enjoyed only the company of George Weightman. Eaton had placed Turner and Ludlam in a cell together, separate from the other two. This gave both pairs more room and some improved physical comfort resulted. The four were kept apart from those others in the now less crowded jail, exercising in the yard as a foursome for one hour a day, and enduring a contemplative solitude for the remainder of their time. Mr Pickering, the Chaplain, and Eaton, the jailer, dipped into their own pockets to provide some better fare for the condemned men. Weightman gladly wolfed down the vegetables and meat so long absent in his diet and Brandreth added to his plate from his own, having lost much interest in food.

Bill and Isaac both took solace in religion and now that the latter had become more lucid, they shared memories of the folk they knew in common. George came to accept that his Captain had need for silence, although he dearly loved to talk himself. Jerry did make efforts to converse with George and, in spite of himself, enjoyed the mundane, but pleasant chatter of his cell mate. When George asked him about his silence he half-expected Brandreth to merely pass over the question, and so was surprised when he received an answer.

"When ah were a fugitive all them weeks, ah learned to keep silent," said his Captain. "Ah found one friend and ah told him everything: Ah must have talked a full night telling it all t' him! After that, there was no need for more words. Ah don't feel as though there's 'owt important enough t' waste time saying it."

George did not really understand this. "Ah know that ah'm not much of a one to talk to," he said. "But Mr Pickering, he's a clever man.

He's helped me accept my fate with what he's said. Ah should have thought you'd have talked t' him. He's a good man and wears t' cloth."

"Ah've made my peace wi' God, George" said Brandreth softly. "Why must ah make any statement for men?"

This answer seemed to satisfy George, and he was silent, himself, for a time. They sat in the oppressive cell, backs against the wall, cramped by their fetters.

"Do you feel angry that you'll be hung?" George asked after a time.

"No, George, ah don't," replied Brandreth with a smile. "Ah've forgiven those who've trespassed against me, as ah hope t' find forgiveness myself. They will get their reward, one day, ah'm sure. Ah don't think that anyone with a conscience that is troubled is happy in this world, and ah'm sure they'll not be in t' next."

"It's that Oliver, that ah'd like to have here," said George, in a voice that was uncharacteristically angry. "That was a filthy trick, that one of his. And that 'friend' of yours, Sampson! How can a man betray his best friend?"

"Let's not talk about 'em, George," begged Brandreth. "What did Mr Wolstenholme have to say when he came to see you? Tell me."

George smiled at the mention of the Curate whose visit earlier in the day had made him feel most important.

"Not good news," he said. "My mother is poorly and Rebecca has taken her in. T' White Horse is closed, because they took her licence off her. It seems folk are frightened t' go there anyway. It must be funny in t' village, without t' White Horse. Ah suppose folk are going down t' Dog and being poisoned by owd Jack's ale!

"Folks are not s' bad off since t' harvest. Flour's cheap and trade has picked up, so that one or two are running frames again. My brothers have found bits of work, lucky devils."

George stopped here, and Jerry could tell that he was thinking of the green hills and fresh air of his home. If they hadn't marched out on the ninth of June they would be enjoying better times with their families. The cell felt even more depressing. He tried to think of words to cheer his friend, but before he had managed to do so, George resumed his news-telling.

"Mr Wolstenholme is having a hard time of it," he said. "He wouldn't tell me much, but it seems that many important folk weren't happy that he buried George Booth and spoke a sermon over him. They didn't like him speaking up for us, or helping collect t' money for t' lawyers, neither. He thinks they might try t' throw him out of his living and put in somebody else. He's a good friend t' me, and ah know they suspect him because ah was taken at his cousin's house. Ah feel guilty that he's suffering because of me."

"Did he have any news of Rebecca?" asked Brandreth, remembering her wild eyes and long dark hair as he did so.

"She's looking after my mother, like ah said," replied George. "Mr Wolstenholme is paying her to clean his house and treats her well.

"He says that she is thinking of me and you as well. She sends her best wishes, and a message: something about playing t' game to the end, ah think. Ah don't really recollect it properly. Ah wish she could have met your wife; maybe they would have been friends like us! "

William Turner resented being confined with Isaac Ludlam at first. It was unfair, in his opinion, as the man was obviously not in his right mind. After a day or two of the efforts of the Chaplain, Pickering, Isaac became much more lucid and Turner was able to have the occasional sensible conversation with him. The talk was mainly on religious topics. Religion was not a subject which William had much time for, previously, but he began to give it much more thought as the day of his death came closer.

Turner was soon as concerned as Ludlam at Brandreth's apparent lack of repentance. Isaac had been convinced early that it had been wrong to rebel and use violence against those who opposed the rising. Turner's remorse at the incompetence of their military preparations had soon transferred itself into a general feeling of guilt for all the events of the rising. Both hoped that Brandreth would voice his repentance along with them, and thereby save his soul. In one of the exercise periods, Bill Turner fell into step with his Captain and engaged him in conversation. The old soldier was interested to know Jeremiah's mind as the hour of their death approached. He was keen to find out why he was not outwardly repentant, and what he meant to do and say on the scaffold.
Jeremiah listened in patient fashion to the questions of his lieutenant. The answers he gave were similar to those he had already given to George Weightman, and they did not satisfy Turner.

"Man," he protested, "We've committed a great wrong. We tried t' overthrow our rightful King, our Parliament! There's t' blood of an innocent man on our hands. We have gone against God. Surely you must repent this?"

"Bill, Bill!" replied Jeremiah, shaking his head sadly. "What is this great wrong we have done? Who is this King you are talking about? He is blind, mad and deaf to our pleas! His son spends a fortune on his mistresses and in building palaces, at t' same time as his people are living on what t' Parish doles out to 'em. Parliament! It's ruled by t' rich and governs on their behalf. It's never done owt for t' poor, except make us poorer! How can we have gone against God in seeking t 'change this? As for t' man who died: ah didn't mean for him t' die; ah pray for his soul and for his forgiveness. But ah have nowt to repent, and mi loyal friend, neither have you. One day the world will turn and folk 'll say Bill and George and Isaac and Jerry were heroes!"

His words made Turner shake his confused head. When Brandreth spoke like this, it was impossible to disbelieve him. Turner knew that if he listened to much more he would find it impossible to agree with Ludlam and Pickering. There remained one question for which he felt he must have the answer.

"When you were on board t' ship for America," he asked. "Did you leave it t' come back to us, like George says, or were you discovered and put ashore?"

"What sane man would come back t' certain death?" laughed Brandreth. "Ah've much more sense than t' do that!"

Turner nodded, but found that his doubts were increased rather than allayed by Brandreth's answer.

On the Tuesday of the last week, Isaac Ludlam received a visit from his wife and eleven-year-old daughter. Mrs Ludlam had been steeling herself for days for the ordeal, and had tried hard to fortify her sentiments through prayer. Isaac had written to her many times during his captivity but she could find little sense in the confused religious ravings of his letters. In his most recent epistle he sounded more sensible and had asked her to visit him. The upsetting part of first seeing her husband was not the sad decline in his appearance brought on by his imprisonment and the mental turmoil he had undergone, nor was she too upset by the obvious squalor in which he had to live. What really shocked her was the fact that she realised how much she had forgotten him in the months since he had been away.

He was so little like her memory of him, being no longer the firm and certain father and the dutiful husband. Instead, he called to mind some Old Testament holy man, with his unkempt locks of white hair, and his wild eyes. Isaac was burning with eagerness to tell his wife of the secret truths which he had discovered in his spiritual wanderings.

He was all aflame with the Lord's message that he was going to declaim from the scaffold and wanted to share this with her and his totally mystified young child. He frightened them both with his uncompromising fire and zeal. For a woman who had come to bid a last farewell to her doomed husband, and a daughter wanting to kiss goodbye to a loving father, his religious fervour was terrifying. Mrs Ludlam's reserve and character buckled quickly as she faced the wild eyes of this stranger, who had been her husband. As he strove to illuminate her with the divine grace which he felt shone from within him, she began to cry.

Her tears were silent at first and he, poor man, presumed that it was the effect of his message which had induced them. The child cried too, joining her mother; their sobbing grew. Soon they were both wailing loudly, while Isaac continued ranting. The prison was soon being disturbed at the sound, and the Eatons came running to the visitors' hatch in the door of the cell where Ludlam waited. Soon, Mrs Eaton was pulling Mrs Ludlam away, her daughter clinging to her skirts, while the incredulous Isaac was taken away to his own little cell and the company of William Turner. Mrs Ludlam paid no more visits to her husband.

Bill Turner was much calmer than his cell mate had been, when eleven of his relatives crowded into the visitors' half of the reception cell, on the next morning. His father was not there, being too sick to come, but his mother had joined the group and was first at the grilled hatchway. His two other brothers (Edward was in prison with him) and his sister were there, too. The Turner clan was mortified by the physical deterioration which they noted in Bill and became very upset before they left. He bore the visit well, though, and reassured them that he was coming to terms with his fate.

Pickering was convinced that the unnatural resolution and unflinching acceptance, which Brandreth had exhibited towards every hardship, was bound to evaporate before he reached the end. To the mind of the Chaplain, it was impossible that anyone should have the spiritual resources to face such a death as was imminent, without the aid of God. In truth, Pickering was made uncomfortable by the realisation that here was a man who could quote the Bible well but did not need the absolution of one of God's ministers in order to die with a clear conscience. It irked him that Brandreth had not chosen to confess and repent his undoubted crimes, but seemed instead to be content to absolve himself of guilt, and make his own peace with his own inner God.

For his part, Jeremiah tolerated Pickering's well-meaning efforts to save his soul, protesting gently that he had no doubts about his own salvation. When Pickering sought to unravel the mysteries of Brandreth's behaviour by talking about his past life, he was quietly deflected. When Pickering inquired whether he meant to die clean-shaven or bearded, Jeremiah replied that it signified nothing to him how his face appeared before those who had come to gawp at him. When Pickering offered the books and religious tracts which Ludlam and Turner had eagerly craved for their comfort, this prisoner declined them, claiming that he had more than enough thoughts with which to occupy his mind, without requiring those of others. When Pickering reported to Eaton as to the spiritual condition of the now famous prisoner, he had to admit that he had found him strong and determined. There was nothing of levity in his conduct: he was sober in his speech, sensible and completely at one with his doom. The reports were sent off to the Home Office where Sidmouth became increasingly alarmed that The Nottingham Captain might not go quietly and would drag Oliver into the public gaze.

Pickering could honestly maintain that in all his many years as Chaplain to the prison, he had not met anyone about to be executed for such serious offences that appeared to be so little distressed, and was so completely ready to meet death without dismay. Now he was instructed by Lockett to find out how much Brandreth and the others knew of Oliver and his part in the rising and what they might reveal on the scaffold.

In his last attempt to induce Brandreth to publicly repent, Pickering appealed on behalf of the many that might profit from hearing of how the condemned man had been led from the paths of honesty and peace, to commit such inhuman crimes as those blamed upon him. Brandreth had given him such a look of pity at this, that Pickering had immediately lost track of what he was trying to say. As the Chaplain left, inwardly admitting that he was beaten, Brandreth had quietly dismissed him by informing Pickering that divine grace was present in all men, and that he was sure of his own salvation; the Chaplain need have no fears for Jeremiah Brandreth.

Ann

Evening had come to the parlour of George Bridget's little home. Ann sat gazing at the fire. With her thin hunched shoulders, she looked for the entire world like an old woman reliving decades of memories. Her golden hair was going to grey, and her face was creased and tense. Her hands were blue-veined and thin, as they supported her chin. Jeremiah was to die tomorrow: both his face and the event were too remote to picture. Ann realised he had left her long ago, when the dreams of a new future had merged into frame-breaking and revolution. Sometime in the last year or two he had gone off on a journey she could not share and now he would never return. She felt that she ought to cry for him, but somehow, Ann was finished with tears. Instead, she sat impassive and empty, her thoughts increasingly on what might lie ahead. Her duty was to the future and the children; she must marry again if she could and put the sadness and nightmares behind her. The baby moved within her; she must sleep soon, for her sake.

George Goodwin

George Goodwin sat up much later than was good for him on this particular night. There would be no work tomorrow: Jessop had considered it politic to allow all the men to have chance to watch the executions, for the sobering effect which it might have upon them. Goodwin had not approved the idea. He was in no way a squeamish man, but he detested the medieval barbarity and spectacle of public hangings and was revolted even more by the prospect of viewing the beheading of a corpse, in front of the drooling masses. To his mind, such circuses belonged to the old world, and had no business interrupting the fabrication of the machines and engines which were ushering in the new one. As the evening wore on, he realised that he was exceedingly sad and sorry that three men were going to die on the next day for wanting to change an old world that he, too, was determined to alter. He was confused at feeling this way, and could come to no rational conclusion.

The Rollestons

The Rollestons had invited Worsley to dinner. They found him in tip-top form, and he had regaled them with tales of his doings on his recent visit to London. His stories were, of course, risqué, but Worsley was too much of a gentleman to give offence to Mrs Rolleston by overstepping the bounds of propriety. All the men's talk could wait until the snooker room. As it was, she had joined in with the merriment of the two men, happy to enjoy such relaxed company once more. As she wiped tears of laughter from her face, Mrs Rolleston reflected that life was at last returning to normal. She looked at Lance and noted how much better he seemed. There was colour in his face once more and he laughed uproariously, his eyes bright as they pictured Worsley's cavortings in the capital. They passed the night in great glee, and the problems of the world outside the dining room did not intrude into their celebration.

Rebecca and Nanny

Rebecca and Nanny sat by the fire. There was precious little left for them to sit on, and the flame was meagre. Thomas, Nanny's son, had brought them some off-cuts of timber, from the saw mill, but they had to use it carefully. Though she had been ill-used, the old woman had weathered the storm quite well, and had lately been buoyed up by the fact that George, the favourite son, was to be reprieved. Her brother, Tommy, had already escaped the gallows, and so things were better than they might have been.

Rebecca was silent and reflective, worn out from the cleaning job which she had undertaken at Mr Wolstenholme's. She too was delighted with the news of George's reprieve, but she was, she concluded, little better off for it. George was to be transported for life to Australia, like Nanny's brothers Tommy and Edward. She would have the comfort of knowing that he lived, but the agony of knowing that she could not be with him. In a way, that would be even more terrible than if he had died. Brandreth's wife would at least know that Jeremiah was dead and be able to pick up the threads of her life. Rebecca chided herself for thinking this way. What must that poor woman be enduring on this, the night before her man met his death? What must the gentle-eyed rebel himself be enduring?

Hugh Wolstenholme

Hugh Wolstenholme had drunk a great deal of wine. Alone in the house after Rebecca had gone he had felt the pangs of sadness and turned to the bottle. He hated himself as he drank. That afternoon, he had ridden out to Crich Stand once more, through the reddening countryside. The harvest was in and trees shorn of their fruit, now shed their leaves like tears, and bared themselves to the cruel mercy of winter which would breathe death into them. He had uncovered his own head to the whistling wind, which had shrieked, tormented, in his face. Below, in the once green valley of the Derwent, the last golden leaves were losing their feeble grip on life, and all was becoming black and bare. He could not look towards the south, in the direction of Derby, without sadness.

The accusations voiced by the local gentry and inscribed on paper by his Bishop hurt him, even though he had dismissed them as being completely groundless. He was berated for neglecting the morals of his parishioners on the grounds that they would surely have never engaged in such crimes as had occurred if they had been given correct guidance by their pastor. Many accused Hugh himself of being one of the prime instruments of provocation, through his unsuitable sermonizing and his persistent failure to condemn radicalism. In the minds of those who controlled his destiny, Wolstenholme was not fit to have a living, and he knew that William Lockett, the Government Solicitor was colluding with his Bishop to have him ousted from the parish of Pentrich.

The wind cleared his head. Eventually, he had realised that it was blowing him back towards his home. Now, as midnight approached, and the rain began to rattle, he grasped the neck of the bottle and tottered unsteadily towards the stairs and his distant bed. As he reached the landing, Wolstenholme rapped against the false panel which had concealed George Weightman, all those months before. He listened for an answering knock, but there was none there to make answer. In a minute more, the Pentrich curate had fallen fully-clothed onto his bed, where he slept far into the next day.

Tommy Bacon

Tommy Bacon shared the cell with his brother John, Edward and Manchester Turner and Samuel Hunt. There was little space and the five men had quickly begun to get on each other's nerves.

Old Tommy was not popular with the Turners who could not find a reason for him being spared the gallows, while Bill was to endure them. It was Tommy's insistent polemics which had induced Bill Turner to become leader of the Wingfield Troop; it was he who had brought them into the rising. Bill had kept faith and done his duty, but Bacon had deserted while others enacted the rebellion which he had stirred up. It was Tommy who had introduced Brandreth into their midst with his wild words and delusions, and who had backed his promises of thousands of men from the North rushing to swell the ranks of the insurrectionary army. What Bacon preached and what he practiced was a long way apart and these former friends of his resented what they saw as hypocrisy, almost as much as they felt bitterness about his old life being spared.

Old Tommy did nothing to endear himself to his cellmates either. He was completely unbowed by the events of the last few weeks, and was insensitively as full of words as he had ever been. He railed against Oliver and Sidmouth repeatedly, cursing them for outwitting the rebels. It irked Bacon considerably that he had not seen through the spy at the outset, because in retrospect he had been such an obvious trickster that he should have been discovered immediately. Eaton had given the old philosopher paper and ink, and he had composed a long statement, giving the history of the whole affair and dwelling long on Oliver's role as agent provocateur. Eaton had passed the statement to Lockett, and he had sent it post haste to the Home Office, where it was consigned to the files, to be lost for many years.

Even Tommy Bacon was quiet on this saddest of eves, as the five waited awake in their cell, keeping a silent vigil for those who were to suffer on the next grim day. Edward Turner was crying softly to himself, as he sat, still chained, leaning against the shoulder of his young nephew, Manchester. He had been separated from his brother since the sentences were announced and was distraught that Bill should be suffering such sadness without himself to comfort him. The others respected his tears, and even the surly and cocksure Hunt felt sympathy for him. They had enough in their own plight to shed tears for, and it took much now for them to weep for any but themselves.

Bill and Isaac

Bill Turner sat on his own, less than twelve hours away from his death. Isaac Ludlam sat on the opposite side of the cell, but his mind had already left this world, for he could no longer face it. Turner told himself that he had been through such nights before on the eve of a battle, for instance, but in his heart he knew that not to be so. The soldier, reflecting upon the action ahead, knows a thrill of optimism and while he fears that he might die, he secretly believes, and passionately, that he will survive. Turner knew that he would not survive tomorrow's encounter. He glanced across at the vacant face of Isaac Ludlam, recalling that it was two days since the white-haired old man had said a word with any sense in it. The old lay-preacher could string religious utterances together at will, but there was no sanity behind them. Momentarily, Bill mourned the ill-luck which had him put into a cell with a deranged man, on the last night of his life. Jeremiah had George to cheer his last hours, but he would have little comfort from Isaac. He dared not reminisce over the life which he must depart, as it brought him nothing but sadness. The present was the state which he sought to escape, and he knew enough about the future to have no wish to call it to mind.

Sleep was beyond him, and anyway it seemed a shame to sleep what was left of his life away. Turner realised that he had never really stopped to sit and think about his existence before this night: all his life he had been concerned with what to do next and how to overcome his immediate problems. He spent the dark hours carefully going over the processes involved in building his parents' house in South Wingfield, laying each stone again in his mind, determined not to cease his thought, till all was finished.

George and Jeremiah

George Weightman could not see Jerry in the darkness, but heard his even breathing. Was the Captain asleep or awake? George could not tell, and nor did he ask, fearful of either waking him or disturbing his thoughts. Eventually, Jeremiah heard George beginning to doze, and smiled to himself at the depth and health of the sounds which his young friend was making. As he waited for the morning, he visited his past life in his memory, each episode vivid in this so peaceful darkness.

The Last Day

William Lockett was up at first light and on his horse within half an hour after rising. The morning was bitterly cold and he found that his breath was hard to come by.

"Thank God it's nearly finished!" Lockett nearly voiced the thought out loud. He had worked harder these last few months than ever before in his life. He mentally listed all the duties he had to perform. First, there were the domestic arrangements for keeping so many prisoners in such a confined, cramped little jail. Food needed accounting for and then there was all that kerfuffle about having the criminals ironed. Eaton had been most obstructive the whole way through. Secondly, there were the trials to organise. Holy God, the trials! Three hundred jurymen and two hundred and sixty eight witnesses for the prosecution must be fed and housed, as well as accommodating the judges and the ten prosecution lawyers. How he ever managed it, Lockett could not bear to think! Thirdly, there were the executions themselves to oversee. This duty included organising the yeomanry to stand guard in case of trouble during the proceedings, finding an executioner, negotiating for a burial place and much more. He also liaised with the military over the deployment of cavalry and foot soldiers to contain what was expected to be an angry mob. Now, at last, thought Lockett, life might soon return to something resembling normality.

He satisfied himself that the new drop outside the jail was clear, and free from any nocturnal attempts at sabotage, and knocked heavily at the door of the old building. There was a long delay, which gave Lockett the chance to notice that Nun's Green was already beginning to fill with folk eager to watch the spectacle which he had come to oversee. After an intolerable time, one of Eaton's tired underlings admitted Lockett through the gates to the early breakfast he had arranged to have with the jailer. Pickering arrived at nine o'clock, fortified by a large breakfast and an hour's prayer. He spoke briefly with Eaton and Lockett, before marching off in a sombre mood to bless the three who were to die.

The noise of the men labouring to erect the scaffold on top of the drop called Jeremiah, Bill and Isaac back from their introspection. They all knew the significance of the sounds which had disturbed them. After a few minutes of solitude with each in turn, the Chaplain led them across the prison yard. As they began to walk towards the little chapel, George Weightman, who had been removed from the cell which he shared with Brandreth a little earlier, appeared before them. He smiled and shook hands with Bill. They exchanged a few words, and then George took Isaac's hand also. Old Isaac did not seem to know him, but gazed earnestly at the young prisoner's face to see what he would say. George could find no words. The four continued into the little chapel and knelt there, as the other Pentrich, Wingfield and Alfreton men came to share in this last service. Only five or six more could fit into the tiny space but the rest formed an extended congregation about the door. It reminded Jeremiah of the time that all his followers were unable to fit into the White Horse Inn. Each of the three took communion.

The service concluded, the Bacons, Edward and Manchester Turner, George Weightman and the rest were ushered back to their cells on the understanding they could say farewell later. The three condemned men remained with Pickering. Isaac prayed desperately; Bill knelt in silence; Jeremiah had asked Eaton earlier, for the boon of more paper and a pen, and he forsook prayer to compose his final letter to Ann.

"My beloved wife,

This is the morning before I suffer; I have sat down to write my last to you, hoping that my soul will shortly be at rest in Heaven, through the redeeming blood of Christ.

I feel no fear at passing through the shadow of death to eternal life; so I hope you will make the promise of God, as I have to my own soul, as we may meet in Heaven, where every sorrow will cease, and all be joy and peace.

My beloved, I received a letter this morning, with a pound note in it, which I leave for you in the jailor's hands, with other things which I shall mention before I have done. This is an account of what I send you: one work bag, two balls of worsted, and one of cotton, a handkerchief, an old pair of stockings and shirt and the letter I received from my beloved sister, with the following sum of money - £1 12s 7d. This I suppose will be sent in a packet to you by some means.

My dearly beloved wife, this is the last correspondence I can have with you, so you will make yourself as easy as you possibly can, and I hope God will bless you and comfort you, as he hath me.

My blessing attend you and the children and the blessing of God be with you all now and evermore.

Adieu! Adieu to all forever.
Your most affectionate Husband
Jeremiah Brandreth.

As they waited in the chapel, Eaton joined them and sat in gentle communion with his charges. Confined in such a narrow place for such a time, the prisoners had grown dependent upon each other, and also upon the humane turnkey who had made their captivity much more bearable than it might otherwise have been. His years in this melancholy occupation had left signs of grief upon his countenance, which did not escape the eyes of Jeremiah as he passed his last letter over into Eaton's hands, with a quiet word of thanks at his captor's answering nod.

At midday, the serenity of the little group was disturbed by the entrance of stubby, little Under-Sheriff Simpson. He had been dispatched by Lockett to deliver the formal request that the bodies of the three be yielded up for execution. He stood before Eaton and officiously read the proclamation which he held, unrolled, in front of his face.

"In the name of the High Sheriff for the County of Derby," he began. "As his Under Sheriff, I command you to bring forth upon the scaffold the bodies of Jeremiah Brandreth, William Turner and Isaac Ludlam, the elder, that their several sentences of death, for the High Treasons of which they have been convicted may be executed forthwith."

Eaton gave the formal reply, and then events began to gather speed. The three were led out into the cold yard of the prison. They could see their friends on the other side being kept back from them by Eaton's deputies. Mr Bamford, the smith who had hammered their irons on all those weeks ago, now reappeared to expertly remove them. The relief as they were able to stretch their arms high over their aching· shoulders was as short-lived as the brief time for which they were free of chains. Mr Bamford had only struck off their prison irons in order to replace them with ones which would unlock to make the task of the executioner easier after the death sentence was carried out. The new chains were lighter than the old.

Eaton allowed Brandreth and the others to mingle with the other prisoners to say their farewells. The Captain shook the hands of each and every one of those who had followed him. They all wished him luck and most had tears in their eyes. Tommy Bacon, who was keeping well in the background, was happy enough to cry when The Captain sought him out, grasped his hand and smiled. He had a final smile for George, too. As they embraced, Jerry quietly told him that of all his comrades, he was the most worthy. He asked him to die well and to remember their heroic enterprise.

Edward Turner clung to his brother, in the utmost distress, his eyes wild with grief. Bill told him not to take on so and tried to soothe him, but Edward grew more and more distraught. Soon he was overcome by trembling and fell to the ground in a fit, to the great sadness of all there. His nephew Joseph and John Bacon removed Edward from the yard. Bill watched them take him in stricken silence.

The reunion lasted but a few minutes. Eaton had a schedule to maintain. A horse was led into the prison yard, towing a low sledge, which would serve as a hurdle. Brandreth sat himself down upon it and was carried ridiculously around the prison yard, the harsh grating of the wooden sled on the cobbles sounding much louder for the silence of those who watched his progress. After his turn was finished, they hauled Jeremiah from the hurdle and put him into the narrow passage which led out to the gate of the prison. He waited there for a minute or so, until he was joined by Bill.

"How do you feel?" he asked him.

"Better than ah thought ah would!" answered Bill.

The two of them shook hands, and embraced like brothers. Ludlam joined them presently, muttering words which signified nothing to those about him. Brandreth and Turner looked at him sadly, then ignored his ramblings and let him pace up and down the passage alone until Eaton appeared behind them. He nodded to the guard at the door as a signal to turn the key and lift the latch. As he did so, the noise of the crowd which had built up steadily during the last few hours, now reached their ears at full pitch. They walked through the door, and found themselves at the bottom of the steps leading up to the scaffold.

Chapter 17: Execution

The cold streets of Derby had been filling from the early morning with people eager to find choice vantage points to view the promised spectacle. Folk who were especially eager turned out in time to see William Lockett, gaudily attired and splendidly mounted, clatter to the prison gate for his early breakfast. Within half an hour of this preliminary event, the eager-eyed among the growing throng spotted a group of workmen emerge, laden with the tools of their trade, through the prison door. The men commenced work above the drop erected in front of the jail.

Two huge, vertical props were already in position at the two ends of the platform. They were fully ten feet above the level of the scaffold, and at their top nearly eighteen feet clear of the ground. The workmen raised a cross-beam, standing on ladders to bolt it firmly into place. Two angled support struts were secured at the corners for extra strength before the men climbed down to view their handywork.

Moments later, a tall, burly man exited from the prison and mounted the scaffold followed by another carrying in his arms carefully coiled ropes. Those in the know whispered that the first man, reputedly a miner, was the executioner, brought in from Chesterfield to do the job, paid at well above the usual rate. The crowd buzzed, fascinated, watching him mount the ladder to fix the ropes to the cross-piece, using the height of his assistant below to measure positions for the nooses. This accomplished, the ladder was removed, and the drop cleared. The executioner and his assistant placed a heavy sack on the trap-door to provide weight; the former took his place at the side, where the handle controlling the mechanism was located. He pulled it sharply and the heavy sack crashed through the drop, brought to a sudden halt by the rope. It shuddered and swayed like a hanged corpse, drawing from the onlookers approving gasps and applause.

The operation was repeated several times until the executioner was satisfied at which point the crew packed up its gear, and disappeared back into the prison.

The crowd tried to cluster around the drop to gain a better look, but half a dozen of the Yeomanry arrived to push people back with their javelins. At this moment, a cry went up from the other side of the green. "The soldiers are coming!" Distracted, the throng turned to see a detachment of the Inniskilling Dragoons marching briskly and rhythmically into Nuns Green. The soldiers halted. The NCO began to bark orders which sent them scuttling in threes and fours to strategic points from where they could control the crowd, and prevent carriages passing into the area. Mounted cavalry detachments were deployed at several places nearby ready to control any crowd disturbances.

As the number of people in front of the scaffold increased, it became a much harder job to police it efficiently. The authorities were determined to leave the principal task of crowd control within civil jurisdiction, keeping the military presence to a minimum, using soldiers only if the situation got out of hand. A real suspicion lingered that the sympathy, so many felt for Brandreth, Turner and Ludlam might provoke an attempt at their rescue. Lockett had hired more than three hundred special constables, and the Yeomanry was turned out in much greater force than any had expected. Lockett justified the expense by reflecting upon how his own career would be wrecked if, after Eaton had surrendered them into his charge, the prisoners were freed by force. As he watched through the jail window, Lockett observed that the crowd seemed in a less festive mood than normal when an execution was to occur. Less merriment was evident than he expected and knots of men appeared in furtive discussions that might include plots to free the felons. But as Lockett looked, he saw something that pleased him: an old quack medicine peddler was setting up stall in the centre of the crowd, diverting the attention of many. He had somehow managed to find himself a platform above the crowd and now playing a fiddle, he began dancing to the encouragement of onlookers.

Today old Hodges the quack was not peddling his patent medicine; he was hawking a ballad instead. Selling at a penny, his boy held dozens of hastily run-off copies. Fiddle in the crook of his left elbow the old balladeer began to sing his piece, and little by little, the crowd hushed to hear him. His voice was unexpectedly fine and strong, and his self-penned words were most appropriate for the occasion:

"Ye kind-hearted souls, pray attend to my song

And hear this true story which shall not take long;

The knitters of Sutton how ill they are used

And by the frame owners so sorely abused. -

Derry down, down, down Derry down."

The crowd there assembled took the spirit of his words, even those on its edges, who could not make out their substance, strained to hear and were silent. The song ran its several verses until the old man concluded:

"My name it is Brandreth, my work is all gone

Paid spies and informers did me this wrong;

Betrayed and abused me I swear it's no lie

And now here in Derby I'm condemned to die -

Derry down, down, down, Derry down. '

His audience joined in the last chorus as one then cheered him vociferously. Within a few minutes, the boy had sold his last ballad sheet and he and his master set off for the inn. They had nothing else to peddle, and shared no wish to see men die.

The crowd waited full of expectation for the main event of the day.

People of every degree and station had assembled; scullery maids to gentlemen's wives; apprentice boys to parsons. The sombre drab of the poorly clad paupers of Derby contrasted with the gaudy raiment of the gentlemen from the County; the whole extent of the huge division between the rich and poor in Regency England was reflected. The rich brought their own armed escorts and peered from behind the curtains of their carriages.

The mood of this gathering was not unrestrained joviality of the sort that normally attended execution of felons: an undercurrent of disaffection and anger among the burgeoning mob was palpable prompting several of the more sage among the gentry to withdraw quietly to a safer location.

Some of the poor had walked in from Nottingham that morning and were reliving scenes from Jem Towle's execution the previous year.

Small groups of grim men began to mutter about rescuing the condemned; the soldiers sensed a feeling of hostility and gripped their weapons more tightly. The atmosphere was charged with tension; Lockett began to wonder whether the distraction provided by the quack singer had, in fact, served to inflame an already dangerous situation.

About six thousand people were gathered in the area in front of the scaffold as the hour of noon chimed out from the Derby church bells. The crowd quieted and became attentive. Those merchants selling pies and sweet meats from little mobile stalls found there was little necessity for them to bellow praises for their stock; their voices carried clearly over the doomed men's audience.

A little after midday, those at the front of the gathering gave voice to their excitement when the prison door swung open permitting the emergence of several figures. First came the executioner, clad in a smock and sporting a black hood with eyelets. Next was Lockett, flanked by two constables. Striding steadily up the steps, he stood gazing importantly above the huge crowd, appearing as if detached completely from his surroundings. In the following group were his assistant and two other helpers, each bearing apparatus required for the executions. One lugged a large basket, contents covered by a cloth; another carried a bulky sack of sawdust.

Four more constables appeared bearing a heavy wooden block, in the form of a bench with a wooden log nailed across one end. The crowd noise grew as the platform party were jeered and hissed, before diminishing into an unreal silence.

The assistant executioner mounted the platform to stand beside his chief, both in masks. The crowd fidgeted through a short period of inactivity during which, most knew the victims were being drawn on the ludicrous hurdle inside the prison.

Somewhere in that press, Nanny and Rebecca struggled to hold on to each other. The Ludlams and Turners had been unable to face the sight of their men being dispatched so horribly, but Rebecca, feeling somehow compelled to be here at the last move in Jeremiah's game, had travelled in a pony and trap driven by Hugh Wolstenholme.

Moreover, she had prevailed upon Nanny to support her. Lost in that huge crowd, they felt helpless and terrified.

Eaton came first, followed by Brandreth, Turner, Ludlam and Pickering. The crowd roared instinctively, but the sound quickly subsided into something near to silence. Jeremiah glanced fearfully at the block lying behind the scaffold, taking a deep breath before following Eaton up the steps. He had expected his body to tremble and had feared that he might stumble, but some power had given strength to his wasted legs. He mounted the platform and looked out at the massed faces below him. He felt dizzy, but a few deep breaths saw him through. The hooded men took a step towards him, anxious to obey the firm instructions of Sidmouth, via Lockett; that the prisoners should be masked and killed before they had time to make inflammatory speeches. One of them took Brandreth's arm firmly, but released his grip when the eyes of the little man looked on him.

The Nottingham Captain stood above the crowd, seeking a familiar face, but finding none. Now it came to it, the speech, he had intended to make no longer seemed important. Instead, he had a desire to wave to all whose eyes were fixed upon him; the chains however, prevented even this simple act; he shrugged and spoke a brief goodbye to the people of England.

"God Bless you all!" he cried, in the voice that inspired the Pentrich Revolution. "Except Lord Sidmouth," he muttered for those nearest to hear. The thousands roared out their salute in reply.

The executioner took him by the shoulders, and propelled him towards the central noose of the waiting three. The crowd groaned as the executioner realised the noose was pitched too high for a man of Brandreth's height. A long pause ensued, punctuated by invective and more hissing from the crowd, while a ladder was brought, the assistant executioner scurrying up to adjust the length of the rope.

From his vantage point Lockett cursed audibly at this incompetence. Jeremiah stood impassively as the alterations were made, smiling towards the crowd. Rebecca stared hard at him, but could not make him see her.

Bill Turner was led up next and, in the few seconds allowed him, managed a sentence of his own.

"This is all Oliver and the Government" he began. Pickering quickly interposed his body between Bill and the crowd.

"The Lord have mercy on my soul!" Bill yelled clearly, as they placed the noose on him. Then he stood beside Brandreth, exchanging smiles of encouragement. The nooses made them keep their heads erect, as the ropes were quite stiff.

Then Eaton helped Ludlam mount the steps. The ruined man was agitated, praying out loud fervently as the noose was placed upon him. Mr Pickering asked Isaac to be silent while a prayer was read, but he did not hear and continued his own increasingly hysterical pleas for mercy from his God.

Pickering continued, despite the competition, and was soon gratified to hear Ludlam joining in the responses with the other two. The Chaplain concluded with the Lord's Prayer and then took a last look at the faces of each. Isaac blinked, not seeming to comprehend his situation; Bill shook a little, but stood to attention, eyes front. When Pickering looked into the bearded, translucent face of the Captain, he was met with a benign gaze he found chillingly disturbing and looked immediately away.

The executioner produced black sacks to mask the faces of the men he was about to kill. Isaac's head was covered first, then Bill's. Jeremiah had time to glance at each; he noted that they were muttering prayers underneath the coarse cloth, rising and falling in front of their mouths. He looked into the crowd a final time seeking a last image to take with him to the next world. There beneath his feet was the horror of a society divided; the obscenely wealthy, guarded and aloof from the impoverished and exploited mob. How could he have hoped to change such an abomination? It was over for him; his part in the game was ended. There would be no victory. Not yet. Not for him. Then in the instant before the hood was lowered, he was looking into Rebecca's eyes.

At twenty-five minutes before one, on Friday, November the seventh, 1817, the muscular Derbyshire miner, who had been hired as executioner, drew the bolt which worked the drop. The crowd pressed forward to see the last struggle of the three rebels.

Jeremiah Brandreth fell straight through and died almost instantly. William Turner too, experienced little pain and a quick death. Poor Isaac Ludlam's pleas for mercy were cruelly ignored by his God, and the crowd watched in horror the sickening sight of his body being slowly strangled, kicking, cavorting and convulsing at the end of the rope. Women screamed, children wept, men clenched their fists in helpless rage and many lowered their eyes in guilt at what had taken place. It was if in that moment the whole world revolted against the disgusting barbarity of it all. Tears fell and the crowd moaned in grim fascination as the life left the hanging men.

Twenty minutes later the bodies were returned to the top of the scaffold. Sawdust was spread around the platform. The assistant unlocked the chains on the legs of the three corpses kneeling on the drop, suspended still by their necks. The constables lifted the block to a position in front the gallows. Three coffins were lifted up too. Those who were closest saw the names "Brandreth, 'Turner" and "Ludlam" scrawled in chalk upon the lids. While this was in progress, the assistant executioner revealed the gruesome contents of the large basket: a pair of axes and two long, black-handled knives. He removed them, placing the basket into position at the end of the block.

The noose was removed from Brandreth's neck, his dead body laid down upon the block, stomach downwards. The lifeless head was propped up on the log at the end of the bench positioned so that the contorted face looked out over the hushed mass of people standing transfixed, fascinated by what was happening.

The executioner took his axe in hand and drew in his breath. The crowd sighed. Nanny held Rebecca's head to her old breast to avert her gaze. The axe was raised high; the blade sliced deep into the defenceless neck of the corpse beneath, but the blow was not bold enough. The head lolled, hanging by skin and gristle for a second or two, until the assistant seized its black curls and severed the stubborn flesh with a knife. Amidst the groans and wails of the thousands present, the executioner took the abused head of the Nottingham Captain from the basket and held it aloft in both his hands, blood dripping onto the sawdust.

"Behold the head of the traitor, Jeremiah Brandreth!" he cried, proceeding to the left and right of the scaffold, repeating the gesture and the grim words at each location. Finally, Brandreth's head and body were placed into the first coffin.

Those nearest the front observed that the hands of the dead man were wound around with a little blue scarf, and wondered what it could signify.

Epilogue

Jeremiah Brandreth, William Turner and Isaac Ludlam were buried together in a single unmarked grave in the churchyard of St Werburgh's in Derby. They lie there still and there is no monument raised to their memory.

Thomas Bacon, John Bacon, Edward Turner, Joseph "Manchester" Turner, Samuel Hunt, German Buxton, John Hill, George Brassington, John Mackesswick and John Onion were transported for life. Thomas Bettison, Josiah Godber and Joseph Rawson and eight others were transported to Australia. Though all survived the voyage, and most lived to be freed, none was ever to see family or England again. A half-dozen other Derbyshire rebels received short prison sentences of less than two years duration.

George Weightman was transported to Australia for life and died in Kiama, New South Wales in 1865, aged 68. He was considered a worthy and upstanding citizen and received a full pardon in 1835.

Rebecca Weightman never re-married, but supported herself and her children working as a charwoman, to all intents and purposes a widow, until her death at the age of 78. She and their three children never saw George again after he was transported.

Nanny Weightman lost her license and the White Horse Inn was closed. The Duke of Devonshire's agents evicted the families of the guilty and removed the roofs from their homes.

Ann Brandreth reared her son and two daughters at her father's home. She re-married in 1825, to another framework knitter, and had a fourth child. Timothy followed his father's trade in Mansfield, before emigrating with his family to America along with his sister Mary, born 1818.

George Goodwin prospered at the Butterley Ironworks and remained there until his death on New Year's Day, 1848.

William Oliver was whisked out of England and given a secure government position in South Africa. He lived the remainder of his

life under the alias of William Jones, suspected of embezzlement by his new employers.

Henry Sampson and his large family were also helped to a new life in South Africa.

Lord Sidmouth continued as Home Secretary. He was instrumental in the passing of the infamous Six Acts, and in carrying out increasingly repressive policies. He was Home Secretary still in 1819 when the Peterloo Massacre took place. He died at the age of eighty five.

Lancelot Rolleston's political career proceeded successfully. He served as MP for the Nottinghamshire Southern Division from 1837 to 1849. He died in 1862, aged 76.

Thomas Denman became the 1st Lord Denman and also Lord Chief Justice.

Hugh Wolstenholme the radical parson who was such a friend to some of the rebels was forced out of his living as curate of Pentrich in the spring of 1818. Hugh then left for America, being shipwrecked at Virginia Beach. He joined the Moravian Church and was known as 'a man of strong convictions, aggressive spirit and fearless utterances' and 'reputed to be one of the most learned men in North Carolina'. He was involved in teaching poor children to read; one of the pupils he inspired was Andrew Johnson, 17th President of the USA, whose presidency is remembered for the Alaska Purchase. He was previously Vice-President to Abraham Lincoln. Hugh ended his days, circa 1875, as a celebrated hermit in a log cabin in a remote area of the Bald Mountain area of North Carolina, which would make him about one hundred years old.

As Hugh Wolstenholme had feared, the bustling village of Pentrich declined quite quickly and began to fade from history. In the spring of 1818 pressure from Lockett and the Church of England establishment forced him out of his living as curate and he and his family left for America.

The following year, his successor, John Wood, issued a circular letter to his parishioners decrying the *"neglect of religious duties and morals, the lamentable effects of which during the last two years are but too well known, and have rendered it an imperious duty upon the well-disposed inhabitants to take some means for stemming the torrent of irreligion and disaffection."*

Last Thoughts

The tale of the Nottingham Captain's last days will be two hundred years told in 2017. His shocking vision of an England where most people could vote, where businesses could not collude to fix prices, where the Press was at liberty to publish, where children's education was free and the government had a duty to ensure that in a land of plenty, no one starved, came to pass long-since.

We must look back upon this tragic episode in English history with disgust and anger. Impoverished Derbyshire villagers were deliberately tricked by the Home Secretary and the Lord Lieutenant into making a ridiculous attempt to capture Nottingham Castle. Their movements were tracked through a network of paid spies, one of whom, known as William Oliver, provided the inspiration, a plan of action and even a date for the rising. The Captain and his band were duped into believing themselves part of a nationwide event involving thousands, but they marched out alone.

Fortunately Oliver was unmasked in time to save many from the gallows, but Jeremiah Brandreth, William Turner and Isaac Ludlam were hanged and beheaded. Fourteen of their comrades were transported to Australia, guilty of the aristocratic charge of "high treason", never before applied to a "commoner" in England, all because they walked thirteen miles in pouring rain bearing medieval weapons and scattered at the first sight of the army.

Amidst the anger and emotion we can be inspired by glimpses of the toughness, bravery and fellowship of the rebels and their families as they faced the consequences of their actions.

Jeremiah Brandreth's dignity and the courage he displayed in his final days invoked loyalty among those he led to disaster and the admiration of many who were repulsed by the conduct of the government.

The Nottingham Captain was killed attempting to bring about a better society. Sadly, two hundred years on, hard won rights and freedoms are once more under threat from the heirs of the self-same aristocrats who beheaded a textile worker, a mason and a quarryman for daring to demand change.

18126773R00181

Printed in Great Britain
by Amazon